The HarperCollins Book of Oriya Short Stories

KK MOHAPATRA was born in 1953 and studied in Ravenshaw College and Banaras Hindu University. His Oriya writings include a collection of stories, *Palabhut*, and a novella, *Photo*, in a not-for-sale, limited edition.

LEELAWATI MOHAPATRA was born in 1953. She studied in Loreto College and Calcutta University. She has published her writings in *The Illustrated Weekly of India*, *The Statesman*, *Indian Literature*, *Indian Horizons*, *New Quest* and *Journal of South Asian Literature*. Their joint endeavours are translations which include *Kishori Charan Das: Wild Peacock and Other Stories* (Grassroots, 1985), *J.P. Das: Spider's Web and Other Stories* (Vikas, 1990), *Fakir Mohan Senapati: Selected Stories* (HarperCollins, 1995), and *Laxmikanta Mahapatra: One Eye Uncle* (Orient Longman, 1998). They have also edited *The Macmillan Book of Short Poems* (Macmillan, 1997).

SUDHANSU MOHANTY was born in 1956. He studied in Ravenshaw College and Utkal University and has published upwards of two hundred essays and book reviews in *The Statesman*, *The Times of India*, *The Hindustan Times*, *The Telegraph*, *The Pioneer* and several other leading newspapers and journals. His translations include *Joy K. Mohanty: Three Mariners* (HarperCollins, 1993). He is currently working on his first novel.

The HarperCollins Book of Oriya Short Stories

Translated & Edited
by
KK Mohapatra
Leelawati Mohapatra
Sudhansu Mohanty

HarperCollins *Publishers* India

HarperCollins *Publishers* India Pvt Ltd
7/16 Ansari Road, Daryaganj, New Delhi 110 002

First published in India by
HarperCollins *Publishers* India, 1998

Translation, Selection & Compilation Copyright © KK Mohapatra,
Leelawati Mohapatra, Sudhansu Mohanty

ISBN 81-7223-312-4

Typeset in Garamond by
Megatechnics
19A, Ansari Road
New Delhi 110 002

All rights reserved. The author asserts the moral right to be identified as the author of this work. No part of this publication may be reproduced, stored in a retrieval system, or transmitted in any form or by any means, electronic, mechanical, photocopying, recording or otherwise, without the prior permission of the Publishers.

Printed in India by
Gopsons Papers Ltd
A-14, Sector 60
Noida 201 301

For Paul St Pierre

Contents

Foreword	xi
1. The Bride-Price *Fakir Mohan Senapati (1843-1918)*	1
2. The Old Bangle Seller *Laxmikanta Mahapatra (1888-1953)*	24
3. Maguni's Bullock Cart *Godavarish Mohapatra (1899-1965)*	31
4. Victory Celebration *Kalindi Charan Panigrahi (1901-1991)*	35
5. Shikar *Bhagabati Charan Panigrahi (1907-1943)*	46
6. The Quest *Nityananda Mahapatra (1912-)*	50
7. The Shelter *Gopinath Mohanty (1914-1991)*	59
8. Bouli *Rajkishore Ray (1914-)*	67
9. The Slanging Match *Faturanand (1915-1995)*	74
10. Dead Flower *Satchidananda Raut Roy (1916-)*	81

11. Oh Calcutta!   87
    Surendra Mohanty (1920-1990)

12. Dispossessed   96
    Kishori Charan Das (1924-)

13. Father and Son   107
    Bamacharan Mitra (1925-1970)

14. Antu Praharaj, the Master Exorcist   116
    Mohapatra Nilamoni Sahoo (1926-)

15. Fig Flower   131
    Akhil Mohan Patnaik (1927-1982)

16. The Emperor   138
    Chandrasekhar Rath (1929-)

17. Parallel Lines   147
    Santanu Kumar Acharya (1933-)

18. The Pilgrim   165
    Krushna Prasad Mishra (1933-1994)

19. Into the Heart of Luvurva   171
    Manoj Das (1934-)

20. The Ghost   179
    Rabi Patnaik (1935-1991)

21. Spider's Web   189
    Jagannath Prasad Das (1936-)

22. Flowering Night   195
    Binapani Mohanty (1936-)

23. Unseasonal Pineapple   206
    Bijay Prasad Mahapatra (1938-)

24. The Stigma   212
    Pratibha Ray (1944-)

25. The Cage 227
    Ramachandra Behera (1945-)

26. Hunger 234
    Nrusingha Tripathy (1945-)

27. Moonlight 240
    Yashodhara Mishra (1951-)

28. A Sita in the Ashok Forest 251
    Jagadish Mohanty (1951-)

29. The Couple 262
    Sivapada Swain (1952-)

30. The Thief 270
    Kamalakanta Mohapatra (1953-)

31. The Rape 293
    Sarojini Sahoo (1956-)

    Notes on the Authors 301

Foreword

The first Oriya short story *Rebati* by Fakir Mohan Senapati (1843-1918) was published in 1898. It marked the emergence of a new literary form out of a long tradition of folklore and the oral literature. The world of swooning princesses and swashbuckling princes living in enchanted castles gradually gave way to an active engagement with the problems and preoccupations of a prosaic everyday world peopled with ordinary beings. The expansive and digressive oral narration of marvellous incidents by a garrulous, avuncular narrator was soon displaced by an authorial presence controlling the economy of the narrative and addressing a literate reading public.

The Oriya short story has come a long way since 1898. It has provided generations of writers with a ground for restless experimentation with techniques of narration. It has also commanded the loyalty of a vast and expanding reading public that sustained innumerable literary pages and weekly supplements of leading dailies, magazines and journals. At a rough estimate, there are at least one hundred thousand Oriya stories scattered in anthologies, collections and magazines. For the poetry-loving Oriyas this switching of loyalty may seem surprising. In contrast to modern Oriya poetry, which exercises only a precarious and tenuous hold on its readers, the short story has never lacked a fascinated and enthusiastic readership. This may be due to the fact that it has remained rooted in tradition while seeking to transform it. It has absorbed alien influences without becoming alienated from its milieu.

The social world which formed the background for Fakir Mohan Senapati's stories has since been transformed. He sought to dramatize in his short fiction the transition from the oral to the written word, from the country to the town, and the shift from a communal way of life to a more individualistic mode of living. The trauma associated with the break-up of a traditional social order gave his stories their special poignancy and continued to shape the vision of a large number of his successors. But the pace of change has accelerated since Independence and the social world of the Oriya short story writer has fragmented under new and irreversible pressures. Modern short stories in Oriya are not so much preoccupied with articulating nostalgia for a lost order as with giving voice to defining the anxiety of coping with a rapidly changing world, which appears hostile and incomprehensible. In the process the form of the Oriya short story has had to be adapted to accommodate the new and unsettling experience of change.

It is impossible to convey the richness and variety of a century-old tradition of short story writing within the compass of a single anthology. What we have attempted here is to bring together thirty-one representative stories which, we hope, will give the reader an idea of the evolution of the form in Orissa. These are not necessarily the best stories of the authors included here. Nor are all of them shining examples of flawless craftsmanship. For instance, *The Shelter* by Gopinath Mohanty, which finds a place in this anthology, may be considered by many to be less powerful and evocative than his other stories such as *Ants*, or *Tadpa* among others. But we selected it because it crystallizes the acute feeling of insecurity of an uprooted lower-middle class adrift in the modern city, and also because it has served as the prototype for several imitations dealing with the same theme. We have opted for Bamacharan Mitra's *Father and Son* for an entirely different reason, because the story captures the eccentricities of a unique individual. Our overall aim has been to highlight the range and variety of Oriya short stories written over the last one hundred years.

We are aware of the fact that several serious practitioners of the genre have been left out because of the constraints of space. But then an anthology is like an aquarium; at any given point of time it can keep a larger number of exhibits out than in. Which, however, does not prove that those outside the pale of the anthology are any less significant. After all, an anthology is just an anthology and not the final word in literary recognition; and a truly good writer will survive the caprices of any anthologist.

May 1998   Editors

Fakir Mohan Senapati

The Bride-Price

Madha Mohanty of Madhupur, a farming Brahmin by caste, was almost seventy. For the first few years after the death of his wife — she died when he was sixty — he had gone around saying that he might get married again; a few people had been sympathetic enough to echo his opinion, and progress had been made, but the old fellow had backed out in the end because the bride-price was too high. For the next couple of years he kept saying: 'Oh dear me, no! What if my second wife gives my little daughter a difficult time? I just can't risk it.' The little daughter, Malati, seven when her mother died, had single-handedly cooked, washed and kept house for her father ever since.

Mohanty had traded off his elder daughter Madhavi — then only eight — to an old man of sixty for a bride-price of seven hundred rupees. That was some four months before his wife passed away. The poor girl became a widow at eleven, but Mohanty never had her home, even for a visit.

By the time she was fifteen, Malati had blossomed into a beauty. Nobody in the neighbouring villages, let alone in Madhupur itself, could hold a candle to her. A lotus growing out of a dunghill, people said. And rightly so. Unlike the other nubile girls in the village, she was never found chattering and gossiping. Her life was spent within the four walls of her home, busy with her chores, and the only time she was seen outdoors was when she went to fetch water from the village pond. With a pitcher on her hip and the upper half of her face veiled, she walked so gracefully along the edge of the narrow path that even the women in the village were impressed. 'But why has old Mohanty kept her unmarried for so long?' they wondered. 'She came of age long ago, didn't she?'

On this subject, Madha Mohanty often came in for sharp criticism from his kinsmen and the villagers, and he was none too happy about it. Getting Malati married was no problem, but who would cook and look after the house if she left? Where would he find a better housemaid? Every morning before going to the paddy fields, he doled out the day's ration, from which the self-denying girl would save part of her share to make an extra bowl of rice-gruel or some rice-cakes for her father's afternoon snack. He allowed only one shell of salt daily. The tamarind tree in the back yard supplied their curry the year round. The old man himself climbed the tree to pick the fruits when they were ripe, not trusting anyone else with it. It was he who shelled them, put them out to dry in the sun, and preserved them under lock and key in earthenware jars. Only two tamarinds a day were allowed.

Malati was a kind-hearted girl. She loved not only her skinflint of a father, but the villagers as well. She had a pet kitten; it was her only company in the lonely house. The kitten would rub itself against her legs all the time, and she let it eat from her bowl and sleep in her bed. Her father loved chilli but wouldn't buy any, so she got two seedlings and planted them in a corner of the courtyard, tending them in summer with water brought all the way from the village pond. When she went out to the fields for her morning and evening ablutions, she scoured the riverbank for edible plants — madaranga, sunsunia, hidimicha, kalamb, meethi. She knew how to make her father a delicious dish out of these.

Madha Mohanty was a man of means. He cultivated fifty acres of land under his own supervision and had turned over nearly half as much again to sharecroppers. There were twelve bullocks and twice as many cows in his cowshed, and he sold every drop of milk. There was very little for him to spend his money on: land revenue was a pittance, and he grew cotton in his back yard, from which he spun clothes for himself and his daughter. His only extravagance, picked up in his younger days, was smoking. A coarse cigar was always clamped between his lips. Every morning he bartered half a seer of rice at Gopia's for a plug of tobacco. Whenever he went out he carried with him a slow-burning stick either in his hand or tucked under his arm.

Malati was getting past the marriageable age, and her betrothal could not be put off much longer. Proposals had poured in from many quarters, but the bride-price offered was nowhere near enough. None of the parties would go above three hundred rupees. However, old Mohanty stuck to his guns: not a paisa under seven hundred would do. Eight-year-old Madhavi had fetched seven hundred! Could that child be compared with the blooming, beautiful Malati? What were the matchmakers thinking? Mohanty was not one to mince his words.

Days passed. Mohanty realized that except for some old widower keen to marry a second or third time no one would offer a higher bride-price for Malati. But he decided he could afford to wait, regardless of how much the villagers spoke ill of him.

Lord Gopaljieu was the ruling deity of Madhupur and the monastery was located in the centre of the village. Though there were other sources of income, the monastery's annual revenue collection from the endowment property alone came to ten thousand rupees.

When the old mahant Raghubar Das passed away, his disciple Lachhman Das became the head. He was a kind and generous soul, with all his predecessor's qualities of head and heart, but without a blemish on his character. Being quite young, he was fond of practical jokes and pranks — anything for good clean fun. He collected and tamed pigeons and bulbuls, and founded an akhada club in the monastery, where the young men of the village assembled to enact the leelas of Lord Krishna and Rama. Sometimes the performances would continue into the small hours of the night. Before the akhada closed, prasad would be distributed. Then a few cronies would follow the mahant to the pond behind the monastery and loll on its banks, smoking ganja and gossiping. The affairs of twenty or more villages were at their fingertips. The mahant had to know everything — he was the judge, magistrate, and moneylender of the area, all rolled into one. Not a single local case could bypass him and go to the courts.

Lachhman Das had a servant called Binodia, a handsome, muscular young man in his early twenties. The mahant had complete faith in him, and the keys to the stores, kitchens, treasury and courtroom all jingled in a bunch on Binodia's waistband. The mahant consulted him on all matters relating to the monastery. Those who knew the equation approached Binodia rather than the mahant to get their business done faster. It could have been easy for him to make a fortune in bribes. The jewels and cash in the treasury were worth some hundred thousand rupees and were all in his care. Nobody would have caught him if he had pocketed some. But Binodia was honest to the bone. He never touched a coin beyond his monthly salary of two rupees, and far from letting the monastery's money be frittered away, he kept a close watch on the sharecroppers and tenants and brooked no cheating. In such matters, he often overruled the mahant's own tendency towards indulgence.

Binodia was a native of Hatagaon, eight miles to the south of Madhupur and also an endowment property of the monastery. Four days back, he had hurried there on receiving the news of his mother's illness. When he returned on this particular morning, he was in low spirits, his mind not on his work.

'Binodia, lad,' said the mahant. 'Why are you squatting here like an anthill? Get up and do some work!'

Binodia prostrated himself at the mahant's feet and burst into tears.

'What's the matter?' asked the mahant. 'What's troubling you?'

'I want to quit my job, sir,' Binodia gasped between sobs. 'My mother said I'd do better to work for the railways, like the other lads around our way. The pay is higher, and Ma said I ought to put something by to get married. My mother would love to see me with a wife before she dies.'

'Is that all?' The mahant chuckled. 'What's there to worry about, you fool? I'll get you a wife. Any nice girl would suit you, I take it?'

'But how am I going to raise the bride-price, sir? It's always quite high, especially in our caste.'

'Don't let that bother you, silly fellow...Marry whomever you please and leave the money matter to me.'

Binodia cheered up and went about his work.

The barber-woman in the village was the widow Padi. Her only daughter had been married off five years earlier and now Padi was alone. It was she who trimmed the nails of the village women and painted their feet with red dye. She was sharp and intelligent, and the women trusted her. Whatever her faults, unreliability was not one of them.

Of late she had been seen bustling in and out of the monastery. She had also often been found knocking at Madha Mohanty's door — when the old man was not home — and the alacrity with which Mohanty's perennially shut doors opened to the gentlest tap from Padi suggested that Malati welcomed her visits.

The first time they met, Padi threw her arms around the girl and cooed: 'My little mother, my jewel, my moonstone! All these long years I have feasted my eyes on you from a distance. Now I hear you'll soon be marrying and moving away. When my own daughter left me I went half-blind with grief, you know. So I had to see you before you left too.' She thrust a handful of mahaprasad into Malati's mouth, declaring: 'From today, you are my daughter and I your mother.'

Malati, who had never had any love and affection shown her before, began to weep. 'Mother, I'll ask no favours of you. Just drop in sometimes and have a bit of a chat with me. I've never had a kind word from my father. He takes offence at the slightest thing and scolds me mercilessly: "Get out of my sight with that ugly face of yours! All you know how to do is to waggle your behind and polish off bowls of rice!". He carried on like this only yesterday, you know; he wouldn't agree to swap some rice for his tobacco; instead he told me to winnow some corn from the chaff-heap to pay for it. Three times I've sifted through the heap, but there's not a decent handful of corn.' A fresh burst of sobs racked the poor girl.

Padi wiped her tears away. 'Don't cry, my pretty little daughter. Lord Gopaljieu willing, we'll see you a princess yet. I've been saying prayers for you every night. Why do you think I go to the monastery so often, if not for your sake?'

Malati's marriage had at last begun to weigh on Mohanty's mind. People were now openly criticizing him. There were a good number of proposals, but Mohanty still would not agree to lower the bride-price. A big bouncing girl of fifteen, in full bloom, he would say to himself; I must have spent six hundred rupees, if not more, on her food alone, and if I settle for a bride-price of three hundred, that will be an outright loss for me, leave alone any profit. No, seven hundred rupees is the least I can accept. The damned girl can wait till she's an old hag. Who cares what people say? After all, I can't afford to lose good money just because of their nattering. Seven hundred in ready cash, yes, seven hundred solid silver coins — not a rupee less. Old Mohanty longed for the day when he would lay his hands on such a sum.

One day it struck him that cosmetics might brighten his daughter's prospects. 'Malati, my girl,' he said, 'take a measure of rice to Gopi Sahu's shop and exchange it for some turmeric. Try rubbing a pinch on your face every day before you go out, and increase the amount when the matchmakers come to see you. But don't forget, young lady, the turmeric has to last you a month.' The poor girl listened, her head bowed, and then ran to the darkest corner of the house to weep in private. But tears were nothing new to her; she often wept until she had no tears left.

A few days later, as Mohanty sat on the verandah rolling cigars, out of the corner of his eye he saw two men striding up to his house. Well-dressed, they looked like gentlemen, but for a moment Mohanty suspected they might be two old spongers come for a free smoke.

He quickly tucked his wad of tobacco into the folds of his dhoti and waited.

'Hello, there,' one of the visitors said. 'Is this Madha Mohanty's house?'

'And what business is it of yours?' Mohanty retorted.

'We've come with a marriage proposal, sir. Are you Madha Mohanty?'

'I am, and you're most welcome. This way, gentlemen. Come right up.' He quickly produced two mats from his house, rolled them out, and, once the visitors were seated, came straight to the point. 'Well, you see, gentlemen, several people have come from different places. They came, they saw and they went away, one and all. The negotiations have always fallen through. Well, you see, if you follow me — you know why, don't you? But never mind, first you must have a look at the girl. If you find her to your liking, we can work out the rest.' He called out to Malati: 'Dear child, these gentlemen have come to see you. Step into the middle of the courtyard, will you? Just as I told you, my dear — you remember, don't you?'

'It's all right, sir,' one of them said. 'We don't need to see her. Her fame has spread far and wide. That's why we came straight to your place.'

'Then, my dear sirs, why waste our breath? The bride-price is seven hundred rupees. Not a paisa, not a half-paisa, not a quarter-paisa less.'

'We couldn't agree more, sir. The girl is certainly well worth a fortune. Besides, our zamindar has given us a free hand to complete the negotiations for him.'

'What!' Madha Mohanty started. 'The bridegroom's a zamindar?'

'Surely you've heard of Sri Binodbihari Gantayatray of Michhupur! He's the zamindar of the entire taluka of Akashpur.'

For quite sometime Mohanty couldn't utter a word. Silently he cursed himself for being a damned fool. Why didn't he go up to a thousand? What's a thousand to a big zamindar? 'But...er...you see,' he began. 'There are the incidentals, you know — the expenses the girl's family will have to incur for the wedding. They'll come to a full three hundred. Gentlemen, I leave it entirely to your conscience. The custom around here is for the bridegroom to foot the bill.'

'Of course, of course! You didn't have to mention it: it's the custom everywhere.'

Heartened, Mohanty was ready to sew up the deal. 'The bride-price and marriage expenses add up to a thousand. I must have the whole of it the moment the bridegroom arrives. Money first, welcome to the bridegroom next — that's my principle. I don't want you to forget that.'

'Fair enough, nothing unreasonable in your wanting that. It's the accepted way, after all, and we've no wish to depart from it.'

'Fine, fine! You seem sensible, men of substance. What better guardians could one hope to talk to? One small thing, gentlemen, before I forget. I would need some cash to get the preparations underway. Twenty rupees or so. But...er...you see, I needn't mention that now, when maybe...'

One of the visitors took a fistful of rupee-coins from his bag and dropped them in front of Mohanty, making no attempt to count them. Babbling incoherently, the old man gathered them with both hands and counted them. Full five and twenty rupees! He couldn't contain his joy. His luck had turned at last, he crowed to himself. After some desultory talk about this and that, the wedding date was set for the seventh day of the month following the Makar festival.

Through the cracks in the door one of the matchmakers noticed a delicate pair of feet in the courtyard. All ten toes turned out, each a charming champak-bud. 'So that's that, Mr Mohanty,' he said, raising his voice. 'We've seen your daughter, whose excellent qualities of head and heart we had heard so much about. You need have no misgivings, we'll give a good account of her in our village. But why haven't you asked us anything about the bridegroom? We feel it's our duty to tell you a little about him. The man has already had two wives — may their souls rest in peace — and this'll be his third; come winter he'll turn sixty-five.' A deep, long-suffering sigh was heard from behind the door and then the feet were gone.

'What does that matter, my friend?' Madha Mohanty said. 'The bridegroom's age is immaterial; he can marry at eighty if he so pleases. But to come back to our discussion, gentlemen, can I rely on you?'

'How can you doubt us, sir, a man of your intelligence and understanding? Do you think it was because we didn't have enough room in our zamindar's mansion to keep our money that we rushed all the way here to throw it down in front of you?'

'Oh no, no! That's not what I meant. You've got me all wrong there, gentlemen. What I meant was — please make sure the bridegroom gets here on the wedding day well before the auspicious moment. Wedding ceremonies must always be timed precisely.'

With many courtesies the two men took leave of old Mohanty.

Never had Malati been shown as much affection as on this day. The old man fussed over her, his voice dripping honey. 'Little mother,' he called her, 'my little daughter-and-mother.' A thousand rupees, no less, were coming his way, and he could well afford to be generous to the girl in his display of affection. But the more affection he lavished on her, the more tears the poor girl shed. Finally, the old man left for the fields, taking with him a piece of sackcloth, a needle and a spool of thread, to stitch a new moneybag while keeping watch over the lazy farmhands.

That day, Malati could not concentrate on her chores. As soon as her father left, she closed the door and, leaning against it, gave way to silent, bitter tears. When Padi came, Malati clung tightly to her feet, her sobs rising to a crescendo. It took Padi quite some time to calm her down and find out why she was so sad. Having heard everything, she said: 'Silly girl, my poor naive little girl! What's there to cry about? Listen, I already knew that some people had called on your father this morning with a marriage offer. There's not even a single word that passed between them that I'm not aware of. Don't worry, daughter — the whole thing was a set-up! Now you open up your pretty little ears and listen carefully to what I have to say. For seven days now I've knelt before Lord Gopaljieu, praying for you. The mahant, too, spoke to Him, on your behalf. And last night he had a dream. The Lord appeared and told him:

"The girl will marry Binodia, the storekeeper of the monastery." Come life, come death, the Lord never speaks falsely. All you have to do is to wait, my darling.'

Malati stared at her, struggling for words. 'But see, mother, I'd rather hang myself than have some doddering old fool come here and marry me.'

Padi grinned from ear to ear, but pretended to be shocked.

Malati went on: 'And another thing, mother. You must help me see Madhavi. I'll die if I can't see her.'

'All you have to do is ask your dear father. He's the one to bring your sister over.'

'Father bring her here? Never. Not long ago she sent a man asking Father for a little money. She wanted it for her fasts and rituals. Father shooed the messenger away, cursing and shouting at him. Another time when Father was ill, my sister sent word she'd like to come and see him. You know what Father's reaction was? "What's there to see in an old man down with a fever? No hurry, the fever won't go away that soon. It's just an excuse to come and have free meals. And once she's here she'll want to stay for a week or two!" There, that's Father for you. My poor sister has had a lot to put up with. She's had a hard life. She lives in a joint family, and she's made to wash all the clothes and the dishes and do a lot of other things. But when she's down with a fever she lies unattended for days. No one offers her so much as a drop of water. Lately she's been getting dreadfully thin. She'll not live long, I can tell you that. If I don't see her soon, it may be too late.' Malati broke into a fresh burst of sobs.

'Wipe away your tears, daughter,' Padi said. 'I give you my word, you'll get to see her.' She left hurriedly, because it was time for Mohanty to return.

A few days later, at lunchtime, Padi banged on Mohanty's door.

'Sir! Are you in, Malati's father? Open the door!'

This was most unusual. When these doors had opened to her before, it had been in response to discreet taps late in the afternoon. Madha Mohanty had just finished lunch and was carding cotton for spinning thread. Ever a suspicious character, he had never entrusted this job to servants or farmhands, because he didn't put it past them to steal a ball of cotton, given the slightest chance.

When the door opened, Padi touched her forehead to the ground and greeted the old man: 'Sir! The news is all over the village. Little Malati's going to be married. How come I haven't been sent for? No marriage takes place in this village without my being hired to wash and paint the walls. I'll start work tomorrow morning.'

'Don't trouble yourself,' Mohanty said, without looking up from his work. 'There's very little to wash and paint here. The girl can do it all by herself. I'm sure your services are not needed.'

'Sir,' Padi droned on, brushing aside his refusal. 'The whole of Madhupur is abuzz. Everyone says how lucky you are. Not only is the groom a big zamindar, but it seems his house is overflowing with gold, silver and money. Rows of granaries full to the brim; two hundred and fifty acres of land! You should thank your lucky stars, sir. They say that he is as generous as can be, that every time you visit your little girl he'll be forcing five hundred rupees on you towards your fare.'

Mohanty stopped his work. 'Padi, old girl' — he could no longer suppress his happiness — 'are you pulling a fast one on me? Are you telling the truth?'

'Nothing else is being talked about in the village these days, sir. They've found out every little detail. Lavish wedding preparations are already afoot at the bridegroom's place. The bride-price has been counted twice over, rupee by shining silver rupee, and put away in a bag. That's the kind of man you're going to be related to and yet not a word from you about preparations!'

'Good girl, Padi. Do wash and paint the walls, if you must. You can start work tomorrow morning, but after breakfast.'

'When do you want me to go round and invite your relatives, sir?'

'To hell with them — I'm not going to invite anyone. They're just waiting for the wedding feast, the freeloaders. I didn't bring up my little girl with the best of everything to blow a good part of the bride-price on my miserable relatives!'

As soon as Padi left, Madha Mohanty called Malati and said,

'Daughter, get that barber-woman to do a thorough job. Look at this part of the wall. It's peeling. Get old Padi to plaster it with fresh mud. But see to it she doesn't start very early in the morning so she can demand a midday meal from us. These village people, they make my blood boil! They won't do a hand's turn of work without asking for a meal.'

Padi promptly carried the tale to his relatives, who accounted for nearly half the population of the village. She spiced it up with a few touches of her own: 'Madha Mohanty won't stand any nonsense from his relatives. He says he'll beat up anyone who comes near his door.'

That infuriated the relatives. None of them even bothered to check Padi's story: Madha Mohanty had not invited them to his elder daughter's wedding, and that had been no small slight. So Padi's words now made them seethe with rage. They waited, gnashing their teeth, for a chance to get even with the old goat.

The mahant was rarely to be seen out of the monastery these days. He practically camped in the grove, surrounded by his disciples and underlings. No matter how important a visitor or a job was, access to him was strictly prohibited. Even the morning akhada had been temporarily shut down. Padi was the only person who went in and out of the grove as she pleased.

Mohanty walked up the steps to his house after his morning ablutions and started as though he had seen a ghost. Padi was squatting on the verandah.

'You're one early bird, Padi,' he said.

'Pity help us!' Padi said in a singsong voice. 'Look at you. You make a game of your responsibilities, while others worry themselves sick! Sir, today's the first day of the wedding ceremony. Have you forgotten? Look at me, I've been up before cockcrow, and have hurried through my chores before rushing over here. Malati has to be anointed with turmeric paste first thing this morning.'

'Nothing doing, Padi. All the rituals will have to wait until the wedding day.'

'No sir, that's simply unheard of. I hear the bridegroom is going to give you three hundred rupees for incidental expenses. If it reaches his ears that you've cut short the rituals and ceremonies, he might have second thoughts. And no one would blame him for that.'

'All right, all right,' Mohanty relented. 'Take a measure of rice to Shambhua's store and buy some turmeric and oil. Paddy prices have shot up — it's now one and a half paisa for a measure. One paisa would've been enough but I haven't the change.'

'Give me a rupee and I will give you back the change.'

'Not bloody likely! Break a rupee and that's the last you see of it!'

'Sir, I'll need more than a paisa's worth of turmeric. Five unwidowed women will have to take part in the turmeric-bath ceremony.'

'Five's a crowd, Padi. One's enough. Once those old hens come along they'll be cackling for breakfast the first thing you know.'

Stifling a grin, Padi showed the old man what she had brought with her: a big bowl of crushed turmeric and a hamper-load of sweetened rice puffs.

'Padi,' the old man stammered. 'What in God's name is all this? Where did you get all this?'

Padi dabbed at her eyes with her veil. 'Sir,' she sniffled. 'I wasn't left badly off, and I do have a little money still. Who will I spend it on, if I don't spend it on Malati? Only the other day you yourself said Malati was like a daughter to me, didn't you? Well then, it's my heart's desire to spend all my savings on my daughter's wedding.'

'Of course, of course, you noble woman!' Mohanty beamed. 'May your praises be sung all around, may your virtues be celebrated in songs and ballads.' He turned to his daughter. 'Girl, what are you waiting for? Take these things indoors. Quick now. Your mother will be upset if you don't accept them. Don't let them spoil.'

'Sir,' Padi said. 'Have you bought the wedding sari? The bride will have to put it on once she's had her turmeric-bath.'

'You have taken the words out of my mouth, Padi! But goodness, what's happened to sari prices? The shopkeeper's charging eight and a half annas for a nine-hand sari. I started the bargaining at five annas and went up to eight, but the fellow wouldn't budge. And he wants a down payment, if you please, no credit! Never mind, let me go and do some more haggling. Maybe I'll have to add an extra half-paisa to my last offer to get that sari.'

'No sir, for a girl of fifteen a nine-hand sari is a bit too small. Listen, I have an idea. I'd have given Malati a good Mangalalata sari in her trousseau anyway. Why don't I give it to her now so she can wear it for the ceremony?'

'Bless you, old girl! No praise will be enough for this gesture of yours. Just think of the punya you're acquiring! Go ahead and buy the twelve-hand Mangalalata sari you've set your heart on.' He reflected for a moment and added: 'One more thing, Padi. Since you're going to the shop, get me a pair of dhotis, will you? I shall need one to wear when I give the bride away. Get them on credit. I'll pay Shambhua down to the last paisa — to the last half-paisa — right after the wedding.' Padi left.

'Shut the door, girl,' Mohanty hissed at his daughter. 'Never leave doors open. And listen, scoop out a little of the turmeric and rice puffs Padi has brought. I'll keep the rest under lock and key. There'll be five women coming to help you get ready. Invite them to breakfast, but don't press them too hard. And once they find out how late the midday meal will be, I'm sure they'll run off home rather than wait. Padi is the only person you need to offer a meal to.'

On the day of the wedding the village was agog with excitement. But Mohanty's household was quiet. His front door remained tightly shut as usual. Not even a hungry beggar stopped there in search of a free meal.

Dusk set in. Mohanty kept his moneybag ready. He rolled a thin wick, poured a drop or two of oil on it, lighted it and put a lamp on the mud platform set up for the wedding ceremony. He couldn't leave that to the girl, for fear she would roll a thicker wick and soak it liberally with oil. A lamp was rarely lit in his house. He always took his dinner and went to bed before sunset.

Padi and Malati spoke in whispers, as the older woman prepared the younger one for the ceremony. Malati was in tears. 'Oh, mother,' she sobbed. 'What am I in for?'

'Quiet, girl,' Padi said. 'Keep your mouth shut and sit pretty. Do exactly as I say. Disobey me once, and the whole scheme might come to nought. Keep saying your prayers.'

The dusk deepened. Mohanty paced the house in growing agitation; from time to time he unbolted the door and scanned the road.

Shortly, two messengers, drenched with perspiration and panting from running, knocked at his door. The bridegroom had suddenly discovered a deficit in the sum he had promised for the marriage expenses, and raising more would take a little time. He would start in the small hours of the morning and reach Madhupur two hours after dawn.

Mohanty digested the message in silence and turned to Padi. 'There's no point waiting. The bridegroom won't be here till halfway through tomorrow morning. I'm going to bed. You and Malati might as well catch some sleep. But for heaven's sake don't sleep too soundly. We've got all sorts of things lying about in the courtyard and there are lots of thieves around here.' With that he snuffed out the lamp and retired to his room.

Midnight drew nearer. The mahant was in the grove, surrounded by his henchmen. The hashish bag was open to everyone. The chillum was not allowed to go cold.

'Hey, Bhima!' the mahant said. 'Hey, Nakula! Is everything ready?'

'Yes master,' the boys answered. 'Just as you ordered.'

'Did you give Padi all the details of the plan?'

'Yes, my lord, word for word.'

'What shape was the girl in?'

'All worked up, my lord, poor Malati was.'

'Hadn't Padi explained things to her?'

'Of course she had, my lord.'

'By the way, how did the two of you manage to sneak into Mohanty's house?'

'We knocked quietly at the back door. Padi was waiting for us.'

Just then another of the mahant's disciples came hurrying up. 'Everyone's ready, my lord — the pipers, the drummers, the palanquin-bearers, the torch-bearers, the barber, the priest, the groom's attendants. Awaiting your orders, my lord.'

'That's fine,' the mahant said. 'Now get the bridegroom dressed up.'

In the small hours, drums rolled and pipes and flutes were heard in front of Mohanty's house. A gaily decorated palanquin stood nearby and on the verandah, on a new reed mat, sat the bridegroom.

Mohanty awoke with a start and, clutching the empty moneybag under his arm, swung himself out of bed, his spirits soaring. Count the cash first, he said to himself — the welcome to the bridegroom can wait.

He rushed out in such haste that he banged his head against the door and slumped to the ground. Blood gushed from the wound, but he had no time to pause and staunch the flow. First count the cash and stow it away in the bag, he thought, as he wrapped a towel around his head. Then he threw the front door wide open. 'Welcome, welcome! Please do me the honour, gentlemen, of coming up the steps and taking your seats.'

The bridegroom's uncle stepped forward. 'Have we the time, father of the bride, to sit down now? The sun is nearly up. The sooner you see off the bride and the groom the better.'

'What! The bridegroom's just arrived, and the ceremony has yet to start, and you're talking about the sendoff!'

'The nuptial knot has already been tied. Doesn't that amount to a marriage ceremony?'

'What about the bride-price, gentleman?' growled Mohanty.

'You've had every coin of it — counted it twice over, haven't you?'

Mohanty's head was already throbbing with pain, and the words came like a shower of white-hot embers. 'What!' he cried in growing indignation. 'You dacoits, bandits, gangsters!'

A furious altercation ensued. Mohanty, demented with anger,

hopped about wildly, shouting, shaking his fists and cursing. But the bridegroom's people displayed admirable sang-froid and remained cool — smirking, tapping each other on the shoulder and exchanging broad winks. The drummers suddenly surrounded the old man and chanted, beating their drums lustily: 'Generous master, give us money for booze. Let's rejoice in your daughter's happiness.' The pipers joined in, blowing their pipes near the old man's behind so that he squirmed like one possessed, his cries drowned in the din. If the idea was to befuddle Mohanty, it succeeded. A scamp lighted a sparkler and threw it at him. It singed his back, raising blisters as big as potatoes. The whole village, from toddlers to old bent-backs, turned up to watch the tamasha — it was a thick crowd. The men, quite a few of them Mohanty's relatives, roared with laughter; the urchins clapped their hands, danced about and sang a chorus: 'Isn't he pleased with his bride-price? The skinflint didn't even pay for the wedding rice!'

Mohanty now realized the full horror of his situation. The whole village was on one side and he on the other, and no one was willing to listen to him. He pushed his way through the mob and rushed out howling, to the monastery.

The mahant had just woken up. 'Who on earth is making such a racket so early in the morning?' he growled, when he saw the dishevelled old man.

Mohanty prostrated himself with a thud at the feet of the bleary-eyed mahant, addressing him incoherently and at the top of his voice.

'Get up, Mohanty,' said the mahant. 'Pick yourself up and tell us what the trouble is.'

Mohanty was foaming at the mouth like a toddy-pot and could neither cry properly nor speak. He gestured that he needed a drink of water, and when some was brought he drank the whole pitcher in one breath, although he had not washed his face nor brushed his teeth. He sat quietly for some time, gathering his wits about him. The mahant kindly patted him on the back and let him take his time. Just then Pari Parida, the bridegroom's uncle, and four of his men came running in and threw themselves at the mahant's feet.

'Get up, my sons,' the mahant said. 'Who are you? What's the matter with you? Speak up.'

Pari Parida folded his hands and said, 'My lord, we poor visitors to this village have been tricked. Merciful Master, lord of the village, we ask only for justice. This Madha Mohanty, who is sitting so innocently in your presence, is our samdhi.'

'Your in-law?' hissed Mohanty. 'What relation am I to your family, you thief, you rascal?'

The mahant intervened. 'Hold on, Mohanty. Let him have his say. You can answer him later.'

'My lord,' Pari continued, 'this man took a bride-price of seven hundred rupees to give his daughter Malati in marriage to my nephew. The nuptial knot was duly tied. After that he demanded another three hundred rupees towards marriage expenses. That is unjust — why should we foot the bill? Now this joker is holding back his daughter from us.'

'Tell the truth,' the mahant admonished. 'Remember you're in the house of God. Did you or did you not pay Mohanty the bride-price?'

'I speak nothing but the truth, my lord. I gave Mohanty the money, rupee by rupee.'

'Incredible! Mohanty's a man of good sense, not a mindless child. To accept the money and then deny it — do you expect me to believe that?'

Madha Mohanty flung himself down before the mahant. 'My lord! Incarnation of justice! Please throw these horrible people out.'

'Look,' the mahant said. 'These visitors are our guests. They might easily spread rumours that justice was denied them in our territory. No, we must examine all the evidence and establish the truth.'

He turned to Pari Parida. 'Parida, do you stick to your story of having paid Mohanty seven hundred rupees? Do you have any witnesses?'

'Hundreds of them, my lord,' Parida said, folding his palms. He turned around and addressed the congregation. 'Come forward, Bhima, Nakula, Makra, Shankra, Radhu Mohanty, Sadhu Dhal and Dharma Patra.'

The mahant cross-examined them one by one. They all sang the same tune: 'Old Mohanty took the money, counted it twice over, put it in a bag and carried it indoors.'

The mahant glanced at the moneybag Mohanty was still clutching under his arm.

Madha Mohanty responded with only one word: 'Thugs!'

'Any witness for the plaintiff?' the mahant asked.

Ten or twelve villagers, all Mohanty's kinsmen, rose unbidden.

'These are sworn enemies of mine,' Mohanty said. 'Their testimony proves nothing.'

'All right, forget the witnesses,' the mahant said. 'We'll make an enquiry on the spot. Let's all go to Mohanty's house. There must be traces of the ceremony, if it did take place.'

The bridegroom's party made a pretence of resistance. 'My lord, what evidence do you hope to find after so long a time? The marriage was solemnized at the stroke of midnight. Many hours have passed since. Please, we beg you, give up the idea of inspecting the site.'

Madha Mohanty, suddenly excited and happy, clung to the mahant's feet, pleading, 'Please come, my lord. Please pay a visit to my humble hut and see for yourself.'

'Please don't go there, my lord,' protested the bridegroom's uncle, looking crestfallen. 'It'll serve no purpose.'

'Of course we shall go,' the mahant said, brushing him aside. 'I must get to know Mohanty's side of the story.'

The crowd followed him to Mohanty's house.

The bridegroom was sitting on Mohanty's verandah in full regalia — a string of kautuk sutra, plum leaves and blades of grass tied to his fingers, a painted sola crown on his head, a nutcracker in his hand. On the deserted wedding platform lay a coconut.

'My lord,' gushed Pari Parida, with folded hands, 'isn't this evidence enough?'

'All very well,' agreed the mahant, 'but let's go inside and look for more.'

'My lord,' insisted Parida. 'Let the look of this platform suffice. Here, my lord, the bride put the customary eight pitchers of water and over there, a handful of roasted rice. There are petals in the water vessels. Over there, my lord, are the remains of the feast. The Brahmins sat on that side; we the relatives and the caste-men, on this. The leftover food is there on the banana leaves we ate from. Nothing has been cleared away yet.'

'But I...er...I can definitely tell you,' stammered Mohanty, 'that my hearth was not even lit last night.'

The mahant strode across the courtyard and pushed the kitchen door open with his walking-stick. The embers glowed red in the oven, and all around it lay big cauldrons with curry, dal and rice sticking to them.

Mohanty's wits deserted him. His back was burning, also his head and his heart. What's all this, he wondered — did ghosts sneak in and do it all? His legs gave way and he sank to the ground. The crowd jabbered and gesticulated. Their words didn't enter Mohanty's ears. A fit of trembling had seized him, and he groaned like a bear with a fever.

'What have you to say, Mohanty?' the mahant demanded.

'My lord, all I can say is my daughter's wedding did not take place.'

The eldest among the relatives, Balaram Nayak, elbowed his way through the crowd, stopped before the mahant and bowed with deep respect. 'My lord, ruler and sovereign, every aspect of our life is open to you except caste matters. Those you must leave to the caste brothers to sort out. Madha Mohanty has withheld his legally betrothed daughter from marriage. If she does not meet her bridegroom before sunset today, Madha will find himself ostracized. Water, fire, barber and washerman will be denied him. And eternal spinsterhood awaits his daughter.'

'A fat lot Mohanty cares for these empty threats!' observed the mahant. 'He could keep a small fire permanently going in his hearth, store water in hundreds of pitchers and jugs. He'll have no need to go out to seek them.'

'No, my lord, that won't work. He'll pollute any pond he dares dip his pitcher into. It'll cost him ten rupees each time to purify it. A pitcher of water will cost him ten rupees. And another thing, he'll pollute any path he treads upon. We'll have to engage a man to follow Mohanty around and splash cow dung water behind him.'

'No, no!' exclaimed the mahant. 'You can't do that to poor old Mohanty. He could never stand it at his age. Who'll come to his aid in times of need if you, his caste brothers, don't!'

'Let this be clear, my lord. When Mohanty dies, none of us will touch his body with the long end of a bargepole. It'll have to be dragged by the untouchables all the way to the cremation ground. And all the paddy, all the grain Mohanty has stored in his house will go to the lower castes, for none of us will sully our hands with the polluted stuff!'

Every word of this sank deep into the old man's mind. They were all in cahoots, he realized, the whole pack of them. That sweet-talking devil of a mahant, too, was on their side. If they literally tore up the foundations of his house and carried off everything he owned, he wouldn't be able to lift a finger against them! Going to court would be a waste of time. A terrible fear clutched at his heart. He rose to his feet, grasped Balaram Nayak by the hand, and cried: 'Nayak, jewel of our caste, I beg you to forgive me. Please go ahead with the wedding ceremony, but under the circumstances, excuse me from taking part. Malati's uncle will see to everything.'

As soon as the words were out of his mouth, Padi, at a sign from the mahant, promptly escorted the bride and groom to the platform. The priest and the barber were at the ready; the mantras were quickly reeled off, and Malati's uncle Sagani Patra gave the bride away. The whole ceremony was over in under an hour.

When the time came for Malati to leave with her husband, she caught hold of her father's feet and wept bitterly. The old man freed himself with such a vigorous shake that the poor girl flew into the air and landed some ten paces away. But she did not take it amiss. She clutched his feet again, imploring, 'Let me stay and look after you for a few days, Father. I haven't the heart to leave you alone in your present condition.'

'Be off,' Mohanty screamed. 'Get out of my sight. I've wasted enough money on feeding you for fifteen years. I'm hardly in the mood to start feeding you for another two months. Off you go, you and your husband.'

Padi drew Malati away and placed her in the palanquin beside her husband. The bearers lifted the palanquin, and their voices rose in a rhythmic chant:

> Yes, brother! Carry, oh brother! Gently, brother!
> Hurry, oh brother! Scurry, oh brother!...

They were already in the fields outside the village by the time the band and the bridegroom's party rose to leave.

Five or six days later, the mahant said to his henchmen, 'What's become of Madha Mohanty? No sign of the old boy anywhere. He complained of fever that day, didn't he? Go and find out.'

Mohanty's door was locked from the inside. Loud knocking produced no response. The mahant's men tried the back door, then the front door again. They repeatedly shouted his name and kicked at both doors. In the end, they climbed over the wall and got in.

What they saw staggered them.

The old man was found spread-eagled on the threshold, head inside and trunk out, his clothes in disarray and body swollen like a barrel.

Half his face had decomposed and maggots were crawling out of it. Clouds of flies buzzed around him.

Evidently, the old man, after shutting all the doors and windows, had retired for the night after the wedding but had never reached his bed. His moneybag lay by his side.

The relatives and the priest approached the mahant for advice. Mohanty had died in a state of sin. Whoever touched his dead body would have to undergo a penance. Arguments raged, until finally it was decided that the mahant's young disciples should first remove from Mohanty's house two poutis of rice for use in the penitential rites, then the priest would recite mantras and sprinkle the dead with holy water to rid it of sin.

'But what sin did the poor soul commit to end up with maggots crawling out of his head and face?' the mahant asked Bishu Rath.

'The answer is there in the Holy Books,' answered the old priest. 'The man who gives his young daughter in marriage to an old man will have worms feasting on his vile head when he dies. Why did no worms crawl out of Mohanty's legs, feet, hands or back? That could not happen: if the Holy Books say it is the head, it has to be only the head.'

The kinsmen, eight or ten of them, returned to Mohanty's house with towels pressed to their noses to keep out the stench. Lest the sin be still attached to the body, they sprinkled it with cow dung water, from head to toe, and the pallbearers hauled it away unceremoniously, with a half-hearted chant of 'The Lord's name is the ultimate truth'.

The corpse, already falling to pieces, was rolled into the bushes, without a proper cremation.

Mohanty's daughter and son-in-law performed the twelve-day funeral rites with due solemnity. The whole village, irrespective of caste and creed, was invited to three sumptuous feasts. Everyone sang the couple's praises.

Binodia, the erstwhile storekeeper of the monastery, now goes by the name of Baboo Binodbehari Mohanty, Esq. He has acquired the whole zamindari of Gopalpur taluka and has two accountants and eight bodyguard-cum-messengers on his payroll. He lives in great style, in a brick house with four clusters of rooms. By any reckoning, he must count as one of the bigger zamindars of the district. Madha Mohanty, rumour has it, had over two hundred thousand rupees salted away, and Binodia found them all. There's a lot of truth in the saying:

> Scrape and scrounge is the skinflint's lot
> Lucky the heir who gets all his honey-pot!

Laxmikanta Mahapatra

The Old Bangle Seller

It was a fiercely hot day in the month of Phalgun. The sun beat remorselessly down on the village road where the old bangle seller was walking, a basket on his head. He was perhaps nearing sixty, or was maybe even older, and toothless like a newborn. Silvery white hair covered his chest and head. Drenched in perspiration, he trudged along.

At the edge of the village he stopped by the big house. It had a high verandah plastered with cement; the straw thatch over the roof was perched high, thick and in seven tiers; the front doorway was massive. The old man gently eased his load down and waited to catch his breath.

After a while, a maid sauntered out from inside the house and noticed the old man. He was someone she knew.

'There you are, bangle seller, after a pretty long time,' she said with a smile. 'Have you got anything new?'

'Of course,' said the old man. 'But daughter, first get me some water. My throat is dry and I'm dying of thirst. Oh, this heat! It will kill me.'

The maid fetched a big jug, which the old man eagerly lifted to his lips. He poured the water down his throat, half-emptying it in one breath. 'Bless you, daughter,' he said with a profound sigh. 'God bless you.'

'Enough, enough!' The maid giggled. 'Come inside. My young mistress wants to see your bangles.'

The old man rose to his feet, picked up his basket and followed her inside.

They went past the main entrance and the hallway, through the enormous, paved courtyard with a cemented platform in the middle, to reach the spacious living quarters at the rear. The young daughter-in-law of the house, the end of her sari over her face, stood at the door. The old man lowered his basket and waited.

'Go on,' the chirpy maid prompted the young lady. 'Ask him to show you his wares. Don't feel shy, little mistress. Come, come, he's an old man. Why don't you rummage through his basket yourself?'

The young mistress pulled back her veil and stepped forward with a smile. The old man looked up at her and was struck by her beauty. Her face was like a sculpture and radiant like a champak flower. The red silk sari she wore down to her ankles revealed her svelte figure. The old man's eyes, lit with joy, stayed riveted on her face. His eyes feasted on her and he wanted to say his bangle selling spiel, but couldn't find the words.

It took him a while to get a grip on himself. 'Choose anything you like, Mother,' he said. He didn't know why he had addressed her as mother but it made him feel good to do so. His heart suddenly brimmed over with happiness.

'You have Asman-tara bangles?' asked the young woman overcoming her shyness.

The old man could not recollect having ever heard a sweeter voice; it was like honey; and her words tinkled in his ears long after she had spoken.

'No Mother,' he said. 'But there are many other varieties — Rangajhiliri, Baulaphulia, Bichhamalia, Chunatipi. Pick out anything that takes your fancy. I will get you Asman-tara bangles as soon as I can.'

The young woman selected some bangles, but wondered if they would fit her.

'Come, Mother,' said the old man. 'Give me your wrist and I'll try them on you.'

The young woman hesitated.

'So shy, Mother?' The old man laughed. 'And of me? Am I not your old son, huh? Do mothers feel shy with their children?'

The perky maid gave a hoot of laughter. 'What luck, young mistress! What a wonderful old son to have, I say!'

'Oh, away with you!' the young mistress giggled, holding out her wrists to the old bangle seller.

What beautiful hands, the old man thought. Soft, plump, pink, full of life and good fortune; the long tapering fingers could put champak buds to shame. Were they ordinary mortal hands or had they been chiselled and honed to perfection by some celestial craftsman? How could he touch them, hold them in his own harsh, calloused and dirty paws? His hands trembled when he finally took her left palm and gently squeezed it to slip a bangle on. Her wrist was so fragile and delicate that the bangles looked earthy and crude; a little carelessness on his part and she could be hurt. With wrists like these he had to be gentle as never before.

As long as her hand was in his, his happiness was boundless. There had been no greater bliss than this in all his sixty-odd years on earth, and nothing certainly half as soul-satisfying. If only he had wrists like these to slip bangles onto every day of his life!

Just then the mother-in-law emerged from the living quarters and the daughter-in-law, hurriedly drawing the veil over her face, scampered off. The old mistress looked at the maid. 'Buying bangles, are we?'

'Yes,' the maid replied. 'The young mistress wanted to have some.'

The old lady turned to the bangle seller. 'What do they cost?'

'Cost?' said the old man. 'How much can a few bangles cost?'

'Tell me how much and I'll pay for them.'

'Nothing. I will not accept a paisa from Mother.'

The old lady, a shade surprised, turned to the maid. 'What's this mother business about?'

The maid giggled. 'The old man has made himself a son of our young mistress.'

The mother-in-law gave a tiny flicker of a smile. 'All right, old son, accept the price of the bangles this time. Next time you may give away some for free. You're a poor bangle seller, after all.'

'It's my gift to Mother. Sorry, I can't accept money for them. A few bangles will make me no poorer than what I already am.' He smiled, picked up his basket, hoisted it up on his head and hurried out of the house. The maid ran after him for some distance, calling for him to stop and take the money, but the old bangle seller did not look back.

So moved was the old man that from then on he unfailingly visited the village every second or third day. But bangles were not something people bought daily; womenfolk wanted them only once in a while and especially during the festivals. But he would religiously go from door to door, hawking his wares. Sales did not matter, he wasn't really keen on his business. All he longed for was a glimpse of his little mother. He would not stop at the outer door of her house but march right into the courtyard. 'Does anyone here want new bangles?' he would trill out, not bothering to lower his basket, and wherever the young woman was she would bustle out and stop by the door. The old man would take a long look at her face, his heart overflowing with ecstasy, half-hoping she would say yes so that he'd have an opportunity to hold her divine hands in his again and slip bangles on them. But the young woman would smile and shake her head, and the old man would slowly leave with a sigh. Sometimes if the young mistress was a little slow in showing up when the old man called, the perky maid would pitch in: 'Young mistress, where are you? Look, your old son's here!' Then the old man too would cry out with professional flair: 'Bangles! New bangles! Wonderful bangles!' The daughter-in-law would appear with an amused grin.

This had come to be a routine, and each time the old man came to see her he vowed to himself that he would make a bunch of Asman-tara bangles as soon as he could. The Rajo festival was not far off and that would be a fitting occasion to change old bangles for new. She would hold out her lovely wrists to him and how he would take them, one after the other, in his own, and slip the bangles on! The mere anticipation could keep him buoyed up for days, even for weeks and months. He couldn't wait for the Rajo to arrive.

Meanwhile it was the month of Baisakh and the heat was unbearable. As old and feeble as he was, the bangle seller could no longer withstand the strain of his visits to the village. He fell ill and ran a high fever for several days, his legs and hands swelled, and the way he clung to bed his neighbours wondered whether he would pull through. But the old man himself was least bothered; his only worry was that he had not seen his little mother for a long time. He could hardly bear the torture.

The Rajo festival was now just a few days away. Two long months had passed since the bangle seller had last seen the young woman. If he had been able to stand on his legs he would have surely dragged himself all the way to her house. But how could he go to her without the promised bangles. It was high time he stirred himself, collected the ingredients and made some Asmantara bangles. True, it was still quite painful for him to sit up, but he couldn't dream of delegating the work to somebody else. So he got down to it himself, summoning every bit of his fifty years' experience of bangle-making. He did not mind if one day's work took all of four; the bangles simply had to be matchless, out of this world. And that's how it went. The bangles were finally finished just two days shy of the Rajo. They were perfect, just as he had dreamed; he had never made anything half as beautiful before. He was thrilled. How lovely these would look on his mother's delicate wrists!

The festival was now only two days away. The old man had not slept a wink the previous night. The girls and young women would put on new clothes and new bangles first thing tomorrow morning. 'What shall I do?' he thought, despair tugging at his heart. 'I can't walk a step and I wouldn't dream of sending her the bangles through someone else. I haven't seen her for aeons. My days are numbered; and if I don't see her now, perhaps I never will. Never will I have another occasion to hold her hands.' He found inexplicable strength surging through his tired, weary, decrepit limbs.

Next morning he had an early meal, carefully wrapped the

bangles at the end of his towel, hung it gently across his shoulder and set out. Every step was an effort, a torture, and the distance of ten miles took him inordinately long; it was well into the afternoon when he reached the village.

He stopped at the same spot in the courtyard where he always had and called out, his voice breaking with joy and happiness: 'New bangles! Mother, come on out. You wanted Asman-tara bangles, remember? I've got them for you.'

But no one came out and no one answered.

'Little Mother!' The old man raised his voice. 'I've got lovely bangles for you.'

Finally, the old lady of the house emerged, with the maid in tow.

'Where's Mother?' asked the bangle seller. 'I've got Asman-tara bangles for her. She'll wear them for the Rajo.'

The maid who had always laughed and joked with him remained solemn.

The old lady gave the old man a cold look. 'Nobody in this house now will ever need new bangles,' she said curtly.

'Don't say that!' cried the old bangle seller. 'I've made these for Mother with so much love and care.'

'She needs them no more.'

'All right, forget the bangles. Call her out and I'll just see her once and leave. I haven't seen her for ages.'

'You can't see her.'

'Can't see her?' The old man felt a bolt of lightning crashing on his head. His eyes instantly welled up with tears. 'But why? Please, please, let me see her. Just once. You can see I'm going to die soon.'

The old lady turned to the maid with a frown. 'Go tell the daughter-in-law.'

The maid left.

After a little while, the young woman came noiselessly to the door and stood exactly where she always did whenever he called. She did not have her tinkling ankle-bells and, instead of her beautiful red silk sari with golden borders, she wore a plain white cotton one.

A tremor ran through the old bangle seller's body. His head

swam and his eyes closed, smarting with tears. He looked up at her again, this time searchingly at her wrists. Those lovely hands were bare, without bangles. He burst into a wail.

The young widow silently withdrew.

'Mother!' lamented the old man, choking in grief. 'Mother!' He unwrapped his towel, took out the bangles he had fashioned with so much love and dashed them on the courtyard. They broke into smithereens. Then he turned and left without a backward glance.

After he had left the old lady and the maid burst into heart-rending sobs.

Godavarish Mohapatra

Maguni's Bullock Cart

Birth and death. The two inevitable phenomena that happened every day among the two hundred thousand odd people of Khalikote town. Such news, however, never travelled beyond the confines of families and neighbourhoods. But when Maguni died, the news spread through the town, and even beyond, and not only that, whoever heard it reacted, after moments of stupefied silence, with 'So the poor fellow's gone! How sad!'

Who was this Maguni? The ruler of Khalikote? The king of a neighbouring state? A major figure in the administration? A big taxpayer, a rich moneylender? A Congress leader spearheading the satyagraha movement for independence, someone used to delivering stirring speeches to delirious crowds? A patriot born to be profusely decorated? Or a prominent native of the town who was always chosen to receive visiting dignitaries? Who was he? Why did just about everyone in the town as well as in the far-flung villages on the forest's edge know who he was?

Not an important man, all Maguni did was drive a Bullock Cart. That was how he eked out a living. All his life he had struggled — not for any exalted goals of his country or countrymen, but simply for himself, for his own little stomach. He and a pair of bullocks — the three of them had forged a bond that had cast an indelible impression on people's minds.

As regular as the sun that rose and set over the fort town, Maguni made his daily trip to the railway station. He was as punctual as a clock, people said. Even in the rainy months, when the sun often remained hidden behind the clouds, his passage announced the time of day. The seasons were at times irregular, the monsoons could be late, or the summer not hot enough, but never did a day go by without Maguni's cart rumbling along the road to the railway station. Even on deep winter mornings, when it was so bitterly cold that people, wrapped in blankets, remained glued to their verandahs, Maguni drove his cart along the serpentine road beneath the hills with a song on his lips.

So what if the king of Khalikote had two motorcars, Maguni sometimes joked. Did the king have a driver like him? His Bullock Cart was far better than any motorcar. He just had to gently pat Kalia and Kasara on their rumps to rev the engine and belt out snatches of the popular ballad 'Rama and Laeekhana followed the trail of the magic deer...' to make the bullocks fly. The hills echoed with his songs and the half-asleep forest fowl and pheasants replied to them, awakening the stray village dogs and making them howl. And, inexorably, his cart rumbled on.

As he carted people across the length and breadth of the town and beyond, he kept them hooked on his stories, which flowed out of his mouth like an endless stream. The stories of his life. Raised with love and care by doting parents, his was a wonderful childhood: a comfortable bed, large meals, not having to do a day's work. Life continued to treat him well even after both his parents had died and he grew into manhood. He married a beautiful girl, whose words were as sweet as her lips. Her breath was fragrance itself and flowers bloomed where she walked. Life was a dream, a glorious riot of joy and happiness. Only this didn't last long. His young wife departed for the other world, where he hoped to join her when his day was done.

The poignant stories of his life brought tears not only to the eyes of the listeners, but to his own too. Discreetly wiping away his tears, he would change tack and launch into something else. The journey would come to an end, but not his stories. With the solitary exception of the king of Khalikote, everyone, from the dewan to the managers, from lawyers and moneylenders to the followers of Mahatma Gandhi, had been aboard his cart at one time or another. And his cart had been witness to many scenes: young widows on their heart-breaking journeys from their in-laws back to their parents; merry brides on their joyous rides from their parents' homes to their husbands'; people like Gada Raul of Mandal village, who went to jail for failure to pay his taxes, and whose worldly possessions, down to his last broom, were transported to the king's court in Maguni's cart; or like Madhu Rath of Bendalia, who was sent to prison for committing a murder; prosecution lawyers; handcuffed peasant leaders who courted arrest with smiles. It had seen sorrow, it had seen joy. Torrents of tears had drenched its straw seats just as bursts of laughter had rattled its bamboo ribcage. So when Maguni spoke, a legend spoke, the living voice of Khalikote's history spoke. He brought so much gusto and excitement to his stories that even the bullocks at times slowed down and stopped. 'Look how these animals love to listen to the stories,' he would chuckle. He could never prod them with the goad.

Came the day when Maguni heard that people would no longer ride his cart. The wealthy Singhs were planning to put a bus on the road. He broke into uproarious laughter. A bus to beat his well-nourished Kalia-Kasara team? Would people ever desert his cart for a godforsaken bus?

Everyone laughed at him, but he was unfazed.

A few days later a monster of a motorbus rolled into town.

Poor Maguni's done for, people remarked. Now his business will fold. How can a Bullock Cart ever match a bus that can carry twenty people at a time and cover forty miles in an hour?

Maguni's heart sank and panic seized him. True, he did not break down and cry, but he came close to tears. He remembered the public meeting at Kodola he had once driven past. A speaker there had asserted that machines were no match for human hands. If so, then wasn't his bullock cart better than the motorbus? He'd go to all those people who had gone to the meeting and listened to the speech. Would they turn a deaf ear to him? If they did, then he'd go to their leader, Mahatma Gandhi. Everyone said he was a great friend of the poor and of the wretched of the earth. Would he turn Maguni away? Would he say let Maguni perish and the Singhs prosper?

The bus plied the same route as Maguni's cart. Day after day after day. The bus went full, the cart empty.

Maguni rose at midnight to go and park his cart in front of the railway station before daybreak, but the passengers chose to wait for the bus, which arrived late in the morning.

Maguni changed the old upholstery of his straw seats for new jute sackings, but people still thronged the bus.

Maguni tried to take the passengers by the hand and cajole them into his cart, but they all headed for the bus.

Some days passed, and then some more.

Maguni stuck it out. He cut his meals down from two to one a day.

A few days passed.

Maguni switched from hot, freshly cooked rice to watered-rice.

More days passed.

From one helping of watered-rice a day Maguni made it once in two days.

Still more days passed.

He did not light his hearth for days on end. There was nothing to cook.

Kalia and Kasara became dreadfully thin. Their ribs jutted out. Often Maguni put his arms around their necks and the three of them wept silent tears.

Gone off his hinges, people commented, crazy from hunger and grief.

More days passed.

Then came the morning when people had to break down the door of Maguni's house to get to his body. He lay on a tattered mattress, his goad beneath it.

A pyre was lit for him. Thick black smoke billowed into the sky, and countless birds, flapping their wings in anguish, flew by. The news swept the town, and nearly two hundred thousand people lamented, 'So poor Maguni's gone! What a pity!'

Kalindi Charan Panigrahi

Victory Celebration

'There you are, Manik,' Mukund said, as he barged into the house. 'Now boil these and stir up a good brew.'

'How much water do I put in?' Manik asked, taking the bundle of dry roots from her brother.

'Not much, I guess. Half a bowl should do. But remember to take it off the fire before the water turns purple. Give Father a cup of it every so often. Oh, that reminds me, keep this lump of sugar. If he complains of being thirsty, give him a little drink of sweetened water.'

'What did Nidhi Maikap say? Father will get well, won't he?' The words seemed to pass her lips only with the greatest effort. Undernourished and thin as a stick, at fifteen she looked like a child of eight or nine.

'Of course he will! Do you think I'd be running around, if there was no hope? Old Nidhi Maikap — why, you should've seen how thrilled he was when I handed him his full fee of eight annas. "Don't worry, son," the country doctor had said with a chortle. "This is a very potent concoction I'm giving for your father. If he doesn't sit up like a hale and hearty bear first thing tomorrow morning, then my name isn't Nidhi Maikap." The old windbag. But listen, Manik. He said Father must have one meal a day of rice gruel from tomorrow on. We'll need paddy for that. But then we don't have a grain in the house, do we?'

Manik stopped in her tracks. She didn't know where in this godforsaken village she could borrow or buy a measure of grain. Even if somebody had a little stowed away, he wouldn't part with it for anything in the world, no matter how hard she banged her head against his door.

'Never mind,' said Mukund wearily. 'We'll think about that tomorrow. Now go and make the brew.'

Nothing had been cooked since the night before, and the fire had died in the oven. Manik pulled out a handful of straw from the thatch, twisted it into a wisp and went out to borrow an ember from a neighbour.

Mukund tiptoed into the small dark room where his sick old father, Guna Parida, lay dying. Six months had passed since he had taken to his bed. Meanwhile his wife and two young sons had passed away, within eight days of each other, bloating up horribly before dying. God alone knew what disease it was, but it had taken a heavy toll in the countryside: thousands of people had meekly succumbed to it. Man is born to die, thought Mukund. Sooner or later. So what did it matter? But this bland philosophizing irked him. Maybe his folks could have scraped through with the proper medication. But where was the money for that? The little he had was barely enough to buy rice for the sick.

Guna raised his withered hand and signalled him to sit down. Mukund slumped to the ground beside his bed. 'Don't worry, my son.' Guna spoke in a hoarse whisper. 'Just wait and see. I'll pull through.'

Hope welled up in Mukund's heart. Yes, why not, he thought. Didn't old Maikap say the new potion would work wonders? A sigh escaped him. He had been able to do precious little for his mother and brothers; they had dropped dead before he knew what was happening. But he wouldn't let his father go the same way.

Guna Parida's four acres of land had dwindled into a small holding, and the produce was scarcely enough for the family. Like others, Guna had had to sell off chunks of land in order to survive. The rains had been unkind two years in a row and, as though that was not enough, the wartime government had declared Orissa a surplus state. It had squeezed the peasantry dry in its procurement drive and had sold off the entire rice stock beyond the borders, triggering a famine.

'Uma!' Guna stammered, staring blankly at his son. His mind was wandering.

Mukund winced as if scorched by a flame. In the early days of the famine, Uma, Guna Parida's eldest daughter, abandoned by her husband, had deserted her children and run off with another man, sullying the name of the Parida clan. Tongues had wagged; some said she had made straight for the poorhouse, others said she had become a whore. The incident had left indelible lines of shame and mortification on poor old Guna's heart. Why didn't the bitch drop dead? Mukund thought bitterly. Couldn't she find a drop of poison to put an end to her shameful life? Starvation and disease took so many people, why not her? Mukund always walked away when her name was spoken. Were his old father well, he wouldn't have hesitated to give him a piece of his mind. 'Is the brew ready?' he called out to Manik, ignoring the old man.

'In a moment,' Manik replied. After a while she came in with a chipped stone bowl.

Guna took a small sip with great difficulty and shook his head. Manik set the bowl down on the floor near his pillow and left.

Outside, dusk had fallen. Clouds had thickened in the sky since afternoon, and now a pitiful drizzle had started. The month of Shravan was on its way out, but there hadn't been a single good shower.

Manik went into the kitchen and found herself a clean white rag, rolled it into a wick, and rubbed it in the bottom of an earthen bowl that had last seen oil ages ago. Oil had been the first thing to vanish from the wartime market.

'Anything to eat, little sister?' Mukund affected an exaggerated casualness.

'What!' A brief smile sprung to Manik's face which resembled a withered bud. 'Oh yes, there's a little rice porridge from yesterday.'

'Good. You eat it up. It's your turn to keep watch over Father tonight.'

'But Brother, you haven't had anything since the day before yesterday!'

'Don't you remember the porridge you made the day before yesterday? Well, who ate most of it, if I didn't?'

Manik recalled having cooked a little porridge two days ago. It was a strange, outlandish dish, cooked out of three-day-old rice-water and yam leaves. 'But I'm sure you didn't touch any of it,' she said.

'Who says so?' Mukund growled, rolling his large eyes, bloodshot from lack of sleep. 'Manik, are you my guardian, eh? Do I have to eat, sleep and do everything under your nose or what? If I told you I've eaten, then I've eaten, and that's all there is to it.' He was the hope of the family, he had overheard his parents saying, he was the breadwinner. Pushing nineteen, Mukund was a strapping lad, and ever since his father took to his bed, he had looked after the land — ploughing, digging and watering desperately. In happier circumstances he would have been married by now. A rueful smile creased his face. His mother had looked forward to it so much. But she was dead and gone, and now Father too was sinking. Why should I let this slip of a girl boss me? 'Watch what you say, you little goose, when I ask you to do something. Who suffers from thirteen kinds of ailments in twelve months, little sister?' He tried to sound as gruff as a family patriarch. 'You're so thin that a whiff of breeze would fell you. And you talk about what I eat, hah! Us men, we take a nibble whenever we can, of whatever we can lay our hands on, from flattened rice to rice puffs. But look at you. You said you had a bite this morning, didn't you? Now let's go out to the street and ask a passer-by to take a look at the two of us and guess which one's starving. You know something, poor Ghania has yet to recover from last year's bruises, I pinned him down to the ground so hard. Now that's something I really enjoy — the bagudi competition during the Rajo Festival.' He gave a croak of a laugh. 'Sister, you'd better stop yapping.' Yesterday's rice porridge, he thought with a sigh. It must have fermented nicely by now. But I mustn't wolf it down. I must wait. Maybe Manik will save a little of it for tomorrow and cook it with a handful of broken rice and both of us can have a helping.

The sick man groaned hoarsely. Mukund and Manik hurried inside and propped him up against the wall. Guna had messed himself. Manik fetched a rag and water and cleaned him. Then she lit a wick in an earthen lamp and brought a bowl of sugar water for him. Guna refused to take more than a gulp.

They came out of the room. Mukund lifted a pitcher of water and poured it down his throat. 'I had some rice puffs, you know,' he said with a snort, forcing out a belch. 'They can make you damn thirsty, rice puffs can. I say there's nothing as good as water. Hunger or thirst, a bellyful of water takes care of everything. Sister, go have the rice porridge before it becomes inedible.'

Manik tucked into the stale porridge without another word. 'Brother,' she said. 'You know something. The Jenas eat hot rice meals twice a day even now.'

Mukund let out another loud belch. 'Oh, don't eye others, my girl. What does it matter to us if they eat hot rice twice a day? Are you going to beg from them or what? Listen, I'm Guna Parida's son. Begging is not in our blood. We ate hot rice as long as we could. It's only for a month or so...' He paused a while. 'Just wait until Father recovers. You can blame me if we don't have nice hot rice meals every second day. But if you think you can't wait any longer, then the doors of the poorhouse are wide open for you. One sister has already tarred our faces, you can go and keep her company. You'll come across quite a few known faces there, I'm sure.'

'Shut up, will you?' Manik cried. 'Why do you always fly into a temper when I tell you any little thing? I'm sick of your sermons.'

'Who asked you to bring up the Jenas? Remember, the stale cold watered-rice of your own house is better any day than the sweet milk-porridge of somebody else's. What business is it of ours to know what others are eating?'

'Have you finished?'

'All right. Go to bed. I'll keep watch over Father the first half of the night. I'm not feeling sleepy. I'll wake you when I'm tired.'

Manik left.

Why do I take it out on the poor child? Mukund thought. Isn't it quite natural that she should long for a bowl of hot rice? I can manage without food for three or four days at a stretch, that's no big deal for a man, scores of my friends are in the same condition if not worse. That reminds me, a little gruel has to be cooked tomorrow morning for Father. Where does one get a measure of old grain? Do I have to run to Banchha Sahu of Nuapara once again?

Banchha Sahu had given him an advance of five rupees against future wages, but Mukund had not been able to put in even a day's work because of the string of deaths in the family. How could he now show his face at Sahu's and ask him for another advance? He briefly toyed with the idea of approaching the Jenas. But why waste his breath? There'd be nothing but a firm no from those quarters. When his mother was dying he had gone and begged them for a lump of sugar, but old Jena was as cold as a stone. I'll be damned if I knock on his door a second time, Mukund thought. He recalled someone mentioning Sadhu Panda of Manijangha and resolved to try his luck there. 'Manik, are you asleep? Get me the moneybag from the hole in the wall, will you?'

Manik fetched him a small bundle wrapped in rags. He opened it and took out the money: two crumpled one-rupee notes and a handful of coins. That was all that was left of the advance.

'All right.' He handed Manik the notes. 'Put this away in the hole and block it securely with a coconut shell. If rats or white ants get at it, we'll be done for. I'll take these nine annas and go to Manijangha tomorrow morning. Oh lord, a good four miles up and a good four down. And a big river of mud to wade through twice besides. Of course I'll run faster than my legs can carry me. Father must have a little rice gruel in his stomach tomorrow.'

'God knows how long it will take you.' Manik sighed. 'Last time you went to buy paddy you took the whole day and bought no more than a rupee's worth.'

'That was different. You're talking about the rations, sister. You know something, there were people who stood in line for three days and still returned home empty-handed. You ought to have seen the mile-long line to believe it. Distribution was slow and the queue crawled a foot an hour. You received your quota only when your turn came. No one would let you jump the queue. Don't ask me how I managed. Anyway, all that's over now. The government has refused to distribute further rations. It's different with Sadhu Panda. No hassles there. Pay cash, collect the rice and hit the road back home. By the way, tomorrow morning you're not going to the swamps to collect marua rice. I want you to sit up with Father.'

Of late Manik had taken to visiting the swamps, a wicker basket in her hand, to collect marua rice from the weeds. Not only she, but droves of women and children, hungry, emaciated and fierce, made a beeline for the place, some getting up at ungodly hours to have a head start. Pausa had come and gone, and the measly harvest — the third in a row — had not even been enough to satisfy the demands of the landlords. People had relied heavily on the bounties of the seasons: raw mangoes and yams in summer; fish, crabs and snails in the rainy months; different sorts of spinach and leaves in and out of season; and now before the advent of winter, marua rice. The swamps, mist hanging over them, presented a unique sight: waves of human beings billowing around the place, revealing a hand here, a bare back there, heads bobbing, wicker baskets swimming in the void.

Manik spread the end of her sari on the floor and lay down, curling up like a puppy. But sleep wouldn't come to Mukund. He was lost in his thoughts: my little sister is such a pathetic rattle of bones and yet she drags herself every morning to the swamps. And I can do nothing about it. I've failed to go for work just for a few weeks and want has closed in on us from all sides. Will I be able to save Father? Will I be able to save Manik?

When Manik awoke before cockcrow next morning, she found her brother gone. She could feel a fever coming on, her body ached and her head felt as heavy as a stone. This was nothing new; she had had fever off and on ever since last summer but had never breathed a word of it to Mukund.

She heard her father stirring in his bed. She got up and went to

him. She washed his face with water and wiped it dry with her sari.
'Shall I get you a bowl of sugar water?' she asked.

Guna's eyes had sunk into their sockets. He raised his hand with the greatest effort and put it on his daughter's head. His lips trembled, but no word came out.

'Brother has gone to buy rice for gruel,' Manik said. 'He'll be back any moment now.'

It was high noon when Mukund bought two measures of rice and started his trudge back home. The road stretched endlessly before him. He crossed the river at its narrowest; yet the mud came up to his waist. When he reached the outskirts of his village, he lowered himself into a ditch to wash himself.

'That can wait,' said someone. 'But not your father. Run along home.'

Mukund swivelled around. It was Ghania. Was the fellow being spiteful? he wondered. 'Joking, boy?' he asked.

'Go find out for yourself,' Ghania said, pushing and prodding a herd of rickety cattle towards the gray grassless pastures.

'Brother, hey, do you still hold it against me, last summer's game of bagudi?' Mukund said. 'All right, I'm ready to accept the fault was mine. There, now forget the old grudge.'

'Run along, boy,' Ghania said, turning and twisting the tail of an old cow. 'You're wasting your breath.'

Mukund's hands and legs went dead. The sky seemed to collapse on his head; the ground sank under his feet. Fighting the daze, he broke into a run. The breeze carried Manik's heart-rending sobs. He reached home, threw the bag down and slumped to the ground.

The paddy came in handy for his father's shraddha ceremony. He engaged a priest and went through all the rites — although in these hard times nobody would have blamed him for negligence — and blew up a full rupee. He couldn't have cared less. His father had died and along with him his hopes and dreams. The wandering mendicant's songs over his doleful khanjani jarred on him. Life's an illusion, is it? he mused. Each passing day brought him more unhappiness.

Then one day he overheard the village schoolmaster discussing the war: 'Oh, quit worrying. The end of the war is in sight. Japan's buckling. Prices will soon come down. Rice will once again be available in abundance.' When? Mukund wondered. Will I live to see it? Manik's fast sinking; how long can a young girl survive on a handful of rice flakes a day? How will she get back her strength without freshly cooked rice?

He had only one rupee left, and he decided to spend it all on rice. He would leave the entire amount with Manik and go to work at the Sahu's. That seemed the most sensible course. But where will I manage to buy rice? Who's going to sell any? I'll have to go through many a village and knock on many a door. Never mind. I can't let my little sister end up in the poorhouse. If the teacher is to be believed the war will be over soon. Then prices will fall and the market overflow with rice. It's just a matter of scraping through until then. He tightened his threadbare towel around his waist as if in determination.

Next morning he set out early. While passing by the village cremation ground, his feet slowed down and he stopped. Heaps of bones littered the ground. Skulls rolled around like pumpkins, teeth bared in hideous grins. The wind whistled through the empty ribcages of the skeletons. Somewhere in these heaps, he thought, are the bones of my people. The bones of my mother and brothers. And now my father's. Soon I'll end up here. And maybe little Manik too. But the sweet old world will not stop turning, will it?

'Patra of Kusupur has hoarded mounds of paddy in his underground vault,' said someone.

Mukund looked up and found he had caught up with a small group of men and women hurrying along the dirt tracks.

'Then let's try his place first,' said another.

'If all of us head there, he'll shoo everyone away,' ventured a third.

Kusupur would have been nearer home, but Mukund was disheartened. He turned his eyes in the direction of Manijangha and his spirits dimmed. Four long miles there and four longer miles back, to speak nothing of the river of mud! He took a deep breath and plunged blindly ahead, picking out a path that wound towards Manijangha.

Late in the afternoon, dead beat, he recrossed the river with a sack of paddy. His stomach rumbled and turned, his knees wobbled, he wanted to throw up, and every four paces he stopped to catch his breath. The sun broke through the ragged clouds and blazed down. He thought his skull would split open. The last stretch of fields before the village cremation ground seemed vast and unending, the giant banyan tree on the edge of the village a speck in the distance. He looked around and spotted a ditch. He ran there and gulped down a few mouthfuls of water. It was muddy and had an awful stink. Things will look up tomorrow, he thought, wiping his mouth. After that we will have one meal of steaming hot rice a day.

Then suddenly, before he knew what was happening, he retched. The sack rolled off his shoulder and he fell to the ground. Mustering the last dregs of his strength, he picked himself up, lifted the sack to his head and took a step. Just the fields to cross, he told himself. Just scramble up the canalbank and you're almost home. He took another step. His legs folded and a violent trembling seized him. The sack fell off his head. He wanted to throw up again and again, as nausea came over him in relentless waves. There was no one in sight. A thin white wisp of a cloud passed overhead, dropping a few futile drops of rain. A breeze sprang up. He opened his eyes and stared at his village. His strength was ebbing fast. Oh, no more walking for me, he sighed, no more worrying. His eyes smarted. He closed them, laying his head against the sack.

The fieldhands brought the news of his death to the village. Manik's fever dropped and she ran to the fields. Tears had dried in her eyes. Her brother had left her a bag of rice.

That evening the village chowkidar strode into the village, breathless with excitement. 'Japan has surrendered!' he announced. 'We've won the war. The government wants us to celebrate the victory with due pomp. So deck your doors with mango twigs and leaves. Sweets will be distributed to school children at the police station tomorrow morning.'

Mukund celebrated the victory no less than the rest, perhaps even more. This was his first chance to be carried on human shoulders — and also his last!

Bhagabati Charan Panigrahi

Shikar

Ghinua was known to be the greatest marksman around, using a bow and arrows he himself had fashioned. To shoot, he would lie on his back, notch his arrow, pull it back right to his ear and send it piercing home. He could hit a target a mile away. He had killed countless deer, sambars, wild boars, bears, leopards, but only two tigers. For shooting the tigers he had received rewards.

One morning Ghinua climbed up the stairs to the deputy commissioner's bungalow with a sack. His bow hung from one shoulder, his axe rested on the other, and in his hand he held the quiver of arrows.

The orderly was shocked to see him in such a state. 'So what've you brought today?' He knew Ghinua quite well. He had often taken a cut from Ghinua's rewards.

Ghinua did not answer. He merely displayed two rows of dirty, yellowing teeth. There was no knowing whether it was a smile or a grimace. Nobody had ever seen Ghinua laugh. On rare occasions he just bared his teeth as he was doing now.

'Hey, why won't you say what you've brought today? What shikar?'

Ghinua pointed to the sack. 'A deadly beast.'

'A tiger?'

Ghinua shook his head.

'A leopard?'
Ghinua shook his head again.
'A bear? A boar?'
Ghinua merely shook his head.
'What then?'
The sound of their voices drew the sahib out of his room. Ghinua promptly prostrated himself before the white man and bared his teeth. When the sahib expressed his desire to see the kill, he opened the sack, took out a human head and placed it ceremoniously at the sahib's feet.

The sahib jumped back.

Ghinua stretched out his hand. 'Baksheesh, sahib!'

With great effort the sahib controlled his fear and indicated with a nod for Ghinua to wait. He went inside and telephoned the police station for an armed contingent. He knew armed policemen would be needed to overpower Ghinua: the man had the strength of a monster and was armed with his lethal bow and arrows.

When Ghinua was led away in police custody, his hands and feet manacled, he could not understand. 'Why did they put me in chains?" he asked, whenever he had a chance. Some said he would be hanged, others that he would be deported to Kala Paani. But why? What crime had he committed? He did not understand what people said.

One day when the deputy commissioner came to inspect the jail, Ghinua asked him what all the fuss was about. The deputy commissioner explained to him that for killing a tiger he had been given his reward promptly. This time, though, he had killed a human being, and the amount of reward would have to be determined by six or seven wise men; therefore, it would take some time. After all, one didn't kill human beings too often. Ghinua found the explanation quite satisfactory.

When the trial began, Ghinua thought perhaps he was to be given his baksheesh now. With much gusto he gave the details of the killing to the judge. It hadn't been at all easy to kill a man like Govind Sardar. There were quite a number of hunters on his trail, but no one had succeeded; Govind Sardar had always eluded them because he travelled in a motor car. The man had accumulated great wealth by cheating others out of their property. A diabolical man, he had murdered countless people, molested many innocent women and reduced numerous others to penury. Not only had he snatched away Ghinua's property, but on that fateful evening he had been on the verge of molesting Ghinua's wife. What audacity the man had! When he saw Ghinua, he quickly hopped into his motor car and tried to drive away. But it wasn't easy to escape Ghinua. He shot an arrow and deflated a tyre, and when the car came to a stop, without further ado he chopped off Govind Sardar's head. Out of breath, he ran all the way to the deputy commissioner's bungalow. Govind Sardar was no mean opponent when it came to a fight. He always carried a gun, and people were more afraid of him than of tigers and bears. He was more dangerous than the wild animals. And Ghinua had shown great courage and skill to hunt down such a fellow. Some years back the sahib had given a baksheesh of five hundred rupees to Dora for killing Jhapat Singh, the rebel leader. But Jhapat Singh was a saint compared to Govind Sardar. Jhapat Singh had never raped a woman, nor taken anyone's property by force; he had merely looted the government treasury and bumped off a few sepoys. Govind Sardar was a far more despicable person. Ghinua ought to get a baksheesh bigger than Dora's for killing him.

Everyone in the courtroom burst out laughing at his story.

'Yes, you'll be given a fat baksheesh,' chortled the judge.

'Indeed, you've been brought here to be given the baksheesh!' the government prosecutor added.

Ghinua did not catch on to their jokes and jibes. He always took everything seriously. He never understood such things.

The sentence was passed. Ghinua could not follow even one word of it. Later, when he was led away to the jail, he enquired about it and was told that the day of baksheesh was not far away.

Not for a moment did it occur to Ghinua that he was a criminal and that he had been condemned to death. How was he to know that killing Jhapat Singh was not the same as killing Govind Sardar? It did not register in his mind that while the first was considered an act of bravery the second was an offence. He simply didn't have the head to delve into the subtleties of the white man's laws. After all, wasn't he just a savage?

If Dora could be given five hundred rupees for killing Jhapat Singh, Ghinua continued to think in his cell, why should he be given a lesser reward. No, he wouldn't accept it; he would throw down the money and tell the sahib point blank: 'Better not give me anything, sahib. But surely I deserve more than what you gave Dora.'

In the dark lonely cell, he thought of this and many other things. He did not have a soul to turn to, nor had he any desire to talk. He was growing restless. All he wanted was to collect his reward and get back home to his wife.

Then came the day of the execution. He was asked what his last wish was.

'My baksheesh!' he said.

'All right, come along now. You'll get your baksheesh.'

He was led away, a black hood slipped over his head.

The government certainly has many fancy rules and regulations before bestowing a big reward, he thought. Look at the fuss. But then after all, it's a big occasion and how can it be done without a little ceremony! When I get back home, I'll show everyone the baksheesh. How happy my wife will be! I'll build myself a new house, buy lands to cultivate and settle down quietly. No Govind Sardar will be around to rob me once again. Maybe, I'll...

Nityananda Mahapatra

❧❧

The Quest

I

'The prince of Avanti, Your Majesty.'
'Avanti, counsellor?'
'Yes, my lord.'
'When will the swayamvara be held?'
'On the full moon day of Phalgun.'
'In how many days?'
'Eight months and ten days, Your Majesty.'

❀

'How many did you say — three?'
'Yes, Your Majesty. Three. Three gems.'
'I see.'
'The older daughters are exquisitely beautiful, but...'
'Go on, counsellor.'
'The youngest is...'
'An ugly duckling, is she? That's all right. What do I care?'

❀

'With all the riches in Kalinga's royal treasury, Your Majesty can buy heads but not hearts!'
'Money buys both, my dear counsellor. I'll show you yet.'

'With one-hundredth of his riches the prince of Kalinga can buy thousands of slaves, but...'

'Go on.'

'With ten thousand times your entire wealth, O Prince of Kalinga, you could not buy a single heart. Hearts are not up for sale, Your Majesty. Hearts are won, not bought. What does Your Majesty desire — a slave or a sweetheart?'

※

'This is nonsense.'

'I beg to disagree, Your Majesty.'

'You mean the prince of Kalinga cannot win the heart of a mere woman?'

'As a human being he can, but all his riches cannot.'

'Do you think the prince will have better luck with the princesses of Avanti if he goes to the swayamvara disguised as a beggar?'

'Your Majesty must never confuse love with infatuation. Infatuation withers away. Love endures.'

II

The youth was handsome, with a broad chest, long arms, large eyes and a broad forehead, but was dressed in tattered rags. Whoever saw him in the streets of Avanti felt pity for him.

In Avanti, resplendent with palaces, riches, invincible and swashbuckling cavaliers astride handsome horses, begging was an evil dream — a crime.

※

'So then, young beggar!'

'At your command, Your Majesty.'

'Didn't you know that begging is an offence in this land?'

'I did, Your Majesty.'

'Are you ready for the sentence?'

'Yes, Your Majesty.'

'The punishment is harsh.'

'What can be worse than begging, my lord?'
'So you hate to beg?'
'With all my heart.'
'It pleases us to hear that. But the law is law. You are sentenced to eight months of solitary confinement. But since you abhor begging and perhaps were led to it by circumstances beyond your control, you shall be allowed one small privilege of your choice during your imprisonment. Name it.'
'I am grateful to Your Majesty for this act of kindness. I pray for your eternal wellbeing.'
'You can state your wish.'
'May I be allowed out of my cell for a while every evening, to play my flute.'
'For how long?'
'An hour or so, my lord.'
'Granted.'

III

Not far from the royal palace stood the prison — a cluster of narrow pigeonholes, built of stone, with a high wall around them. There were no windows; only a tiny hole below the roof in every cell to let in a little air. The heavy iron gates closed like the bloodthirsty jaws of a monster.

Every evening the young beggar came out of his cell, sat on a large stone in the courtyard and planted a warm lingering kiss on his flute.

Every evening the palace trembled with the liquid melody of his music. Cuckoos trilled out of season, the still waters of the crystal-clear bathing pools broke into gentle ripples. And in the remote recesses of the royal chambers the princesses' hearts beat uncontrollably.

IV

'Prisoner!'
'Yes.'
'Where are you from?'

'Kalinga.'
'Who gave you this flute?'
'The prince of Kalinga.'
'The prince himself?'
'Yes.'
'I hear he's very handsome.'
'As handsome as Lord Kartikeya.'
'Will he come to the swayamvara?'
'He may or he may not.'

◈

'Prisoner!'
'Yes.'
'Are you from Kalinga?'
'That's right.'
'Who taught you to play the flute?'
'The prince of Kalinga.'
'The prince?'
'Yes.'
'I hear he's extremely rich.'
'Even richer than Kuber.'
'Will he come to the swayamvara?'
'He may or he may not.'

◈

'Stranger!'
'Who's that?'
'Are you from Kalinga?'
'Yes, I am.'
'Oh, stranger!'
'Yes?'
'Can you tell me...?'
'Tell you what?'
'Something...'
'Ask.'

'Why does your heart echo through the notes of a little bamboo flute?'

The prisoner started and tried in vain to see the questioner in the deepening gloom.

'Stranger!'

'Yes?'

'Does the prince of Kalinga play the flute as hauntingly?'

'Even more hauntingly.'

'Is he kind?'

'Very.'

'And learned?'

'Like Lord Ganesh.'

'And brave, too?'

'Like Arjun.'

'Will he...will he come to the swayamvara at Avanti?'

'He may or he may not.'

V

There where sunflowers wilted by the prison walls, when the deepening dusk hid the rough contours of the monstrous stone edifice, and the sky shivered with the tremulous notes of the prisoner's flute — a young woman was seen to appear for a brief while and then disappear. And so it went for many days.

On the other side of the prison, where the nightflowers spread their intoxicating fragrance, where the great green bowl of the earth and the diabolical dome of the prison mingled in the darkness, and the lilting notes of a flute twirled through the pastures of the sky — another young woman, shorter than the first, appeared and then disappeared. And so it went for many days.

When, in the hushed silence of a late evening a light breeze stirred within the prison, the frail figure of a young woman stole into the courtyard with a bowl of fruit and placed it before the prisoner's cell.

'Who's there?' the prisoner asked.

'Someone.'

The prisoner ate the fruit and the young woman collected the bowl and disappeared. They never saw or spoke to each other and only the darkness saw their eyes swimming with tears. And so it went on for many days.

VI

The evening before the full moon of Phalgun.

The following day the swayamvara for the three princesses of Avanti would be held. The same day the prisoner would be freed.

'Prisoner, play your flute.'

'The flute shall play no longer.'

'Why?'

'For eight long months I played my flute. People stopped to listen. But, but...'

'But what?'

'But I could never touch the heart of the woman I played for. Maybe she was thrilled to hear me play, but she could never divine the anguish in my heart. She did not respond because I'm a beggar and a prisoner, and she a princess.'

'A princess?'

'Yes, a princess of Avanti.'

'Of Avanti?'

'Yes. Did that startle you?'

'What insolence! For a lowly beggar, you aspire for the most exquisite flower in the land? Don't you know the grand swayamvara for the princesses of Avanti will be held tomorrow and princes from other lands will gather here to try their luck? Maybe the prince of Kalinga will win the princess.'

'Maybe.'

'One word from me and you'll be sent to the gallows.'

'I couldn't care less. Of what use is *my* life to me?'

'Very well! Know then that I'm the eldest princess of Avanti.'

'Stranger, why is your flute silent?'
'The flute shall play no longer.'
'But why?'
'I broke it.'
'Why did you do that?'
'There was no one to appreciate its melody.'
'Far from it. Many people stopped to listen.'
'But no one understood what my flute was crying out for.'
'How do you know?'
'I asked myself.'
'Did you care to explain to your audience?'
'I cared a lot, and for far too long.'
'How long?'
'One day less than eight months.'
'But who is it you played your flute for?'
'The person I pine for.'
'Who is that precious person?'
'I dare not say.'
'Go ahead, I'll keep it a secret.'
'She's a princess of Avanti.'
'What — a princess of Avanti?'
'Did that startle you?'
'Impudent fool! You're a dwarf and you aspire for the moon! How dare you fall in love with a princess of Avanti who might adorn the throne of Kalinga tomorrow? Do you know what would happen to you if I reported you?'
'Death holds no fear for me.'
'Very well! You had better be ready for it. And know that I am the second princess of Avanti.'

❈

'Traveller!'
'Yes?'
'Why didn't you eat today?'
'Hunger has forsaken me.'
'But why?'

'No food can satiate the hunger of the heart.'
'Why aren't you playing your flute?'
'The flute played for only one person.'
'Isn't that lucky person here this evening to listen to it?'
'She hears but she doesn't listen.'
'How do you know?'
'I asked myself.'
'Stranger, is the heart of a princess a stone?'
'Yes, like a gem, a stone — hard and cold.'
'She sees nothing?'
'Only the outside.'
'Not the mind?'
'Not the mind but the wealth.'
'Can she not fathom the sorrow of others?'
'No, only her *own* happiness.'
'You're wrong.'

VII

'Prisoner!'
'Who's that?'
'Psst, keep your voice low.'
'Why should a man condemned to death fear his voice will be heard?'
'For heaven's sake keep your voice down. If you wish to live, do as I say.'
'But I've no wish to live.'
'Oh no, you *must* live.'
'For whom?'
'For someone.'
'Who's that someone?'
'There's no time to explain everything. The prison doors are open, and you'll find a horse outside. Please get away from here as fast as the wind, otherwise tomorrow morning you will have to go to the gallows.'
'But who are you and why have you come to set me free?'
'No time to go into all that. I may only say that I'm carrying

out the orders of someone who has looked into your soul and suffered your sorrows.'

'I can't thank that person enough. But may I know who this mysterious *someone* is?'

'I am not allowed to tell you. All I can say is that the haunting notes of your flute have touched *her* deeply.'

'So it's a woman! But she never asked me to play my flute!'

'She didn't.'

'I decline the offer. It's not fitting for a son of Kalinga to steal away in the dark of night. But please tell me who this lady is who's been so kind to me.'

'Would you believe me if I told you?'

'Why not?'

'Are you sure?'

'Of course!'

'She...she...'

'Oh, stop torturing me.'

'She's the youngest princess of Avanti.'

VIII

The day of the swayamvara.

'Your Majesty!'

'At your command, Prince of Kalinga!'

'Your first and second daughters have hung their garlands on my statue, not on me. When I was a prisoner...'

'Forgive them their follies, Prince. They didn't recognize you.'

'Neither did your youngest daughter. Lord of Avanti, I might be a rich and mighty king, but for those eight months in your prison I was the lowliest beggar in your land. The young woman who could fall for such a wretch...Well, she alone shall be my queen. Give us your blessings.'

Gopinath Mohanty

The Shelter

The train from the south brought Sadasiva, his family and their luggage to Cuttack. Sadasiva, a government employee, had been transferred to the capital.

'Father,' his daughter Mandakranta asked, as they came out of the station. 'Our house — where is it?'

'Our house, our house!' Sardula-Bikridita, younger than Mandakranta by two years, ran around, yelping with joy. Little Anustup and Gayatri guessed that here was an occasion for celebration. 'Our house, our house,' they chanted, throwing their arms around each other's neck.

Walking behind them all, their mother, Damayanti, wondered aloud: 'I hope we haven't left that earthen pitcher in the train?'

'No,' Sadasiva said. 'I have it. You'd better walk carefully.' And turning to his children, he added sternly, 'Hey kids, stop that racket, will you?'

The milling crowd at the railway station gave them funny looks and sniggered. That wasn't surprising since Sadasiva had an enormous amount of luggage. 'Cab, sir?' the eager cabbies swarmed around them. 'Cab?'

Mandakranta could not contain herself. 'Father, how far is our house from here?'

Sadasiva did not reply. He dumped the luggage into one cab,

herded his family into another and began his journey into the city.

'How do you feel?' he asked his wife, who was in an advanced stage of pregnancy.

'Fine,' she murmured.

'Hey children!' Sadasiva admonished his brood. 'Don't crowd against your mother.'

'Our house!' Sardula-Bikridita came up with a throaty slogan. The rest immediately joined in in a shrill chorus: 'Our house, our house...'

The husband and wife looked at each other. Damayanti began to smile. Sadasiva hung his head.

Sadasiva was coming back to Cuttack after twelve long years. True, he had visited the city on official business a couple of times during this period, but here he was now with a family and the accompanying burden of their luggage.

He looked out and sighed. Good old Cuttack — the city of his childhood and youth. He remembered his lovely little village, just eight miles from the city, on the other side of the river. Chillies and aubergines would perhaps be growing around his deserted house, pumpkin vines crawling all over, the velvety leaves so round, so green. Sadasiva let out another deep sigh.

Buildings, buildings and more buildings! A veritable concrete jungle; buildings everywhere, some already finished, others rising. Stacks of bricks, heaps of sand. Loaded trucks, groaning under the weight of bricks and sand and iron. Oh God, somebody's been run over, poor fellow...Well, it's sad, but what can be done? Wouldn't the poor chap have died one of these days, anyway? Surely the wheels of progress couldn't be brought to a halt because of one little mishap! The great city, the progressive city. Well! The infinite variety of people — well, well! Sadasiva sighed.

He had been heaved out of this city twelve years ago. What a sprawling state Orissa is, he thought. What large districts, what remote nooks and crannies to be pushed into! Mandakranta was born in Balasore, Sardula-Bikridita in Koraput, Anustup in Boda-Sambar, and Gayatri in Rosulkunda, the land of the great Bhanjas.

But what about this one who hopes to see the light of day in Cuttack, this little life that was conceived in the jungles of Mankadanacha? Where's the shelter for him?

'This has become a place for the rich,' he burst out. 'We don't belong here.'

'Wait and see,' said Damayanti.

'You know,' he told her, 'the problem is that those who ought to die don't at the right time!'

'Why are you so upset?' Damayanti consoled him. 'We'll surely find a place somewhere.'

'Some hope!' His scorching glance fell on the dusty road.

From behind came cars and trucks honking their horns.

They were heading for Ratnakar's place. Ratnakar, an old friend, had started a small hardware business after the war. His house, a small shabby affair with a thatched roof, had only one living room and a narrow passage. In the living room cots were placed one beside the other without a gap, with old tin trunks shoved underneath. The household belongings hung from the ceiling in jute slings. Ratnakar's family included his wife and five school-going children, a couple of servants, a dog, a cat, and some mice and cattle. Still he had generously offered to put Sadasiva up at his place. 'Come and stay with us for as long as you wish — a fortnight, a month,' he had written to Sadasiva. Ratnakar of all people! Sadasiva had smiled.

Wonders never cease, Sadasiva thought. How many times have I been pushed to the brink of insolvency and doom? Yet haven't I always scraped through; something would happen at the last moment and I would bounce back. What would life be without surprises, accidents and unforeseen events? Oh, how they co-exist — unexpected charity and wanton cruelty!

The tiny, tumbledown shed adjoining Ratnakar's house yawned, as if it was tired of waiting for Sadasiva.

'This is the place!' Sadasiva whispered to his wife, his voice catching.

Mud walls, threadbare thatch, no windows, and a door of bamboo trellis. Stacked inside: assorted wooden boxes, all sorts of junk, three almirahs full of children's textbooks and notes, two tables, five chairs, and two cots placed side by side. Mercifully there was a little space on either side of the joined cots.

Darkness. A torrential downpour. Snores.

Sadasiva awoke with a start, he didn't know why. He looked out. Why doesn't this miserable life end? he wondered. Why doesn't it simply end? How does it withstand all these strains, this darkness, this rain and cold, this utter hopelessness? One wonders. Really, how it lingers on with a little nudge here and a little push there, with a little help now and then! But where do I go from here? Where, after Ratnakar's house?

A mouse scampered over his hand, startling him. The house was crawling with mice; he had seen them scurrying about in broad daylight. He listened to the silence of the night. The stillness was eloquent.

A strange intermittent sound, accompanied with a stink, seemed to come from under the cot. He fished out the flashlight from under his pillow and turned it on. A mangy old dog without a wisp of fur on its body lay curled underneath the cot.

Why, of course! Sadasiva reflected, not without a little sympathy, a dog, too, has its claims! But the slight tinge of sympathy suddenly vanished and Sadasiva sprang to his feet to chase the dog away.

The dog seemed determined not to be hustled out into the pouring rain and spooky darkness. A game of hide-and-seek ensued, among the cots and tables, almirahs and piles of luggage. The dog joined in with great enthusiasm.

Half an hour into the game Sadasiva gave up; he flung himself on the bed and buried his face. The dog crawled back under the cot and curled up. The scratching died down but the stink remained.

Bracing himself to meet the new situations in his life, Sadasiva listened to the patter of rain and drifted back to sleep.

He got up with a violent start in the morning, wondering if the world had taken him for a Kumbhakarna. The din was ear-splitting. That was the city's way of welcoming him on his first morning, in its very own language — the clank of pounding metal.

He lifted his head and shuddered at the sight of a flock of sheep and a pair of bullocks tramping into the room. He sprang to his feet.

Sadasiva got right down to looking for a house in earnest. With a paancase, a bundle of beedis and a matchbox, he set out on a bicycle. A whole Sunday lay before him. This country is a place for the enterprising, he reminded himself. It provides great opportunities to explore the multiple dimensions of one's personality. He mentally divided the city into four zones, to be covered in four days — each at a time.

He spoke to the paanwallahs and brokers, to his friends and colleagues. He collected voluminous data, tracked down many houses, made many acquaintances. Each time he got some information, he dutifully jotted it down in his diary and made a dash for the place.

No house.

'But this is vacant!'

'Someone has already taken it...'

'What about the one you're building? Can I have that when it's finished?'

'Sorry, someone has already paid an advance — the bricks to lay the foundation were bought with their money!'

No house.

He learnt a great deal about the topography of the city. What a city — unheard of streets, frightening lanes, godforsaken alleys, how bewildering! The city had moved on. It had grown and expanded while he had wandered from the back yards to the back of beyond doing his job. Houses had been built and roads had been laid. Lakshmi, the goddess of wealth, had visited house after house, and many had become rich.

Whichever way he looked at it, Sadasiva found the city a great mystery. The familiar spots and landmarks had vanished; the place had become unrecognizable. A grim two-storeyed building stood where once a blue pond swarmed with ducks. What was once a swamp with wild plants and flowers had become a bustling slum. Buildings were rising even out of waist-deep water: nothing seemed to stop the frenzy of construction. Sadasiva felt as though the buildings were laughing at his misery and mocking him. 'We've grabbed every inch of space; there's no room for people like you here. Go back.'

And yet, not long ago, he had lived in this city. A walk down a familiar road brought back a horde of memories. Why, wasn't this the good old neem tree? And this, the same old row of houses? So there'd been a little facelift here too? Good God, even a homeopathic clinic! Sadasiva reached the house in quick strides.

'Looking for somebody, eh?' A gruff voice enquired from within.

'Well — er — no. Just passing by.'

It was no longer his house; it belonged to the past.

In the next lane stood another house, where he had once lived for four years. Peeping through the door, Sadasiva recalled what it had been like. Fragments of his youth came floating into his mind: the study, the girl next door, the moonlit nights and the girl's melodious voice trembling over the notes of a harmonium. He lingered near the door. Now there'll be a big commotion, he imagined. Old Bhalu will perform a canine waltz in my honour. How the poor dog loves sweets.

'Who are you looking for?' barked someone from inside the house.

Sadasiva started.

'Does Sadasiva live here?' he stammered awkwardly.

'No.' A hulking figure waddled out of the house. 'Move on. Go look elsewhere.'

Sadasiva hung his head and walked away. Who did I say I was looking for — Sadasiva? Am I off my hinges or what? But what did that fat slob say — go look elsewhere? Move on indeed! If I have to look for myself anywhere it'll have to be in the debris of the past.

He jumped to the side of the road just in time to avoid being run over by a speeding car. His clothes were spattered with mud. He turned round and caught a fleeting glimpse of the car. There was a plump man in spotless white clothes inside. Did he see what his car did to me? Sadasiva wondered. Perhaps not. Perhaps he was too preoccupied with his precious thoughts. The proud car-owner and the poor pedestrian, they'll never know each other, they never will.

The dirty water, seeping through his clothes, touched his skin. His reverie came to an end. Why have regrets, he thought. Haven't I lived in many parts of the country? Haven't hearths been lighted for me in distant places? Haven't I stopped at godforsaken holes to wipe the sweat off my brow? My life has been shaped in such environments. And now all those places belong to my past. Several times I've been crushed, sometimes mercilessly, but haven't I risen from the ashes, phoenix-like, and blossomed forth again? Haven't I died many a death, and haven't I been restored to life each time? So why have regrets?

After roaming around the city all day long, Sadasiva returned to Ratnakar's house in the evening. The sky had become heavy with dark, ominous clouds, and he had found no house.

After combing the city for four days, Sadasiva joined his new office. The joining was an empty formality because there was no place for him to sit. The office resembled an old beehive and the officials busy bees, flying in and out. Some big, some fat, some quite small, and some awfully thin; some droning loudly, some stinging sharply. Together they produced a sad, muffled hum.

With difficulty Sadasiva managed to get a little spot at one end of the corridor, then a table, a chair and two benches. With relief, he sat on his chair, straightened his back, stretched his hands across the table and stared out. This is my domain, he smiled to himself.

His eyes fell on the floor and he flinched. There was goat dropping and cow dung everywhere. Well, well, he sighed, isn't the smell of goat supposed to protect against tuberculosis, and cow-dung to be a disinfectant?

As he watched, a peaceable nanny goat with three kids came ambling down the corridor. They stopped and looked at Sadasiva in surprise. Sadasiva stared back at them. So I'm not the sole master of this tiny domain of mine! He chuckled.

Sadasiva put in an application for government accommodation. 'That's none of our business,' the boss said. So once again he had to fall back on his own resources. Advice poured in: personal endeavour is the best thing, you know, self-help is the best help; observe how big companies are floated, how big businesses run and big houses are built — all by individuals; what is impossible? Nothing! If you happen to achieve nothing, you are either bone lazy or plain unlucky.

He spoke to many people, made frantic requests, and received ample assurances. Everyone seemed to drip with sympathy. Paan-drenched smiles and politeness all the way: 'Don't worry. Ridiculous, it should be easy to find a house for you. All right, I'll keep my eyes open.'

He went through the same routine the next day, and the day after that — it went on, apparently without an end in sight.

'Did you find anything for me?'

'Find what?'

'Why, a house! You said you'd keep a lookout.'

'Did I? Oh yes, I'm still on the lookout. I'll let you know as soon as I find something.'

Assurances galore, but not a single house.

Ratnakar was as nice as ever; he never grumbled. Days passed. Every evening Damayanti enquired about the house. The baby in her womb clamoured for shelter outside.

Finally, it was Damayanti who came to Sadasiva's rescue. She applied to the hospital for a cabin for her confinement and got a one-room house in the hospital compound. Sadasiva moved in there with the children.

'Our house!' Sardula-Bikridita cried, hopping all over the little patch of grass in front of the cabin. 'Ho ho ho! Our house!' Anustup, Mandakranta and Gayatri joined him. Damayanti beamed at them from the verandah. Watching the clouds gather in the sky, Sadasiva wondered what name to give to the child soon to be born.

The door of the cabin opposite their's swung open and a funeral procession filed out. Sadasiva started. 'Children, children, get inside the house. Quick!'

Rajkishore Ray

Bouli

It all began in the gathering twilight of an innocuous day when the old duffadar, on his way back from the police station, crossed the narrow village path sandwiched between screwpine bushes and climbed the steps to Bhajani Pradhan's verandah. Stooping a little, he carried on his ageing shoulders the enormous burden of a dozen or more schemes and plans — to incite new litigations, to find quick out-of-court settlements and others. The brass buttons of his uniform, scrubbed with ashes, gleamed. The bulging bundles of papers under his arm, held together by soggy cardboard covers from which a string limply hung, were dark from the inky stains of a million thumbprints.

Bhajani's wife Sarasi was sweeping the mud platform around the sacred basil plant in the courtyard when she saw him arrive. Quickly pulling the veil over her head, she fetched a reed mat and spread it on the verandah. She was his goddaughter, and his visits were a routine. Invariably he would ask after her welfare and, once the polite enquiries were over, gush about the smoothness of the aubergines in her vegetable patch, the thickness of Ujala's milk, the richness of Patani's cream, all of which he secretly hankered for.

Bhajani hired himself out as a farm-hand and raised a few head of cattle. But it was Sarasi who really looked after the animals. She was poor, but her heart was full of love and devotion for her husband and the cattle — Ujala, Patani, Manguli, all cows; Jagannath and Balabhadra, a pair of bullocks; and Bouli, a pretty little calf. They were the apples of her eye. She was grateful to Goddess Laxmi, whom she worshipped by painting a symbolic patter of tiny footsteps in the eastern corner of her house, not only for a bountiful harvest but for the health of her cattle too. At the crack of dawn, just when the sun's chariot rose in the sky, lighting the pale blue horizon, she would tug at the udders of her cows and direct the jets into the vessel balanced between her knees. The thrill of it was so pure, so satisfying that it helped her bury the pangs of childlessness, that most acute pain of womanhood, deep within the recesses of her heart; indeed, neither her workaholic husband nor the loving animals had any inkling of these feelings. As the vessel gradually filled to the brim with Ujala's milk — pure, snow-white, and frothy — little Bouli's wet muzzle would roam all over Sarasi's back, hands and arms. She found the touch so delicious that she often imagined how much more thrilling the touch of her own child would have been. In the village community hall she had often heard the stories of the dalliances of Lord Krishna recited, of His life and pranks at Gopapur. She had been to the village theatres put up by the untouchables and had watched the tears and suffering of Jashoda overwhelmed with love for the young Krishna. She had been fascinated by the mischievous capers of the Lord behind the cattle in the streets of Gopa, the way He broke the milkpots with a slingshot, and then the sudden fear of His mother which made Him stand glued to the wall. Sarasi had absorbed every last detail. Where was her tiny toddler, scampering about on unsteady legs, smiles dimpling his chubby cheeks, playfully attacking the milkpot? It was a dream which never left her, and the more the frisky Bouli carried on with her antics the more she felt the lack of a child in her life.

'Daughter, where's Bhajani?' The duffadar was all smiles. 'Away in the fields, eh?'

'Yes,' said Sarasi, half-hidden behind the door. 'Must be on his way back now.' Knowing how much the old man loved rice flakes with cottage cheese made from Ujala's milk and fresh jaggery, she bustled about to get a meal ready for him.

'Sara,' the old man said, while doing justice to the spread, 'there'll be a livestock fair in Cuttack. Why don't you ask Bhajani to take Ujala and Bouli? I'm sure the cow and the calf will steal the show. You've kept them so well-groomed, so scrubbed and polished that even flies will slip off their skin. They're a feast for the eyes. A prize-winning cow will fetch the owner a cash award of fifty rupees.'

'Fifty? How much is that?'

'Two score and ten.'

'So much!'

'Yes. Down at the police station the boss told me to spread the word around. Rural folks should participate in large numbers. Pucca arrangements have been made for food and shelter for the animals and their owners in the fair grounds. Remember to tell Bhajani. If I run into him on the way home I will try to convince him.'

'But it will be a waste of two precious days,' she remarked. 'And he will need money to spend on the way there. If he wins the prize he will get it only at the end, isn't that right?'

Panchu, with his dog Kalia in tow, had stopped to listen to them. Although Kalia was just a country dog with no pedigree to boast of, he was so audacious that at a nod from his master he would attack a cow or a bull ten times his size. His devotion to Panchu and their love for each other had earned them the respect of the villagers.

'Panchu,' the duffadar said. 'Why don't you take Kalia to Cuttack? A brave dog like him stands a good chance of winning a prize.'

'He's a country dog,' Panchu said. 'Will anyone even look at him?' He ran his fingers over Kalia's head. The dog thumped his bushy tail on the ground and clawed up a little mud as though to suggest that he was game, that it was well worth taking a chance.

Kantha the priest had stopped by too. He was as famous for his evening services in the village's Shiva temple as for slitting the throats of rams which defied the expertise of seasoned butchers. For a fee of two rupees he could decapitate the most obstinate goat or sheep; his patrons, mostly school and college students, were many; and as a result Kantha didn't lack for money. This was a skill he had apparently picked up in Puri, where as a young boy he had gone to an akhada for wrestling lessons. The vertical line of vermilion from the base of his hairline down to the tip of his nose was a nostalgic commemoration of his arduous training. The towel around his broad shoulders, rising and falling rhythmically with each step, had become an inalienable part of his self; it responded as much to his talk as to his walk and every time Kantha raised his voice the ends of the towel twirled and danced.

'Priest,' the duffadar said. 'Make your ewe dance.'

'Want to see a performance? All right, all right.' Kantha slapped his arms and called to his dear ewe. Although it was a familiar sight, it always had an air of freshness about it because of the Puri slang liberally interspersed in Kantha's flow of words.

Kantha had brought up his ewe with great care and tenderness. It was a large animal, glossy black, the hair on its neck as deep and dense as a lion's mane; the horns curling around the sides of its head gave it the look of a warrior with spruced-up sideburns. Kantha spent more money on this animal than any man of comfortable means in the village did on himself. Madhav Mian, the local butcher, had once offered upto forty rupees for it, but Kantha had rejected the very idea.

Two days later, at the crack of dawn, a unique procession was seen on the riverbank: Kantha in front with his ewe at his side, followed by Panchu tugging at the rope around Kalia's neck, with Bhajani, Ujala and Bouli bringing up the rear.

The huge animal and agricultural fairground in Cuttack. The eye-catching contrast between the rugged, mud-splattered appearance of hard-working, tousled-haired, swarthy village folk and the urban sleekness of a sprawling city.

Lost in the welter of faces, Panchu, Kantha and Bhajani wondered what it was all about. Their animals were hungry, tired and jittery. The ewe, startled by the sound of a motor horn, had twice snapped its rope; Ujala, a trudge of eighteen miles behind her, was unable to stand and had tears streaming down her cheeks; Bouli lay on her back, limp and exhausted, her legs stiff as sticks, although for a large part of the distance Bhajani had carried the four-month-old calf on his shoulders. He had brought her up on a diet of green gram powder, but in the town nothing but hay was available. He had already appealed to one of the organizers only to be directed to another, who in turn had directed him to a third and so on. Bhajani had neither the energy nor the zeal to follow the trail.

Suddenly lusty shouts went up: 'The minister! The minister's car!'

Kalia was in a frenzy, he had always reacted to sudden noise of any kind; he who had eyes only for a brood of plump hens began to bark his head off.

When the speeches began, the stomachs of Panchu, Kantha and Bhajani rumbled with hunger.

'...Learn from Holland and Denmark.' The minister's voice resounded over the public address system. 'Look after your cows as they do in those countries. Feed them well and they will multiply. And yield more milk, too. Several treatises on cattle-rearing are available nowadays. Read and profit from them. We have with us today a Denmark-trained cow-expert who will enlighten you on how to build an ideal cowshed. We have another expert to explain at length the methods of poultry-farming...'

Words, words and more words. The three friends heard it all. They couldn't see the minister from where they were and wondered what a minister looked like.

'An important announcement!' The microphones rumbled on. 'The Hon'ble Minister congratulates the department of agriculture for making this fair a grand success and as a token of his appreciation he shall now present a cash reward of one hundred rupees to the employees of the department.'

The speeches finally over, the prize-winners were declared: Paata, owned by the mahant of Cuttack was the best cow; deputy magistrate Bhattacharya's bitch Lily, the best dog; My Darling Ewe of Abu Hassan, a prominent businessman in the city, the best sheep; somebody else's goat, the best goat.

The three hopefuls who had come a distance of thirty-six miles listened to the announcements in silence. Panchu and Bhajani stared at each other, and Kantha's eyes were fastened on someone who was none other than the meat king of Cuttack, Sharif Khan. Khan's sharp business antenna was seeking out signals and his roving eyes were sizing up the animals for likely transactions. Animals could be had for a song after the fair.

Panchu, Kantha and Bhajani were in the throes of despair. They had no money and the prospect of trudging back another thirty-six miles made their heads reel. The twelve-and-a-half annas Sarasi had given Bhajani had been spent on fodder for Ujala and Bouli and on a measure of flattened rice for himself and his companions. Kantha had some money of his own but all of that had been spent on opium, which he couldn't do without.

The country dog Kalia was not a saleable commodity. Panchu was safe. Ujala and Bouli, the mother and the daughter, were an inseparable part of Bhajani's life. That left only Kantha's ewe — Sharif Khan's eyes had never strayed from this magnificent animal — and he sold his pet for five rupees. The raging fire of hunger in his and his two friends' stomachs had to be put out.

The return journey was made in total silence; no one had a word to say. Bhajani's shoulders, red and raw, hurt from carrying Bouli all the way from the fairgrounds. The poor little calf, it's belly distended, was in awful shape. She groaned constantly and brought up blood with every cough. Behind them, Ujala limped, dragging her hind legs; the tears which had been flowing since she had left the village had never dried. At every little opportunity, Kalia put his muzzle beside her ears and sniffed.

A few hours later Bhajani put Bouli down on the ground. 'It's all over for the little one,' he said.

Panchu and Kantha stopped.

The poor calf was dead. The trickle of blood with which her life had ebbed out was all there was to show.

Bhajani raised his head and looked at the sky. It was teeming with stars. 'Kantha,' he cried out, his voice catching. 'Priest, how will I face Sara? What will I tell her? Will she survive the shock? Can I stop her from hitting her head against the wall? God didn't give her a child, but He had given her Bouli. The little calf was her daughter.'

Kantha wiped the long vermilion line off his forehead — he would never wear it again. 'Bhajani, brother, roll Bouli down the riverbank and forget her. The fair's over. She didn't matter. Neither did we.'

Only Kalia hung back where Bouli's carcass was left. With his head bowed, he stood rooted to the spot.

Faturanand

The Slanging Match

Unrelieved gloom overhung the Five Head. Things were in a bad shape. Quite a few days had already passed in acute boredom, with Bookworm buried in his books and One Anna Yogi in his deep meditations. Both had sorely tried the patience of the other inmates — a cook who was also a handyman, and the two amiable ruffians who were the in-house orators, listeners, spectators, discoverers and inventors of all sorts of fun, pranks and practical jokes. Except for the cook, all the others were in college. The Five Head had a name for its air of mirth and merriment, and in the evenings several uninvited friends and college-mates dropped in to hotly debate, denigrate and satirize college and national politics and economics. They gossiped and lampooned, often in swift limericks between tepid tea and soggy biscuits, much to everyone's delight. But there were occasions when it looked as though an evil eye had cast its spell: Bookworm would be found staring at a textbook like a heron in a fish-pond and One Anna Yogi would be seated cross-legged in the lotus position on a reed mat, lost in blissful samadhi, one or both refusing to participate in the proceedings. (Yogi had achieved yogic perfection worth only an anna — hence this peculiar appellation.) With such wet blankets around, no heart-warming, mind-boggling talk and banter was possible. Quite a few glorious summer evenings had already passed in silent despair and desolation.

'Listen,' Long Sideburns said one day, when both the spoilsports were away. 'It reflects poorly on the Five Head. Our friends feel rotten. Not only are they not entertained, but they feel positively neglected. And all because of these two scoundrels.'

'But what can we do about it?' asked Sword Moustache.

'Well, suppose we hire a couple of goons to come and create a pandemonium? Anything, any damn thing, to put an end to this unbearable reading-meditating syndrome.'

'Press a two-paisa coin into a street urchin's hand and get him to beat a tin drum under our window. How's that for an idea?'

'But what excuse will the boy have for creating such a disturbance?'

'He can always claim he's trying to shoo monkeys away from the neighbourhood.'

'Shucks! You don't know these two scoundrels. They may just catch him. One tight slap and the tiny mite will spill the beans. Bookworm and One Anna Yogi will then go for our jugulars and I for one wouldn't blame them.'

The conspirators suddenly stopped in the middle of their deliberations. The whole neighbourhood was crackling with noise-waves. Long Sideburns and Sword Moustache cocked their ears.

'You child-chewing widow! May cholera, malaria, pox and plague carry you off. You who sleep with an infidel, may your ugly mug go up in flames!'

'That's Serenta's Ma,' said Long Sideburns, with an appreciative chuckle. 'She's a treat when she blows her top. But wait until you hear the other siren wailing. Sukuta's Ma is no mean opponent. The slanging matches between the two are out of this world, enormously enjoyable. Open your ears wide and try not to miss a single word. But it seems Sukuta's Ma isn't home. Judging by the delay in her retort, she may have gone to do number two, you know, the big call.'

Scarcely were the words out of his mouth than the second loud-speaker began blaring.

'You eighty-eight-time widow! You barren bitch, mother-in-law-eater, husband-eater, father-in-law-eater, why don't you go dig a pit and bury yourself alive! May you contract all kinds of unmentionable sexual diseases.'

'There!' said Sword Moustache. 'As the poet says, if one is here, can the other be far behind?'

'Look at the great waste of energy! All of it going down the down train, I mean, the town drain. If we could only harness it for our own benefit! Think of the Hirakud dam. Don't we produce electricity by harnessing water? If we only knew how to store the energy unleashed by these two old crones and use it against Bookworm and One Anna Yogi!'

Both agreed that with a little planning these two human engines could be revved up the moment Bookworm and One Anna Yogi showed the unmistakable symptoms of getting down to their irritating preoccupations, the first to his reading, the second to his meditating. 'Regular bouts of slanging matches between the two old hags and all this reading-meditating syndrome will vanish from the Five Head,' said Long Sideburns. 'Also, we'll pass a law: henceforth all reading-meditating shall be done only in the morning hours. Evenings and holidays shall be left absolutely free for shooting the bull.'

'But the problem is how to get both the engines started at the right moment. Who'll press the buttons?'

Long Sideburns gave an enigmatic smile. 'Leave it to yours truly.'

One Sunday afternoon not long afterwards, it so happened that a lot of friends had dropped in at the Five Head to wash away the stale stink of books from their noses. But after a brief round of gossip and badinage, just when things were warming up, One Anna Yogi showed the characteristic symptoms of lapsing into a yoga-coma.

Long Sideburns did not waste a second. He slipped out of the room and ran to Serenta's Ma. 'Hello Auntie! What are you doing? Don't you know that Sukuta's Ma is cursing you under her breath? Does she think nobody can hear her or what? I heard every word she said. Chhi, chhi, chhi, such vile swear words!'

That was enough. Hurling thunderbolts, Serenta's Ma charged out of her hut. 'You shit-smeller!' The sluice gates opened immediately. 'Son-eater, husband-eater, may maggots crawl out of your rotting flesh. May leprosy make a quilt out of your dirty face. Mud-eating bitch, may jackals jump and frolic about on the ruins of your homestead.'

Sukuta's Ma was putting an earthen cooking pot on the oven when she heard it. She smashed it on the floor with a bang and rushed out. 'You family-drowner, you fallow widow! Go jump into the river and be dead for ever and ever. May you be stricken with leprosy and roll about limbless on the streets of Puri. Famine-bitch, hole-worm, you who sleep with untouchables, may your jaws lock, may your eyes drop out of their sockets...'

One Anna Yogi snapped out of his trance. It was impossible to concentrate. He turned to his friends and soon their conversation picked up.

The two old hags roared like lionesses. After pouring venom on each other like snakes, the two engines gradually sputtered to a stop an hour and a half after they had started. It was great fun for the inmates of the Five Head and their visiting friends. But a mere half an hour later Bookworm started fiddling with his books again. It was an ominous sign. Others despaired: it was nothing short of disaster.

Long Sideburns lost no time. He went out, collected a red hibiscus and a handful of rice and hotfooted it to Sukuta-Ma's place. He sprinkled the rice and the flower on her verandah and went inside. 'There, Auntie,' he said. 'Have you seen your front verandah? Go have a look. Serenta's Ma is trying to cast spells on you. She's thrown rice and a hibiscus on your verandah. My, what a red flower! Just like blood!'

Sukuta's Ma stomped out to have a look. 'Blood-drinking witch!' she screamed, shaking with anger. 'You choleric she-devil, succubus, lamia! You dare give me the evil eye? Wait, you pox-ridden bitch, I will sit on your chest and take a bath. Shit-eater, how dare you...'

The riposte came instantly and with great gusto. 'Oh you filthy whore! Who's casting the evil eye on whom — you on me or I on you? Daughter of a knuckle-sucker, shit-worm, since when have you become so brazen? May your face go up in blazes! May your past, present and future generations be wiped off the face of the earth! May low untouchables drag your corpse all the way to the cremation ground. May paralysis strike you...'

Laughter and applause rocked the Five Head. Bookworm slapped his book shut with disgust and, though far from happy, joined his friends. 'These two old hags are about the most quarrelsome and cantankerous pair you can ever hope to see. Foul-mouthed, ill-natured and destroyers of public peace. They should be put behind bars.'

The Five Head was no longer a dull joint; whenever academic or spiritual preoccupations seemed to threaten the general air of merriment, a slanging match could readily be organized between the volatile Serenta's Ma and Sukuta's Ma. But the job was too much for Long Sideburns alone: running between the two huts, and playing up the two harridans, always on the sly. It was therefore decided that the duty of egging on the two would be shared. They drew lots: Serenta's Ma fell to Sword Whiskers and Sukuta's Ma to Long Sideburns. Both the rascals discharged their duties with considerable skill, and for some days everything went according to plan. The atmosphere of the Five Head was no longer claustrophobic; the Yogi's one-anna worth achievement had dwindled to one-paisa; and the Bookworm, like a repulsed bedbug, stayed away from his moth-eaten books. But the inmates and their friends didn't dare slacken their vigil until the two had completely forsaken their natures.

Meanwhile the curses and abuses hurled by the two old crones had become stale, cliched and worn-out, and the daily exchanges had lost their sting as a result. Instead of making the audience double up with laughter it left them cold. Something had to be done about it and quickly too. So one day, when Bookworm and One Anna Yogi had gone out, a meeting was convened and Long Sideburns and Sword Whiskers were entrusted with the task of enlivening the slanging matches with crisp, brand-new, ultra-modern cusswords.

But that was easier said than done. How could new cusswords be collected and from where? And how to get those two ancient hags to quickly absorb an expanded vocabulary, most of which was in a foreign language and real tongue-twisters at that? Long Sideburns and

Sword Whiskers racked their brains. And then one fine morning it suddenly dawned on them that the collection part was easy indeed: newspapers, political manifestos, handbills and graffiti on the city walls were full of interesting words. It took them a month and a half to draw up an exhaustive list. They made two copies.

One day at an opportune moment Long Sideburns went to Serenta's Ma. 'Auntie, have you heard? Sukuta's Ma is busy lea_ning a whole dictionary of firinghee cusswords. I'm afraid you'll not understand them. How will you ever give it back to her? Sukuta's Ma will easily become the world-conquering queen of the slanging matches. But don't worry, I'm with you. I'll coach you, no matter how long it takes. I'll whisper into your ears the words you can hurl at your opponent. That will knock the stuffing out of the old witch, her tongue will wither inside her mouth and no words will come out any more; she'll even forget her own father's name, crawl back into her hole and stay put there until the end of her days.' In the middle of their deliberations Sukuta's Ma opened fire all of a sudden, without any provocation: 'You fasistee bitch! You think you can put me down with your angrezi swearwords? Self-seeking pig, how dare you...'

'What did I tell you, Auntie?' said Long Sideburns, glancing over his list. 'Let's have a crack at the bitch.'

The air was filled with words unheard of before. The two prompters performed as admirably as the two old women.

'You lefetist fembale, you stinking ritist whore...'

'You, you, you. Middilist slut! Ekstereemist. Demn you, you soptist...'

'Whore of first water! May kilass strugale cook your goose. May porgesive lend reforms finish you off...'

'Slut! Harlot! May you become a Schedal Cast. Piss on your head, you handmaiden of terroristies...'

'You showey slut! You shelf enriching boorokrazy! May you disappear in the kilassless chociety. May the devil drop his dung on you, whore, counter rebolusonary, barren bitch...'

'Demn you, dog demn you, right rebisionist. You dare reap dubious poltical gains...'

'Devil take you, you agenti of red tepism. You running dog of anti social govment...'

'Devil's urine on you, you rapist of dembokracy...'

'Violator of low and order, down with you! Promoter of pooliceraj, goondaraj, loot taraj, I shit on the fourteen generations of your ancestors. Immoralist, poorhouse-grub-eater, symbol of repressive, athoterian admenistasun, may you live the rest of your shortened life in your stinking hell-hole...'

'Crap on you, public enemy number one, C.I.A mole...'

'KGB plant, branded turncoat, political mouthbottom, Naxal, Anandmargi...'

'Woman with seventeen husbands, you! Billak marketer, hoarder, unscrupulous profit monger, may people's wrath come down heavily on you. May taxmen strangle you, DRI lick you, MISA chew you. May you suffer for becoming an obscurantist...'

'Drop dead, opposer of deblopment, right rexonary, neo kepitalist, leo colonialist...'

'Death to you, bloody witch, fifthy coloomnist, ekespansionist...'

'Purty boorjooa! May civil war engulf you...'

'Swollen-headed mongrel, may ekonomik deskrimnasun ruin you. Adulterer, black marketeer, tex evader, profit monger, may you rot during Emergency...'

The two women stopped, frothing at their mouths.

The next morning they were at it again.

After a few such exercises, Bookworm turned into a harmless housefly and One Anna Yogi threw away his prayer mat and loin cloth: both had ceased being wet blankets. Happiness and mirth returned permanently to the Five Head and the evenings were simply delightful. Sometimes, just for the heck of it, the buttons were pressed for a slanging match. It had tremendous entertainment value.

Satchidananda Raut Roy

❧❦

Dead Flower

Jagu Tiadi — an opium-addict, a lusty drummer, and the undisputed leader of the brahmin kirtan singers of Podabasant village — had made a name for himself as a cremator. When it came to burning a body there was no one, even in the neighbouring villages, who could hold a candle to him.

Corpses, you see, can cause plenty of headaches: some slowpokes refuse to catch fire; others, as sly in death as in life, suddenly thrust out a stiff hand or leg, upsetting the carefully arranged pyre; some burst open at the seams at the slightest heat and their abundant body fluids douse the fire. Only a few go without a fuss. Faced with such difficulties pallbearers would look to Jagu for help and advice. Fighting off sleep and an opium-induced languor, he would struggle to his feet, pull out a smoking log and land a couple of hefty blows on the unyielding corpse. 'Go quickly, or I'll hand you a second death,' he would curse, as he saw to it that the skull was smashed to smithereens, the legs broken into splinters, the stomach deflated like a pricked balloon, the body caught fire and turned to ashes.

Until it was all over, Jagu would lumber about the cremation ground littered with ash-heaps, winnowing-fans, broomsticks, shards, rags and knotted balls of hair and nails. A smooth cremation never failed to warm his heart. 'Thank God,' he would say, slapping oil on his thighs for the mandatory ritual dip in the village pond. 'There, that's a decent corpse for you.'

When cholera and smallpox struck the village and almost every home had a body to cremate, Jagu naturally was in great demand. If a family tried to reduce his fee by so much as a paisa, he would leave the body to rot in the house. He would not budge an inch unless he was paid a quarter-rupee coin and a tola each of ganja and opium. These, of course, were in addition to the customary offering of rice, new clothes and invitations to three funeral feasts.

For Jagu, the death of a married woman while her husband was still alive was nothing less than a bonanza. If she belonged to a prosperous family Jagu was entitled to her gold nose-stud or earrings; if she came from a humbler home he took her silver toe-rings. Before placing the body on the pyre he himself would remove the jewellery. Sometimes when the piece did not come off easily, Jagu would impatiently yank it off and if in the process the corpse bled, it did not upset him in the least. Why, he never even hesitated to strip a dead woman to the skin just to make sure he had not missed out on anything valuable.

He rejoiced most in the death of a pregnant woman, or better still a death during childbirth. On such occasions, he would refuse to lift the bier unless he was paid a full rupee. People who haggled with him were damned; he would have nothing to do with the cremation. He could even talk the other pallbearers into a strike. But once he got his silver coin, he would get on with the job with the elan of a professional. Belting out lusty shouts in praise of God to the rhythmic beat of drums, he would dance down the village path, his spotless white sacred-thread girdling his black-as-granite body. His big booming voice, echoing through the village, scared the little children off the road. At the cremation ground, once the washerman had slit open the swollen belly of the dead woman he would pluck the foetus out. Sometimes he beat the half-formed child into a pulp before unceremoniously throwing it into the fire. No one dared comment upon his outrageous behaviour. After all, there was no one more efficient than Jagu to take care of the dead!

The relish with which Jagu often described his exploits left no one in doubt about the pride he took in his calling. 'Who kept Narasingh Mishra's wife's pyre going in the pouring rain? Who found the way to reduce Nath Brahma to cinders when the bloated-up old bounder was a wet mass?' he would ask. Even when cremations took a long time and were tiresome, Jagu would linger patiently until the end, sometimes just about the only person around. And the nether world notables he encountered on these ungodly occasions! There was the Headless One roosting at the fringe of the Seven Tree grove; the old witch in the crotch of a mango tree by the Muktajhar stream roasting a new-born baby over a pale cold fire. Pausing only for a deep drag on the chillum or to clear his throat, he reeled off his stories so vividly that the listeners in the village bhagavatghara, covered in gooseflesh, huddled closer to each other.

One late evening in the month of Ashwin, when the sky hung low with dark clouds, Jagu sat on his verandah, nursing a splitting headache. He had a muffler around his head, his temples smeared with dabs of quicklime. The village priest was reading aloud the holy *Harivamsa*. Suddenly a loud wail pierced the stillness of the evening. Somebody had died. Jagu grew restless wondering who it was. But soon someone who had gone to the shop at the other end of the village brought the news. It was Jatia's deserted young wife. Jagu sat up. Here was a big chance for a shiny silver coin. Not often in this sinful world did women predecease their poor husbands. It did not matter that Jatia had abandoned his wife long since.

His joy, however, was shortlived. The grapevine had it that the young woman was pregnant and that the local abortionist's potion had brought on her death. Jagu realized he could cremate her only at the risk of excommunication.

All Jatia's old mother had been left with in the world was this young daughter-in-law, and now she too had died in the most disgraceful of circumstances. Jatia had left home three years ago to seek his fortune in Calcutta, and had broken all ties with his family. The rumour had spread that he had taken another wife. Abandoned by her son, and now by her daughter-in-law, Jatia's mother rolled in the dust, bewailing her fate.

Although the village elders blamed the old woman for not keeping a strict eye on her daughter-in-law, it was no longer her private misfortune. If the police got to know about it, it would be a slur on the honour of the caste and on the village as well. The body had to be disposed of as quickly as possible, for there was no lack of sneaks in the village to carry tales to the police. Jatia's mother felt so mortified that she held a straw between her toothless gums and prostrated herself before the village elders.

A few young men volunteered to cart the corpse to the cremation ground. Straw ropes were plaited, a bamboo bier was readied, and the winnowing fans, broomsticks, pots and slings were collected from inside the house. The dead woman was wrapped in a sari and tied down to a bier. The cremation seemed far from being a tame affair: the rains threatened to come down any moment, and if the police arrived before it was over the whole village could be put in the dock. Urgent summons were sent to Jagu.

But Jagu would have none of it. The young woman had died in sin and he did not wish to pollute himself by cremating her. Jagu found his moral qualms too strong to be overcome — until an offer of five big silver coins was made, and he reluctantly accepted.

Jatia's mother dug out her nest-egg from a hole in the wall, but it was barely enough for the wood, kerosene, rice, and fees for the barber and washerman. So would Jagu kindly relent and have the gold piece the dead woman wore on her nose?

'Jai Hari.' Jagu turned to the pallbearers. 'Praise Hari. Ram Nam Satya Hai. God is the only Truth.' The bier was hoisted.

The wind had dropped, and a rank smell hung over the cremation ground. Jagu cleared a little space among the debris, dug a pit, and filled it with dry wood, stick by stick. The dead body was placed on the pyre.

The moon suddenly broke from behind a bank of clouds as Jagu removed the veil from the woman's face. The gold nose-stud glittered in the moonlight.

A shiver ran down Jagu's spine.

The moon disappeared behind a cloud for a moment and sailed out again, the light and shadow playing hide-and-seek on the pale face of the corpse.

Jagu stretched his hand towards the jewel and stopped. The woman's face was like a wilting blue lily, her thick tresses resembled the clouds the moon was flirting with. Jagu felt a knot in his stomach.

The moon again slipped behind a cloud. Jagu waited. A lump rose in his throat. Why did he feel so sad? Had he not burnt plenty of young women? Why did he find the job so awful, so difficult this time? Many a woman had been prettier than this one.

He caught himself thinking about her. On her nose she had a little trinket of gold and in her faintly swollen womb an unborn child. Another four or five months and she would have become a mother. Why did she have to come to an end like this? It wasn't her fault that her husband had deserted her within a fortnight of their marriage. It wasn't a crime to be young and vivacious, to thirst for love, to crave male caresses, to exult in the excruciating passions of the flesh. Was it her fault that the repressed passion of her starved body had overcome her sense of right and wrong? What was right and what was wrong, anyway? Who could judge?

'Come on, Jagu!' the pallbearers fidgeted. 'Hurry up. The red turbans might swoop down on us any moment. Take the nose-flower off the corpse and light the pyre. For heaven's sake, don't waste time.'

'I don't want it,' Jagu said, coming out of his reverie. 'Let it go with her.'

'The gold nose-stud? Are you sure? All right, then torch the bitch. God knows how long she'll take.'

'Douse her with kerosene. It'll help.'

'Are you sure you don't want that piece of gold?' The pallbearers quizzed Jagu. 'How come?'

He did not say a thing.

The tongues of fire leaped up. The wood crackled. The body turned and twisted a little. The skin crinkled and turned black.

Jagu's eyes remained riveted on the pyre. After about an hour he took his stick and probed the lump. Soon it would be time to smash the skull. A sigh escaped him.

An owl began to hoot at the far corner of the cremation ground and vultures flapped their wings; a male jackal let out an eerie howl. The putrid stench of burning flesh hung thick in the air.

The cremation proved a smooth business. The rains held. The pallbearers chatted gaily among themselves.

'Good for him, he didn't touch the tainted jewel of the whore,' remarked someone. 'That gold would have done Jagu no good.' There was a chorus of agreement. Jagu winced.

'Whoever goes whoring around and killing the fruit of her womb,' said someone else, 'deserves a miserable death like this. There is dharma, after all. You can't escape it.'

'Shut up,' Jagu Tiadi said, a raw edge to his voice. 'Do me a favour and shut up.'

Surendra Mohanty

Oh Calcutta!

...We need to set about complete destruction, but not in word: in deeds. Everything you have borrowed from others will go up in smoke. What remains will be essential to you. Do you agree?
— Jean-Paul Sartre (*Troubled Sleep*)

'Guru! Tops! A top! All rolled into one, damn it!' shouted the fellow with long sideburns from inside the empty restaurant, gawking at the girl. 'Guru! Tops! A top! Holy shit, three in one!'

The underworld's language.

The girl darted a frightened glance at the hoodlums in the restaurant and quickened her pace towards the college. She wore a skimpy, sleeveless blouse revealing a heart-stopping slice of soft inner arm. She had full breasts and a midriff seductively exposed down to the navel. 'To accelerate the tempo of life — so dull it's become — what's needed is sex,' the fellow declared. 'Sex and revolution. But these bloody reactionary class enemies, damn them, the buggers are up in arms against both.'

He let off a lusty wolf-whistle. He remembered Guru's remark that these whistles were like the mating calls of animals. What's the difference between animals and human beings, anyway? Aren't cities primeval jungles?

Guru kept on gravely filing his nails with a knife. His silence was like the proverbial lull before the storm. He snapped the knife shut with a loud click, put it back in his pocket and turned towards the street. It was always a mystery to his cronies what he saw from behind his dark glasses.

On the other side of the road, leaning against the graffiti-covered college wall, stood a decrepit garbage dump under a dusty, gnarled tree. It sported a new poster: 'Grand Cultural Evening in Deshgaurav College Auditorium.' Crows were picking crumbs from the garbage heap. A large brown kite came winging towards them and flew away only at the last moment, perching gingerly on the tree. A mangy pariah dog came sniffing along, lifted its hind leg and pissed on the wall.

What a goddamn strategy on the part of Bhabatosh Das, Guru thought. This is how the bastard hopes to sweep the college union elections, eh? Cultural evening — balls! A little speechifying and plenty of ass-waggling. That's your big *cultural* event. Stupid sentimental songs and eunuch dances. Some scum of a fat-assed minister to inaugurate the tamasha.

'Bloody reactionaries!' Guru gnashed his teeth. 'Dogs of the Establishment!'

They looked up at him.

'The wretched dogs,' Guru said. 'How cocksure, how unruffled and unconcerned they are, even while sitting right over the epicentre of an imminent earthquake! And they have time for pop music and dancing, too!'

He fished the knife out of his pocket and snapped it open.

Surely Guru's hatching something, they figured.

A ramshackle restaurant in a blind lane in the city. Called Sujala; the tea and coffee here are appropriately watery. It is their little People's Republic. Here they gather, ogle at the college girls, make comments and lewd gestures and discuss revolution, counter-revolution, left revisionism, Che Guevara and Vietnam. A little distance away, where the narrow lane meets the main road, stands Deshgaurav College.

The old alma mater — hah! Guru snorted. That sonofabitch

Bhabatosh must be driven out of the college union this time. By hook or by crook.

Guru took off his dark glasses and glanced around. His empire, so snugly hidden away inside the Sujala, and his cronies did not flatter him. Although he seemed mysterious behind his dark glasses, without them his eyes were pensive and wistful.

The young man who had joined Guru's gang recently was not yet fully familiar with their language. 'What's a top?' he asked rather innocently. Only the other day he had learnt that doublebread was the underworld slang for bombs. And at what cost! He shuddered.

'Why on earth had Guru taken a fancy to this delicate girl-boy with a slender waist?' Sukant wondered aloud. 'The fucker's a Lachak all right. And a dimwit to boot.' The other day, in the thick of battle, Guru had told Lachak to get two doublebreads and, oh God, this bloody asshole went and actually bought two buns from the nearest bakery. The battle against Bhabatosh's gang was at its peak. Bhabatosh's boys came in through the park and pelted us with stones and soda bottles. Guru naturally called for doublebreads to retaliate. Imagine Lachak turning up with two buns! Guru could have knifed him then and there, and no one could ever for the world guess why he didn't. Was it out of pity? Come to think of it, as a hoodlum of long standing Guru had never experienced such a crushing defeat as on that day. Wiping the blood from his forehead, he simply stared at Lachak and the buns. 'Idiot!' Guru said, with a sick smile. 'Oh, you bloody fool!' Guru could be so goddamned enigmatic at times.

'What's a top?' Lachak repeated diffidently. 'What is it?'

'Idiot!' snarled Sukant. 'Go look it up in your bloody dictionary. A top is a top is a bloody top. Understand now? Didn't you notice how that bloody sexy wench walked past — swivelling, spinning, turning on her stilettos like a top?' Turning to Guru, he added, 'Guru, where did you unearth Lachak from? All he needs is hot halwa up his ass. Good hot halwa — the kind that's the soldiers' delight!'

Guru did not respond. He glowered at the poster on the garbage dump, thinking up schemes to sabotage the cultural show. He nursed a pathological hatred against culture and such stuff. Culture was always the tool of the counter-revolutionaries. And on top of that, Bhabatosh was the brains behind the show tonight. Just a matter of blowing the electric fuse, Guru chuckled. Toss in a doublebread or two and the cultural evening is fucked up!

He knew what chicken-hearted creeps the raving votaries of culture were. Damn the dogs of establishment, he spat. Tied to their chains they barked an awful lot, but merely for another helping of the leftovers, for another bone; they never broke their chains, they knew that would make them lose their few crumbs from the Establishment's table. But look at their highfalutin speeches extolling the revolution! What fever! What fiery poetry! Even Bhabatosh claimed to be a poet, the bastard. Sala, all poetry's doublebread today. Doublebread is the best poetry.

Guru's serious thoughts were disturbed by Sukant's impudent babble. 'Sutka!' he barked at him with sudden vehemence. 'Say sorry to Lachak! Delay a minute longer and I'll loosen your ass with one swift kick. What the hell do you take Lachak for — a branded antisocial, a criminal, a rusticated student like you, huh? Why, the poor little asshole must still have a first-class degree certificate — his passport to the Establishment.' He paused and, turning to Lachak, added, 'Buddy, it's a full house over there!' He guffawed at his own witticism. 'Ha-ha! No vacancy. No admission.'

'Sorry,' Sukant mumbled. The unexpectedness of Guru's reaction had rattled him.

Guru wasn't wide off the mark, anyway. Lachak was indeed a brilliant student. He had a real name as well: Subhendu. He never ever cheated in examinations and always dreamt of an ideal life of virtue and conformity. Little did he know that there was a cruel world outside the university. What a world, what a life! The queues at the employment exchange, no vacancy - queue - interview - no vacancy - queue - interview - queue - no vacancy - get lost! The unrelieved rhythm. Nor did home bring an escape from this cruel world — home, sweet home, ha! — a hovel of two tiny cobwebbed rooms that resembled ancient caves. In one room lived his asthmatic old father, wheezing and gasping for breath all night, his unblinking eyes glazed with the fear of death. Until the small hours the old man would sit on the bed, fretting like a caged animal. Subhendu's harried, overworked mother slept on the floor in the same room; she no longer needed even a mat to lie on. He and his sisters were cooped up in the other room, so tiny it was impossible to make up three separate beds, even overlapping each other. The girls hadn't the ghost of a chance of marrying. Ever since Subhendu had started college he had taken to spending nights outside home. Like a canny hunter his old man kept a close vigil on his arrivals and departures and lamented above his asthmatic wheeze that the boy had gone to the dogs. Subhendu didn't care what he thought. The mystery of 'no-vacancy' gnawed at his heart. 'You need pull,' one interviewer had observed airily. 'Backing! Do you have backing?' Subhendu had fallen from the skies. 'Backing?' he had asked. 'What's that?' The interviewer had laughed scornfully. 'The patronage of a godfather,' he spat out the words, as though he were flinging scraps of paper into a waste basket. 'Get a politician or a top official to back you!' Subhendu thought, 'I've got my own back, that's all. Get someone's backing — no!' Finally, forced to eke out a living, he decided to sell Hindi movie tickets on the black market. It won't be so difficult after all, he thought. The poor fellow did not know that quite another kind of backing was necessary for that as well. He had barely got started when he was flushed out by two toughs and whisked off to a spooky restaurant behind the movie hall. That had brought about his first encounter with Guru. With his feet, shoes and all, on the table, Guru slouched in a chair. He slowly tilted his head back, glowering over a bottle of rum at the offender, and took a knife from his pocket, snapped it open and thrust the tip against Subhendu's belly. 'Why this mastaani here, boy?' he growled. 'Don't you know whose territory this is? Did you get my permission to operate here? You're from which gang, hey?' Subhendu trembled in fear. 'Sir, I'm jobless, unemployed. I don't have backing,' he squeaked, his voice catching. 'The hell with backing, man!' guffawed one of the toughs. 'Look at his back. Smooth, isn't it? Guru, I tell you here's a damn good Lachak.' From that moment Subhendu became Lachak. 'Hey Lachak!' said Guru, staring at him, his eyes suddenly softening. 'I'll let you go this time. Don't make the mistake of straying into my territory a second time. I don't want any unpleasantness.' Lachak did not want any either. 'But I've got to survive!' he stammered, as if his life and death hung on Guru's decision. Blowing a string of perfect smoke rings, Guru grunted, 'Man, one survives in this world by liquidating the reactionaries, the class enemies.' Lachak was ready for anything. 'But who are these reactionaries and class enemies, sir?' he asked timidly. 'Our enemies,' said Guru. 'The class enemies!' Mere slogans, Lachak realized, his heart sinking. Empty words.

'Bloody Bhabatosh!' Guru exploded, much to the consternation of the gang. 'Class enemy number one!'

Sukant wondered why Bhabatosh's stock had fallen so low. Till the other day Guru and Bhabatosh had been great buddies. Together they had hurled doublebreads at the hapless cops, and committed quite a few crimes. Why did Guru pick on him now? Was it because Bhabatosh had managed to cling to the college and the Students Union? Bhabatosh had remained on the rolls for so long that he seemed to have become a permanent student at Deshgaurav. Sukant remembered when he had joined as a fresher, Bhabatosh was in the second-to-last year. Three years later when Sukant was chucked out for cheating in exams, Bhabatosh was in his final year. Bhabatosh's tenacity had baffled Sukant. 'In a bourgeois society,' Guru explained, when he had brought up the topic once, 'the colleges too are footholds of power. To capture these footholds, there are the unions, and all this politics.' But surely Bhabatosh couldn't be damned for this alone.

'But Bhaba has links with the naxalites!' Sukant said, in an unguarded moment. 'How can he be a class enemy?'

'Shut up, Sutka!' Guru bellowed, hitting the table hard. 'Bloody fool! Either you're a police spy or an agent of the class enemies.'

Rattled to his very bones, Sukant cowered.

Lachak stared from Guru to Sukant, wondering at the thin line between a class enemy and a comrade. Who was a class enemy and who a comrade? What was the difference between the two? 'Bhaba might not be a class enemy,' he ventured, yanking at his long, unkempt hair, 'but he serves those who are. Hasn't he been canvassing for the right revisionist ministry?'

'You're bright, Lachak,' Guru beamed. 'Holy shit, you really are. It's time I changed my opinion of you, comrade.'

For so long Lachak had been some kind of hanger-on, a mere stuffy, sterile intellectual, afraid of class struggle. Now he was a comrade.

It was beyond Guru's expectations that Lachak would improve so much in such a short time. 'Let Lachak have the honour of transacting the little doublebread business at Deshgaurav this evening,' he said. 'Okay, Lachak?'

Lachak glowed under his skin. Here at last was the chance to prove his revolutionary ardour. He had come of age. But the prospect daunted him as much as it thrilled him. 'Me alone?' he asked diffidently. 'Isn't Sutka coming along?'

'Remember,' Guru said dreamily. 'One guerilla's enough for a whole bloody gang of class enemies. One against many — that's our buzzword.'

Lachak jumped up excitedly. He felt as if he was savouring the taste of life for the first time. He was no longer the helpless little leaf flying from office to office in search of a job. Now he was someone to be reckoned with. The life of society was in his hands. Tighten the fist, strengthen the grip and toss two little doublebreads, and...Lachak laughed. Up they go in smoke!

The doublebreads inside his bag reminded him of his one-time girl friend Jamuna's beautiful breasts. After college she too had stood with him in the queues of the employment exchange. But after a few months she had dropped out of sight. Only the other day Subhendu had stumbled upon her in a shady nursing home. 'I'm not well,' she said, with a wan smile. Her lips were white, bloodless. 'Hit a bad patch.' It wasn't easy to pull the wool over Subhendu's eyes. He found out she was convalescing after an abortion.

Poor Jamuna! Lachak sighed. Such a lovely girl — how could she become a whore? Anyway, what am I but a g... g... guerilla!

Oh Calcutta! Oh, why had this city turned into a jungle at the height of its culture and civilization? Why did I, Subhendu Das, turn into an urban guerilla? Why did my love have to get admitted into a nursing home under a false name for a third, maybe a fourth abortion? He pulled at his dishevelled hair, half expecting the answers to tumble out like rabbits from a conjuror's hat.

In the college auditorium the cultural programme had already begun. A profusely garlanded minister was in the middle of a ponderous speech: 'C...C...culture, our great Indian culture, has the backing, strong backing, er, heritage of two thousand years and more. I call upon the youth of today to become worthy of this culture. Come, let's take a vow that...'

The hall suddenly plunged into darkness.

'The lights!' shrieked the minister. 'The lights!'

'Oh God, those savages!' screamed the girls. 'Those beasts!'

A bomb exploded outside and the smoke drifted into the hall.

'Police!' cried the minister, his voice hoarse with fear and impotent rage. 'Police!'

In the darkness, Bhabatosh led him to a corner of the platform. 'This must be the handiwork of I know which bastard!' he said. 'Does he hope to upset the evening by blowing the electric fuse and bursting a firecracker or two? What's there for the police to do? Wait here, sir. I'll set everything right in a minute.'

As Bhabatosh jumped down from the dais, someone whispered into his ear, 'Boss, it's someone from Guru's gang. The bastard has already knifed one or two of our guys. Patla's palms are badly cut, he was trying to hold the fellow's hands.'

'Trap him,' Bhabatosh hissed. 'Shut all the exits. Don't let the bastard slip away.'

In the deep dark forest Subhendu pranced around like a drunken peacock. The pent-up despair, defeats and humiliations of his life had found an outlet. He experienced a heady romance in violence.

The darkness and chaos afforded the hoodlums in Bhabatosh's gang the chance of a lifetime to indulge in their lewd pastime. An orgy was on.

A brassiere landed on Subhendu's shoulder. 'Oh fuck!' someone whispered into his ears. 'Are these boobs or bran-sacks?'

At last the police came and cordoned off the hall. The electric fuse was mended. When the lights came on, the floor was littered with broken chairs, blouses, brassieres, torn garlands, shoes, and blotches of fresh blood. In the midst of the chaos, the blood-soaked body of a young man dangled awkwardly from a chair, blood still oozing from deep cuts in his belly and chest. A card from the employment exchange peeped timidly out of his shirt pocket.

Puffing frantically on his cigarette, Bhabatosh lurked under a tree in the darkest part of the sprawling campus. As a shadow stole across towards him, he enquired agitatedly, 'Who was it?'

'Not a hot shit, boss!' came the reply. 'We found his employment exchange card on him. Name: Subhendu Das. Education: M.A. (Mathematics). Age: Twenty-two.'

'Some bloody class enemy!' Bhabatosh spat.

Kishori Charan Das

Dispossessed

He isn't here, he's gone. But wasn't he here only a moment ago? Didn't he press his face against mine while I caressed his neck, soothing the prickly heat on his shoulder? His damp hair had a mildly pungent odour of perspiration. And how he had blinked at me with his sleep-laden eyes! But these people wouldn't believe it. And why would they? After all, they hadn't given birth to him!

'Come on, Bhauja,' said Chhabi, the youngest sister-in-law. 'It's almost five. Bhai will be back from the office any moment now.'

Shaken out of her trance, Nirmala abruptly sat up on the bed. 'So what?' she snapped. 'What do you expect me to do?'

Chhabi remained silent.

Perhaps it's Chhabi's turn this afternoon to see I have my tea. Oh, these people! Such a silly lot! Or are they a damn sight too clever for me? This Chhabi, this chit of a sister-in-law, is perhaps one of them. I can already feel her prying gaze shooting its probing needles into my skin. Now she will go and regale them with her stories: *you know what, Bhauja slept like this, she stared at me like that, she said this, she said that, she's growing a horn on her head, yes, I saw it with my own eyes, and she wouldn't touch the tea until I begged and begged her on bended knees.* Oh, my God, how she will gloat! Then they will descend on me, one by one, the whole lot, from the oldest to the youngest, every one of them. They will paw and pat me, sniffle, and vie with each other to parade their sympathy. Who cares for their sympathy, ha! My son's gone. And what do I care for their sympathy?

She smiled bitterly and burst into a flood of tears. Hiding her face between her upraised knees, she tried to stifle her sobs. No, she decided, I'll stop making a spectacle of myself. In fact, I should join *them* — giggle and gossip, bake cakes and peel vegetables, and...Listen, can't any of you bring my son back just once? Just one more time. Just for two minutes. I'll tell you what I'll do. I'll take a good long look at him and maybe talk to him a little. Then I'll wipe the sweat off his forehead. Am I asking for too much? I'm not asking for the moon, am I? Won't he come to me once more? Just once. Why not? What sin have I committed?

A disconsolate Nirmala raised her head and found Chhabi waiting for her response. 'Still here?' she asked weakly. 'What for?'

Chhabi quietly left the room. The tea had gone cold. Whose turn next to pester the life out of me? Nirmala wondered. Would it be the old servant or the brother-in-law? Or the mother-in-law herself?

Umesh beat them to it. He stole in softly, glanced at his wife and hurried to change his clothes. Pretending to be oppressed by the heat, he looked up at the ceiling to see if the fan was moving at full speed. Then he desperately looked around to fasten his attention on something, anything, no matter how trivial, as though his whole life depended on it. His furrowed brows and sagging cheeks conveyed the unmistakable impression he had reached the end of his tether. There was a limit to what a man could take, he thought, he was just a creature of flesh and blood, not an epitome of endurance.

Nirmala stared vacantly at her husband. She had no urge to speak to him. I know this man, she mused. He's my husband. I don't need to arrange my crumpled sari and look nice. His presence makes no difference to me, it just doesn't. It brings no solace, no balm to my aching heart. Look how he's peeling off his clothes and sighing! Oh, poor husbands — well, what else can they do?

Umesh stood directly under the fan, drying himself. 'Hasn't the tea gone cold?' he asked.

She did not respond.

He sat down beside her. 'Shall I ask for some more?' he enquired rather timidly.

She shot him a scalding glance. Her moist eyes sparked fire. 'Tea! Tea! Tea!' she exploded. 'No one in this house seems to bother about anything else! For heaven's sake, why can't you people leave a person alone?'

For a moment it seemed he would throw his patience to the winds and take her on. But he knitted his brows and clamped his lips shut. We are passengers on the same boat of grief, he mused, victims of a common tragedy. Why doesn't Nimu realize she isn't alone? How long can she go on like this? Little Biju was my son too, damn it. Everyone said we had the same complexion, the same nose and the same dark brown hair. Had he lived long enough, we would have gone out on walks, played football and chatted about a whole host of things. Maybe he would have hurt himself playing. Then I would have sat with him, cheering him up with stories. Another time he'd have done something naughty, and I'd have given him a box on the ear. The little imp would have scampered off to his mother, wailing and seeking consolation. Oh, my son, why did you have to die!

Billowing in the breeze, the ends of Nirmala's sari brushed gently against Umesh.

This proximity, this physical presence. Nirmala sensed even his sighs kept pace with hers. It irritated her — this petty, superficial harmony.

'Aren't we supposed to go shopping this evening?' she said suddenly, springing up from the bed. 'Come, let's go.'

Umesh winced.

They dressed in silence and went downstairs. The hushed family members watched, silently. It was the first time husband and wife were going out together after the tragedy. Umesh's father had the urge to tell them to take the car, but he kept quiet.

Umesh tried to keep up a chatter of small talk: 'The weather's nice, isn't it?...Where shall we go to buy Nani's sari — Kishanlal's or The Ladies' Emporium?...I was to go on a tour next week, but the boss had the good sense to cancel it, you know...'

They walked side by side, as if in a ceremonial procession. Even as they weaved their way through a knot of people in the crowded Clock Tower Square, Umesh resolutely clung to his wife's side. He didn't realize how unusual this was of him.

The market. The hurrying throng. The cacophony of buying and selling, the brisk air of commerce, the sweaty odour of enterprise. A hawker shouted beside a pile of cheap red and blue handkerchiefs. A rustic girl picked one up admiringly as her harried mother tried to drag her away. A bird-seller dangled an aviary of irate, screeching mynahs. A Sikh boy, his hair tied in a bun on top of his head, was bawling. His nylon-clad, heavily lipsticked mama, who had vanished into some shop, waddled out. In a small, cramped shop two young workers rolled beedis, seemingly absorbed in their work. An old man at the fruit-seller's examined each mango painstakingly to gauge its ripeness.

A peddler advertising a wonder ointment for scabies shoved a leaflet into Nirmala's hand.

They don't know, she sighed, this multitude. They don't know a damn thing about me. They don't know that my only child left me not even a fortnight ago.

She gloated in the secret pride of her private grief. I know what these people, steeped in ignorance and indifference, don't know. Am I not like a God incognito in this crowd? Or maybe I'm just an unredeemed sinner, still at large and on the loose, sullied by the putrid blood of death, who could pollute the whole of humanity with her faintest touch. My, why's that little brat staring at me? Could he have seen me for what I am?

'Not that way, Nimu,' Umesh kept up, keen not to relapse into silence. 'Why are you heading towards the vegetable market? We have to go to the cloth shop, don't you remember?...Watch out, there's a garbage heap ahead...You must be very tired. Come, let's have a cold drink...'

As she waited for the cold drink, Nirmala contemplated her husband's hairy hands and heavy face, and suddenly felt very tired. This fellow's not just a husband, she thought, but a man, a male. His gross, unperceiving maleness, his remorseless male body. God,

how large he looks! And what is it he's so much at pains to convey
— that he understands? Does he, huh? How dare he imagine he has
plumbed the mysterious depth of my grief? Is it because he had laid
his body over mine and fathered my child? Oh God, even this
marketplace is no different from the bedroom. Can I ever get rid
of this man? Or will he always hover around me? How I would
love to fling the drink in his face and run off — run off and get
lost in the crowd. At least I could be alone then. I could laugh, cry,
dance, or do anything. Even strip — strip myself of the exteriors
and whirl within the recesses of my suffering. And nobody would
watch me. Least of all this man here. There would be no one but
me. Only me. Me, my sorrow, my son. He would steal softly in,
my son, and like an eager little calf press his face against my breasts
heavy with milk. That three year old child! Yes, I used to suckle
him still. What concern is that of yours? Who are you to decide
everything for me?

Nirmala stiffened.

It did not escape Umesh. He felt a stab of panic. One never knew,
he thought. She might dissolve into sudden tears, or flare up
inexplicably.

Old doctor Gobardhan's words came to mind: 'Listen, young
man. Pull yourself together. You can't afford to give up. You must
be a source of strength to Nimu. In times like this women need
careful handling.' But why? he wanted to know. Am I not
suffering? Am I not supposed to, because I'm a man, a male? Am
I not the father of the child who died? Ah, it's easy to preach,
damn it.

He felt anger rising in him, but he collected himself quickly. He
looked at Nirmala sadly and hoped her black mood would pass.

Once they had finished their drink, they bought the sari and
walked back home, enveloped in a funereal silence. Nirmala made
up her mind to sleep alone on a bare mattress on the verandah from
then on.

That night Umesh tossed and turned on the bed. Why is it so
dark outside? he wondered. Where has the moon gone and hidden
itself — in some godforsaken corner of the sky? Why is the night

so quiet, so still, so devoid of its healing touch? Does the night ever calm the ruffled mind? What comforts the soul? Nothing! The poor damned males are condemned to fend for themselves forever.

His burning eyes ran over the cold lonely flower standing in the flower vase. It had not wilted yet. One must either face one's grief manfully or succumb to it, he sighed. There's perhaps no other way.

He had a sudden urge to hug somebody tightly, breathlessly. Oh God, my son is dead, he moaned. My wife has forsaken me. She won't even sleep with me. Isn't she mine any longer? Oh, this ghastly, this crippled, fetid old night! My wife sleeps out there on the verandah. Oh, let her. I won't go to her. Damn it, I can't stoop so low. I'm a man, I can't grovel before her, I can't cry out for help!

Yet a few seconds later, he crossed over to the verandah, lay down by her side, unbuttoned her blouse and buried his face between her breasts.

Half asleep, Nirmala stirred and pulled him closer, pressing his eager mouth to her breast. A sharp thrill ran down her spine. My little Biju's come back, she thought. Oh, what a state he's reduced me to, the naughty thing!

She fondled his face. Waves of warmth and dizziness rolled over her. My Biju has grown so much, she smiled. So what? He's still a little child to me — the same face, the same nose, the very same greedy moist lips.

Then she felt the unmistakable stirring of the male body, the slow surge of its desire. Oh God, this is not my child, she woke up. Why, what have I been dreaming of?

'Aren't you ashamed of yourself?' she hissed, recoiling from him in disgust. 'Who the hell asked you to come here?'

Nirmala looked down from the balcony. The cobbled courtyard was still damp from an early morning shower. Everything is so real, so solid, she smiled bitterly. The house with its high ceilings, the cracks in the boundary wall, the iron vaults, the tall almirahs, the bathtubs, the chipped flowerpots, the pigeon cotes, the new garage, the fresh coat of varnish on the wall, the brand new radiogram...Everything was so solid, so permanent — the strength and pride of the unchanging frieze. But oh, not me. Not my son. We fade, we pale, we die.

How long has he been dead, my son? Ten days or fifteen — how long? A year? I no longer sink into despair nor cry as bitterly as before. Maybe I shall soon learn to giggle again, to play cards and strut about in new saris, to guzzle like a pig and chatter endlessly. Sometimes I shall remember my child. Of course, I will. But then I'll not be so heartbroken. Maybe only the lustrous drop of a tear — my poignant homage to his memory — will glisten in my eyes: *Oh, once I had a little child!* Oh no! It's not going to be like that. I'm not going to sit and embroider covers for the radiogram, or cook mutton curry. I'm supposed to stitch and cook well — ha! Damn it, I couldn't care less about what other people think. Just give me a little more time, I beg you. Don't rush me. Have pity on me. Please. I know I'm beginning to forget my son — there's a current carrying him down, a breeze blowing him away. Soon I'll forget him completely, oh God!

'Nimu,' her mother-in-law called. 'Nimu!'

There, Nirmala sighed, how her voice drips tenderness. Perhaps the spices have been ground and she's waiting for me to cook the mutton. Or maybe it's time for Father-in-law's sherbet. I don't mind doing the work, but what I can't stand is her stuffing me with sweets. Why does she do that? But then the blame isn't hers alone. Don't I love sweets? Don't I love being fussed over?

'Coming,' Nirmala responded reluctantly. She went down the stairs, almost brushing against the wall.

From the landing, she could see several pairs of shoes on the verandah. A particularly battered brown pair stood out from the rest. A chill ran down her spine. So the wise old heads have gathered for a morning session, she groaned. I know who must be stealing the show — the owner of the battered pair, the family physician and Father-in-law's closest friend to boot — that old fogey Gobardhan.

'Roll some paans for them, will you?' her mother-in-law asked her. 'Two for Batadada. You know what he likes, don't you? Without lime. Why didn't you have the dessert last night? I told you to so many times!'

Nirmala did not answer. She began to prepare the betel leaves. As fragments of the conversation floated out of the drawing room, she craned her neck and caught a glimpse of the gaunt white-haired profile of the doctor.

'You know, Dasarathi,' the old doctor was saying, with the finality of clinching an issue, 'your doctor, father, mother, grandfather, grandmother and the rest are of little avail when you're up against fate. What are we all worth? Mere straws in the wind.' In a gesture of reverence, he raised his hands heavenward. 'What didn't we do to save that child! While there was the faintest chance, I didn't give up hope. But he was beyond cure, beyond all our mortal efforts. We couldn't have held him back. Do you remember what I told you that evening about a week before his death?...'

Which evening? Nirmala tensed. Nobody ever told me anything! Till the last minute you all led me to hope that my little Biju would pull through. Even on the last day, you, doctor, you patted his head and said, God's there, everything will be all right. Why couldn't you come out with the truth? Why couldn't you say, God is in His heaven, but your child won't survive?

She glared at the doctor's large dome of a head. Biju had never taken to the old goat, she recalled.

'You know what happened to my sister-in-law's daughter?' Batadada began. 'You people ought to have seen that plump little angel. Absolutely healthy that child was, nothing wrong with her. Then one fine morning she complained of a stomach ache and the same evening she died...'

Oh, my God, what's all this about! Nirmala felt giddy. Has my son been dead so long that these people can talk so unfeelingly? Don't they have any compassion?

More instances and more illustrations of untimely deaths followed. Each vied with the other to recall as many incidents as possible.

Nirmala cocked her ears when she heard the deep voice of her father-in-law.

'My father had an elder brother,' Dasarathi began. 'He died before he was three months old. When my grandma was around, she used to tell us about him. You wouldn't believe how her eyes would instantly well up with tears, as if the boy had died only the night before... A mother is a unique creature. She never can forget the child she carries inside her for nine months.'

'True,' chimed in the rest. 'Very true!'

Dasarathi fell silent. Nirmala was relieved. She imagined his broad face twitching in deep understanding of a mother's grief.

'Whatever the Lord does is for the best,' the old doctor droned. 'Who are we to question His intentions? More often than not what He snatches away with one hand He gives back with the other. If He plucks a fruit before it is ripe, He bestows another in no time. That's the underlying principle of creation. A purely biological necessity. I tell you Nimu will have another child within a year. I say, Dasarathi, old boy, cheer up. You will surely behold the face of another grandson. That will make you live for another decade.'

Nirmala froze, gripped by a sudden fear. Why did he speak like that? Wasn't it downright cruel and mean? Did my father-in-law believe in all that rubbish?

Now it was Batadada's turn. Vigorously munching paan, he reeled off yet another story.

They must be enjoying the whole thing, she sighed, these august, venerable judges. They must be smacking their lips while pronouncing their precious, irrefutable verdicts. Creation and biology my foot!

As she walked into the room with the paan-tray, she glanced out of the corner of her eye at them. She knew she was right. Behold, she thought to herself, the mighty Lords sitting atop the celestial Mount Kailash! What am I but a mere dancing girl before them! A nimble dancing girl to provide them with a little distraction!

She was not angry; on the contrary, she felt very small and insignificant. She could sense the mute blessings of the Lords bestowed upon her. She suddenly felt a child growing inside her as their divine eyes remained riveted on her, and they smiled benignly at her rapidly swelling belly. She flushed. So it's just a matter of one child following another, huh? One fruit after another? Damn you, Lords. Am I a cow, or a tree?

Nirmala did not feel like going back to the kitchen. Excusing herself to her mother-in-law, she walked off. She could feel the old lady's fond gaze. Was she too dreaming of the next fruit? she wondered.

She stopped on the stairs to catch her breath. To whom can I speak? Who'll understand my tangled thoughts?

Dressed for the office, Umesh came down for his meal. Nirmala paused in her tracks. Haven't I been looking for this man? she wondered. Yes, of course, who else? Who else will understand the contours of my mind? Ah, the poor dear looks so pale and haggard. No, I must restore him back to health, and together we shall put up a brave front against the rest. These people, they don't know us yet.

Overwhelmed with love, she took another step towards him. Umesh looked away.

Nirmala realized he was sulking. It's all my fault, I know. I've spurned him, I've pushed him away. All this while I haven't even bothered to see if he existed. Maybe he wanted to say something last night. Oh, why did I push him away? Why is he so hurt? Aren't we adrift in the same boat? We're so helpless, the two of us. Why should we resent each other?

She looked up at him with beseeching eyes.

Her unarticulated feelings had not failed to reach him, but he thought he should wait until she was her usual self. She's unhinged, he reminded himself as he shuffled nervously towards her.

They came face to face near the staircase window overlooking the lawn. Then, suddenly, oblivious to the world around her — the sand heap, the chained dog, the labourers — she threw herself on him with outflung arms. 'I can't stand this place any longer,' she burst out, holding him tightly. 'Take me away. Please!'

Umesh was taken aback. Raising her chin, he looked into her eyes. 'What's the matter? What's wrong?'

'Promise me,' she stammered. 'Promise me you'll not want a child again. Give me your word.'

He did not know what to make of this sudden, garbled entreaty. 'But who says I want a child?' he comforted her, lowering his head on her shoulder. 'I don't want anyone but you.'

When she opened her eyes, Nirmala found the congregation dispersing. The old doctor was struggling to open his tattered umbrella.

Watching them, she felt very small again. But now it did not hurt her, this feeling of smallness; on the contrary, there was something lovely about it — as lovely as a bee buzzing or a butterfly flying, or a little red fish splashing.

Early that night they lay in their bed and made love with abandon, their body and mind achieving a rare fusion.

But shortly afterwards she began to feel restless. Did they bury or burn my child? she wondered.

A long unresolved question gnawed at her. What happened to the half-eaten lozenge he'd hidden in his shirt pocket?

She turned to ask her husband, but he was already asleep.

Bamacharan Mitra

Father and Son

In this weary old world of ours where there is as much haggling over a bunch of spinach as over policies in august international bodies, where the struggle for existence is as much in evidence in the village market as in the United Nations, there are still some people who treat life as one big joke and methodically make a mockery of all struggles, rat races and crises. If you threaten to whip them for their insouciance, they unashamedly plead: 'Look, why flog a dead horse? Can't you see I'm already down and out!'

Old Kanhu in our office belonged to this blessed tribe. He was a sort of grandpa to everyone around, old and young; even the newcomers promptly became his little grandsons, swapped jokes with him, pulled his leg, tugged at the ends of his dhoti and scribbled 'ass' on the back of his wide avuncular shirt. Serene, collected and unruffled, Kanhu didn't mind their pranks. It was well nigh impossible to nurse a grudge against him; he simply left no room for that. He had already seen to it that he posed no serious threat to the promotion prospects of his colleagues, having, in the infancy of his career, settled for rank inefficiency. Forty long years in the service and he remained exactly where he had begun. Strictures, warnings, denial of increments and threats of suspension made little difference to him; Kanhu, the old bounder, was incorrigible, and one could never catch him trying to better his lot. His was apparently a small family and his wife was permanently hidden away in a distant village; with his meagre salary, as Kanhu argued, bringing her to the town even for a change was out of the question. He would have dearly loved to dump his son in the village too, but the boy had his studies to do. When the son passed matriculation, albeit after several attempts, Kanhu began to hope that sooner or later the boy would step into his shoes in the office.

It was Kanhu's assiduously cultivated life-long habit to come to the office in a black buttoned-up cotton coat, so shabby and threadbare that even beggars wouldn't dare touch it, and a smelly moth-eaten shawl of undecipherable colour flung across his shoulder. It took him a little over half an hour to say his prayers, touching his forehead gently to the doorframe, before setting out for the office.

On his way he would stop by all the roadside shrines, whether in small mud temples or, as is common in an ancient town like Cuttack, simply under trees and eaves, and offer prayers, ten minutes to each. He never reached the office before twelve o'clock. Meanwhile the boss would be furious, asking for him after every five minutes. Panting and puffing from climbing the stairs, Kanhu would stagger into the office, his dhoti hitched up, and plunge into his chair with a deep sigh, trying not to look at the slip of paper placed on the table. The message, scribbled in angry red ink by the head clerk, was meant to remind Kanhu to see the boss the moment he came in.

This had become a ritual, and a blasé Kanhu who saw through it sometimes took his own sweet time. Occasionally, Dhanu the peon would accost him: 'Kanhu Babu, the boss has sent you his fond greetings for the fourth time this morning. Run along, man. You'll have enough time to cool yourself afterwards.' Heaving a huge sigh, Kanhu would reluctantly spit out his half-chewed paan, smooth the creases in his coat and slowly move towards what he called the torture chamber. Even lambs led to slaughter showed better spirit. He would stand in the boss's presence with his head deeply bowed, ears shut, and hands folded behind his back — you couldn't tell him from a statue. Once the harangue was over, he would bustle out of the chamber with the happy air of a bride, an inscrutable grin furrowing his face. He would then head straight for the records room, a dim deserted hall stacked with old records from floor to ceiling. Here, once the files had been removed from the bottom shelf of one of the almirahs, there was enough room for a man to stretch out and sleep. A reed mat, ragged from continuous use, served as a bedroll and a bunch of old files tied together with a piece of rope did well for a pillow. Save a few trusted 'grandsons' no one knew about this lair. If by any chance the boss looked for Kanhu yet another time the same day, the grandsons would cover for him. The harried head clerk would stare balefully over his glasses at Kanhu's vacant chair, mutter under his breath, tear a slip from the bunch of papers tied to the leg of the table and scribble a note. 'Peon!' he would bark hoarsely, making us all jump out of our sleep-inducing chairs. 'Yessa,' Dhanu would shout back irritably. 'Go straight and give this to the boss,' the head clerk would order. But Dhanu was a friend of Kanhu's — not only did the two hail from the same village, they also shared a damp little hencoop on the edge of the town — and would never dream of betraying him. He would make a detour to the records room on his way to the boss. (Kanhu and Dhanu were alike in many other ways, too. Ever since taking up jobs in the town they had never lived with their wives, nor ever taken a vacation long enough to make a visit to them in their far-off village worthwhile. The bus fare alone came to fifteen rupees — a sum well beyond anything they could afford. Besides, leave did not come easily and so the number of occasions they had visited their wives could be counted on one finger.)

This was the story of Kanhu's life. It never swerved out of its groove. Meanwhile bosses came and went.

One day the new boss, a young man full of vim and vigour and bustling with new ideas, tried to reason with Kanhu: 'Look, Kanhu Babu, your gross dereliction of duty would make some sense if we were still under foreign yoke. Maybe then it would've been seen as patriotic, as a gesture of protest. But now the foreign power is gone. Our country is independent. Or do you have doubts about that? Don't you think that now it's a crime to shirk your duty?'

As was his wont, Kanhu let out a huge sigh, his chin on his chest, his lips hermetically sealed.

The boss was intensely irritated. 'What's this stupid habit of yours, Kanhu Babu? Why don't you answer when you're asked a question?' He drummed on the table with his pen.

Kanhu gave him a shy, sidelong glance. 'Sir!' he gulped. 'Sir...'

The boss glowered at him.

'Sir,' Kanhu hemmed and hawed. 'Sir!'

'Yes, go on.'

'Sir, you think I'm dumb, don't you, sir? But I'm not as dumb as I look, sir. I understood every word of what you said, sir. But sir, please pardon me for saying so, sir, the trouble with me, sir, is that, sir, I can't put my heart into my job, sir.'

'Why the hell not, *sir*?'

'Sir, I know I ought to work. And very hard too, sir. The country would benefit if I chipped in. But sir, pray take a good look at poor me, sir. My life, sir, is nearly spent. But have I ever known any happiness, sir? No! Have I ever been able to live with my wife, sir? No! Have I ever brought her to the town for even a week? No! I have never had even an iota of her company, sir...'

The boss was silent. The conversation had taken an unforeseen and embarrassing turn.

'All right,' he said. 'You may go now.'

Kanhu, as always, showed more agility and enthusiasm at the moment of dismissal.

'By the way,' the boss said, 'when are you retiring?'

'That day is not far off, sir. But you can hasten it, sir. My son has applied for a job in this office, sir. If he's given my post, I'll call it a day right away, sir.'

'Is that so?'

The meeting was over and, as his feet instinctively led him back to his lair, Kanhu was happy that at least one boss had taken some pains to talk to him; others had merely shouted.

The day his son received the appointment letter, Kanhu submitted an application to extend his own service. The head clerk wrote a blistering note: it had been a crime to appoint someone like Kanhu in the first instance; to view his prayer for extension with any sympathy would be a calamity.

When the application reached the boss, he nearly fell out of his chair and called for Kanhu. As usual, Kanhu was missing from his seat. Sensing what the hullabaloo was about, Dhanu hurried to the hideout and shook the sleepyhead awake. Kanhu grumbled, spat out his paan, washed his face with cold water and tiptoed into the hallowed presence of the boss. There, his head bowed parallel to the ground, he waited.

'What're you up to, Kanhu Babu?' The boss was scowling. 'Why have you sent in this application?'

Kanhu did not answer.

'What's the big idea? Didn't you tell me you'd retire the day your son got a job here?'

'Sir,' said Kanhu, after what seemed like a respectful delay, 'that's how I viewed it then. Now I have changed my mind, sir.'

'It's high time you called it a day, Kanhu Babu. Forty years in service is long enough for anyone. Forget about the extension and go home. Turn your mind towards God and religion. Get your boy a wife so that you'll have a little daughter-in-law to look after you. Go back to the village and enjoy whatever years you have left. Why cling to the office?'

'Not a question of clinging to the office, sir. The fact is, sir, if I get pensioned off now I'll wilt and die inside of a week. Sir, I can't face the prospect of leaving the town and going back to the village. What attraction does the village hold for me, sir? I don't possess an inch of land to keep myself busy with farming. I wouldn't know what to do with myself, how to spend my days. Tell me what to do, sir. You're my boss, you tell me, sir. I beg you to kindly enlighten your most obedient servant, sir.'

'But you have your wife. She'll give you company. You've been missing her. Now...'

'Now what, sir? There's a time for that; there's a time for everything, sir. Of what use is a woman to me at my age? To tell you the truth, sir, she's a stranger to me.'

'Hmm.'

'I married but stayed a bachelor all my life, sir. For all practical purposes, sir. Sometimes I wonder if I've a wife at all. The woman in the village is a stranger to me. All I've had from her is her thumbprint on the monthly money order receipt — even that, I'm sure, was forged once or twice. I've visited the village only five times since I married, and I've never spent a night with her. Sir, you can imagine the amount of contact I've had with my wife. The government in its wisdom has not allowed me more.' The discussion had stirred old Kanhu deeply.

The boss wrote a note recommending an extension.

A few days afterwards Kanhu boldly asked to see the boss unbidden. With exaggerated trepidation he handed him two applications and stood staring at his toes.

The boss glanced at the papers and broke into a smile. 'Fast work, eh, Kanhu Babu! Barely has the boy joined and you're getting him married. Well, who's the lucky girl?'

'Dhanu's daughter, sir.'

'Dhanu — our peon?'

'Yes sir. We're from the same village.'

'Fine. But three days is the most I can allow. Although the flood relief operations call for a total mobilization of manpower, I'm willing to make an exception in your case.'

'Thank you, sir!' Kanhu spluttered with happiness. 'Very kind of you, sir!'

Anybody else would have haggled for at least four days so that the marriage could be consummated, but not old Kanhu.

Three days after the wedding Kanhu and his son returned to Cuttack, leaving the bride in the care of her mother-in-law.

Time wore on. One day, about a year later, Kanhu received a letter from home. He had been blessed with a grandson. The old fellow leapt out of his chair with joy and went around spreading the good news. He could not even keep it from the boss.

The boss stared speechlessly at Kanhu. He had always joked privately about the three days he had allowed for the marriage.

'Sir,' Kanhu begged him, 'may Your Kindness grant us leave for two days to visit the village and feast our eyes on the auspicious moon-face of our descendant.'

'Why, yes, of course,' the boss mumbled, looking away.

Kanhu looked for his son. The boy was missing from his seat.

'Have you seen him?' he asked Dhanu.

'My son-in-law is his Pa's spitting image.' Dhanu gave a croak of a laugh. 'Before you retire to your nook your son goes there to catch a few winks.'

They shared a hearty laugh and marched to the records room.

'Wake up, son, wake up.' Kanhu shook Ajay by the shoulder. 'Get up, we're going home.'

'What's up, Pa?' Ajay, groggy with sleep, was bewildered. 'Leave the office before five o'clock — what's the matter with you? Why do you look so excited?'

Kanhu practically dragged him along. 'Come along, son. I'm going to give you a great little piece of news when we get home.'

On the way he went on a shopping spree.

They reached home at a trot. 'Here's some sugar,' Kanhu told his son. 'And you know where the tin of flattened rice is. Have a good bellyful and get down to packing the bags. I must run to the market again and buy some chewing tobacco for your mother.'

'What's all this fuss about, Pa, why this bustle, this shopping spree? What's happened to you?'

Kanhu took the letter from his shirt pocket. 'Here, read it for yourself. But get the bags ready. I won't be long.'

He hurried off to the market, bought tobacco for his wife and a colourful cotton shirt and some toys for his grandson. When he returned home he found Ajay sitting on the bed like a stump of wood, dead to the world, tears streaming down his cheeks.

'What's the matter, son?' Kanhu did not mask his irritation. 'The train is due in thirty minutes and you haven't done a spot of packing! Why are you crying, for heaven's sake?'

'Oh Pa, how could the news make you so happy?'

'Why, what's wrong with it?'

'I'll be frank with you, Pa. Remember we had only three days for the marriage? I had to take leave of my wife before consummating the marriage. I've visited her only once since then, and on that occasion she had her period. Tell me how could she go and give birth to *my* son.'

Kanhu was nonplussed, but only for a moment. An angelic smile appeared on his face. 'Is that what's eating you, son? Ram, Ram, Ram! Son, how can we afford to be so touchy? Listen, I've visited your mother no more than six times in all my life, and each time there was something or other the trouble with her, you know; and that was that. Besides, government servants like us who live far from our homes and wives should not make a fuss. You know how it was in the ancient times, don't you? The big rishis couldn't care less who fathered their brood. To bring up a child was bliss enough.'

'Pa, am I too...?' Ajay looked incredulous.

'Yes, of course!' Kanhu laughed. 'Come, get a move on, boy. We're getting late for the train. I hope for once it's not running on time. Cheer up, my boy. Give us a smile. Hey, whose son are you, anyway? If you take a close look, you'll find that being a biological father means nothing. It's the paternal feeling that matters. That's the real thing — the fatherly feeling. That reminds me, I ran into my old friend Kadam the other day. The poor devil was legging it to the hospital like a wild horse, a sick child clasped to his breast. I was taken aback.

"Smart operator!" I stopped him. "Gone and got married and even produced a bonny boy and not a word to old friends!"

"This isn't my boy," Kadam stammered.

"Whose is he then?"

"No, I mean, yes. He's mine all right."

"Explain, man, this is getting curiouser and curiouser."

"Not mine, you know. This is the child of the woman I'm living with."

The poor fellow was nuts. "Are you out of your senses, Kadam, old boy?" I said. But then, suddenly, the realization struck me, and I hung my head in admiration for Kadam.'

Kanhu paused.

Ajay stared at him.

'Son,' Kanhu continued. 'Haven't you read the great Shankaracharya's *Mohamudgar*? *Who's your wife and who your son? The world is nothing but an illusion.* Come, hurry if you hope to catch the train.'

'Yes, Pa,' said Ajay, rising to his feet. 'The world is an illusion, a strange illusion. And strange too are we human beings. Hurry, Pa, we mustn't miss the train. I forgot to ask you, what did you buy for my son?'

Mohapatra Nilamoni Sahoo

Antu Praharaj, the Master Exorcist

'Come on, all of you. Move aside,' ordered a village elder. 'Hey children, go away. Why have you gathered here? Do you think sweets are being distributed, eh? You girls, clear off. Kamali, Mena, Jhumpuri, all you little ones, please leave. Folks, make way for Antu Praharaj. Here he comes!'

Anant Narayan Praharaj was the most famous exorcist within fifty miles. When he was eighteen he had run away to Kamakshya, the land of sorcery and black magic. He had lived there for three years, three months, and three days with a flower-woman who turned him into a billy-goat during the day and a virile man at night. It was from her he learnt the arts of conjuration, bewitchment, enchantment, bedevilment, mesmerism, magnetism, spirit-rapping, counter-charm and voodoo. Once he had learnt everything he needed to, he had escaped with a lot of scrolls.

Antu Praharaj was a big hulk of a man, with a copper-brown complexion. On his left arm he wore a string of rudrakshya shaped like cowfaces and on his right a snake-shaped copper armlet. Three strings of the five-faced rudrakshya adorned his neck, and below them hung a pendant of a five-headed Hanuman made of eight metals, along with many other talismans, amulets and charms. His nine-strand sacred thread, spotlessly white from much washing, girdled his bare chest like the snake on Lord Shiva. On his broad forehead a dab of vermilion graced the horizontal stripes of red sandalwood paste. His eyes were heavily lined with kohl and his lips were perennially red from betel juice. He wore a bright saffron dhoti and wrapped a stole around him with 'Hail Kamakshya' printed all over it. Under one arm he held a patchwork bag with a rolled-up tiger skin peeping out of it and a twin-cane decorated with blue jay feathers under the other. Pieces of coloured cloth tied to one end of the cane fluttered like pennants in the breeze.

There was an audible gasp of relief from the crowd on his arrival. The spectators fell back out of deference. Praharaj strode towards the inner verandah where Kausalya was sitting. He did not bother to look at anyone else.

Eighteen-year-old Kausalya, Dama Mohanty's third daughter by his first wife — he had three other daughters and a son from his second marriage — had been possessed by a spirit since the previous evening. With turmeric paste rubbed all over her body and her hair plastered down with oil, she had gone to the pond in the back yard for her ablutions. It was there she heard a woman giggling in the sahada tree next to the twin palms. She looked around but saw no one. Dusk was falling. Suddenly, without a whisper of a breeze, the sahada tree began to sway violently, and Kausalya felt someone climb down the tree and get inside her. She let out a scream and collapsed. Hours later, after much searching, her people had found her on the bank, unconscious.

When she came to, she began to behave strangely. She refused to eat or drink, sat rooted to the spot, alternately crying aloud or laughing her head off like a shameless hussy. Sometimes she thrashed about in wild paroxysms, her sari in disarray. Medicinal roots, herbal concoctions, holy water and exorcism — nothing helped.

'The girl is faking it! Oh, how she carries on!' said her stepmother, an old hag and a terrible shrew. Shouting and screaming was her forte and she would peck like a vicious crow at whoever came her way. 'Why should a ghost bother to possess her? The rotten bitch wants to make us the laughing stock of the village, that's all.'

Poor Dama's head was in a whirl. As if his backbreaking labour from morning till midnight to fend for his brood was not punishment enough, his eldest daughter had eloped with a Muslim. The second girl, already twenty-four, had settled into spinsterhood; he had not been able to scrape up a dowry for her. And now Kausalya, his gentlest and quietest daughter, had been possessed by a spirit.

The villagers, from the youngest to the oldest, milled about his house, avidly watching Kausalya's fits. A string of quack exorcists had come and gone without success. Kusunu Malik, the last of the lot and who enjoyed some reputation, had chanted incantations for a very long time, burnt bitter dried-fish with the knotted balls of hair of a dead person and made Kausalya inhale the putrid smoke. He had applied a red-hot poker to her body, which had been left covered with awful blisters. But the ghost was stubborn.

The plump, well-built Kausalya showed unmistakable signs of sinking. In despair, Dama Mohanty cupped his head in his hands and slumped to the ground.

The sight of Antu Praharaj the renowned exorcist gave Dama heart. Praharaj had the reputation of plucking the stars out of the sky. He could make the moon rise on a moonless night and blot it out on a full-moon night. Even a charging cobra would recoil like a worm at the sight of him. He could reduce wild tigers to harmless kittens. Ghosts and spirits of all kinds — incubi, succubi, lamias, vampires, ghouls, gremlins and imps — even Muslim or Christian ghosts bolted when he was present. No wonder he was the master exorcist, the crown-exorcist, a jewel among men, a paragon of virtues. There was no branch of black magic unknown to him. He could make himself invisible right under your nose. One minute he would be talking to you, the very next he would be seen buying eggplant in Dasarathapur market.

Huddled in a corner of the verandah, Kausalya sat sobbing, tears streaming down her cheeks. Spit dribbled from the corners of her mouth. God alone knows what happened when her eyes met Antu Praharaj's, for she pulled the end of her sari over her head like a married woman.

Antu Praharaj looked at her searchingly for a moment and broke into a broad smile. He took a silver container from his bag and helped himself to a paan. Then he spread his tiger skin on the ground and sat down. 'All right,' he ordered, 'get me some water in a brass vessel, a bowl of turmeric paste, seven haridas, seven betelnuts, seven blades of grass, seven plum leaves, seven fig leaves, seven yam leaves, seven bitter dried-fish, a pinch of vermilion and a measure of parboiled rice.'

Within minutes everything was ready and placed before him on a plantain leaf. He started burning incense in an earthen bowl, filling the whole place with smoke.

He fished a vermilion-stained box out of his bag. Roots, herbs and powders of various colours poured out of it. For a while, he sat stockstill, staring at Kausalya. Then he sprinkled a mix of the powders into the fire and a horrible smell spread through the place. He touched the things spread out before him with his twin-cane, dipped it into the vessel of water, raised his voice and chanted: 'Om hling, kling, sling, hring, khring, phat, phat, phut, ding, dhing, thing, om, namoh Chandikeyah! O water! O water! Water of the brass vessel, water of the earthen bowl, water of the well, water of the pond, water of the Bindusagar, water of the Narendra, water of the Markanda, water of the Ganga, water of the Yamuna, water of the Narmada, water of the Baitarani, water of the Mahanadi, water of the Kedar-Gauri, water of the seven seas, water of the four clouds, water of the nether world, water of heaven; bathwater of Lord Jagannath, bathwater of Bimalei, bathwater of Saralei, bathwater of Charchikei, bathwater of Bhagavati, bathwater of Kakatei, bathwater of Katakei. O water! O water! Water of this kind, water of that kind, water of the fourteen worlds, water of the seven islands. All waters unite, mingle! Rush to the east and west, rush to the north and south. Go, flow into the tank of Goddess Kamakshya, into the cooking pot of Nitei the washerwoman, into the pitcher of Pitei the witch. Come, Chandis! Come, Chamundis!

Devour the fish, dried-fish, fowls, goats and sheep. Occupy the ten horizons, be everywhere, take possession of all places...Thuh thuh, phus phus phus!' He turned to Kausalya. 'Hey, who are you? In which tree do you stay? The tamarind tree? The mango tree? The jack-fruit tree? The palm tree? The coconut tree? Whatever tree it is, go back there. Don't come out again. Stay there happily. Eat fish, eat dried-fish, eat fowl — but go you must. Leave this body, leave this house. Go in peace. Go in water, go in air. Clear out. That's the order. Whose order, you dare ask? Well, the order of Goddess Kamakshya, the order of the guardian of the five-faced forest — dhund! The order of Dhandola Maharaj — ah, phus phus phus, phus phus phus!'

He sprinkled a few drops of water on Kausalya and she began to shiver like a malarial patient.

'Oh!' she screamed. 'Oh, my body's burning... I'm dying, I'm dying. Oh, this horrible fellow's killing me...'

Praharaj lowered his twin-cane on her head and thundered, 'Who are you?'

'Raghua's wife Parbati,' replied Kausalya.

'Where do you live?'

'In the sahada tree on the bank of the pond.'

'How did you get here?'

'Kausalya had been out there in the evening all dolled up. I couldn't resist the temptation to possess her.'

'What do you want?'

She did not answer.

'Speak up, hey! What do you want?'

'Why do you ask?'

'Shouldn't I, eh? You have been torturing the hell out of this little girl since last evening. Can't you see what she's become? Why, she may not even survive!'

'What does that matter to me? I tell you, I'll possess the entire womenfolk of this village one by one and finish them all off.'

Praharaj touched Kausalya's head, shoulder, breast, belly and feet with his cane. 'Listen, Raghua's wife Parbati!' he commanded. 'I command you to leave this girl. Don't torture her any further.'

Kausalya threw her head back rather haughtily. 'And what of these people who tortured and ruined me?'

'Ruined you — the villagers? Come out with it. Name the culprits.'

'There, there,' said Kausalya, pointing at Markand Satpathy and Bana Mohanty. 'Look at those two sly bastards standing over there watching the tamasha. They're the ones. They cajoled my poor husband into accompanying them to Puri, put poison in his bhang and when he was out of his senses, pushed him into the Bhargavi, where he drowned. Then back in the village they demanded from me the money they claimed my husband owed them. Two thousand rupees to each, with interest. I am a poor woman, I pleaded with them. What do I have? From where will I get so much money? I didn't even know my poor husband had borrowed from them. Every evening they came and threatened to throw me out of my home if I didn't pay up. Then, then...hey bastards, shall I come out with it? Markand Satpathy and Bana Mohanty, shall I divulge your sins? Oh sir, these two bastards...they took me against my will. Fifty times each. Night after night. I couldn't stand it any longer and tightened a rope around my neck.'

'Shut up, you snivelling bitch!' bellowed Satpathy and Mohanty, jumping up and down. 'What the hell are you yakking about?'

The crowd looked at them.

'Markand Satpathy! Bana Mohanty!' said Antu Praharaj, in his booming baritone. 'Answer her! Come clean!'

'Lies!' cried the two men in chorus, after a moment of hemming and hawing. 'Damn lies, sir! The bitch wants to malign us. Why don't you apply the red-hot poker to her buttocks? She's out to make fools of two honest men.'

Praharaj glowered at them. His eyes seemed to bulge out of their sockets. 'Listen,' he said, 'ghosts and spirits never lie. I've been dealing with them all my life. Some of them are too despicable for words, some inveterate hooligans, but lies they never tell. I ask you to confess it all. I have invited sixty-four yoginis here. If you utter falsehoods in their presence, you will reap the consequences. Don't blame me afterwards. Things will no longer be within my control then, let me tell you.'

The crowd looked at the two men, as if demanding an answer.

Bana and Markand looked at one another, each perhaps expecting the other to come out with it. The silence was deafening.

'All right, sir,' Bana began. 'If you really command the ghosts and spirits, and if the spirit of Raghua's wife Parbati has really possessed Kausalya, and if the spirits as you claim never tell a lie, then let this girl now divulge the sins of the rest of the villagers. Let's see what kind of a truth-telling bitch she is!'

Praharaj turned to Kausalya and touched her head with his twin-cane three times in quick succession. 'Well, Raghua's wife Parbati!' he said gently. 'Could you tell us the sins of the other villagers?'

Kausalya remained silent. Her bloodshot eyes closed from weariness and she swayed from side to side. After a while she perked up and stared wildly at the crowd. Her plait had come loose and her hair hung down like storm clouds. Her sari had slipped off her shoulder, revealing her full and shapely breasts. The village boys ogled at her, nudging and whispering to one another. Kausalya's poor father nearly died of shame and mortification.

'Now you know, don't you, sir?' cried Bana and Markand, turning to Praharaj. 'Give the slut a good beating, sir. That's what she needs. It will bring her back to senses.'

'Look here,' Praharaj replied, 'I can't beat her just because you say so. She is a poor unclean soul, wracked with torment and out to make others suffer. She must have died with her desires unfulfilled. Maybe nobody offered a shraddha on her death. Just because I have the power to command the spirits and wraiths it does not mean that I can indulge my whims and subject them to further suffering. As far as my knowledge goes, in this area sixty miles across, there are about fifty lamias, thirty-one ghosts, four demons, nine ghouls and one imp. Two Muslim ghosts and a Christian one as well. I know them all through and through — their temperaments, idiosyncracies and activities. Normally they do not go out of their way to harm anyone. But if they have a score to settle with you, or if you happen to cross their paths, they throw their scruples to the wind. In thirty long years of my profession I have had to imprison only three vampires. They had become too big for their boots. I had no option but to nail them to a tamarind tree. But my approach is to coax them, to cajole them. Sometimes when they get headstrong, I scare them stiff. But beat them? Well, that's not my style. Don't ask me to do that now. You had better answer her. Tell me, is her allegation true or false?'

'Do you expect us to own up to this drivel out of fear?'

'Not at all. No one's forcing you. But don't blame me later.'

Antu Praharaj touched Kausalya's head with the cane. 'Raghua's wife Parbati,' he implored. 'Let bygones be bygones. Please leave this girl alone. Don't torture her any longer. Go away. Go in peace. Go back to the tree you came from.'

Kausalya's eyes dilated and she rocked from side to side like a drunk. 'All right,' she said heavily. 'I'll leave. But let me tell you, the wives of these two bastards will soon become widows. Their husbands have defiled me, embezzled the village funds, stolen the valuable Madanmohan statue from the temple of Makareswar and sold it to a white man. They have brought ruination upon this village. Thanks to these two scoundrels, litigations have doubled and scores of poor helpless people have lost their lands and homesteads.'

'You bitch!' bellowed Bana and Markand, charging at her. 'What do you take us for? Who do you think you are fooling?'

Bana grabbed Kausalya by her hair and gave her a push. Markand delivered a vicious kick on her rump.

Kausalya's father burst out wailing. People were stunned. Antu Praharaj did not utter a word for a few seconds.

Then a strange thing happened. Markand could not bring his foot back down to the ground. And Bana could not straighten his back. They struggled desperately, but failed. They remained in their grotesque postures.

'I'm dying of thirst,' screamed Kausalya. 'Oh, my throat's so dry! Give me a drop of water. O Lord, my heart is going to burst!'

Antu Praharaj pushed the brass vessel of water towards her. 'Pick it up with your teeth and run off,' he ordered. 'Go to the bank of the pond and drink your fill.'

Kausalya effortlessly lifted the heavy vessel by its rim between her teeth and carried it off as a cat would a tiny bowl of ghee. She ran toward the pond like lightning.

Praharaj stopped the curious onlookers from pursuing her. 'Follow her at your own peril,' he warned.

After a while, he took Dama Mohanty along and went to the back yard. Kausalya was lying unconscious on the bank. Dama wrapped her with a sari and carried her back. The spirit of Parbati had left her and she looked her own self again.

Meanwhile the travails of Bana Mohanty and Markand Satpathy continued. Bana straightened himself up with a mighty groan only to slump down the next moment. Markand gritted his teeth and planted his foot on the ground, only to see it spring up again. They were pale with fright. Instead of coming to their rescue, the villagers clapped, laughed and jeered. It did not occur to anyone to find out how such a weird thing could have happened.

Finally, tired from their efforts, Bana and Markand slumped to the ground. They avoided looking at each other.

Night fell. The ranks of the spectators swelled with urchins and adults from the nearby harijan colony. Dama's house was full. The people laughed and made rib-tickling comments and observations.

After a long period of inactivity, as the spectators grew restive, Bana and Markand raised their heads at the same time as though predetermined and glowered at each other. God knows what happened, but they started slapping each other. This continued for almost an hour. The crowd roared with laughter. Some of them egged the two wretches on: 'Come on, Bana! Don't let Markand get away with it! Hit him hard, man! ...Come on Markand! Give the bugger a good wallop!...Hey, Mohanty, don't lag behind! ...Buck up, Satpathy, split the fellow's cheeks!' Bana and Markand slapped each other with renewed vigour. Their cheeks swelled up. The crowd fell on one another, laughing.

After a long time Bana and Markand stopped abruptly. They hung down their heads and remained motionless. The crowd fidgeted. The two men straightened up again, looked at each other, threw back their heads and started howling like two miserable dogs. This set the audience off again.

'Come, folks!' shouted a village elder. 'Shut up, now. You've had enough fun. Now go look for Antu Praharaj. Let's ask him to free these two wretches from the spell.'

The crowd took heed. The noise died down. Everyone started looking for Antu Praharaj. But the exorcist — who caused the moon to rise on a new-moon night, who commanded the ghosts, spirits, betals and the sixty-four yoginis, who had mastered the arts of casting spells, hypnosis, bewitchment — had already vanished into the sepulchral darkness of the night.

The crowd dispersed. Bana and Markand were left alone to howl through the night. Their poor wives sat beside them, shedding bitter tears.

I do not know what else took place that night. The following morning I left the village, ending my visit to my eldest sister's place.

A couple of years later a brass-worker from Kausalya's village was in our village on business, and I learnt from him that Bana Mohanty, Markand Satpathy and their wives had all gone mad. One of the wives drowned herself in a pond and the other succumbed to a mysterious disease. Satpathy fled the village and was untraceable. Bana became a shrunken lump and lay rooted to the ground, howling like a stricken ewe until his death. His sons left the village with their families and settled in faraway places like Rourkela and Paradeep.

Another time a mason from that village, who came to work on the construction of the block development office, told me that Kausalya had not been able to marry within her own caste for lack of an adequate dowry and had eloped with a harijan boy. They settled in Bhubaneswar, where they built a house of their own. Her husband worked as a personal assistant to the minister of tribal welfare.

Four decades have since passed. Many cataclysmic changes have swept the land. Many things, hitherto unheard of and beyond anyone's dream or wildest conjectures, have taken place. Dazed and dumbfounded, we simply watched as events overtook us. And all these years I have been assailed by an intense longing to see Antu Praharaj, the mighty Antu Praharaj in his element.

It was perhaps destiny that brought us together again. On a sombre wintry afternoon in 1978 I discovered him in a small wayside tea-shop near the city-office in Bhubaneswar. Blowing on a hot glass of tea to cool it, he was sipping it slowly. His teeth had all fallen out and he kept wiping his moustache and beard after every sip. I would have taken him for some old baba had someone not told me who he was. He had grown very old and looked pallid. He wore a pair of thick glasses and had lost all his hair save a few measly strands of matted locks. But the beads, the vermilion dot and red sandalwood marks were all there. So were the bracelets, talismans and amulets. His patchwork bag and his staff rested beside him on the bench. In spite of the ravages time had wrought he still looked handsome in a tired way — profound, serene and detached.

People crowded around him in ostensible reverence. A young disciple, dressed like a tantrik, stood beside him, waiting to do his bidding.

I jostled my way through and touched his feet. He looked up at me for a moment and concentrated on his tea. I waited. He did not utter a word.

He finished his tea and stood up. His disciples hailed a rickshaw.

'Maharaj,' I began, unable to restrain myself. 'Are you still exorcising ghosts and spirits? Do you still practise the secret art?'

He looked up at me, his broad, wrinkled face creasing in a smile. 'No son!' he said playfully, in a whisper. 'I have given it up. My teeth have all fallen out. The spells do not work when your teeth are gone, you see!'

'Sir, why don't you pass on your knowledge to someone else? It would do people a world of good. Such an important branch of learning should not be allowed to lapse into oblivion.'

'This vidya will work no longer, son! It's not easy to master it. Besides, in the hands of monkeys it will become avidya and do more harm than good. Don't feel bad, many branches of knowledge have disappeared from this world without a sigh of regret. Now this too will go.'

Perhaps he would have added something more, but his disciple wouldn't let him. 'Baba!' he implored. 'Let's go. The winter here is harsh. You might catch a cold. Please get on to the rickshaw.'

Antubaba took a step and stopped. The disciple picked up his patchwork bag and handed him the staff. Baba supported himself by leaning on the disciple. Quite a few in the crowd touched his feet. He raised his hand and blessed us all silently.

After the rickshaw had vanished onto the busy, crowded street, I felt forlorn. I sat in the shop and ordered a cup of tea. Another tea-drinker ambled over and sat down beside me. He seemed eager to strike up a conversation. I was hardly in the mood but was helpless.

'Do you know why the old man gave up exorcism and all that?' he began.

I shot him an undisguised look of discouragement, but it was lost on him. He rattled on with great gusto:

'When he grew old, this man took four disciples and started teaching them all the stuff he knew. The seat of learning was the village cremation ground by the side of the river. They had put up a small thatched hut under a tree.

'Within a few months the disciples had mastered everything, from spells to hypnosis to spirit-rapping. Producing a sudden fire out of nothing and making shit rain down into your cooking pots were just some of the small things they could perform. As it happened, power went to their heads and they started defying everyone.

'Then one day one of them got into a row with the local tehsildar. "Pull down the hut and leave this place," ordered the tehsildar. "You people are occupying government land. I want it distributed among the harijans." The old exorcist was ready to quit. But his chelas wouldn't listen and issued dire threats. Now this tehsildar happened to be one of those tough characters, you know. A hot-headed stubborn man, if there was one, with scant respect for gods and godmen. He was the same fellow who had a Trinath temple razed to the ground just because it had been built without his permission. He was honest to the bone and worked strictly according to the law. He couldn't be influenced even by his wife and children. He issued an order that if the old exorcist and his boys did not leave the place within twenty-four hours he would have the hut burnt down. The old man went and pleaded with him: "Sir, please don't pick on this small ashram of ours. We haven't occupied much land. The government should not grudge us this little chunk of the cremation ground. Let the harijans have all the land they want, but let this one guntha be left to us. We need this place to go on with our learning. If I don't pass on this vidya, it will be totally lost after my death. And I'm already so old. Huzoor, I request you not to push the issue further."

"Humbug!" said the tehsildar. "What's your mumbo-jumbo worth in this age of science? You are a bunch of bums. Your spells and abracadabra are useless in this atomic age." He repeated his order and hopped into his jeep.

'As he drove off, one of the disciples picked up a handful of dust and, chanting an incantation upon it, blew it towards the receding vehicle. Immediately it screeched to a halt. The driver got down and tinkered with the engine but it wouldn't start again. They had to push it all the way to the office. "Sir," the driver told the tehsildar, "this is what comes out of antagonizing the old exorcist. You don't know Antu Praharaj, sir!" "Tell me another!" scoffed the tehsildar, in utter derision. "Antu Praharaj, huh? I'll scoop out his entrails. What does he take me for? I'll teach him the lesson of his life. Let me ring up the police as soon as I reach the office."

As he walked to the telephone, he found a black cat snuggled up beside it. "Get off," he cried, in irritation. "Get out." The cat only mewed. The tehsildar picked up a stick and tried to hit it. But it kept mewing and wouldn't budge. The tehsildar got so mad he gave a heavy blow to the cat's head, splitting it in two. The animal fell off the table, writhed for a moment or two and died. The tehsildar couldn't have cared less. He picked up the receiver. But not a word would escape his lips. At the other end, the police kept screaming: "Hello! Hello! Hello!" The office staff, the sarpanch and the ward-members, the chairman and the block development officer all came running. Everyone was stunned at the sight. "This must be the work of Antu Praharaj," said someone.

"He must have sealed the tehsildar's lips." People went running to the old exorcist. When he was approached, he merely said: "What a pity! Never mind, the tehsildar will be able to talk as soon as you go back to him."

'Once he got back his speech, the tehsildar lost no time in ringing up the police. He asked for an armed contingent. The villagers pleaded with him, but he wouldn't listen. He had gone mad with anger. He called for some harijan youths and instructed them to throw the old exorcist and his disciples out of the hut and set it on fire the moment the police reached the bazaar. The elderly harijans tried to talk the youngsters out of it, but failed.

'The old exorcist asked his disciples to either run away or retaliate with physical force. He wouldn't dream of casting spells on his enemies for his personal safety.

'The two groups fought a pitched battle. The police were waiting in the wings, and the old man and his disciples were promptly arrested. Prosecutions were undertaken against them. The whole episode was described by the police and the newspapers as an atrocity against the harijans. The old man was handed a sentence of one month's imprisonment and his disciples got six months each.

'After his release the old man gave up sorcery and black magic. He left home and visited the places of pilgrimage, returning to his land only last year. One of his grandsons is now a big shot in the government. Perhaps the old man has come here to stay with him a while.'

Having rattled off his story in one breath, the fellow paused and lit a cigarette. Taking a deep drag, he surveyed the crowd that had gathered around him. Just then a motorcycle stopped in front of the shop with a deafening roar and our narrator rushed towards it. He jumped behind the driver, who looked every inch a demon, and off they went.

Depressed and tired, I looked at the people around me. Everyone seemed so unreal, so surreal. Maybe they are all ghosts and spirits, I thought. Or at least possessed. And all the happenings of the world are the handiwork of these ghosts and spirits. Antu Praharaj, the master exorcist, the crown-jewel among them all, the ocean of virtues, seemed to be the only sane person, unaffected and unpossessed.

Over the years this feeling has taken deep root in my mind. I do not know whether a ghost has got into me. Maybe one has. Why else should I feel so low and depressed all the time? That all of humanity is possessed — you can see the morons jumping and shouting about — is small consolation for me. The question is who is going to save us, to release us from the spell? The master exorcist Antu Praharaj has lost his teeth and with them his powers. Is this earth then going to spin through the rest of its existence possessed and ruled by ghosts and demons? Oh God!

Akhil Mohan Patnaik

Fig Flower

From the moment she laid eyes on me the lady mistook me for Sanjay, and I somehow didn't have the heart to put her right. Let me tell you about it. I was doing my postgraduate studies at Allahabad University and had gone to Guwahati for a holiday. I had found myself a cosy little room in a small hotel in a posh part of the town. On either side of the street stood identically designed houses, in neat rows, all beautifully built; indeed they seemed to have come out of the pages of a book on architecture. Yet something was lacking in their perfect symmetry. They did not have the distinctive features associated with homes. Anyway, it's not these fancy houses I want to talk about. Let me get back to what happened.

One evening towards the end of the vacation, as I was heading back to the hotel after a long walk, the sky suddenly darkened with heavy clouds and a strong breeze came up. Before I knew it, fat drops of rain began falling. I made a dash for the nearest house, yanked open the inhospitable iron gate and scampered up on to the verandah, throwing the fear of dogs and darwans to the wind. The skies split open not long afterwards. And how it poured!

Reconciled to a long dreary wait, I looked around the verandah, which was done up very tastefully. On the wide mosaic floor four cane chairs were placed in a cosy little circle. A shining teakwood nameplate was nailed securely to the wall and a pretty letter-box with exquisite carving hung a few inches below it. The cement trellis on the southern end was covered with a luxuriant vine with large green and yellow leaves. And among the many varieties of cacti in porcelain vases were some which were quite rare.

The rain fell in sheets, there were claps of thunder and flashes of lightning snaked across the sky. There was no sign of life in the huge house; it was ghostly silent. The doors and windows were open and the snow-white lace curtains flapped and fluttered. I could see into the drawing room, where the wind caught the pages of a magazine lying on a round centre table. It sounded as though a drove of desperate pigeons were flapping their wings.

The downpour continued with wild abandon. Night fell suddenly and the street lights came on. I watched the shiny rain drops as they slid off the lamp post breaking into a thousand silvery particles.

The sight had me so enthralled that I nearly jumped out of my skin when a big black car suddenly drove up to the portico through the gates I had left open and screeched to a halt. The headlights caught me full in the face and I sensed a shiver of mortification run down my spine. I felt as helpless as the lost son of the poor kotwal in the fairy tale who had unwittingly ventured into a demon's lair for shelter.

The headlights went out and an eerie darkness engulfed the place.

'Is that you, Sanjay?' gushed a breathless feminine voice from inside the car.

I didn't know what to say.

A lovely, elegant woman hurried out of the car, grabbed me by the hand and pulled me into the house with such a huge rush of warmth that I was swept off my feet.

In the well-lit drawing room I was able to examine her properly. She was distinctly middle-aged, but very handsome, very chic. She had taken pains to preserve her good looks, but the efforts hardly showed.

We regarded each other in intense silence. It occurred to me it was high time I pointed out her mistake. But before I could clear my throat she started babbling: 'Oh, you dear boy! Why, you haven't changed a wee bit. You look just the same, my dear Sanjay. When did I see you last?' She called out to the cook, who materialized from the mysterious womb of the house, and ordered tea. 'You prefer tea, isn't that right, Sanjay? A mother always remembers the tiniest thing about her children. We poor mothers truly do, don't we? But the children, well, they couldn't care less. Let's see if you remember how much sugar I take in my tea!'

One spoon? Two? Perhaps a cheery but enigmatic silence was wiser than a wild guess. But in those brief moments I took to debate within myself, a sad, faraway look stole into the lady's merry, twinkling eyes. She slumped back into the couch with a sigh and said, 'The young don't care at all about the old, do they? Take Manju, for instance. What great research is she doing that she can't find time to fly back home for a weekend and come and see us? Imagine, four years have passed since she went away to college. Her daddy keeps telling me he's already sent her the air ticket. Summer is drawing to a close but there's no sign of the girl.' She brightened inexplicably and added, 'Thank God for making you drop in on us. Oh, how nice to see you again, my dear!'

I sat in a daze. The situation was getting out of hand and until the rains abated I hadn't a ghost of a chance of escaping.

The rain drummed down relentlessly.

'Manju must be excited to be going to England this winter,' she went on. 'Her daddy has it all planned. Once she's off, who knows when we'll see her again.' She paused and smiled to herself. 'How I wish children would remain children, always small, helpless, dependent, always in a cocoon, and never grow up and go away. If going away to college makes you forget your parents, then I wish colleges didn't exist.'

Her voice and demeanour took on a sudden note of sternness. 'Of course I could stop the handouts any moment and compel her to come back.' She softened instantly. 'But a mother can't be so cruel and heartless.'

The rain let up as abruptly as it had begun; I could hear the water dripping slowly from the cornice. I took several glances at my watch, but when that did not register, I had to tell her I had an appointment to keep.

I could see her reluctance, her unhappiness to let me go without dinner. She asked for my hotel address, she wanted to know my plans. Before she could ply me with further questions I got up and ran down the steps.

'You mustn't walk to your hotel in the wet.' She forbade me, her voice authoritative and maternal. 'Get in the car. The chauffeur will drive you.'

I climbed into the car. The drive to the hotel passed in silence. I was burning with curiosity but couldn't ask the chauffeur anything.

Early next morning, soon after tea had been served, there was a gentle tap on my door. I arranged my rumpled clothes about me and asked the visitor in.

In walked a tall, handsome, elderly gentleman with pensive eyes and a shock of silver grey hair. He wore a white dhoti and kurta. His walking stick was elegant, his carriage straight and dignified. Stopping in the middle of the room, he took off his glasses, wiped them slowly with a handkerchief and put them on again. He leant his stick against the chair and examined me closely.

'I had an uncanny feeling that my wife had made a mistake,' he began, as he sank into the chair I had shown him. 'But in all fairness, I must admit it's a mistake even I could've committed had I not looked into your eyes. Young man, the house you stopped by last evening is my house and the lady you met there is my wife. She practically bundled me out of the house this morning to come and see you. Sanjay's back, she said. Poor dear!'

'Look, sir,' I began apologetically. 'I'm not who your wife thinks I am. My name's Ashok, and I'm awfully sorry about what happened last evening. It was stupid of me to be so tongue-tied. Maybe I was overwhelmed by your wife's warmth and affection. But whatever it was, it wasn't nice of me to perpetuate the pretence. I should have dispelled her illusion...'

'You know something, young man. You do look so much like

Sanjay!' he said, waving me aside. 'Uncanny resemblance, I must say. But of course you aren't Sanjay. One has to look closely at your eyes and nose.' He paused. 'And there's no earthly reason why you ought to feel sorry for whatever happened last evening. It was a cruel joke of fate.'

'Who's Sanjay?' I asked him.

'My daughter's fiancé.' His voice caught. He stared straight ahead at the tea-tray in front of him.

I poured him a cup. He lifted it absent-mindedly, held it for a minute and put it down. 'Why am I telling you all this? Last night when I reached home I found my wife glowing with happiness. I hadn't seen her like that in ages. She had taken you for Sanjay and instantly rushed to the conclusion that you'd come back to ask for Manju's hand.' He left it at that.

I sat in silence. The unspoken explanation hung heavy in the air.

'Why do I have to straighten out this error to her? Why do I have to shatter her illusion? After all, what's the harm if she carries her little illusion to her grave? As long as it gives her some happiness, it's all right with me.' He took his glasses off and wiped his sad eyes. 'Young man, you're young enough to be my son. May I call you by your name? Ashok you said, didn't you? No, on second thought, that would be a mistake. I better call you Sanjay. Is that all right with you? I do not wish to slip on that in an unguarded moment and undo my poor wife's mistake.' His face was flushed and he was shaking a little. 'I can depend on you, can't I? From now on you're Sanjay, if only for me and my wife, just for the two of us, and I've one big favour to ask of you — you must come and spend a little time with us here next year, the year after next, and the year after that, until our death.' He seemed eager for my reply. 'Money is no object. It never was, it never will be. All we want is that you visit us from time to time. There's this one gaping void in our life,' he warmed to the proposition like a maniac, 'and you alone can fill it. You will, won't you?' He leaned forward with feverish expectation. I thought he looked just as high-strung as his wife.

'You will go on being Sanjay, won't you?'

I stared at him.

'Well?'

The man was in evident agony.

I was so moved that I found myself mumbling, 'Well, all right, if you insist. Please stop worrying.'

'Do I have your word of honour?'

His face lit up. As if a great burden had been lifted from his heart. 'We'll be seeing you off at the airport in the evening.' He had obviously spoken to the reception clerk downstairs. 'My wife might ask you to carry a packet for Manju. Please don't turn her down.' He paused briefly. 'I'd better go now. I've taken plenty of your time already. Goodbye, young man. God be with you.'

I saw him off at the door and tottered back to the bed. The tea had gone tepid. I began to wonder about the couple, their daughter Manju and her fiancé Sanjay.

In the evening as soon as I reached the small, sleepy airport I scanned the lounge for the strange couple. I needn't have bothered, for very soon a friendly hand squeezed my shoulder from behind and cooed into my ears: 'Hello Sanjay!' I turned round and came face to face with Manju's parents. They looked transformed. They looked eager, warm, full of good cheer. I felt I had known them a long time.

'This is for Manju,' the lady said, handing me a beautifully wrapped packet. 'You don't mind the trouble, do you, my dear?' She gave me a conspiratorial wink and squeezed my arm.

I looked at the packet. In big bold handwriting just one word was scrawled across it: Manju. There was nothing else — no address, no telephone number.

The flight was announced and the passengers were requested to proceed to the aircraft. The lady tightened her grip on my arm. 'Excuse me,' I said, unplucking her fingers from my arm. She had a serene smile on her face, but there was something in it that hurt.

I took the gentleman aside. 'Will you please give me Manju's address and telephone number? Your wife's forgotten to put it down here.'

Never before had I seen human eyes turn so glassy and distant. His tall, thin body shook with suppressed tremors, and the bitterest of smiles leapt to his lips. 'Manju's address?' he whispered. 'Do I know it myself? She's been dead a long time, if you must know. It was a train accident. Just before my wife showed signs of softening in the head.' His hoarse whisper poured urgently into my ears. 'It's been kept from her. It would have killed her. It's been almost four years now. Manju was in the final year of her B.A. when she died. If she were alive today she'd be on the last leg of her doctoral work. You understand it all now, don't you? Very soon Manju will have to be packed off to England for her postdoctoral research. Anything, just anything, to keep her away from Guwahati. All mapped out, you see...' He gave a croak of a laugh.

The microphone shrieked my name several times.

'There you are,' he said, shaking my hand.

I said goodbye to them and hurried across the tarmac. Before I walked up the gangway I turned around for a moment. There they were, two forlorn figures, waving wildly to me. They looked like two marionettes, the way their upraised hands twirled and twisted. Were they waving at me or gesticulating at the Supreme Puppeteer?

Chandrasekhar Rath

The Emperor

When he returned home, his wife said, 'Someone came looking for you a little while ago. Shortly after you went out for your walk...'

'What did he look like?'

'I didn't bother to look closely,' she replied. 'Shall I get you a cup of tea?'

His wife seized the chance to get away, and he was overcome by the desire to close his eyes for a long time. His face, pinched from melancholy, took on a faraway look. The voice declaimed: *Fools! Nincompoops! How on earth can a man attain victory if the wheels of his chariot sink into the mud at the height of battle! There are strategies to chalk out, campaigns to command, countries to conquer, and when you're set to do all that and more, the very ground on which you stand starts to give way!*

'Sir!'

He opened his eyes a crack and saw two young boys, thin, starry-eyed, enter the room. His reverie interrupted, he stared at them with evident displeasure.

'This is the second time since yesterday that we've come to see you, sir,' the boys said. 'If you turn down our request we'll bang our heads against this wall.'

He remained silent.

'You must agree to take the role of the emperor in our play *Swargadwar*. Nobody else can do justice to it. So what if you do look a little old and decrepit? A touch of make-up and you'll look better than a real emperor. You've always played the emperor and you're going to play him one more time.'

He remained silent.

'We simply refuse to take a no from you. The handbills have already been distributed.'

Who are these fellows? He wondered, straightening himself with a sigh. His neck looked longer than before. The furrows on his broad forehead and chin gave his face the look of a squeezed inverted triangle. Everything had withered away: the imperious hauteur, the bushy eyebrows, the big brooding eyes, the Grecian nose; everything was gone. On his unshaven face the sweat looked like the churned muddy waters of a ploughed paddy field — the face pockmarked with the footprints of nameless dark monsters. The gaping holes, the furrows, the stubble. Where had the famous face gone? He looked up.

'So it's arranged, sir!' the boys cried out together. 'We'd better run along now.'

His eyes closed. Reflections rose on the life-size mirror of the auditorium: *the haughty, swaggering Karna in his red robe, golden waistband, heavy crown, and gilded pendants hanging from his neck like rising suns; the strapping Kartyavirya guffawing uproariously; Prataparudra, Mukundadev, Kharavela in exquisite dresses, gold necklaces, glittering armbands, flinging their glorious arms about; the puny, deferential make-up man tiptoeing in and out of the greenroom, touching up an eyebrow one minute and a sideburn the next...The stage floods with light. There the sun rises; there the night sets in; there the lion growls, setting the papier mache mountains and the cardboard fortresses atremble. The tumultuous sea of the enthralled audience stretches from the mouth of the cave to the deep night sky — every spectator a pair of wide unblinking eyes, a pair of cocked ears. Oh, the festival of applause! The sea rolls with joy, the sky showers petals, and someone climbs on to the stage to pin a gold medal on the emperor's* vast chest. The emperor does not deign to bow his head in acknowledgement, his crown touching the sky...

'Here's your tea,' his wife interrupted. 'Who were those boys?'

'What-er-who?' he fumbled for words. 'I don't know, who were they?'

'What did they come for?'

'Weren't they telling me something — well, what was it?' He lifted the cup gracefully, as if he was picking up a bouquet. 'Oh yes, they wanted me to play the role of the emperor in their play *Swargadwar*.' Fine, you find me a crown and I'll give you an emperor as good as they come. Age does not put an end to class. He lifted his cup and took another sip. That's how Mukundadev took his goblet of wine from the hands of a bewitching dancing girl. His mind wandered again: foggy dreams, thin as swirls of mist, filled the still, upturned eyes of a sleepy man.

From her experience of twenty-five years as his wife she realized he had already drifted off to another world. She waited, drank her tea, looked out, and waited some more. Hadn't she waited like this, night after night? The nights were so still that if a straw fell it could be mistaken for a winnowing fan. A sudden gust of wind, and the front door would creak as ominously as her heart. Sometimes, on the thatched roof a cat pounced on a mouse; a battle ensued and blood was spilled. She could hear a squeaking lump of flesh being torn to shreds. She would flinch and cover herself with a blanket, her nerves in tatters: so this is what life is for a mouse! Strange fears and sadness would grip her. In the kitchen the egg curry remained on the stove and, outside, the dew fell in drops. In the deafening stillness of the night, she throbbed with anticipation. The darkness was filled with the aroma of the new mosquito curtain. And then it was gone as a strange perfume wafted in from god knows where. She felt somebody stealthily walking around the bed, closing in on her. Goosebumps rose all over her body. Then sounds of conversations came floating in from afar — the actors were returning from the rehearsal. The footsteps stopped near the front door. A thick, soft knock. No mischief of the breeze this time. She would hurry out of bed, light the lamp and open the door with a yawn, feigning she had been awakened from a deep sleep. The emperor would stride in, declaiming his dialogues in his deep baritone, and sit down to a cold, dull dinner of rice and egg curry as though it was the greatest banquet. Who knew how far gone in the night it was.

She sighed, and the curtain fell. The glowing stage limped back to darkness, and the lonely old couple drank their tepid tea. She wanted to begin a conversation, anything to hold his attention, but didn't know how. The minutes ticked away, and in the disquieting silence the curtain lifted once again. Hectic preparations were afoot in the greenroom.

How I'd love to straighten out some of these fellows, he thought. Why doesn't someone show these Kalamandir fools the door? Who brought them here? Their props are filthy, the curtains tattered and discoloured and they smell to high heavens. These costumes have never been washed and reek of a thousand different odours of sweat; they're crumpled and the brocade is coming off. How can anyone put on such clothes and keep his head? But of course the costume the other night was the very worst — it was crawling with ants. Luckily, there was time to take it off and put on another. With all those ants biting me, what would have happened to me on stage?

His eyes opened abruptly, dilating in anger.

His wife collected the cups and walked off.

His eyes closed. *Were the Royal Painters people any better? First-rate crooks! And that seedy-looking dwarf of a manager — how he would giggle at every silly word of yours! Never was there a greater giggler. Nor a more glib talker. He could charm the birds out of the trees. But to give the devil his due, he had the best costumes. His emperor costumes were magnificent, simply magnificent. But where did that son of a bitch of a manager get the foul-smelling glue to stick the emperor's moustache on with? It was a lovely prim moustache twirling divinely at the ends. But the stink was so awful he had to hold his nose. Once a damn fine scene was nearly ruined because of it. Of course the audience didn't catch on; maybe they thought he had improvised this mannerism, this royal habit of stroking the moustache at every second word. Little did they know that the poor emperor was in a cold sweat. His voice sounded so hollow to his own ears that it hurt him. He couldn't tell people about the glue, could he? He would happily have murdered the manager.* He shook in anger and scowled as if he was going to send everyone to the gallows.

As she washed the cups in the kitchen sink, his wife fell to thinking. Nobody had ever understood the full extent of her husband's histrionics. Nor would anyone ever. The time for that had passed. The time had passed for a great many things besides: a house of their own, good clothes, good food. The only silver lining was that their two children had turned out well, after all. Mamuni had married an army officer and now lived in Darjeeling, Babuni had got a good job and moved to Bombay. That's what the world's like — you can't latch on to the children all the time. How nice it would be to go on a pilgrimage now, just the two of us, husband and wife! How her heart yearned to step outside the four walls of the house! But she knew that that was just a pipe dream. Her husband was gravely ill and deteriorating day by day. His rock-like muscles had melted away and the big hulk of a man was already a bag of bones.

The emperor sat stock-still, lost in his reverie. Craning his neck, he glowered angrily. Already in some invisible execution ground, rows of nondescript make-up men and managers were climbing the scaffold at his command. How he had wanted to buy himself costumes, swords, wigs and beads nobody else would use! He had made plans to buy them from Calcutta, but Calcutta always remained a distant place. He had plans to record his famous declamations for posterity. He had plans to go on air. Kartyavirya's bellows would have rattled the ribs of the radio sets. From the burgeoning void of the lonely cave a stormy voice rang out: 'Nothing achieved! Nothing at all!' The emperor's head drooped. His eyes watered. Hurriedly the old actor retreated into his drawing room, to the safety of its wicker chairs, old cotton cushions, and odours of familiarity.

The voice from the cave chased him.

He suddenly remembered Radharani, the actress who had played the role of queen in most of the productions. She was every inch a queen, a stunning beauty. And when she played Padmavati how provocatively her silk sari would climb up her slim legs. What a wonderful lilt she had to her voice and how sweetly she sang! He had wanted to learn to sing, but the guru he went to said it was too late in the day. He had tried hard but could not go beyond the seven notes. He had wanted to be a sculptor and chisel incredibly beautiful shapes and forms out of rock; he had wanted to be a painter and create vivid dreams in colour on canvases as large as the wall. The slabs of stone ended up as steps around the well; termites got at the unpainted canvases; the paint tubes dried up and hardened to stone.

The voice from the cave rose to a shrill crescendo: 'Nothing achieved! Nothing at all!'

The emperor sank into his chair — his neck, spine, ribs, hands, legs, all in a sad heap, like an old sack of broken coloured glass of tinkling dreams.

The front door creaked.

His wife hurried back into the drawing room. 'It might be that man again,' she said.

'Which man?'

'The one who was looking for you.'

Would her husband, a full six feet and two inches, get to his feet to receive the visitor? she wondered. Would he use the occasion to stretch his limbs? But he continued to sit like a shrunken lump, even as Beni Madhav Samant, his friend, strode in. A forest contractor, Beni Madhav, was a jovial, fun-loving man.

Beni Madhav's sudden appearance triggered off an unpleasant reaction: Why, I never thought Beni could be so mean! Just because he's lent me some two or three hundred rupees, here he comes barging in. Maybe the tightfist has come to remind me about it.

'Hey, old boy,' Beni Madhav said. 'I hope nothing's the matter with you. God knows I've come running all the way. Didn't even stop to have tea.' He turned to her. 'Bhauja, do me a favour and make me a steaming hot cup. But first listen to what I've to say.

You remember the patch of sal forest, don't you — that dark, eerie place? Damn it, I've never been able to walk past it without trepidation. Ever since I was a child. This evening, what happened you know — I was returning from work...'

Bloody skit! He smiled. A load lifted off his chest. Beni isn't here to ask for his money. He's afraid of walking by a ragged cluster of trees. Calls it a forest. Hah!

'Give me your ears, Bhauja and brother, will you?' Beni Madhav raised his voice. 'It was simply incredible. A fellow materialized from nowhere and stood in my path.'

'Who?'

'Someone who's been looking for you.'

'Was he a short, slovenly man?' Bhauja enquired.

'Why, yes! But how did you know?'

'He was here this afternoon and said he'd come back.'

A brief silence, heavy as a fog, hung over the room.

'Oh leave it, Beni,' said the old actor. 'If he's looking for me, he knows where to find me. Don't you think there's a chill in the air?'

'A chill in the air?' Beni Madhav was surprised. 'It's so hot and sultry. You're feeling cold, huh?' He turned to his friend's wife. 'Bhauja, get the old boy a sheet. Let him wrap himself up in it.'

The front door opened again with a creak. Beni Madhav started and stole a glance at his friend's wife. 'Perhaps it's that man.'

Old doctor Dhanurdhar swept into the room and flopped down on a chair. The chair groaned.

'What's the matter with you?' the doctor enquired, looking at the actor. 'Are you ill?'

The old actor eyed Dhanurdhar without a word. So you've come to collect your fees, huh? Don't I know you! Come out with it and end the suspense.

'Why have you wrapped yourself in a sheet? It's so hot. Come, give me your hand. Let me see your pulse. Never mind, that can wait. Let me first tell you about the funny fellow I met on my way here. He scared the life out of me. Why was he lurking about under a tree like a ghost? He suddenly rushed out and planted himself in front of me. A short, unkempt, sheepish-looking man. And he enquired...he wanted to know where to find you. I don't know why he's looking for you so desperately. He sure gave me a jolt. I couldn't get here fast enough to tell you. Now, if you'll give me your hand.'

The doctor turned to Beni Madhav Samant. 'Do you see, Samant, this elephant of a man, how he's been reduced to skin and bones!' Turning to the actor, he continued, 'Do you have to keep yourself covered and sweat buckets for nothing? You don't have a fever! Come over to the bed and let me examine you properly. You know something, your obsession for the stage did you in. Keeping late hours, taking meals at odd times and drinking god knows how many cups of tea a day, have taken their toll.'

There was a brief silence. The old actor's big brooding eyes wore a faraway look. 'Get me the box of medals, will you?' he asked his wife.

She brought the box, wiping the glass cover with the end of her sari. There were ten rows of gold and silver medals pinned to a velvet cloth — ten twinkling medals in each row but one, the ninety-nine medals shining like stars. He had worn everyone of these on his proud chest amidst deafening applause under blinding floodlights. Just one more and there would have been a hundred and his sky would have been filled from end to end.

All eyes inevitably rested on the vacant space in the last row, and a feeling of acute discomfort permeated the air.

'You realize, doctor,' said Beni Madhav. 'He's a rare talent in this land.'

The doctor fiddled with his stethoscope, a scowl on his face. 'You don't feel good, do you?' he enquired, looking at the patient.

There was a knock on the door and they all started. The door opened and the actor's grandson Jhampu, his daughter's son, parted the curtains and skipped in. The rapid patter of his tiny feet brought a sense of relief.

'Back so early from your lessons?' Jhampu's grandmother asked. 'The tutor didn't show up or what?'

Jhampu said nothing. He went straight to his grandfather and looked at him intently. Then he took his arithmetic book from his bag and said, 'Look, grandpa, there's one sum even the tutor couldn't solve. I told him my grandpa could. You bring any sum and he'll solve it. It's not for nothing that his pictures are in the history books!'

Suddenly everyone grew restive. A lump rose in the old actor's throat. Stretched out on the bed, he whispered hoarsely: 'Turn back, Queen Mother, go back. Mother of the Pandavas, go away. Consign me to oblivion. I'm but the offspring of a lowly charioteer. Humiliation, defeat and death are in store for me. Mother, please go away...' *The audience held its breath. Tears glistened in every eye. The gaslights sputtered and hissed. The sound of a falling straw could be mistaken for a winnowing fan...* A wan smile creased the old actor's face and tears welled up in his eyes. Who's that dwarfish, seedy-looking man waiting in the wings? Why is he grinning like the manager of the Royal Painters?

'Grandpa,' said Jhampu. 'I've got a medal for you.' He took out a tin badge distributed for Army Day and pinned it on his grandfather's chest.

The old actor was overwhelmed. The seas roared. There were peals of thunder and flashes of lightning. A tumultuous commotion. The sky opened up. The emperor stood in the wings. The mighty Karna, clad in hibiscus-red robes, glowed like the fiery sun. A small, seedy-looking man stood beside him, holding him by his little finger, ready to take him backstage. The audience would see the emperor no more.

Who are these people pulling and tugging at the old white sheet? Why are they doing that? What are they looking for in the folds and wrinkles of an old dress? Who are they looking for?

Santanu Kumar Acharya

Parallel Lines

'Saar!' The fellow greeted me with effusive politeness. 'Namaskar.'

'Namaskar,' I answered without warmth, looking over my shoulder. Whoever he was, he seemed to be catching up with me. 'Namaskar,' I repeated, increasing the pressure on the pedals. Why did I do that? Did it have something to do with my nature? Maybe, I'm not sure. Or was it because of the vile mood I was in? I had noticed the fellow as he was pushing his bicycle along the canal bank that ran parallel to the road all the way to the town. He switched over to the road at Game Leg's store.

We travelled a fair distance before he began to catch up. Quite imperceptibly the race was on. Have you noticed a cooing cuckoo in springtime getting agitated when it hears a mocking voice? To put the impudent intruder to shame, it starts singing a halting but more melodious trill. If the mocking persists it becomes edgy and, hopping from branch to branch, calls rapidly but still quite melodiously. Finally, with a long, plaintive, ridiculous cooo-oooh, away it flies to a distant tree. The race between the stranger and I followed a somewhat similar pattern: we raced neck and neck, one outstripping the other, the other not lagging behind for long; we panted, we sweated, we didn't give up until our lungs were ready to burst. The whole thing was as ridiculous as the cuckoo's vehemence.

'Well, saar,' he began, bearing down on me. 'Visiting your village, were you?'

I pedalled faster.

'Where does your father stay these days, saar?'

I ignored the question. Who was this fellow? Why was he tailing me? Did he think he could catch up with me? Did he think I could not see through his ruse of slowing me down by engaging me in conversation?

My studied indifference was lost on him.

'Where's your younger brother these days, saar?' His cordiality and effervescence continued undiminished. 'Still with Tata?'

I glanced at him. How come he was so up on my affairs? Where did he come from? Were there still people hereabouts who remembered me? Apparently, there were. And of course, I had been in the newspapers of late.

I had indeed slowed down, quite unconsciously. But a voice inside me kept prodding: Pedal harder, put a decent distance between you and this wretch; he's not even a nodding acquaintance, don't fall into his trap of an easy camaraderie en route, he simply wants to pass time.

I pedalled harder. But he caught up with me. As we tore ahead side by side, I watched him out of the corner of my eye.

'Going far?' I asked, with a studied casualness, raising my voice a shade over the rattle of the wheels.

'Who, saar?' he responded enthusiastically. 'Me?'

Did he snigger? I couldn't be sure, but I had the unpleasant feeling that perhaps he did.

'Well, if you must know, I will go as far as you, saar,' he continued. 'Heh! Hush, you bugger!' He bent forward over the handlebar and thumped the front mudguard on his cycle. 'Hush! You make such a racket I can't hear myself talk. What are you up to, eh? And you've already nibbled away half the tyre — damn you! Now stop it and let a man carry on a decent conversation!' He straightened up with a smile. 'Makes far too much noise, saar.' His breath came in jagged pants.

I looked him over. Thickset, dark, of medium height, he wore a short-sleeved artificial silk shirt and a pair of cheap but clean cotton trousers. The cycle he rode obviously belonged to an office.

We cycled for a while without a word, but then he became gabby.

'Heading for Cuttack, aren't you, saar?' he asked. Getting no reply from me, he added, 'Me too. Been to the village for the weekend, you know.' He paused. 'What's the day tomorrow, saar? Monday, is it? I should have returned tomorrow but the boss said you must report on Sunday morning. Tell me, saar, is it possible to wrench yourself away from home on a Sunday morning? Especially if you've got there only the night before! Then there's this twenty odd miles between the village and the town. True, the distance isn't much, but with a ramshackle thing like this, cycling is no fun. Add to it the bumpy canal bank and your cup of happiness is overflowing!'

There was a silence.

'Which department?' I asked with a remoteness in my voice that one reserves for an inferior.

He stared at me.

'What's your job?'

'Whose — mine, saar?' His reply came without a twinge of shame. 'I'm in agriculture. Khosla Sahib is my boss.'

'Khosla Sahib's peon? The Agriculture Department? Very good, very good.'

'Thank you, saar.'

'Fine, fine.'

'Thank you, saar.'

Again there was silence.

'And where are you these days, saar?' he asked.

'Huh?' Staring straight ahead, I wondered how to fob him off. The village visit had turned out to be a pain in the neck. My sleepy little ugly backwoods village had changed enormously over the five years since I had been there last. My lectureship job was no longer good enough for it. As much as I resented it, I had been weighed and found wanting. Snatches of it came back to me: *Hello, son, how are things with you? Does your job let you make a tidy pile on the side?*

It's time you built a brick house in the village...Oh hullo, brother! Say do you get a fatter salary than our Harekrishnabhai?...There's no big money in those government jobs any more. What our village confectioner makes in fifteen days you lecturers don't earn in a month. And starting from clerks to officers who does not queue up in front of his shop? Who doesn't want to sweeten his mouth?...Gone are the days when you could live like a prince on a government job. These days the salary is peanuts. Not even enough for one person...Take our Ramakrishna. For the sweet life of me I don't understand why he sticks to that silly teaching job. I've told him umpteen times: son, forget teaching, go into politics, run the village panchayat, and in two years you'll be where your colleagues can't dream of being in twenty years, but does the moron listen to me? Teaching is a lousy job. In my opinion, if you have to do a government job you had better go into one which lets you make a quick buck. There ought to be ample funds to eat and ample to treat friends and relations with, what!...Whoa, brother! We heard you sat for the IAS exams this time. No? Why? Our Rabibhai took the exams, you know. He's been called for the interview. If he gets through — ah, by God, we're all going to have a rollicking time. One IAS officer in the family is more than enough.' Having had to swallow all these disagreeable remarks how was I going to answer this goddamn peon of some Khosla Sahib?

'You didn't answer me, saar.'

I wondered what to tell him. How well did he know me? Why not tell him I run the Zilla Parishad? But a poor illiterate peon might not have heard of ZP. What then — BDO, SDO? IAS? No, that'd be too much. Big lies always unnerved me. What then? Irrigation engineer? Hell, no, the fellow was obviously from a village by the canal and might know half a dozen irrigation engineers. Oh God, the bastard had me in a cleft stick all right.

Suddenly he threw me into greater consternation. 'Saar, we hear you have a lectureship or some such thing somewhere — true?'

I winced.

'A boy from our village got into lectureship this year,' he continued. 'At Bhadrak College.'

I winced like the mother of a sick child when her child is

compared, even if without malice, with someone else's dying baby. I found my tongue. 'At Bhadrak College, huh?' Contempt dripped from my voice. 'A private college!'

'A private college? Are there government colleges too? You mean there are colleges among colleges, saar?'

'What did you imagine, eh?' I pitched in, seeing his look of incredulity. This was a wonderful chance to gloat. 'Yes, my dear fellow, there are private colleges and then there are government colleges.' I glanced at him and repeated it with slow deliberateness, with perverse delight. 'In private colleges you start with a salary of a mere one hundred and eighty rupees. In government colleges...do you follow me?'

He did not.

'What's your grade, saar?'

'Grade, huh?'

He had pushed me into a tight spot. How to explain to this peon just how much space a lecturer occupied in the government hierarchy? 'Well,' I hemmed. 'It's the deputy grade. We are at the same grade as the deputy magistrate, you know.' The words had tumbled out of my mouth before I could think. I had blown a chance to compare my job with the august IAS. Roping it in somehow would surely have done the trick. Who bothered whether a lectureship was two-thirds or three-fifths of the IAS?

He stared at me in wide-eyed wonder. 'The deputy grade, saar?'

'What else did you imagine, my good fellow?' I measured him with a haughty glance, pleased at the amazement on his face.

'Great, saar! Just great! What a fantastic life you must have!'

I glanced at him. Did his voice betray a touch of sarcasm? You could never take this peon of some blessed Khosla Sahib in the agriculture department for a fool.

'Grade is not the only thing.' I had a sudden urge to talk, perhaps to quell the rising waves of dissatisfaction within me. 'We lecturers are gazetted officers. We wield power, too. Oh yes.'

This produced no reaction. That got my goat. I expected he'd gape at me with profound awe and respect. My glance would scald him and he wouldn't dare raise his head again until we reached the town. He would stop yapping, keep a reverent distance, soaking in whatever I deigned to talk about and nodding his pumpkin-head away.

Hadn't he grasped my answer or what? Was he thinking of something else? It was necessary to din it into his head.

'Look here,' I persevered. 'We have power. Now you might be thinking who the hell is bothered about that sort of power anyway. Fine. I wouldn't blame you if you thought like that. That's quite in keeping with the current attitude towards academics. But let's analyse power. Power! What is power and who wields it? Gone are the good old days of brute power. Now's the age of knowledge, you understand? Knowledge is power. Power is knowledge. No knowledge, no power. Next, we have long vacations. The only other institution which enjoys such long vacations is the High Court. A full five months out of twelve we academics are off. Read as many books as you can, write as many books as you like, acquire knowledge and, through knowledge, power. Now, now, don't for a second imagine that we go without salary during the vacations. No, my good fellow. We get full pay, not a paise less. That's one reason why other government departments can't stand the sight of us. Even the secretary of our own department envies us. And why not? The poor devil doesn't enjoy as many holidays. True, he belongs to the blessed IAS and gets a fatter pay cheque, but doesn't he work his hind quarters off for it? My dear chap, the point is that no one wants to get down to the bottom of the matter. Do you think the government's a damn fool that it gives us these long vacations for nothing? You see we work like the dickens during the vacations — oh, we really sweat it out. We study, we grind away. The government knows this all too well. And doesn't it stand to benefit from our studies? That's the crux of the matter. Without knowing all this why should anyone envy us?'

He was staring straight ahead.

'The fact is that the more we study the more the government profits from it. It exploits the fruit of our knowledge for its own ends. We don't get our vacations for twiddling our thumbs. You've heard what's happened in Turkey, haven't you? All the professors there have been rounded up by the military junta. Yes, rounded up. Not for execution though. They are now the right hand of the Turkish government — its friends, philosophers and guides. They are drafting the new laws of the land, those brainy professors. Not a piddling job, mind you! Same is true in all other countries of the world, practically. We the professors, we the enlightened, we turn on the tap of our knowledge for the government to slake its thirst. We write books, project reports, seminar papers and minutes of discussions and what have you. If the government does not pay heed to them, we freely air our criticism, and oh boy, once we academics take it into our heads to blow our top, are we virulent! The poor government comes reeling back to its senses. We are the necessary brakes upon the wheels of the government. You must have seen my articles in the leading dailies and journals...'

My eloquence was wasted on him. He remained stubbornly unmoved, disquietingly so. Did all that Turkey and stuff go over his head? I eyed him wearily. His face was blank.

I was silent but not for long. What I had spewed forth was nothing compared to what I wished to. It would have been one thing to hold off from the beginning, but having started I had to go the whole hog. Something goaded me from within: come on, you're a born teacher. True, the fellow is a dumb, dimwitted peon but make him understand. This is a test for you, this will prove how good a teacher you are.

'Look here,' I droned on, taking a different tack. 'A professorship doesn't mean we sit and spoon-feed the students from morning till night like the poor village schoolteachers do. No! We leave the boys pretty much to themselves most of the time and carry on with our own studies. You know what that means, don't you? Research, my dear chap! Pure research. We professors carry on research day and night. We shut ourselves up in big-big labs and carry out tests and experiments. Can you imagine what'll happen if we stop our research? Why, man, the world will grind to a halt! It'll simply fall apart. Yes, under your very nose it will, yessir. You people will be left high and dry. Tell me who invented your atom bomb — the government, huh? No! We the poor professors. That should give you a fair idea. Now suppose you wish to go to the moon...'

He stared at me with interest. I bucked up. Taking an enormous breath, I slid into the narrative. 'Power in itself is not a great thing. The real thing is knowledge. Knowledge, wisdom, humane feelings, devotion, mokshya, nirvana...'

'Saar, did you lecturers make the atom bomb?' he asked, cutting me short.

So the atom bomb of all things had clicked. Good, I could now bombard him. 'Who else, eh? And making that bloody bomb took a good bit of our dear old colleague's brain. Old Einstein, if you remember. As I was saying, research, devotion — these are the hallmarks of true professorial power and glory. What we achieve through our donkey-labour and hermit-like self-denial, the rest of the world enjoys. You know, we...'

I could feel he was drifting away and tried to fell him with a withering look.

'Saar, we hear there's a move to raise all grades, true?' He was alongside me.

Oh God, I groaned. What a twist, what a fall from the sublime to the mundane! I felt my throat tighten. 'Don't know, don't give a damn. Where's the time to think about the grade and all that? Research absorbs us body and soul, day and night, awake and asleep. No time for trivialities. You know, I wrote a piece on this theme sometime ago. Wouldn't be surprised if you read it. My stories and essays are published in the newspapers every week. I showed a little piece to our village schoolteachers this morning and the whole bunch was in stitches. My stories are generously larded with humour and wit. Only the discerning few discover the tragic vision underlying it all. Now, let's see, who do you think wields the finest humorous pen in the Oriya language today? You must have heard that my...'

'Saar!'

I found my hackles rising at the interruption.

'Day before yesterday there was something in the newspaper,' he said. 'Our memsahib, poor woman, she nearly died from all that laughing. She can't read Oriya script but she understands every word, even the most colloquial expressions, when something is read out to her. And she makes me read out the paper from beginning to end.' He turned to me with a huge smile on his face.

'What was it?' I asked. It was a relief he was talking about writing and not grades. 'Who wrote it? In which paper?'

'Where's Pati these days, saar?'

'Pati who?' I was flummoxed. The man could jump from one thing to another with the agility of a monkey.

'Saar, is it true that Professor Pati turned down the government offer point-blank and flew back to Allahabad?'

It certainly wasn't gratifying to be told of the antics of some Pati chap when I was riding my hobby horse. That he belonged to the tribe of professors was the only consolation.

'Is it by any chance Sitakant Pati you're talking about?'

'Right, saar. Sitakant Pati. We hear he's gone and invented such a wonderful machine that scientists all over the world are going gaga over him, true? It was in the paper.'

Some other time I'd have brushed this aside, but not now. After my harrowing village visit I needed to unbosom myself, to bolster my ego. And here was a chance for vicarious self-glorification. 'Oh, Professor Pati! He's my man. He is what an ideal professor ought to be. You know something, three times in a row he turned down his selection to the IAS. A truly great man. A great scientist. And the range of his research! What does it not include? One doesn't become world famous for nothing. You may visit Dr Pati in his house anytime you like, but you'll always find him immersed in his research. The sun will rise in the west the day he lifts his head from his research to say hello to you. So absorbed he is in his studies! In this respect we professors are all alike, you know — sunk seven fathoms deep in studies and research...'

I stopped with the sickening feeling that he was no longer listening to me.

'Saar, this research,' he piped up, out of breath.

I brushed him aside. 'Yes, research. Research. Dedication. The job of a professor is...'

'Research, saar? If there's one man who's really into research, it's our Khosla Sahib.'

I gaped at him.

'A madman, saar,' he went on excitedly. 'Completely off his hinges. Dotty about plants, plumb crazy. And his wife — our poor memsahib — oh saar, how can I describe her? What a tantalizing woman, saar! Stately figure, a wee bit on the plump side, tall and regal, gleaming complexion, unmatchable profile. The poor thing always snuggles up to that madhatter of a husband, saar, but does he waste a glance on her? For hours on end he'll crouch over some godforsaken plant or other, God knows observing what all with that instrument of his. It doesn't bother him if his wife stands sulking beside him the whole day. But saar, it rips you apart to see a lovely young thing sulking her prime years away...'

'Research,' I cut in, 'is a jealous mistress...'

'The sad sulky face of a beautiful woman! Now, saar, that's something which kind of kills me.'

I stopped in exasperation. Jabbering, like humming or singing, can be infectious, and now that Khosla Sahib's peon had caught it from me, there was no stopping him.

'Today's Sunday. And it's already evening. As you can see for yourself, saar, I'm returning from home. I was supposed to report to the memsahib early this morning! Go on, ask me why I'm late? Did I oversleep? If I didn't, why didn't I jump onto my cycle and start at cockcrow? Because, saar, my wife, she put on the longest face a woman can first thing in the morning and began to sulk. You couldn't tell her from a log of wood. Sulking women, pouting women, saar — they're my bane. They get on my nerves. They knock me out cold. That explains my delay. What's the time now, saar? Five o'clock already, isn't it! God save me! The memsahib insisted that I show my face in the morning. I just don't know what to do — keep away from home, or the job? The best solution of course is to keep your family with you wherever you are, but that's easier said than done. Look at Cuttack town, saar. Is there an inch of space for folks like me? Where will I get a house? The ones I come across hire out at thirty rupees a month.'

'How much do you people in the agriculture department get? The peons in our colleges...' If he didn't want to hear about the professors, maybe I could interest him in the lot of his counterparts in the education department. But no, the loquacious peon of the mighty agriculture department would not let me.

'Oh, what's the use of discussing it, saar! The point is neither do I do justice to my job nor can I chuck it. Back home, I've my wife and a two-year-old boy. Once I had about four acres of land, but the delta irrigation projectwallahs have already nibbled away six bighas. Things are not shipshape on the homefront. But do I have a cushy time at Cuttack to compensate for it? No saar. Of course, I can't expect wonders as I have to work under a looney boss. I pray to God he'll either transfer me to some other section or give me a raise.

'A madcap, saar. A madhatter, a nut. Absolutely crazy about those damned plants. They seem to have cast a spell on him. He potters around them day and night. God knows what he sees in them and why he studies them. And here his poor little wife's withering away. What good is a big job, saar, when you can't even find time for your wife? Compared to the sahib, we peons are much better off.'

Suddenly, without a hint, he switched his attention. 'Where do you keep your family, saar — with you in the town, or in the village?'

'With me, naturally,' I said, not without a tinge of sudden intimacy in my voice. 'I wouldn't dream of living away from them!' I didn't mind talking about my family.

He nipped the intimacy in the bud. 'You must be in government quarters. After all, you're at the deputy grade, aren't you?'

I broke out in a sweat. My wits nearly deserted me. But luckily the fellow didn't press for a reply.

'Yessaar, it's unthinkable that you would have any housing problem. How can the government not give bungalows to a deputy grade lecturer who's doing so much research! I bet there are big, big bungalows for you wherever you're transferred. You can set up your study in one room, your children's in the next, so that you can keep an eye on them. Though I don't see how on earth you'd have time to do that, taken up as you are with research...'

I felt expansive. The fellow had humbled himself. I could become a little more agreeable out of charity. I was getting back the thrill I had been robbed of in the village. There was no longer the compulsive need to talk about myself. I didn't mind listening to the little peon for a change. True, he was not an equal, but he did all right as a companion *en passant*.

We were silent for sometime. I wondered what he was thinking.

'Why doesn't the world ever acknowledge that a peon's job is as fine as any other?' he began.

I waited.

He smiled weakly.

'Of course a peon's job's fine,' I said. 'If you ask me you peons have a cushy time. And from what you've told me I think you're having a jolly good time at the Khosla Sahib's.'

He tensed and glanced furtively at me.

'Cushy time? What cushy time?'

I turned my head and looked at him. Our eyes met. Since I had accepted him as a companion it was all right if I joked and bantered a little without weighing words. Perhaps fathoming my mood, he burst into a guffaw. It was so unexpected that I felt a stab of embarrassment.

'What can I say, saar,' he said, picking up the thread. 'What else would your fate be if you worked under a mad boss? You know something, saar, you aren't the first person to get at this.'

Get at what? In my bewilderment I searched my mind — good God, what've I gone and driven at?

'Take my wife, for instance. She too drops wide hints. How can one explain things to her? Is she prepared to listen to me? The whole village is agog with gossip. The villagers have gone and convinced my dimwitted hen of a wife that in the government service Sunday is a holiday which even a governor cannot steal away from his peon. My woman has gone and swallowed it. Once her mind digs in, it won't let loose. Now she's haranguing me for working for my memsahib on Sundays. If I try telling her, look here, my good wife, for a peon government service is such that he has to sell his soul to the devil and work round the clock, she puffs out her cheeks or makes a long face. Have you ever seen the clouded face of a sulking woman, saar? Something happens to me every time I see a sulking face. I see red. Something snaps inside me. You tell me, saar, how can I explain these things to an illiterate woman?'

I did not reply.

'No saar, the bottom of the matter's elsewhere,' he chuckled and droned on. 'Women — they're all alike, birds of a feather! No man can ever explain a thing to a woman to her fullest satisfaction. Take my wife. She can't stand the memsahib. The merest mention and she blows her top. Take the other woman, that memsahib. She can't stand the idea of my having a wife, a home and a village. God knows what's in her mind, every time I ask for permission to go home she pouts and sulks and tells me to stick around. She finds all sorts of vague work for me, even on a Sunday. Now the village dame, she simply can't digest this. I'll tell you what happened this morning. Until breakfast my woman was in fine fettle, full of vim. The moment I began to put on my clothes, she sat down with a thud, making a face. Then suddenly, for no earthly reason, she started heaping curses on the poor mad sahib. I told her, woman, come on, don't curse the poor sahib, what harm has he done you, can't you find another person in the whole wide world to lavish your curses on? Did she scalp me for saying this! I can't bring myself to repeat half the things she spewed forth. The whole morning passed like this and I was able to leave home only in the afternoon. And mind you, only half the trouble is over. The other half awaits me at the sahib's. Who knows what the memsahib's up to?'

I did not hazard a comment.

'The sahib — hah, he doesn't notice a thing. Lives only for his plants and his research. If the plants are OK, he's OK.' He stopped. His voice changed, as if he was daring a stranger. 'From what I see, I don't have a ghost of a chance unless I give up this job.' A faint smile played on his lips.

'Suppose your sahib turned madder if you quit?' I said casually, without much thought.

'That's the size of it!' he beamed at me. 'You've got it right, saar, by God, you have. Only an educated man like you could get to the bottom of the matter without beating about the bush. Not until now had anyone caught on to this simple thing. I can neither part company with that madhatter nor breathe in peace in his house.'

'And what does your pretty little memsahib have to say about it?' I asked flippantly, giving a wicked little laugh.

He stiffened. 'You didn't get me wrong, did you, saar?' He looked me dead in the eye. 'Chhi, chhi, don't even imagine that. Our memsahib is a gem of a woman, a jewel. No riffraff, hanh! She's beautiful, she's educated; she can sing. A classy woman, yessaar, she's...'

I had stopped listening to him. But his last few words awoke me, and I stared at him.

He fell silent again, but not for long. He glanced at me and started babbling. 'You haven't seen her otherwise you wouldn't have spoken like this. She's like no one you've seen. She's religious, she prays, she observes all sorts of fasts and penances. You know something, she even observes the *sudashavrata* like our native Oriya women! The yellow string of charm and good luck looks so pretty on her plump, creamy arm, saar. And she has tremendous devotion for our local goddess Cuttack Chandi, too. You'll nowhere find a more refined woman, saar. But what's there to all that? People like her are out of this world. This world isn't for good people like her, nah, naaah!'

There was another brief silence. He fell back a little. My mind was wandering. Dusk had fallen. Moths and insects swirled about. I was blinking furiously to keep them out of my eyes. I could feel his gaze on me.

'People have loose mouths, saar. And who can shut them? That memsahib is like a goddess, I tell you. I've seen the memsahibs of many officers. Such brazen hussies most of them are, saar; no male-female sense left in them any more. But our memsahib? Not only does she not chase a man, she doesn't encourage fawners around her. No colleague of the sahib ever comes to our bungalow. I tell you, no outsider can ever set foot on our bungalow, not even the peons and clerks in our department. I'm the only exception. And me she won't let out of sight. After all, she's got to have someone, no? In a lonesome household, as the saying goes, even dogs and cats are company. To tell you frankly, saar, in the beginning the whole thing got on my nerves. It's all right if you don't know your boss as a man. But when you do...'

Columns of insects rose, and we whizzed through them. We pushed along slowly. I kept switching my breath to avoid inhaling the insects. Every snort seemed to feed my companion's irritation. Keeping pace with me, he watched me with suspicion.

After an uneasy silence he fired a fresh volley of explanation. 'You aren't laughing inside, are you, saar? You think I can't make that out, huh? Look here, saar, I may not be as educated as you but I can certainly guess what's going on in your mind. Let me tell you something. You've never seen a woman like the memsahib in your whole life. You'd start crying, no matter how cold you are, once you were face to face with her. I told my wife all this till I was hoarse, but did she understand?'

He was quiet for a moment. 'They haven't laid eyes on each other, these two women, but when it comes to hating each other's guts, both vie for the top slot. One sulks in the village, the other in the town. To tell you frankly, I dread Saturdays. The moment I ask the memsahib to let me go home for the weekend, she begins to sulk. If I pester her, the cunning thing that she is, she says, all right, go, I can't stop you, but come back on Sunday morning. Sunday morning, mind you. Not Sunday evening, leave alone Monday morning. If I persevere with her she invents all sorts of errands for me: milk to be bought, wheat to be crushed, so on and so forth. Who knows what's in her mind, but honest-to-God, saar — why would I tell you lies at this sacred hour of dusk — she cordially detests the idea of my leaving her alone to go home to my old wife. That's her one little blind spot.

'But who would blame her for this quirk? The sahib's such a crazy cat — the way he's hunched over the plants and stuff, glued to his research day in and day out. The bungalow's so huge, and there's just this one woman, so lonesome, so uncared for. It's the loneliness that makes her invent work for me. Yessaar, she has her little idiosyncracies, why deny it! You wouldn't know how many times I've explained it all to my wife, but she won't even try to understand. At the faintest mention of the memsahib's name her face swells up with anger. She's a great one for sulking, she can go on for days on end, without food, water and sleep. You'll find her sitting like a stump in one place for hours together. And the memsahib, she too won't make an effort to understand. I find myself between the devil and the deep blue sea. And what's my fault? Why should a poor peon like me be in such a pickle?'

He scanned my face in silence. 'What's my wife but an illiterate, rustic woman? Once she gets an idea she won't let it go. No amount of explanation helps. These days she's up to a new trick. From the moment I reach home she starts nagging me: "Either take me to the town or give up the job." Now tell me, saar, what can a poor man do? Look at my salary. It's a pittance, not even enough for a single person to make do with. I haven't told you, I get free meals at the sahib's. Tell me, can I afford to bring my wife and child to the town? Do I have the financial means? All right, just for the sake of argument, let's say I bring them over and we manage to live in a corner of the sahib's bungalow. How do I ensure that this wife of mine will not do something preposterous like picking a quarrel with the memsahib? I'm at the end of my tether, saar. The looney sahib refuses to see anything. He'll be my death, I know. I wish he'd throw me out of service. Anything would be better than this, I swear.'

He sounded so comical that I choked with suppressed laughter. He cocked his ears.

'This world's a rotten hole,' he hissed like a whiplash. 'A huge stinking rotten hole. That shrivelled bitch of a wife of mine has driven me nuts. And that memsahib's no better either. I'll be damned if I don't see through her tricks. You know something, she knows pretty well my blood boils when I see a woman sulk. My hackles rise, tears well up in my eyes, my mouth goes dry. Why do women sulk? For heaven's sake, why? I can tell you in black and white that the memsahib must be in a mighty sulk by now. Sulking away to high heavens. Bloody hell, you're a high-quality memsahib, damn you. Good-looking, young, vivacious. What ails you that you sit and sulk, enveloped in sadness, as if somebody's pinched a pretty penny from you! What a woman, saar. Who knows what's in her mind! You can't figure out a woman.'

'How old is she?' I asked, cracking a smile.

'What?' His voice crackled with indignation.'What did you ask?' I felt crushed.

'Truly, truly, saar! The world is a rotten hole. Who can survive in this stinkpot? Who understands you? From officers to clerks to peons to my wife to the villagers, everyone's mind's in the same groove. Whatever they say is heavy with hints. But curse my luck that even the stranger I take pains to explain things to also starts thinking along the same lines. Chhi, chhi!'

His voice grew severe. He pedalled vigorously and came abreast of me. 'I'm ready to swear by my little son. Not a bit of what you imagine is true. There's nothing between me and the memsahib. How could an educated deputy grade lecturer like you think such dirty...chhi, chhi!'

I was abashed.

'It's my misfortune that my boss is a nut. What have I done to get thrown into a mad household? Why does this brood of fools from the office to the village suspect me of an entanglement with the memsahib?...What a nut I am, by God! Why the hell do I have to go on explaining? For six years I've been explaining and explaining and explaining. Whatever for? I'm just a peon, a poor little peon, a wretched peon, worth one, two, three, forty rupees a month — why should I fancy that the crackpot sahib can't do without me? Why should I fancy that the memsahib can't survive without me? Why should she invent odd jobs for me on Sundays? Why should my wife mock me? Why should people slander me? Why should everyone imagine passionate goings-on between the memsahib and me? No, from what I see I've got to quit this job. Let the madman dawdle over his damned plants — what's that to me? Why should I take the blame? After all, where's his position and where's mine! What's he to me? Let him come off the hinge completely. Let him wind up dead. What do I care? I've got to get out of this mess. Nobody understands. Nobody cares to understand.'

He was frothing with anger.

'Come on,' he dared me. 'Tell me who understands! But one thing I know for sure. The day I chuck the job the sahib will drop dead beside his damned plants and his little woman will collapse in a dead faint in that lonely bungalow. Who'll look after them? When I tell people all this, they laugh and mock me. To hell with them. Why should I explain at all?'

A frigid silence hung over us. Chagrined, he scanned my face. Then he opened his mouth and poured forth explanations, vehemently, shouting as he began and choking towards the end. The more he protested his innocence, the more I was convinced that he lusted after his memsahib.

Then, with a sudden burst of speed, he shot ahead. I tried to catch up with him. For a while we didn't talk, cycling wearily through the gathering twilight. We were fast approaching the town. The road had more traffic and lights twinkled here and there.

'Goodbye.'

He turned and went back to the bumpy canal bank that ran parallel to the road.

Krushna Prasad Mishra

The Pilgrim

The crowd eddied around the huge stone lions on either side of the temple's Twenty-two Steps, and the Bazaar of Joy was chock-a-block with people. A priest was holding forth. A miracle had taken place! And hanging on to every word of his, the goose-pimpled devotees swayed back and forth in ecstasy, while the doubting Thomases' suspicions lay uprooted like trees after a storm. Between the pauses the roar of the sea could be heard, and as soon as the priest was finished the tremulous cries of Haribol rent the air.

What a miracle indeed!

A middle-aged, turbaned, upcountry pilgrim squatted in the courtyard of the temple of Lord Jagannath, facing the image of Goddess Laxmi, silent tears coursing down his craggy cheeks — no unusual sight this, considering the many ways God can affect His devotees. Only an hour ago this man, having discovered that he had been relieved of the wad of money he had so carefully tucked in the waist-folds of his dhoti, had brought the place down with his bawling. Like a madman he had scurried around the sprawling courtyard in search of the culprit, bumping into pilgrims and badgering them for information; and now, tired, defeated, with all hope gone, he sat shedding copious tears like a simple, innocent rustic villager. Many a pilgrim, moved to pity, had offered him money and consolation, and one of the priests had even promised to pay his train fare home. But the man was inconsolable: of all people why had he, a pious, god-fearing man, who had done no wrong, been dealt this blow? What had he done to deserve it? From where he sat he could behold both Lord Satyanarayan and, with a slight tilt of the head, Goddess Laxmi; a priest had pointed out this unique spot to him only the evening before. He kept silently pestering Them for an answer.

As the morning progressed the sun grew fierce and the marble floor, dotted with memorial slabs in a multitude of languages, sizzled like a frying pan. The heat simmered in the courtyard, and the pilgrims thinned, but this man sat rooted to the ground, his head between his knees, a few futile coins strewn around him.

In the late afternoon two young men suddenly materialized before him and one of them gently shook him by his shoulder, while the other shoved a big handful of mahaprasad into his mouth.

This little scene excited no great attention; stranger sights of generosity and conviviality were witnessed in the temple day in and day out.

'Uncle,' the dark young man said. 'Come, have another mouthful.'

The startled pilgrim stared at them.

The fair one explained: 'We vowed to distribute mahaprasad if our wishes came true. So here we are.'

'And you're the last person to partake of it,' the dark one added. 'Want a little more? Please help yourself. Now we'll go into the temple for a darshan of the Lord.'

The soft deep voice of the young man cast a magic spell on the pilgrim; the words were like balm to him. Entranced, he gobbled up one mouthful after another.

The dark young man pressed a packet into his hands, patted him on the shoulder and said goodbye. Dumbly he watched them walk into the sanctum sanctorum of the Big Temple — from where they did not emerge. He waited for a long time and, his appetite whetted by now, he tugged at the strings of the packet, hoping for sweets.

Thick rolls of hundred-rupee notes and a train ticket to Raipur fell out. The poor man leapt to his feet.

Dusk was falling and the lights were coming on in the courtyard, which was slowly swelling with devotees for the evening darshan. The pilgrim stared at the money and the ticket: What was all this? Who were those two young men? Why did they have to press so much money on me? How did they know that I come from Raipur?

Then in a blinding flash it dawned on him. 'Oh Lords!' he began to scream like one possessed. 'Woe to me, I did not recognize You when You appeared before me! Oh, blind little fool that I am! Oh, thick-headed blundering me!' He ran wild in the crowd, jostling and showing everyone the crisp currency notes, enquiring if anyone had seen a pair of young men, one fair and the other dark.

The story made the rounds.

As old Dash, his energy sapped by a recent bout of typhoid, and already late for the evening darshan, staggered painfully up the Twenty-two Steps, he heard a voice over the din: 'Sirs, brothers and sisters! How can I leave Puri and return to hell after what has happened to me? Is that what the Gods want me to do — return home? Answer me, brothers, what did the dark Lord Jagannath and the fair Lord Balabhadra tell me when they stuffed mahaprasad into my mouth — catch the train back to Raipur, eh? Ah, my friends, does anyone ever desire to go back to the world after a glimpse of the divine Lord? Blessed are the eyes which have beheld Him, blessed the ears which have heard His voice; blessed is he and blessed are his parents. Who said that in this kaliyug God does not show Himself?' The speaker paused for breath. His words shot through Dash like an electric current.

'So what use do I have for this wretched ticket?' the speaker continued. 'Let me tear it up and block the road to hell.'

'Hold on,' Dash shouted, pushing through the crowd. 'Don't tear up anything yet.'

But he was several seconds too late. The man had already scattered the shreds to the wind.

Dash looked the pilgrim over: knee-long dhoti, sleeveless cotton vest, turban, a typical outsider; his furrowed, sun-baked, sweat-stained, mahogany face made Dash wonder for a moment if the saints of yore looked any different.

An elderly devotee, a regular to the temple whom Dash knew a little, took Dash by the arm and babbled, 'Oh, who can belittle the Dark Lord, the Round Eyes? He makes the impossible possible. Only one must know how to pray to Him.' He raised his hands skywards and Dash slipped past him.

The memories of his village filtered back to Dash. How fervently he had prayed when his only child lay dying: 'Almighty, you accepted coconut from the hands of Dashia Bauri the low-born; you let your chariot procession be interrupted by Balia the fool. Beloved Shyam, will you not grant this poor Brahmin beggar of Chandanpur a small favour and spare his little daughter's life? She's not yet five and she's all I have. What sin has she committed that she must go? Give her a chance, Lord. I'm not asking for the moon — am I?' But did the Lord — may one never belittle Him — listen to Dash's prayers? His little girl died. His poor wife simply cracked up from the shock; she swept the idols and images of his prayer-room into the garbage dump at the back of the house. Dash left the village and came away to Puri.

But now the Lord needed old Dash more than he needed Him. After all, what was He but a log of wood without Dash's mercy? He needed Dash to bring Himself to life. That was what Tulsidas had done to Lord Rama, Mirabai to Lord Krishna, and Ramakrishna to Goddess Kali.

Dash took up a corner of the temple courtyard, explaining, day after day, all this to whoever bothered to listen. His admirers grew in number and soon he had a crowd of people turning up regularly for his evening discourses. His intense fervour and vivid descriptions cast a spell on his audience. He did not confine himself only to miracles of the past, he dwelt upon recent ones, little-known ones, ones unheard-of; he even spun some, and what did it matter. If such a miracle had not happened already, it surely would sooner or later some day, if not here then somewhere else. And often Dash's own fabrications proved more thrilling than the stories from the

Scriptures. Such was his fame that pilgrims from all corners of the country came to listen to him. The priests and attendants held Dash in high esteem; his daily discourses had quadrupled their income.

Is this rustic oaf taking us for a ride? Dash wondered, his eyes riveted on the pilgrim. Or is he another madman out to boost the sagging prestige of the Lord? Dash's heart suddenly prickled with jealousy: what if the man was telling the truth? It was difficult to believe the miracle, but to dismiss it as rubbish was harder still. He elbowed his way through the throng and reached the pilgrim. 'So you claim to have seen Him?' asked Dash, as the fellow's stench of sweat hit him. 'You did, huh?'

With the elan of a magician the pilgrim produced wads of hundred-rupee notes from his vest pocket and held them high above his head. 'Brothers, take a look at this — the prime cause, the root of all evil.' The words now seemed to roll off his tongue with great ease. 'This filth is the real culprit. Make no mistake, lucre is the villain. It was the loss of a little money that reduced me to tears, to heaping curses on the Lord, to denying His very existence; I was livid with His sense of justice. But how He took pity on this sinner! Not only did He appear before me with His fair brother, He fed me with His own hands, consoled me, loaded me with these and a ticket to Raipur to boot! But He can no longer pull the wool over my eyes. I shan't be taken for yet another ride. In my own humble way I've understood the mystery of life. No more of this miserable mundane world for me, no more. No one can lure me into it again!'

He paused for breath. He could see the priest who had offered him consolation and money for a return ticket. Beside him stood the chubby little priest who had recounted the miracle of Dashia Bauri the untouchable. How the good priest had concluded: 'God does not discriminate between the low and the high, birth matters little to Him, it is the devotion that matters!' The pilgrim turned his head a little and spotted the thin sprig of a priest who had described to him the story of Balaram Das the possessed. A fresh wave of inspiration rolled over him.

Droves of pilgrims rushed up the steps toward him.

'Brothers!' he resumed, his voice rising. 'Do you know what keeps man apart from his Maker, what stands as an impenetrable barrier between you and Him? Mammon! Lucre! Money! One way or the other money kills God. Look at me, the poor bastard. I came to Puri for a darshan of the Lord, had my purse pinched by someone, but the Lord has given me a thousand times more than what I lost. So I ought to be happy and getting back home, shouldn't I? No sir! Not me! No more! Watch this, brothers, watch how I shred these damn bundles of hundred-rupee notes into pieces. I advise you all to take out whatever money you have in your pockets and tear it to pieces. Only after you have done this shall the Lord appear before you. That's the only way to behold Him. Kill Mammon, brothers! Exterminate money!'

He shredded the hundred-rupee notes and scattered them. The scraps swirled like insects around neon lights, and a thousand eager hands stretched forward like lizards.

The pilgrim fished out another wad from his pocket. 'Hurrah!' he cried. 'Here they go. Come brothers, empty out your pockets. The sooner we rid ourselves of this devil the better. Destroy the demon, brothers! Now! This very moment!'

The incredulous crowd lunged forward before he could finish. They had had enough of a lunatic tearing up precious hundred-rupee notes. In the stampede that followed the pilgrim was the first to fall.

After the temple guards had succeeded in dispersing the crowd, they found the pilgrim lying in a pool of blood. His eyes were closed, but the Lord's name was on his lips and a faint smile played on his face. The scraps of the hundred-rupee notes in his hands had turned into petals.

Picking up some which had dropped from the pilgrim's half-clenched fists, old Dash headed for the Bazaar of Joy.

Manoj Das

❦

Into the Heart of Luvurva

Dear Editor,

The report is forwarded along with my personal regards. I only hope I have succeeded to some measure in approximating the high standards of investigative journalism expected of us. It's been a long hard assignment in Luvurva.

A sense of utter surprise awaited me at the borders of Luvurva. The whole forest seemed to be in the grip of a wild orgy. Everyone was celebrating I know not what — democracy? In one place I found a brood of cheerful young donkeys braying — sorry, *singing* — at the top of their lungs, and with what gusto! So touching, so unshakable was their faith in their musical prowess that I realized any attempt to distract them would be of little avail. In hindsight I am mighty glad I kept quiet.

It was, however, the queer behaviour of a herd of wild pigs which landed me in the first of a series of scrapes my tongue got me into. Can you believe it, the pigs were dancing? And as they danced, as only they could, they cast meaningful sidelong glances at me, clearly expecting me to burst into applause. 'Hats off to your persistence!' I, like a fool, shot my mouth off. 'But hasn't it ever occurred to you that one needs a slim waist to excel at dancing? Maybe if you looked you'd find you are all good at some other form of performing arts.'

The pigs flew into a towering temper. 'We didn't expect such an undemocratic remark from you. No sir, not from a journalist of your stature,' grunted their venerable dance-guru. 'Our Constitution has guaranteed all its citizens the right to dance.'

'A constitutional right is one thing,' I persisted. 'But having the anatomy and the aptitude quite another, don't you think?'

'Thank you, we've both,' the pigs retorted. 'And you, sir, are an ass. But no problem. Now that you're in Luvurva, we will din some sense into your thick skull.'

They promptly gheraoed me and continued their frenzied dancing. Three long, miserable hours later, much wiser and almost on the brink of a nervous breakdown, I begged them to take pity on me. 'Thank you, thank you, thank you,' I spluttered on bended knees. 'I've been much enlightened. Never before had I witnessed anything as fascinating as a porcine dance.' I was made to follow this up with a written apology before they would consider freeing me. The incident is symptomatic of the spirit of rampant democracy now permeating every class and every aspect of life in Luvurva.

As soon as I secured my release I couldn't hurry fast enough to go and find our old friend Jackal the Junior. His older sibling Jackal the Senior is currently the *de facto* ruler of the land.

Jackal the Junior was palpably cool. Coming from someone who had made much fuss over scribes in the past, his behaviour was surprising. He gave me a wink and enquired casually, 'So how are you?' Then he lapsed into silence, fretted and repeatedly glanced at his watch. His mood, however, changed dramatically when I dropped a broad hint that we were planning a special report on the revolutionary changes sweeping Luvurva. He cast aside his studied indifference, hugged me warmly, made a great display of affection and whined, 'Oh, you hot-shot reporters, you've completely forgotten us! But the minister and I often remember you.' Never once during our tête-a-tête did he refer to Jackal the Senior as his brother; it was always minister this and minister that. I spent one whole day with him and gleaned many useful tidbits.

The next two days passed in a whirl of interviews. I met the delegates of the Federation of Wild Buffaloes, the convener of the Association of Boars, the secretary of the Association of Owls, the lady president of the All-Luvurva Deer Union, the president of the Association of Poisonous Snakes, the spokesperson of the Association of Non-poisonous Snakes, the honorary treasurer of the Union of Tigers, and last but not least, the Personal Secretary of Lion the Glorious, the deceased ruler of the land. (The poor P.S. is languishing under house-arrest.) Except for the P.S. everybody could sketch only the superficial outlines of the event under investigation.

Now to the event. Lion the Glorious, the president of the council of ministers, had been at the helm of affairs for nearly two decades. The one and only time the Luvurva Council met was when the president was elected; a second meeting was never convened. Some of those whom I interviewed were of the opinion that from day one the council of ministers was a lame-duck for all practical purposes; all powers were concentrated in the hands of the president, who did not burden his ministers with the onerous responsibilities of administration; they hastened to add that that might be because the president looked upon the ministers as his children, but there it was. Others were of the view that since the presidential administration went smoothly — no bottlenecks, hassles, or red-tapism — there was simply no work for the ministers.

My investigations revealed that not until the promulgation of a fateful ordinance did the ministers have any cause for grievance either. As long as they had access to loudspeakers they were in fine fettle. Microphones in hand, and in love with their own voices, they strutted across the length and breadth of Luvurva and made interminable speeches. They all lived in a state of frenzied ecstacy. Some of them, more inventive than the others and with an unslakable thirst to drink deep the nectar of their own words, even wore hearing aids, can you beat that!

The addiction to microphones seemed to have proved more and more overpowering until it assumed such proportions that nothing was ever done without them. No longer confined to ministers, the virus had possessed the rank and file. Be it a marriage or a funeral, or merely day-to-day business, the use of microphones was much in evidence. Even wedding music was served up like commercial jingles by powerful amplifiers. Those reported to have taken the keenest interest in the use of microphones were the jackals. They had begun to deliver their ritual howling at sunset over microphones; not only that, announcements regarding the time and venue of all future congregations were also made periodically over the public address system.

Rumour has it that once Lion the Glorious upbraided the jackals for their new-found enthusiasm. 'Look,' he is supposed to have said, 'this communal howling is an ancient tribal ritual of yours. It hasn't changed even a wee bit, in content or in style, since it was thought up by your illustrious ancestors. And for centuries you folks seem to have done quite well without microphones. Why do you have to use mechanical devices now?'

Apparently, the president's gentle remonstrance bore no result. Hence the ordinance banning microphones. The justification, briefly stated, was something like this: Respect for one another is one of the significant aspects of any civilization. Luvurva is, and ought to be, no exception. At the same time technology has made rapid strides of late and many new gadgets have come to stay. Indeed, some of them are taken as symbols of progress. But unrestrained and unregulated progress can also kill culture and civilization. Take microphones, for example. The question is whether we shall use a device like a microphone for collective joy with the consent of one and all, or ram it down the throats of an unwilling multitude. There can be no two opinions that loud noise is a menace to all living beings wherever they are, whether on the streets or in the depths of the forest. A doe might be unwell, a rabbit might be composing a poem; someone else might be simply longing for silence. No one has the right to cause pain or discomfort to others while pursuing his own pleasure.

The promulgation came into effect immediately. Peace returned to Luvurva. The calls of doves and cuckoos were heard once again after ages.

But as it happened the ordinance also began to kindle the flames of unrest; it began to blaze more fiercely in the bosoms of the distraught ministers. And something they could not dare to imagine even in their wildest dreams began to take possession of their minds: how to dislodge Lion the Glorious from the seat of power.

I ran into an old owl, a well-known psychologist thereabouts, who had this rather interesting light to throw on the subject. He said it wasn't quite correct that the president had become such a megalomaniac that he had usurped the powers of the state. Far from it; the ageing president had simply forgotten when to step down and had continued to discharge his functions as head of the state as befitting his animal-like simplicity of vision.

Two years had passed since the promulgation of the ordinance. The president was going strong, exhibiting the same zeal and zest for administration as before. But meanwhile the ministers were on the brink of barking madness; the lack of microphones had eaten deep into their vitals.

So when Lion the Glorious invited Jackal the Senior for lunch one afternoon, he noticed how pale and woebegone his minister looked. What ailed the poor fellow, what made him so miserable? The presidential enquiry slowly unravelled the cause of the minister's misery. He was worried to death about the future of Luvurva.

For the ageing president, it was a pleasant surprise. 'It gladdens my old heart, Jackal the Senior,' he beamed. 'I never thought anyone else worried about Luvurva as much as I did. You see, I am never entirely free from the fear that after me there'd be the deluge. Happily for me, that apprehension has been dispelled today. There's no denying that I'm getting on in years and my death is not far away. But when my time comes I'll be ready to depart with a lighter heart.'

It had never occurred to Jackal the Senior, or for that matter to anyone else in the council of ministers, that Lion the Glorious might die one day. The mere possibility sent such a shiver of excitement down his spine that he lifted a jug of wine and polished it off. The old president did not much care for wine, but he too had to drink a jug, just for the sake of table manners and etiquette.

Lunch over, Jackal the Senior hurried to the riverbank on the edge of the forest, yodelling away to glory. All the symptoms of advanced inebriation were evident in his demeanour and movement.

The sun was setting when he arrived at the venue of the jackals' ritual howling. The entire tribe had already congregated there.

Jackal the Senior opened his mouth, and it was then that the liquor took its toll: instead of sharing with his fellow beings the exciting possibility of the president's death, he declared that the president was dead.

The jackals were hushed; for minutes they were speechless with grief. Then they burst out wailing. So great was the commotion that the whole forest reverberated with it and all the other animals thronged there to find out the cause. When they heard that their father-like, god-like president was no more, they all began to howl and then marched towards the presidential quarters located a little above the foot of the hill. The president's residence was a spartan affair, just a large cave, inside which the old president, because of excessive drinking, lay in a deep slumber.

The moon had risen and all Luvurva, bathed in soothing light, looked solemn and mysterious. All the denizens of the land, from toddlers to doddering old folks, assembled near the cave. True they were no longer wailing, but the collective sound of their convulsive heaves and sighs could be heard miles away.

Jackal the Senior entered the president's cave, and instantly his intoxication disappeared. He realized what a blubbering blunderbuss he had been and began to tremble uncontrollably like a palm frond in a storm.

Outside, squatting on a rock, a monkey, an ambitious young member of the council of ministers, began to sing the praises of the late lamented president and the audience erupted into sobs.

The noise awakened the president. He lifted his head and peered out. The congregation was truly massive, awesome; all of Luvurva seemed to have turned up. Then he became aware of Jackal the Senior's presence inside the cave. It was all so bewildering.

'President, sir,' began Jackal the Senior, his heart in his mouth, 'You're dead.'

Lion the Glorious, groggy with sleep, nursing a nasty headache from too much wine at lunch, stared blankly at him.

'Sir, the citizens of Luvurva have assembled,' Jackal the Senior pressed on, 'to mourn your death.'

'Am I dead?' enquired the president, still in a daze. 'Are you sure?'

'We all are, sir.'

The president surveyed himself. 'But why do I have this twinge of confusion? I'm not sure I'm dead.' He was on the verge of tears. 'Is there a way out of this dilemma, minister?'

'The dilemma does not reflect well on a wise and able president like you, sir,' answered the minister, confidence slowly returning to his voice. 'You must gracefully accept that you're dead.'

There was silence for a moment.

Suddenly the congregation outside burst into encomiums for the deceased president. The walls of the cave shook, and the president fearfully rolled his eyes up at the roof.

'So what do I do now?' he asked, his voice catching.

'Don't worry, sir,' answered Jackal the Senior. 'I'll give you just the advice you need.'

He ambled out of the cave and ascended a jutting rock nearby. The noise dwindled down.

'Citizens of Luvurva,' declaimed Jackal the Senior. 'Our father-like, god-like president is dead and ready to depart for heaven. Because of the infinite love and affection he bore us, he has ensured that the migration of his immortal soul will be visible to all Luvurvians. The great soul will carry with him his carapace of flesh on his celestial journey.'

A hush fell over the citizens.

Jackal the Senior hurried back into the cave. 'Did you hear that, sir? Well, don't delay a minute longer. As soon as I step out and raise a slogan in praise of you, bolt out of the cave like an arrow and don't stop until you've scaled the summit. The whole thing must be accomplished with lightning speed. You may catch your breath once you're on the other side of the hill, but for heaven's sake leave Luvurva as quickly as you can. Don't pause for a moment to wonder whether you're dead or alive. You'll have enough time for reflection afterward.'

Jackal the Senior trooped outside and belted out a booming slogan. The denizens repeated it in a million voices, their eyes awash with tears, riveted on the mouth of the cave. And then, in the bright moonlight, they saw a golden arrow shoot out of the cave, fly towards the summit and vanish. The president was gone, body and soul.

The rest, as they say, is history.

This is the background to the mysterious midnight appearance in our town, a couple of months ago, of an old, decrepit lion who met his eventual end at the hands of the local population with a little help from the police and the fire brigade.

Jackal the Senior is the current ruler of Luvurva, although no one's quite sure whether out of modesty or out of deep political calculation he has not declared himself president. He prefers to be known as minister. As I was leaving Luvurva, the Right Hon'ble Minister had the forest in a frenzy; his umpteenth address to the nation on matters of national interest was being broadcast in every nook and corner of the forest. Hundreds and thousands of microphones were blaring.

Rabi Patnaik

The Ghost

Sumi suddenly let out a volley of eerie, bloodcurdling shrieks from the bathroom verandah. It was around nine at night.

'What's the matter, Sumi?' Mother screamed, rushing out of the kitchen. 'What happened, my girl?'

I jumped up from my seat in the front room and ran inside.

Mother was holding Sumi in a tight embrace. The poor girl was shivering from top to toe, her eyes dilated and jaws locked; she was trying desperately to speak but could manage only a few incomprehensible grunts.

'Say something!' Mother ran her fingers through Sumi's hair, apparently to soothe her. 'Answer me, did a snake bite you? Oh Ramu, where are you? Go get the doctor. Quick. Sumi has fainted!'

I made a quick sortie around the bathroom. I couldn't see anything.

'Let's put her in bed,' I suggested. 'We'll check if she's been bitten and give her first-aid. It'll be quite some time before the doctor arrives. Come, hurry up.'

We carried Sumi to her bed and gently laid her down. She had taken an evening bath to beat the summer heat and her hair was all wet. Her sari was in a mess; she had somehow wrapped it around her. Maybe a snake bit her when she was changing in the bathroom. Thank God she had the presence of mind to quickly unlock the door and step out. Otherwise the door would have had to be broken down.

Mother pushed a pillow under her head, while I switched on the fan at full speed and began minutely examining her legs. But there was not a scratch anywhere, let alone blood. Mother, in the meanwhile, fetched some water, which she sprinkled on Sumi's face.

Some ten tense minutes ticked by. Sumi lay still and motionless. I stood by her side, wondering what to do next.

'Why are you standing here like a log of wood?' Mother shouted at me. 'Go fetch the doctor.'

It was as if this brought Sumi back to life. She opened her eyes, stared wildly about her and shrieked: 'A ghost!' She fainted away again. Just then auntie, our next door neighbour, arrived. I left Sumi and Mother in her care, jumped on my bike and pedalled furiously in search of a doctor.

The bathroom in our quarters, like all others in Unit Six, is located at quite some distance from the living rooms. The thick canopy of the banana, papaya and guava trees made that part of the compound quite dark. Maybe Sumi had spotted a thief beneath the trees and taken fright. Lately, there had been a boom in thieves in Bhubaneswar.

By the time I returned with the doctor Sumi had recovered. Nevertheless the doctor examined her thoroughly. 'No, not an epileptic fit,' he declared. 'Nor even a bout of hysteria. A slight psychological shock more likely. Anyway, there's nothing to worry about. It happens sometimes, you know. If you're too deep in thought about someone you tend to see a vision. But it's all an optical illusion. Something like mistaking a stunted tree for an apparition in dim moonlight. The ghost is all in the mind. Anyway, let her have a cup of hot milk and go to sleep. She can take a sleeping pill too. By tomorrow morning she'll be fine.'

I teased Sumi after the doctor left. She was the youngest child in the family and had recently enrolled in a Master's course in psychology.

'Sumi, I didn't know you were such a skit. How could you mistake a banana tree for a ghost! Girls of your age don't see ghosts, you know.' I turned to my Mother. 'Ma, high time you looked around for a boy. The earlier Sumi's married off the better. Or else we'll have to keep a strict vigil on the ghost in the back yard.'

Sumi wasn't her usual self; she did not scream at me. And I found her wild stares quite disconcerting.

'What's got into you? Why are you staring so wildly? Did you really see a ghost? Who was it?'

'Moni Bhauja!'

'What!' I started.

'Believe me,' Sumi said quietly. 'That's who it was. She wore her red polka dot sari with a red sleeveless blouse and had a shy smile on her lips. I thought I was hallucinating and went into the bathroom again to splash water into my eyes. When I came out I found her standing under the trees. She was as real as you and I. Go on teasing me all you want, but I did see her.'

'Rubbish!' I said after I had recovered from the shock. 'As the doctor said, you must have been thinking of her a lot lately. Ghosts don't exist, much less show themselves to the living. So get that nonsense out of your head.'

Mother overheard us. 'Not only did the bitch commit suicide, she has the cheek to come back as a ghost to torment us! I'm going to ask your father to move out of this house. Or else let's get an exorcist to get rid of the spirit. Ramu, can't you go to Balakati first thing tomorrow morning? I'm told there's a famous tantrik camping there. Nothing like getting him here right away. Don't bother about his fee, I'm ready to pay any sum. Maybe we can ask him for a charm for Sumi. She's a grown girl, and you never know. These ghosts and evil spirits are very mean and spiteful and they single out young unmarried girls.'

Moni, who was now being reviled and denounced by Mother as mean and spiteful, had been, a mere fortnight ago, someone dear and close to her, in fact to all of us. She was more than a family member. She was our neighbour Sridhar's wife, married for eight years; their wedding had taken place just a year after Sridhar had moved into his quarters next to ours. When my elder sister Roni's wedding was celebrated sometime before theirs, Sridhar, then a bachelor, had given us a free run of his house for the occasion. Ever since then we had become very friendly.

Moni had not had a child. In those eight years she had tried every conceivable thing: opinions from medical experts, spells, fasts and vigils. On my mother's advice she visited gods and goddesses of all kinds — from Akhandalamani to Nilamadhab. She brought water from Gourikund, she started Saturn-worship. Name a thing and she had tried it. Only late last year she gave it all up. She grieved all the time, but it didn't show.

Moni was plump, not too tall; her complexion, though dark, was smooth and glowing; and she was forever smiling. Her eyes were deep and shiny. She was good at everything she did — household chores, stitching and embroidery, interior decoration, textile designing, everything. When bored with housework she resumed her education and took a Master's degree in Oriya literature the same year I did. She wanted to take up a job but Sridhar wouldn't agree. She dropped in at our place everyday — giving rise to the joke that she couldn't digest her food if she didn't — and snatched work from my mother's hands and did it herself. She had grown so close to our family that many a time she was consulted before an important decision was taken. 'Why don't we ask Moni? Let's see what she thinks,' was Father's constant refrain. As if everything depended on Moni's opinion.

I was in the last year of school when Moni Bhauja first came here. She was older than me by a year or two. Mother said she was younger than Roni, three years senior to me.

Why did a woman as vivacious, as spritely, as lively as Moni Bhauja commit suicide? Sridhar was, and still is, a decent sort. We hardly ever saw them quarrel, much less fight. They did have arguments sometimes, but all low-key; nothing came anywhere near a no-holds-barred showdown. Financially, they weren't badly off either. Nor did Moni have to put up with terrible in-laws. Sridhar's mother was long dead and his father, who lived in the village, seldom visited them. There were occassional visitors but none overstayed their welcome. Never once did we sense Moni's disenchantment with life. Whatever her feelings, she camouflaged them very well.

But the big bitter truth was that Moni committed suicide.

I've swallowed a sleeping pill but sleep seems to elude me. I'm wide awake, though my head is as heavy as a rock. The room is dark. Mother is fast asleep in the next bed. Her breathing is heavy. I clutch the end of her sari for protection. My fear has lessened, but I can still see Moni Bhauja's face. She was on the verge of saying something. What was it she wanted to say? Had she found out my secret?

Oh, Moni Bhauja, did you commit suicide because of me? Please don't blame me, please. I swear by all that is holy that I am entirely blameless. You know me well, don't you? And for a good eight years. Do you think I am capable of telling you a lie? Besides, now you must be able to see it all, lie or truth, and see everything that goes on in our minds. Then why do you torment me? Why look at me with sorrowful eyes, why blame me for what happened in your house that terrible afternoon? Believe me, I had gone over looking for you. How was I to know that you had already slipped out your back door and walked in through ours? And why should I fear Sridhar, who I'd always looked on as an elder brother, and who had always treated me affectionately as a distant sister-in-law? He might have joked with me but he had never made any advances. How was I to know that he was so worked up that lonely, sultry afternoon? He caught hold of me, pressing me to his chest. Before I could let out a whimper of protest he had stripped off my clothes. Fear, anger, shame and surprise had turned me into a statue. He pawed me all over, bit into my lips and cheeks, but Bhauja, believe me, that's all he ever did. All of a sudden he released me. I picked up my sari and ran into your bathroom. A little later he knocked and pushed my petticoat and blouse through the gap over the door. And then when I came out your back door, I bumped smack into you. If I didn't speak to you then it was because I was burning with shame and mortification, because I was trying to choke back my sobs. What would you have done in my shoes? And look at my plight: on the one hand there was you, my dear sweet little Moni

Bhauja; on the other, that husband of yours, who had been so polite and correct until then. I was flabbergasted by his behaviour. Never once had he eyed me. And I had spent so many quiet afternoons in your place, sometimes all alone with him. Never once had he betrayed a trace of desire. So why did he suddenly go crazy? Did I provoke him? But how? I'm a student of psychology but this is beyond me. Now that you're in the realm of the spirits, Bhauja, you must know the answer. Please enlighten me. Tell me whether this was an act of destiny. I know how deeply you must have misunderstood me that day, how deeply you must have suspected me of carrying on an affair with your husband. Had I dared to speak one word against him you would have only blamed me. Moni Bhauja, more than anything in the world I didn't want to be misunderstood by you, for that would have hurt me the most. And believe me, I had made up my mind to tell you about it, and soon enough, but you never gave me the opportunity and went and committed suicide that very night. Moni Bhauja, you must know by now that I'm not to blame. I did nothing wrong.

Just when the grief was beginning to fade, Sumi had to reopen the wound. Moni, Moni Bhauja, do you really believe I was beginning to forget you? Can I ever forget you as long as I live? You exist within me — then, now, forever. You do not have to appear as a ghost to remind me of you.

Show me a place in this room where you do not exist. I feel you everywhere — this cot, this bed, the counterpane and the pillows, the door and window curtains; there's your touch everywhere. The tablecloth, the pens, the clothes and the shoes — everything was chosen by you. Every particle of dust, every speck of colour here speaks of your touch. The shirts still retain the smell of your perfume, the bed the fragrance of your body, the air your eternal presence. You're everywhere — in the room, in the clothes, in every corner of my mind, in the depths of my heart, in every drop of my blood; I see with your eyes, hear with your ears, smell with your nose; my fingers remember the softness of your flesh, my lips the taste of your kisses.

Moni, Moni, Moni. Did you find my love so wanting that you suddenly upped and went? What was my fault that you had to punish me so heartlessly? Was it a crime to fall in love with you? Did I bring on your death?

Did anyone come to know of our relationship — this relationship of love, warmth, understanding and intimacy which spanned eight years?

Did you for a moment consider our relationship sinful, immoral? And did it weigh you down so much that you chose to put an end to your life? I do not know what constitutes sin, but never once did I feel there was anything ugly or immoral about our relationship. It was sacred, pure; there wasn't an iota of dross in it.

Moni, it's still a mystery to me how you graduated from Moni Bhauja to Moni, how you entered the orbit of my life, how you made a sculpture out of as shapeless a block of stone as I, how you transformed an arid, bohemian male into a soft, quivering lover. All I know is that it was you who made me what I am today. You were the artist, I your art. You endowed me with a soul. Every minute, every second of my life I've felt the rustle of your soul deep within me. Of all your pieces of art I was, and still am, the best, though you're gone and I continue to go on.

Moni, I remember the moist twilights at Khandagiri and Udayagiri, the lazy afternoons at Nandankanan, the moon-drenched evenings at Dhauligiri, the perfumed dusks on the lonely beaches of Konark and the divine dawns breaking over the golden sands of Puri. All that is gone. But I have no regrets. In two years you gave me the experiences of two thousand years, the life-essence of two hundred thousand years.

The strangest thing, Moni, was that when Sridhar turned up that morning and broke the news of your death, everyone dissolved in tears except me. I couldn't. There was not a drop of tear in my eyes. Can you believe it, I felt you were standing beside me all along and together we were watching someone else's funeral. Even afterwards, whenever the acuteness of your physical absence tormented and tortured my mind, I'd suddenly sense your presence around and would instantly feel revived, consoled, soothed, the flames of pain and suffering doused. That is why I believe that you have not deserted me, that you have stuck by me.

True, never again shall anybody see you sitting behind me on my scooter, never again shall anyone discover you with me in Konark, but I know, I feel it in my heart of hearts that anytime I go to Konark or Nandankanan and Khandagiri, you'll quietly perch behind me. That pillion seat will never go empty. Never again shall anyone find you accompanying me to the shops to choose clothes for me, but I know you will continue to make me buy what you think will look good on me. You will not come and tidy up my bed, dust my bookshelf, restore order to my cluttered table, go with me to our favourite Chinese restaurant in Cuttack, but you'll be there with me, your spirit will be with me, making me do what you wish.

Moni, you're present even though you are absent. Or so I feel. Although you're physically gone, you still exist. Whenever I am reminded of your body I think how strange it is that it was there till the other day and is now gone forever. Sometimes I feel you've been with me since my birth, we two inseparably tied together. You envelope me. Always, you are within me and without. Sometimes when I look at myself all I find is you. Maybe you aren't dead really. Maybe I'm the one who's dead. Maybe I'm you.

Moni, what was my fault, where did I go wrong? I know I'm the one to blame. I was so madly in love with you that I could not rein myself in. The deeper my love grew for you the deeper became my fear of losing you. It's strange, isn't it, Moni, that our tears should be directly proportional to our love!

Moni, remember those three months after our wedding? That was the entire extent of our relationship as man and wife. But you never breathed a word of it to anyone. To imagine you spent eight long years, laughing and joking, as though nothing was amiss. No one had the ghost of a suspicion about us. Oh Moni, what an accomplished actress you were! No, how great your self-sacrifice was! I found it stifling. You were always up, I down.

Did you imagine I didn't know about you and Ramu? I knew

everything. There was someone who snooped around and passed on all the tidbits. Are you mad with me for setting a spy on your trail? Tell me what else could I have done? Does anyone like to lose a pearl? He may not wear it, he may keep it forever stashed away in a safe, but the sense of possession is bliss enough. You were my pearl. I wanted to own you. Forever. Yes. True I didn't use you. I couldn't, I had been robbed of my manhood.

Moni, I am not sure you could ever fathom the depth of my sorrow. It was not possible for you, nor for anyone else. It was a terrible sorrow, utterly soul-corroding. Then there was the dilemma — something akin to what a leper woman feels when torn between her maternal love for her new-born and her fear of passing on the disease. Eight long years I lived, torn by my love for you. You were just a breath away but I couldn't touch you; you slept by my side but I couldn't feel you. It was as if I could not cross the chasm of flames that had come between us.

You couldn't know how much I envied Ramu. Oh, I envied him greatly. Sometimes a maddening desire to throttle him would seize me, but I knew I would lose you forever if I ever tried anything of the kind. It drove me nuts nonetheless. And that crazy little incident with Sumi — well, it was symptomatic of my insanity. The poor girl was shaken to the roots of her being. I doubt if she understood that I was, and had long been, a toothless tiger. How could she know that a mere three months after our wedding I had lost my manliness!

Why do such things happen, Moni? Why? Why was such a miserable fate in store for me? Why didn't the scooter accident prove fatal? Why didn't my head, legs, hands break instead? Why did my second and third vertebra have to break, rendering me impotent for the rest of my life?

Who can I blame, Moni — fate, God, the scooter, the pedestrian, you, my father who wanted a scooter as a part of the dowry, or your father who gave in to the demand?

As days passed, my life became increasingly unbearable and I constantly toyed with suicide. But to tell you the truth the more I saw you the less I desired to die. I didn't want to die alone, leaving you behind. That's why I've outlived you. When I cottoned on to your affair with Ramu, I began to dry up and wither away within; it was a kind of slow death.

Moni, I knew of your pain and suffering. That was why I never put a spoke in the wheel, why I never prevented you from having a good time with Ramu. It was sheer joy to see you alive and beaming; my envy and frustration took a back seat. Your smiles lit up my day, gave me inspiration to go on living.

But something snapped inside me the day I learned you were pregnant. My reasoning suddenly failed me and I hated you passionately. I couldn't stand your happiness. Hate, envy and desire for revenge filled me. Your smiles inflamed my insane anger, and anger fuelled the flames.

Before dawn broke that fateful morning, when the whole sky eagerly awaited the rising of the sun, I awoke to the cold touch of your body beside me. Your face was still radiant and calm, and I detected a flicker of a smile in the corners of your lips.

It was at that moment that I felt the fire smouldering inside me suddenly go out, the despair clutching at my heart quickly subside. For the first time in years I felt at peace — with myself and with the world.

Moni, I don't know if I cheated you, but I admit I cheated Ramu and the rest. But the point is why should I have continued to burn alone? Eight years was a long time, wasn't it? I know my misery will continue to haunt me until the end of my days. But why shouldn't Ramu share a part of it? Why should he have had the nectar, leaving me with the cup of poison?

Now you know, don't you, dear Moni. That evening when you and Ramu were busy with each other I dissolved thirty sleeping pills in your glass of milk and waited for you.

Forgive me, darling Moni. But am I the one to blame?

Jagannath Prasad Das

Spider's Web

'A bad omen,' Sadhna whimpered, wringing her hands.
'Hmm.' Rohit lolled in the bed, exhaling a plume of cigarette smoke.

'An ill omen, I tell you, this twitching of the left eye.'

Rohit blew a perfect smoke ring. 'Hurry up or you'll be late for the office. Don't let your boss give you a dressing down.'

'Dressing down?' She looked at her watch. 'Oh God! Pass me the hairpins, will you? If I'm not ready in two minutes flat, I'll have to report sick.'

Rohit swung off the bed and rummaged through the things on the dressing table. 'So cluttered,' he said. 'Here, take all six of them.' He tried taking her in his arms. 'By the look of it, you won't be ready in two minutes.'

'Let's see.'

'Mmm, that's a maddening perfume you're wearing.'

She wriggled out of his embrace and started changing her clothes.

Rohit watched with fascination. Until recently she had insisted that he look away. For him, it had been a long journey from her drawingroom to her bedroom, from nodding acquaintance to passionate lover. She was most definitely not the greatest beauty on earth, but as far as he was concerned there was no one more adorable. Everyone else paled into insignificance in her presence. And the day she accepted him, naive that he was, he wished he could die and not outlive the moment of his greatest happiness. The future held such perilous possibilities that he felt dizzy. His body ached with a fulfilling bliss. What did he have before meeting Sadhna, anyway? Success? Status? Prosperity? What did all that amount to? Nothing! The day she slipped her hand into his she made him forget his work, profit and loss accounts, friends, relations, acquaintances, the earth, the stars, the planet, the solar system, heaven, hell, birth, death, rebirth, all at one go. She exuded the magic fragrance of oblivion. Her first embrace wiped out his childhood and adolescence, her first kiss his youth of fanciful dreams, imagination and aspirations. In the moist twilight of her bedroom he lost and regained and lost again his identity, memory and all his tomorrows.

He hugged her from behind.

'Lay off. I'm late already.'

To hell with the office, he thought. May it catch fire. May your fat boss drop dead. May the third world war break out. Let you go, my girl? Forget it.

But he did not say a thing. To him, she always remained an enchanting enigma, and he was as unsure as ever how to deal with her.

He released her and went back to the bed.

She tucked the pins in her hair, smoothened her sari, and put on a pair of earrings. Strapping on her shoes she sprayed perfume all over herself yet again.

Then she turned and fastened a liquid gaze on him. 'But who says I'm going to the office?'

'Hurray!' His heart leaped. The gloomy uncertainty was over. He jumped off the bed and took her in his arms, and they kissed.

She pushed him away gently, wiped her mouth with her handkerchief and applied a fresh coat of lipstick. 'Wait, I'll make you some tea.'

He retreated to the clammy corner of the bed, resigned to her unpredictable ways.

She kicked off her shoes, unpinned her hair and threw the

hairpins on the dressing table. As she emptied her purse, she threw him a mysterious smile and vanished into the kitchen.

Rohit lit another cigarette and stared vacantly at the wall.

A spider was crawling across it.

He wondered where it would go.

It stopped in the corner near the door and set about spinning a web. First the deft outlines of a hexagonal field. Then the quick, sure threads from the corners to the centre.

He sat back and watched.

The spider bustled about, an air of vibrant mystery hanging around it.

Sadhna walked in noiselessly. 'Here's your tea.'

Rohit started.

'What's the matter?'

'Look, there's a spiderweb in the northeast corner of the room. What does it portend — good or evil?'

'Whichever, I'm going to dust it away right off.'

'Oh, no!' he interjected as though he was himself woven into the grand design of the web. 'Leave it alone. The poor spider has taken great pains to weave it. Don't you find it lovely?'

He remained engrossed in his thoughts for a minute or two.

'A penny for your thoughts!' she said.

'Sorry.' He looked up at her. 'Our relationship — er — relation — er — don't you think it's a bit like the web?'

'What makes you think so?' She was suddenly very serious. 'Is it so fragile?'

'Far from it. It's so lovely, so shimmering, so out of the world!'

Sadhna cut him short. 'Perhaps you find it a deathtrap?'

There was no answer to such a question, he knew from experience, and an unguarded conversation could only lead to a bizarre conclusion. 'Come closer,' he said, 'and I'll whisper the answer into your ear.'

She moved away from him, but came back and took a chair next to the bed.

Every movement of hers was full of mystery.

Presently she put her cup down on the table, rushed into his arms and pressed her lips onto his.

'Did you know,' he said, 'that the thread of a spiderweb is stronger than steel wire of the same thickness?'

'Rubbish. Whoever sold you that yarn?'

'Well, I read it somewhere.'

'If it were true people would use spider's web rather than steel wire. And the poor wretched spiders would be forced to devise some other method of catching their prey. Come, let's hear what else you know about spiders.'

'The female of the species gobbles up the male.'

'How wonderful!'

She slowly unbuttoned his shirt and peeled it off. 'Want to see how she goes about it?'

Before he could answer she sank her teeth into his arm.

An incredible pang of ecstasy spiced with pain shot through his body.

She bit into his arm again.

Tears came to his eyes. 'Leave me,' he begged hoarsely, 'or I'll scream.'

'Go ahead. Scream,' she said. 'Don't ever talk to me about spiders, right?'

He glanced at his arm. It hurt. The tooth-marks glistened; a little blood began to ooze out.

'Oh dear, I've gone and bitten a little too hard,' she said, wiping the blood with her sari-end. 'Does it hurt? I hope nothing will happen. Shall I wash it with a little dettol or something?'

'Never mind. I'd like it to fester so that I'll have to have my arm amputated. Anything to remember this afternoon by.'

'Don't talk like that.' She moved away from him. 'I promise I'll never do it again.'

'Why don't you change your sari if you aren't going to the office?'

'Makes little difference now. It's already crumpled. Now tell me, do you want to stay here or push off?'

'Stay here. Till eternity, if you allow me to.'

'But what about your business? What'll happen to it? You may be losing good money this very moment.'

'Maybe. Who knows?'

'Hey, I haven't the foggiest idea of what you really do. You never tell me anything about your business. But look at me, I keep filling you in on the most trivial details of my office.'

'But you know, business is such a drag. The humdrum affairs of the hardware trade would certainly not interest you. Your office, on the contrary, is so damn lively, so terrific. Interesting people, interesting goings-on. Besides, Sadhna, you love talking about them, don't you? And how I love listening to you!'

'You do?'

'And business is full of problems...'

'Don't give me that dope, love. I too have a bunch of problems. In and out of the office. I live in this flat all by myself. That's a problem, isn't it? I skip office at the slightest whim. Isn't that another? Who knows what music I might have to face tomorrow? Anyway, the point is you keep your affairs pretty much to yourself. Just shows how little you care for me.'

'What's the point of burdening you with such details? They won't interest you, I'm sure. You aren't a business rival; I don't purposely keep things from you.'

'The other day you ran into somebody in the lobby of the hotel we went to for dinner. I asked you who he was, but you wouldn't say.'

'When? I don't even remember. I must've been a little absentminded. But why didn't you ask me a second time?'

'Why should I? What did it matter to me who he was? All I'm saying is you can be awfully indifferent at times.'

'Oh, my God, indifferent to you?' How could he explain what she meant to him, how she occupied every bit of his mind?

'The other day I begged you to spend the evening with me, but you marched out.'

'But didn't I tell you I had a client to look up?'

'That just shows how little you care for my feelings. Your business is always more important. Are you sure you don't have a client to look up today?'

'Come, I'll never make that mistake again. Forget my engagements. I'll keep you company for as long as you wish.'

'That's up to you. I'm not asking you.'

'You wish me gone, do you?'
'That's up to you. What do I know of your engagements?'
'Why don't you tell me clearly?'
'I'm not saying anything either way. You're free to do as you please.'
'Do you mind if I stick around?'
'I don't care either way. If you feel like staying on, stay on. If you feel like leaving, the way out is the way you came in.'

He propped himself up on the bed and looked at the wall. Its web completed, the spider had vanished. He hurried off the bed, put on his shirt and shuffled for his shoes.

'On your way already?' she asked.
'Yes.'
'When do we meet again?'
'Whenever you wish. I'm only a phone call away.'
'Must you come only when asked and never on your own?'
He said nothing.
'Are you cross with me?'
He didn't answer.

She unbuttoned her blouse and offered him a generous slice of her shoulder. 'Bite here and call it quits.'

He tied his shoelaces.
'So this is how it ends, huh,' she said.

His head was in a whirl. He was feeling weak in his legs and his lips were numb. Dazed, he took a step towards the door.

'Leaving?'
'Yes.'

He stopped by the door. The web hung inches above him. It was woven of strands of vivid silver, an enveloping hammock of intricate, transparent weave. The air seemed full of billowing snares. He stretched a finger towards it, and a thread snapped at his faintest touch.

He came back to bed and slowly began to take off his shoes. 'Sadhna, my dear,' he said, with an inscrutable smile on his face. 'I'm not leaving. Not even if you throw me out.'

Binapani Mohanty

Flowering Night

Lipi dragged her tired, weary feet up the stairs. The house seemed deathly quiet and the front door was wide open. She felt a flutter of apprehension. Where was everybody? Had Naresh taken the children out for the evening? Was her mother-in-law in her prayer room? Anyway, she didn't matter, for lately she had withdrawn so completely into her shell that she didn't hear or see a thing. What about the servant boy? But of course it was foolish to expect anything of him. All he ever did was sleep or twiddle his thumbs. Why didn't anybody care that the front door was open?

She parted the curtain and looked in. Naresh was sprawled on the divan reading something and down on the floor Runi and Jhuni were hunched over sheets of white paper. It was the sight of the pen, which the children took turns dipping into an enormous inkpot to draw pictures of houses, cows and crows, which made her heart skip a beat. The golden nib was already crooked, perhaps chewed, and Lipi felt blood rushing to her head. The pen was a present from Vikas on one of her birthdays — something she had preserved with a lot of feeling and rarely used herself. How could Naresh hand it over to the kids? He himself had asked for it a couple of times but she had always been able to put him off.

She swept into the room, as if possessed by a demon, and

delivered two stinging slaps to the cheeks of her two daughters. 'Scoundrels!' she hissed. 'Couldn't you find anything else to play with? Wasn't the pen in the almirah, on the top shelf — how did you get it? How dare you...?'

Naresh seized her hand when she raised it again. 'What's so bloody special about the pen that you're hitting the poor kids? For years it's been lying unused...'

'Shut up. What does it matter to you how long it's been lying unused? Aren't there pens galore in this house? Runi and Jhuni have several sets of sketch pens. Why do they have to take this pen?'

'Mummy,' Jhuni blubbered, rubbing her tear-filled eyes. 'Daddy gave it to us. He made us draw pictures with it. What's our fault, tell us?'

And then breaking into a phlegmy sob, Jhuni repeated the same thing.

Lipi stared at Naresh a long moment and stomped out of the room. Hardly able to walk, she slumped onto a chair in the dining room. Naresh's jealousy was hard to comprehend. Or was it his secret anger? Why was he so curious about the pen? Why did he always want to know who gave it to her and why had she preserved it so lovingly? She had been able to skirt the issue. It's a present from a friend was all she could bring herself to say.

Only a few days ago, Naresh had noticed the novel a friend had given her and had repeatedly asked who it was. Somehow he had not been able to decipher the illegible signature on the front page. Lipi had laughed and merely said it was a present from a friend. A few days later she found the page flying about in the garden. When she asked Naresh about it, he answered irritably: 'Anything might have happened. The breeze might have gotten hold of it. The kids could have torn it out. It might have fallen off by itself. Why are you getting worked up over something so trivial?' Lipi had remained silent. The incident had perhaps stayed in his mind; for since then his replies had become cryptic and strange.

Then there was the incident the other day which refused to leave her mind. She had reported sick and stayed home. Naresh too was around, having just got back from a long business tour. The whole afternoon he kept rummaging in the trunks, suitcases, cupboards and almirahs, scattering the contents on the floor. The room was in shambles but he appeared in such a high sulk that Lipi thought discretion was the better part of valour and kept quiet, letting him carry on as he pleased. She was pretending to be asleep when the sound of a loud crash made her sit up with a start. Naresh had succeeded in breaking her favourite china doll, a childhood possession.

'Why did you have to break it?' She seethed with suppressed anger. 'I'd preserved it for ages. And it was right at the back of the shelf. How did you manage to knock it down?'

'What's so special about a silly doll? You played with it when you were a child, eh? Brought it as a part of the dowry, did you? Have the heavens fallen because it's broken?'

'Don't speak like that. You won't ever understand why I cherished that doll. I bought it at a fair...'

'Aw, shut up. You women, you only know how to wallow in stupid sentimentality and clutter up the cupboards with useless bric-a-brac.'

Lipi stared at him. What was wrong with this man? Why was he deliberately destroying everything she loved? The search was just a pretext. Perhaps he was going to break the pots and pans next. What madness had come over him?

'Tell me what it is that you're looking for,' she said, trying to calm herself down, 'and I'll help you find it. Why don't you go and get some rest? You need it. After all, you're just back from an exhausting tour. Didn't you say you were feeling feverish?'

Naresh impaled her with a sharp glance. 'How come you didn't go to the office today? What made you stay home? As far as I can see there's no work here requiring your presence.'

'There is.'

'What is it?'

'Something personal. Satisfied?'

'Waiting for somebody, are you?'

Lipi couldn't help smiling. 'You're right. Yes, why else would

I take leave and stay home?' She put her hand on his arm. 'Honestly, tell me what are you looking for, please?'

'Nothing.' He spun away from her.

Twelve years of marriage had passed but Lipi did not find Naresh easy to fathom. Why did he do what he did, why did he say what he said, what was it that he really wanted from her? She was often quite scared.

He had positively encouraged the girls to break her pen. It was a costly pen, but more importantly, a loving present from a dear friend. Why was Naresh eager to destroy every little thing she loved? Wasn't this house hers too? Couldn't she keep a single thing of hers safe — a doll, a pen, a few memories? She never desecrated anything Naresh was fond of. On the contrary, she always picked up even a scrap of paper with his scribbles and preserved it, never made snide remarks if he liked something, never opened his briefcase.

Naresh's screams jolted her out of her reverie. He was shouting at the houseboy. 'Romu, bring me the tea. And be double quick about it, boy. I need to go out.'

Whenever she was home, Lipi always made him tea, no matter how busy she was, but today she couldn't care less. She let Romu make tea and stepped into the bathroom.

'Master left,' Romu informed her when she came out, 'without taking tea.'

'Never mind.' She didn't owe Romu an explanation.

She looked out and saw her daughters standing forlornly near the fence watching children play in the street. Are they thinking about their parents' fights? she wondered.

She went out and gathered them in her arms. Her mother had always fussed over her when she was shouted at by her father. The memory of it made her eyes water. Why couldn't she show the same consideration towards her own daughters? Why did she behave as if somebody had taken away the words of comfort and sealed her lips, had deprived her hands of the loving touch? What was it that stood in the way — her job, her university education, her ego, her anger towards her husband?

She brought her daughters in and made them sit at the table. 'Don't break any more pens,' she said gently. 'I've given you so many pens, what did you do with all those?'

'Mummy, we didn't ask daddy for this pen,' said Runi, tears welling up in her eyes. 'It fell off the shelf when he was rummaging for something. He deliberately stepped on it and it cracked. Then he gave it to us and told us to draw pictures with it. He got angry with us when we didn't want to touch it.'

Tears streaming down her cheeks, Jhuni added, 'Daddy always beats us when you're not here. Mummy, please don't go to the office.'

'All right, all right!' Lipi made a feeble attempt to laugh it off. 'Be good girls now and get down to your homework.' Wiping their tears away, she went into the bedroom.

The bedroom was a mess. The adjoining storeroom was in a bad state too. The trunks and suitcases lay open on the floor. Even her own suitcases hadn't been spared. She had never bothered to keep the keys with her. But if Naresh was so careless nobody could blame the houseboy or the part-time maid if they stole something. Even Runi and Jhuni might take something. Lipi's head was in a whirl.

The doorbell rang and she hurried to open the door.

'Hello there, Nirmal Babu,' she greeted the visitor. 'Come in. Long time no see. Your friend has gone out, but will be back soon. Won't you please sit down?'

Nirmal glanced at his watch. 'When did he go out? We were supposed to go to Sukumar's this evening. Didn't Naresh tell you anything about it?'

'He must have forgotten. It's good you're here. Left to himself, he doesn't remember a thing.'

'One tends to forget,' sighed Nirmal. 'It's the pressure of work. Business can take a heavy toll. Look at me, I haven't been able to spend a quiet moment at home for ages. Sarojini and the children are pretty sore about it. But do I have any free time?'

'Really, what's time for you people? It's the lot of the wife and children to worry but daddy has time only for his business. Even evenings out with friends are a part of business.'

'You've got it right.' Nirmal lit a cigarette. 'Naresh might have discussed his problems with you. The investment he has made in shares isn't quite enough. He really needs a much larger sum, otherwise business won't pick up. We had planned to discuss this with our other partners, Sukumar and Vinay. Hasn't Naresh said anything to you?'

Lipi gave a sick smile and remained silent. Naresh hadn't breathed a word about it to her. Maybe this was what had been eating him up lately, this business venture.

Nirmal glanced at his watch again. 'Naresh might have gone to Sukumar's already. I must hurry there. I've a train to catch for Madras tomorrow morning. In case I don't get to see Naresh, tell him I came... Well, couldn't you perhaps pitch in with a little help.'

'What do you mean?'

'You could give Naresh some money. You could ask your brothers, you could raise a bank loan by pledging your jewellery. Maybe you have some money in your personal bank account. Look, don't take it amiss, this is just a friendly suggestion. Think it over. Bye.'

More out of politeness than anything Lipi went to the door to see Nirmal off. The moon was bright and she could see Nirmal's car parked around the bend in the road. Naresh stood with his back to the car door, smoking a cigarette. One minute he was there and the next he had ducked behind the car. Was he scared she might see him? A chill of unknown fear ran down her spine and her heart began to race. So Naresh was capable of doing things behind her back! She had never imagined that. And since when had he gotten smitten by the moneybug? Why couldn't he confide in her? Hadn't he turned to her when he didn't know where to go to at the time of his sisters' marriages? Hadn't she taken a lot of her jewellery from her safe-deposit box and handed it over to him? She had been genuinely happy to have been of help. Why couldn't he be half as considerate? Like everybody else he looked forward to her help and was happy when he got it, but Lipi didn't expect anything from him, or from anybody else for that matter. All she wanted was a little concern, a little consideration, a little affection, a little love. She simply wanted to preserve the little life had given her. But the way it seemed to dwindle, perhaps like the waning moon, who knew how quickly darkness would overwhelm her? Her daughters were not old enough to understand. They were perhaps scared of the parents they once loved. She herself had become increasingly indifferent — to herself, to her children, to the outside world. She was tired, spent, finished — from being too considerate. But nobody bothered about her.

She went inside and began to tidy up the storeroom. How many pieces of jewellery was she left with? she wondered. A pair of earrings, two rings, two bangles. The bangles had been given her by her mother-in-law and she intended to save them for her daughters. Was there nothing else? She racked her brain. No, there was something else. The first time her grandmother had come to see her after her marriage she had given her a silver vermilion container. It was bigger than an ordinary container and under the vermilion the old lady had placed five gold coins — something nobody else knew about. Once while talking to Naresh about the container she had impulsively shown it to him. Naresh was a little careless, and it had fallen from his hands; the contents had spilled out. Lipi had been quick enough to scoop up the coins. 'Old granny had nothing other than these coins,' she had explained, burying them under the vermilion. 'She didn't want to visit me empty-handed.' That was all right, Naresh had remarked, it was the spirit that counted more than the gift itself. Lipi had been careful to hide the container amid the clutter in a wooden almirah. She knew someday the coins would come in handy in a crisis.

Looking at the empty container, she was filled with sorrow and anger. I must confront Naresh, she decided, and not let this pass. Why didn't I have the sense to check up on it from time to time? She caught her reflection in the mirror. Why am I such a fool? Why am I so naive? Who dinned it into my head to trust, to trust blindly?

She was in a frenzy. She rummaged through her things again. But the gold coins were just not there. Who could have pinched them — the houseboy, the children, her mother-in-law? Most unlikely candidates these, she decided.

Sick to the core of her heart, she bustled into the bedroom, switched on the fan, placed a stool in the middle of the room and sat down. Her heart was bleeding. She felt numb and heavy. Of late everything had become a strain. Neither the office nor home was a happy place. She found it tough to concentrate on work. Meeting dear old friends didn't make her feel happy. All she wanted these days was to sleep like a log for days on end, with nobody around to disturb her. Her dreams had shattered, her tree of life had sprouted thorns, and the more she clung to it the more she bled. Is there an escape? She often wondered. Why don't I die?

Suddenly she sensed that Naresh was back home. Hours had passed but she wasn't aware of time.

'Why are you sitting like a stump?' Naresh arched his eyebrows. 'The houseboy said you didn't have dinner. What's wrong with you?'

She could smell liquor on his breath.

Naresh's glance swept over the chaos. 'What the hell have you been up to?' His voice rose. 'Isn't your head working?' He shook her by the shoulders.

'Just now it's started to,' she said, shrugging him off. 'It had stopped for a long time.'

'What are you looking for? The room is a mess...'

'Shut up. You know damn well what I'm looking for. Where are the gold coins? Why did you touch my vermilion container without my permission?'

'Your permission?' He glared at her. 'Don't you forget this is my house and you're my wife and everything you own belongs to me because you are mine.'

'You're mistaken. Sadly mistaken. And if that's how you feel I'll find it impossible to live with you. In fact, right this moment...'

'You want to leave me, eh? All right, leave. Go away. But keep in mind that a woman without a husband has no place anywhere. Society will look down on you. Of course, financially, you may not face any problems since you have a good job. And I hope you won't demand alimony, or will you?' He picked up a glass of water, drank it in one gulp and threw himself on the bed with a thud.

Lipi stood leaning against the wall, assessing things, taking stock. A void loomed before her whichever way she looked. But somehow the fire of discontent which had been burning within her for so long had suddenly been extinguished and she felt utterly calm and peaceful. Hadn't she been longing for a state of bliss like this? All her life she had been frightened of precipitating a crisis, but now that a major one, perhaps the worst of all, was about to overwhelm her she felt a strange rush of relief. Maybe she had worked it out for herself. The feeling of exhilaration far outweighed the sorrow, and she decided she mustn't do anything to stray from the path she had set herself. For so long she had played the role of a woman who could get along with anyone, cope with any situation — how foolish she had been! How naive of her to expect that if she pleased others they'd leave her in peace! For years she had daily looked forward to a new beginning, a new lease of life; all she had hoped for was the night to end and dawn to come, but each new day had been as cruel, as painful as the one before and had added nothing to her wealth of happiness. Was there anything less than nothing? If there was she wasn't aware of it.

She heard Naresh snoring. Come morning, she decided, she would leave. And take her daughters away with her. The woman who might take her place in this household might find the two young girls millstones around her neck and do them some harm. Naresh had already said he wouldn't have to pay maintenance because she had a job. What did women who didn't have jobs do when they were kicked out by their husbands? Go to the poorhouse, live off the charity of relatives? Thank God, she was spared that misfortune.

She came out of her reverie to find Naresh standing in front of her. His face was close to hers and his breath stank to high heavens. Only minutes ago he was asleep and snoring like a pig. Lipi knew what his staring meant, the message was loud and clear. She shrank away in revulsion. Night after night her body had been a prey to his lust. Is this what happened to all women? Didn't their wishes and willingness matter?

Naresh grabbed her hands and pulled her towards him. She spun on her heels, struggling to free herself, but Naresh grabbed the end of her sari. Her husband. Naresh. No, she would have to leave this animal.

She was about to say something when Naresh clamped his hand on her mouth and hissed, 'Don't forget that you're my wife until you've left this house. Until then you'd better obey me. Try disobeying my command and I'll beat the shit out of you.'

She knew better than to call for help. No one would come to her rescue. On the contrary, she would become a laughing stock. She could put up a fight but she didn't have the strength. Ironically, just when she was beginning to find her mental strength she would have to taste her first physical defeat.

She looked at Naresh. He looked more hideous than a primeval monster.

He began to undress her. 'Scared to go out into the dark, eh? Scared to step out of the house, eh? Stay until morning by all means. But till that time you can't rob me of my right over your body, understand?'

She prickled all over. Her eyes fell on the window. The worm-eaten wooden frame had crumbled and the iron grill had been removed. Down below there were heaps of broken glass and clumps of thistle bushes. But anything was better than what Naresh was planning.

She took the plunge.

She felt a million thorns piercing her body.

She felt a sudden weight on her back pushing her down into the bottom of the bushes. A cement bag had tumbled down, she realized. All round her, it was dark, inky dark. But she no longer felt any fear. Nor pain.

Dawn was not far away. Naked, bleeding, she lay and waited for it. Why didn't the cement bag hit me on the head and crush it to a pulp? she wondered. Death would have been infinitely more welcome but then it never came when one most longed for it. She smiled to herself. Maybe I will have a little peace in the remaining days of my life. How wonderful it would be now if I were able to bounce back on my nimble toes like a film heroine and effortlessly scale the boundary wall and escape!

Her eyes began to close. With a mighty effort she rolled over and looked up at the sky, her nails clawing into the earth. The stars shone bright like tiny white flowers. Dawn had been all night coming.

Bijay Prasad Mahapatra

Unseasonal Pineapple

The neighbours, the relatives, and even Mithi's parents, brothers and sisters all seemed to have come to the same conclusion: Mithi would pull through only if her old grandmother died. As days passed with no perceptible deterioration in the old lady's condition, their desperation mounted.

Although nothing was said within earshot of the old lady, she had begun to sense it all. The children had taken to repeating to her every morning: 'Granny, pray to God to put an early end to your suffering!' A couple of days ago the second granddaughter had stopped in the middle of her history lessons and told her: 'Granny, do you know what they did to old people in the olden days? They shoved them into big earthen jars and buried them alive in the fields.' The old lady was shocked: 'Really!' The granddaughter had blithely prattled on: 'Yes. Many jars containing their remains have been excavated...' The grandmother's lips had twisted into a bitter smile: 'That was a wonderful thing to do — to bury the old alive! What else could be done to them if they refused to croak? As a matter of fact, my dear, no human being should be allowed to live to a ripe old age.'

After dinner one night her son and daughter-in-law came and sat with her for awhile. 'Let me give you a massage,' said the daughter-in-law, handing her a tiny paan with just a pinch of tobacco and finely sliced areca nut. Before the old lady could say no, the daughter-in-law had pulled her shrivelled legs onto her lap and begun pressing them gently.

'Are you sleepy, Ma?' her son asked. 'Did you like the pineapple this afternoon? It's not the season for pineapples, you know. It must have been a little sour, wasn't it? Remember you said you craved pineapples?'

'Did I?' The old lady sighed. 'Are you sure I said I craved pineapples?'

'See you've plumb forgotten.'

'Oh, have I? Maybe, maybe. There are so many things one forgets at my age.' She paused. 'Yes, maybe I did say I wanted to eat a slice of pineapple. Now that wish has been fulfilled I hope to quickly pass away.'

'Ma!' The daughter-in-law protested. 'How can you utter such inauspicious words!'

'Daughter-in-law,' the old lady said. 'The life of the old is like a drop of water poised on a yam leaf. Until the last wish is fulfilled, it will not fall off. Have I ever told you what happened to my grandfather-in-law?'

The son and daughter-in-law remained silent.

'He was paralysed and bedridden for a long time. His whole body mushroomed with bedsores. The blood that sometimes came out of his nose and mouth was almost black. He failed to recognize anyone, neither their face nor their voice. Every second hour he drifted into unconsciousness. But he would not die. Often he lay so deathly still that the visitors took him for dead. We'd rush to his bedside and hold a mirror to his nose, and the mirror would take nothing short of an hour to fog over a bit. "Thank God," we'd cry out in mock relief. "The poor dear is alive, praise God!" One day he puckered his lips as if he wished to say something, and an experienced relative commanded us: "Find out his last wish. As long as it remains unfulfilled, he won't breathe his last." His eldest son pressed his ear to the old man's mouth and asked, "Father, what is your last wish? Is there anything you want?" The old man's lips trembled. His son pricked up his ear. "Can't make out a thing," he said, shaking his head. "Perhaps he's asking for a blackberry." The entire area was combed for the fruit, but it was the month of Pausa and not a blackberry was to be found anywhere. Meanwhile the old man refused to die. Pausa passed, Magh passed and then Phalgun — three full months. In the month of Jaistha blackberries ripened, and the day the old man's eldest son brought home some ripe blackberries and put one into his father's mouth, the old man passed away. He didn't even wait to swallow the ˜ruit.'

The old lady fell silent. She was fast asleep. The daughter-in-law removed her feet from her lap and the son drew the sheet up to her neck. Then they tiptoed out of the room, like two dispirited cockroaches.

Mithi lay in the next room shrivelled up like a sick kitten. She was eighteen, but who would believe that. She was just a bag of bones. Her mother often sobbed into the end of her sari: 'What sin did I commit in my last life? Whose household did I destroy, whose food did I poison? Why is my grown-up daughter, who should be in the full bloom of youth, reduced to skin and bones?'

That was how it was — young Mithi in one room, her old grandmother in another, both dreadfully sick. The old lady's son wondered how long his mother would survive, whether she'd quickly pass away, now that she had had a slice of pineapple. Maybe it was time for the proverbial drop of water to fall off the yam leaf.

The daughter-in-law tiptoed into the room and stealthily held a mirror to the old lady's nostrils. The mirror misted up.

One more day had passed. Would Mithi pull through another day? With both her kidneys failing, her days were numbered; each passing day only made it worse. A transplant was possible, though as a last resort. The chances of survival had been left to the patient's luck.

'How much will it cost?' they had asked the doctor.

'Money is not important,' the doctor had replied. 'First get hold of a kidney. If someone's willing to donate one, we could carry out the operation right away. If Mithi is lucky, her system may not reject the transplant.'

But a kidney was not like hair or nails for which there would be eager donors. Hair and nails grow back in again, but not a kidney. Mithi's father, mother, sisters and brother had all backed away.

'If no one's willing to donate a kidney,' the doctor had said in the end, 'take Mithi home. Leave her to her fate. Meanwhile keep a lookout and let us know when an old person dies or someone meets with a fatal accident. It'll be worth trying a kidney transplant. It'll be an experiment, of course. If Mithi's luck holds...' Teary-eyed, the parents had brought Mithi home.

Back home, they went into the old woman's room, silent, grim, and dark with despair.

'How's Mithi?' the old lady enquired. 'What do the doctors say?'

'Her kidneys have failed,' the daughter-in-law said. 'If someone is willing to donate a kidney, the doctors might try a transplant. I offered to give her one of mine, but your son put his foot down. The children are too young and need a mother to look after them, he said. Then he offered one of his and I said no. He's the only breadearner in the family. That left the children. How could we have the heart to ask one of them for a kidney? They have their entire lives ahead of them.'

They sat in silence for a while.

'Why don't you take one of mine?' the old lady asked.

The daughter-in-law sniffled. 'Ma, you're so ill yourself. You wouldn't survive a kidney removal. Besides we're not so shameless that we'd broach the idea with the doctor. But they said they can remove a kidney from somebody who passes away, within two hours of death. There's no certainty the transplant would work, but it'd be worth a try.'

They sat in silence again.

'Don't worry, daughter-in-law,' the old lady said. 'I'm a dry leaf liable to fall off at any moment. Alive today, gone tomorrow. May my years be added to Mithi's!'

They looked at her — the dry leaf on whom Mithi's life depended. Should it fall soon, Mithi would get well. But who can tell how long it takes a dry leaf to fall? Would Mithi survive until then? They saw the gaunt old lady as their only hope. Everything was in her hands. If she earnestly desired she could pass away that very moment, and Mithi would be up the next, hale and hearty, very much the eldest daughter of the family whose every footstep had once put the blooming lotus to shame.

The night passed and the next morning the old lady awoke and looked around. The young grandchildren had surrounded her.

'Granny, pray. Pray to God that He may take you soon.'

She looked at them with a twinge of guilt. Why hadn't she passed away during the night? Why did she have to wake up alive this morning? She had had her slice of pineapple, she had had everything she craved. Why wasn't she dead? Maybe tomorrow the children would ask her the reason. What answer would she give them?

Her son came in and stood by her bedside, his face drawn.

'These godforsaken oldsters!' the old lady said, hoping that everyone around heard her. 'Their life is like a water drop on a yam leaf. Until their wishes are fulfilled they'll stick around. Did I ever tell you what happened to my grandfather-in-law?...'

They left her alone.

In the evening the son came home with another unseasonal pineapple. 'Ma, remember you said you wanted a slice of pineapple?'

The old lady's eyes filled with tears. 'That's right,' she said, picking up a slice. The daughter-in-law had seasoned it with salt and chilli powder. Her grandfather-in-law had waited until he had a blackberry. Maybe she was waiting for this second helping of pineapple, and now that she had it she had no right to tarry longer. She should pass on right away.

Next morning she awoke with the children crowding around her and was filled with remorse. 'I want to see Mithi,' she said with tears in her eyes. 'I want to see how she's doing.'

'There's nothing to see, Ma,' the son said. 'Mithi's no longer the girl you once knew.'

But the old lady insisted, and in the end her son picked her up from the bed and carried her to Mithi's room.

Mithi opened her eyes and looked at her grandmother. They smiled at each other.

'Now you may take me back,' the old lady said. 'I wanted to see her just once. Now I'm satisfied. Put me back in my bed.'

At ten o'clock, when her son was ready to go to his office, the old woman called her daughter-in-law. 'Has Nilambar already left for the office? Tell him to get me some palm fruit kernel if he can.'

The son and daughter-in-law looked at each other. Nilambar's eyes became moist.

'Where'll I get palm fruit kernel now? It's out of season.'

But as he stepped out of his house, he was determined that no matter what, he would get the palm fruit kernel somewhere.

He turned up at home unexpectedly at noon.

His wife opened the door. 'What's the matter? Why have you come back at this odd hour?'

Then she noticed the palm-leaf packet in his hand.

'Got it?'

Nilambar nodded. 'I had to ask our peon Dina to cycle down to his village and get me some. This isn't the season for it, you know.'

Together they hurried to the old lady's room.

'Ma,' the daughter-in-law said. 'Wake up and see. You wanted palm kernel, didn't you? Your son has got you some. Eat them up before they harden.'

The old lady did not respond. The water on the yam leaf had dropped off at last.

Pratibha Ray

The Stigma

Sarami was seized with a shameful bout of hysteria yet again. She clenched her fists, flung her legs about obscenely, rolled her head and yanked out her hair, shook her body and stuck out her tongue, threw her sari off her breasts. One moment she lay limp, exhausted, her eyes closed and the next she was up, fiercely rolling her eyes, hissing like a snake and frothing at the mouth. It took four or five stout young fellows to restrain her. Alternately she laughed like a shameless hussy and wept like a wretched waif. Sad like a silent grey afternoon one minute and riotous like a crazy sunset the next. Then the spell was over just as suddenly as it had begun.

Except for these periodic bouts, Sarami was every inch the typical shy bride, sensitive like a mimosa creeper. She never revealed herself, neither her moon-like face from behind her veil, nor her mind. The ankle chains she wore on her reddened feet tinkled ever so faintly when she tiptoed around. She was so gentle, so serene, so unruffled that she often resembled a sculpted image. It was of course quite another matter that despite her damnedest efforts to smother her youthful figure under layers of clothes, her voluptuousness was apparent. Her brother-in-law devoured her with his eyes; even Sudam, the young unmarried nephew of her husband, unabashedly ogled her, mentally mapping her exciting contours. When a lovely flower blooms in somebody's garden, it belongs to the garden owner but don't others get to feast their eyes on it and inhale its fragrance? The same held true for Sarami: she might have been Raghu Tiadi's wife but there was no earthly reason why others could not appreciate her beauty or flirt with her a little. It was accepted social behaviour that a young brother-in-law could banter and take some verbal liberties with the new bride in the house. Even if Raghu Tiadi didn't like the idea, he would have to put up with it. To think that in the beginning he had even tried to shield his wife from Sudam, his nephew, the orphan of his own elder brother! Hadn't he raised him since he was a little boy? If Raghu's first wife had borne him a son instead of a daughter the son would have been the same age as Sudam! What evil stars! The wife passed away in childbirth and the girl grew up, got married and had three girls herself. It had dealt a blow to Raghu's pride to be a grandfather to not one but three young girls. His second wife was a shade better: she bore three sons, but God alone knows what sins she had committed that she and her sons should have died when the evil goddess of smallpox visited the family. Sudam's father too fell to the scourge. Raghu's stars were bright, maybe he had the benefit of accumulated merit from previous births; he managed to claw back from the jaws of death, though losing an eye and developing a game-leg in the process. And of course plenty of tell-tale pockmarks on his handsome face. Young Sudam and his mother were away at his maternal uncle's place and had thus escaped unscathed. The mother had lived a long life and had died only two years ago.

True, Raghu Tiadi had lost an eye and his good looks, as well as his erect gait, but he had not altogether been robbed of his manhood. He had the grave responsibility of preserving the family line from extinction. Sudam, already on the threshold of adulthood, could have been trusted to keep the line alive but Raghu Tiadi couldn't bear the thought that his name would be completely wiped out. No wonder he had seriously toyed with the idea of a third marriage. His well-wishers too had egged him on, and a search was mounted to hunt for young brides for both the uncle and the nephew. Regardless of the difference in age both wanted young girls, and nubile young things were not exactly in short supply. But there weren't many from respectable, well-to-do families. And what did sweet sixteens from poor families amount to — nothing! Sudam had made it clear that he had no qualms about tying the knot with a girl short on looks but long on dowry. Paragons of virtue and beauty from humble homes could try their luck elsewhere. Why take on the eminently avoidable responsibility of providing food, clothing, jewellery, children and conjugal bliss to a girl from a poor family! There was only one way out for a good-looking girl from a poor family: she could escape the curse of spinsterhood by hoping to be accepted as a second or third wife of some doddering old man.

When the matchmakers brought a proposal for Sarami, both Sudam and Raghu Tiadi went to inspect the prospective bride. Sudam took a shine to the girl but not to her father, who was as poor as a church mouse. Flowers and fruit were all such a man could offer as dowry. Agree to the match? No way. The girl had great looks, but so what? Her father didn't have enough money, he could never come to the son-in-law's rescue in his hour of need, and what's a father-in-law if he couldn't do that? Neither Sudam nor his uncle could give the go-ahead.

Sarami's father, who was blessed with not one but three millstones around his neck (grown girls were, proverbially, worse than fire, one never knew when they'd burn the good name of the family to cinders), grasped Raghu Tiadi's hands and begged: 'Gosain, you're a big man. You command respect in ten neighbouring villages. Surely you do not lack for anything that you too will look for a dowry to fill your house! Please accept my daughter as your wife and I'll remain eternally grateful to you. You will be doing a good turn, for which the gods will reward you. My daughter has strong stars in her horoscope and she will bring prosperity to whichever home she goes.'

Raghu Tiadi was not easy to melt — he had heard enough spiels and sales pitch before — but a lingering look at the exquisite face of the girl touched a chord in his heart. On a sudden impulse he consented, and the wedding date was fixed on the spot. Sarami's eyes briefly met Sudam's. There was a flutter of gratitude in hers but all Sudam's piercing gaze held was the hint of an erotic welcome.

'Aunt,' he gushed, only a few days after the wedding, 'aren't you breathtakingly beautiful! The aunts before you were not equal to your toes! Uncle is one lucky man!' The new aunt had looked into the nephew's eyes: was he being facetious? A bitter question flashed through her mind: What about your new aunt's luck? Or are girls from poor families not supposed to have any? But her face remained as serene and her lips as tightly shut as ever. It was her first lesson in deceit in her husband's place and in the days ahead she would need it aplenty. She would have to learn to stifle her innate candour, honesty of opinion and easy and open manners. She was an aunt to Sudam and must continue as such, and as nothing else, in the young man's eyes. He could afford to behave like a lecher; society wouldn't condemn a man as much as a woman. One little scandal and Sarami would be handed a one-way ticket to purgatory; no amount of penance would absolve her of her crime.

Sudam married shortly afterwards and got a fat dowry. He kept it all but sent his wife back to her parents before the year was out. Obviously she wasn't as handsome as the dowry: she was toothy, squint-eyed, pitch-dark and loud-mouthed. 'Display one girl and palm off another? They dare do this to me?' was what Sudam alleged. God alone knew the truth. Not long afterwards he married again. His second wife was not half as beautiful as Sarami, although in a matter of speaking, quite nicely put together, but that hardly mattered anyway, for a few days after the wedding she drowned in the family pond. No one knew whether it was an accident or suicide. Evidently Sudam wasn't lucky in marriage. Nonetheless there was no dearth of girls, and the young man was still in his prime.

Meanwhile it warmed Raghu Tiadi's heart no end that his nephew had taken to his wife regardless of her aloofness and unmistakable display of annoyance. Of late she had badgered her husband one time too many: 'Why don't you break with Sudam? Just because I'm around to work myself to death and keep the house, the fellow doesn't seem to bother whether his wives live or die, stay or leave. I can't be expected to look after him forever. In the future our own family will grow...'

Raghu Tiadi turned a deaf ear. Weren't women proverbial house-wreckers? Why start worrying before the family has expanded? Cross that bridge only when you come to it. Moreover Sudam wouldn't be without a wife for long. His horoscope indicated a bad patch for three years but after that everything would be all right. Split with a nephew? No way, a nephew was as good as a son. The trouble was that Sarami was not prepared to look upon Sudam as one. Petty, jealous, selfish woman! Take Sudam. He never complained about his aunt. On the contrary, her name was on his lips all the time. Ten words from him would fetch a monosyllabic reply from her. Never once did she pull the sari off her head and show him her moon-face. Why be so stiff, so standoffish? After all she was his aunt, wasn't she, although some seven or eight years younger? And wasn't an aunt the same thing as a mother? Besides Sudam was such a help. What would Raghu Tiadi do without him? He was freed from everyday cares and anxieties only because of this young man, who looked after the land and farming, the farmhands and harvests; he made it possible for the old man to devote his time to worship, adjudication meetings, teaching Sanskrit, and reciting scriptures. Raghunath Tripathy, alias Raghu Tiadi, was a learned person who had a name in society; people stepped back when he passed by. Wasn't Sarami a lucky woman to have become his wife? What did it matter whether she was the third or the fourth? She must thank the good karma of her previous births.

A woman's good fortune was judged by the social standing of her husband, the amount of jewellery she could laden herself with, the quality of food she ate, the weave of the clothes she wore — her state of mind, happiness, emotional fulfillment, wishes all counted for nothing. Better that way, otherwise poor Sarami would have chosen to drown herself. She had learnt not to reflect, not to mull things over, not to dwell on her condition; she had painfully acquired the habit of not thinking too much about herself. The abyss of darkness within her was fathomless and frightening. Sometimes she wondered what would happen to her if she lost her looks and turned into an ugly toad. Anything could happen. As long as she lived with her parents a fire had been in her stomach, but ever since she moved into her husband's home it had moved to her heart. The fire in the belly could be extinguished with food, but neither food nor clothes nor jewellery could douse the flames in her heart. On the contrary, the tongues leapt higher and higher. Sarami would gaze at herself, her beautiful body in an exquisite sari and bedecked with jewellery and her face would darken with anguish.

She had everything, yes she had everything she wanted. Raghu Tiadi never denied his wife the good things. To say that she was virtually like a queen was no exaggeration. Nobody ever caught Raghu Tiadi being harsh to her. As the saying goes, he kept her on a pedestal. If despite all this she wasn't happy, she had no one but herself to blame. Admittedly Raghu Tiadi was a lot older and had lost his looks because of smallpox, but that didn't mean he was any less a man. Why, he was in the pink of health, his manliness undiminished. Although he favoured his game leg, the ground literally shook when he walked. His emergence from his doorway — lines of shining sandal paste across the wide forehead beneath his bald dome — reminded many of Lord Jagannath's pahandi during his ceremonial chariot ride. He had successfully impregnated his young wife not once but twice, and in quick succession too; the blighted woman had only herself to blame for the miscarriages; they were no reflection on Raghu Tiadi's masculinity. Yes, yes, Sarami was squarely to blame. Particularly when there was no comfort under the sun that she lacked — she had plenty of food, clothes, jewellery! Perhaps all that had made her too lazy to even hold on to the foetus in her womb. Whereas her own poor mother, waging a daily battle against hunger and poverty, had ritually delivered babies every second year until she finally dried up, Sarami, on the other hand, had become too pampered in her husband's home. Even she herself sometimes tended to agree with this view. How she wished she had had two or three children! Then there would have been no free time to look into the depths of her soul. Everyday cares would have ensured that life pass faster and the hungry looks, the suggestive gestures, the audacious flirtations of her brother-in-law Dibakar and nephew-in-law Sudam wouldn't have troubled her so much.

To think one time she had nearly married Dibakar! The match had come unstuck at the last moment because her father could not scrape up the two thousand rupees Dibakar had demanded. The same fellow who had rejected her for the blessed money was now so full of love for her, the scoundrel!

But no matter how hard she steeled herself, how rudely she behaved towards Dibakar and Sudam, she couldn't hide from herself that she secretly relished the advances of the young wastrels. Sometimes when she served Sudam food, the fellow made a point of grasping her hands to say 'Enough, enough, aunt!' and although she jerked her hands free and scolded him sternly 'Why do you have to grab my hands? It's enough if you speak. I can still hear very well', she did feel giddy and delirious at the touch, her face aflame, her heart pounding away like a husking paddle. 'My dear lovely aunt,' Sudam would flirt outrageously, 'I'm forced to hold your lovely hands because I'm afraid my words don't ever enter your beautiful ears!' Sarami would shriek, a flaming snake of desire slithering inside her entrails, 'There's God above, Sudam. He's watching. You're going over the limits of decency. An aunt is like a mother.' Sudam would burst into a guffaw: 'You wouldn't have become my aunt if your poor father had been able to scrape up a good dowry. Don't think I didn't notice the look in your eyes the day Uncle and I turned up at your place to see you. Don't tell me you didn't feel attracted toward me, that you didn't find me desirable. Listen, ours is a quiet household and there's no one around to spy on us. It's an open secret that you don't get enough physical satisfaction from your husband.'

Turning crimson as much from anger as from contempt, Sarami would rush into her bedroom, slam the door and throw herself on the bed, sobbing convulsively. A wild desire to spit Sudam in the face would seize her. When it was a question of marriage the fellow hadn't thought twice before rejecting her, but now he was so eager to start an affair! He might come to no harm but what would happen to her? Society would denounce her as an immoral bitch, a whore, a sinner. But who could she tell all this to? Once or twice she had tried to tell her husband ever so subtly, but the old man had retorted, fixing her with a hard, one-eyed stare, 'Don't ever talk against our innocent Sudam. If he wanted to have you for himself he could have had got you on a platter. What was there to prevent him from marrying you? Remember, I decided to step in only after he had turned you down. How can you insinuate these things against him?'

More than Sudam it was Raghu Tiadi who was responsible for her unenviable plight. He had damned her by his kindness. Surely her father could have found a young man for her, even if only from a nondescript family. She would no doubt have had a tougher life, maybe she would have had to work like a donkey, but anything was better than the kind of deprivation she was condemned to. Raghu Tiadi could give her the moon but not the physical bliss and pleasure for which she ached and ached no end. Their cohabitation was and would always remain an act of deceit, a sham, a pain. On the other hand, although with one part of her mind she hated Sudam and Dibakar, with another she feasted her eyes on their handsome, muscular physiques. A stray touch sent her pulse racing wildly, her heart beating furiously. Sometimes when Dibakar playfully tugged at the end of her sari she was scared she might swoon; she could hardly speak, she stuttered, stammered, became tongue-tied. True, she was able to fend off their advances but could she dam the surging tides of desire and passion in her heart? When her marriage with Raghu Tiadi was being finalized, her parents should have realized that the man was old enough to be her father and could give her no physical satisfaction. But did they give it a thought? Raghu Tiadi too should have given it one. But did he? All of society should have protested against the mismatch. But did it? And now there were the likes of Dibakar and Sudam hovering around her to take full advantage of it. How they ogled her and propositioned her at every turn! Leave alone the most virtuous woman, if you work on a goddess ceaselessly, sooner or later she'll give in — it's as simple as that. In fact, the deeper the need the faster the opposition ended, sweeping aside the barricades of taboos society artfully clamped on relationships between a sister-in-law and a brother-in-law, an aunt and a nephew, and between cousins. Swept away like dry leaves in a torrent. Hunger made a person lose all sense of morality, drove him to beg crumbs from any source, compelled him to leftovers on the sly. No matter what little saints, holy men, sati Savitris people posed as, deep inside they were tormented souls on fire. Hungry, tormented souls, driven by lust.

There were examples galore, many of them from that very village. Similar events might well have occurred elsewhere, in other villages as well. Nothing under the sun can remain forever under wraps. Yet the ones who ate the forbidden food nonchalantly wiped their lips and continued to pretend they were holier-than-thou, purer than the sacred waters of the Ganges, more sacrosanct than the consecrated prasad of the gods. Many clandestine affairs were embarked upon. Take the relationship between a man and his wife's sister, for example, or between a woman and her husband's brother, or between a woman and her godbrother. On the outside it was all very prim and proper, very correct, with just a whiff of flirtation maybe but nothing discordant, displeasing to the eyes, but inside it was all body. Something society was only too well aware of. At times the body drove one so crazy that he or she broke even bigger taboos. Perhaps, in the ultimate analysis, there was only one relationship which remained beyond the pale of corruption — the relation between a mother and her child. Everything else could prove rotten, even the relation between a father and a daughter, oh the shame of it! Man was nothing if not an animal underneath his clothes. Not long ago in this neighbourhood one wretched girl had chosen to hang herself because of the persistent attentions of her own father. There was a clandestine affair between a widowed aunt and her nephew which produced a child, whose dead body was discovered under the screwpine bushes at the edge of the village. In another incident, a man split open the skull of his brother because of the brother's carryings-on with his wife. For many a woman the loving attention of their devoted godbrothers had taken the sting out of their long separations from their husbands, who had to remain away from home on work. There were many, many more instances. But not a ripple on the surface — all was very placid, fine, within bounds.

Sarami was not the only one of her kind in the village — there were quite a few second and third wives, and none of them badly off either; in fact, they lived quite happily with their decrepit husbands, who were also dark and ugly into the bargain. How outrageously they flaunted their clothes, jewellery, authority and offspring! But were they really happy? Didn't they have regrets? How was it that not a shadow of their internal turmoil showed on their faces? How did they manage to look so serene, calm, collected? What were they made of — flesh and blood, or wood, stone and metal? Where had they put their minds — in a cave? And shut the mouth of the cave with a slab of stone? Did their bodies clamour for nothing besides food, clothes and jewellery? That was hard to accept. Why, Sarami was afraid that her mind and body were ready to betray her at the slightest provocation. How her mind yearned, hungered, lusted! Were there any tricks to wish one's mind away?

If only she could ask those women on the quiet, 'Do you really find the social canons as sacred as the scriptures? Don't you ever feel tempted to break them? Don't you ever feel tormented? How do you manage to put on such serene expressions? If you are above all torment, what's the secret?' But she knew she could never bring herself to ask these questions. She could do so only at the risk of revealing herself, rendering herself vulnerable to tongue-wagging. The whole village would be abuzz with gossip: Sarami's got a filthy mind; all she ever thinks of is sex; she can't be too far from the path of adultery and infidelity. Without committing any wrong she would be roundly condemned as a whore, a sinner and an immoral woman, her reputation in tatters. Just as society sometimes dismissed the truth as idle gossip it could seize a rumour and hammer it into a truth. Truth and rumour were like two sides of the same coin, and how quickly both travelled through the air! Better to keep her thoughts to herself. Thank God, thoughts were invisible. What total chaos there would have been otherwise! Would it ever have been possible to maintain even one perfect relationship, be it between a man and his wife or between a sister-in-law and a brother-in-law, or between cousins? All of society would be turned on its head. The flaming red vermilion dot on a woman's forehead was only a facade; she sinned enough in her mind to be damned to perdition until the end of eternity.

Sarami's self-flagellation often left her mind lacerated and badly bloodied. Her conscience was like a shark-tail whip — sharp, thorny, stinging. Ultimately that was what kept an affair away, though starting one or even several at the same time would have been terribly easy. A lonely house, the quiet afternoons; a deserted back yard, the dark evenings. She could get as many men as she wanted. A tiny nod from her and droves of brothers-in-law, nephews-in-law, uncles-in-law, stiff-lipped village elders, pontificating priests, stern-faced guardians of morals, men of high principles would have descended on her back yard, barnyard, pond-bank, cowshed, seeking trysts; and no one would have been the wiser. They could come and go, each at his appointed hour, without bumping into one another. There wouldn't have been a blot on their reputation. Not a blot on Raghu Tiadi's either. And of course Sarami's virtue would be left as dazzlingly bright as ever. Everything would continue smoothly, just as the hidden lives of all others did. But who prevented her? Who stopped her from crossing the strait of morality and fidelity? Sometimes she suspected that even her revered lord and master too was encouraging her to stray from the straight and narrow path. Why else did he leave a young and beautiful wife alone in the house under the care of a virile young nephew and stay away for days on end on the pretext of arbitrating disputes, giving scholarly advice and what not? Didn't a worldly-wise man like him know the consequences? Sudam might be his nephew, his blood relation, but he was nothing to Sarami. A little change in the script and the young hound could well have become her husband. A towering rage would possess her at times — a rage directed as much against herself as against her parents, her husband, society, the gods, everyone; her tortured soul sometimes taunted her to go whoring around to her heart's content. But a stern voice from within would stop her — what was it, her ego, her samskara, her notions of self-respect, her ideals of perfect womanhood? Adultery, she knew, was like a bowl of borrowed curry — good enough only for a gulp or two, it could never amount to a square meal. It would never fully sate her appetite, but leave her reputation in the mud. Even if it remained under wraps, she would never be able to hold her head high the rest of her life, forever ashamed to face herself.

But those who erred the most, those who made a profession of seducing and bedding women other than their wives, were the first to vilify an erring woman: 'There goes the adulterous whore, pity her poor husband!' Sarami could never in her dreams bring herself to be reviled by these lowlifes. Even Sudam, who never ceased his broad hints, was scared of her. One frown from her petrified him into a block of wood. If she gave in to the temptations of her flesh even once, this very same Sudam would start treating her like a doormat. Once he was past the first flush of the fling he would seize every opportunity to rub her infidelity in. Life would become intolerable.

In fact, although her physical craving was as deep as an ocean, her mental resolve was as hard as a mountain. One pitted against the other in a no-holds-barred fight; no quarter given nor expected. Sarami was a battle-scarred ground.

Just as the molten fire in the womb of the earth sometimes flares — the fiercer the fire the greater the intensity of the tremor — and breaks free, spitting smoke, lava and ash, burying green vegetation, ruining nature, underlining its own ugliness, so too the repressed sexual desires smouldering within Sarami would sometimes erupt like a volcano. It was then that she went into sobbing hysterics, uncontrollably, unpredictably. Raghu Tiadi, with his slack, ageing muscles and slothful manhood, completely failed to rein her in and would steal away like a thief into the farthest corner of his verandah, subdued, crestfallen, morose, his copper-coloured face turning bitter black, ruing the day he had wedded a girl who was to bring him shame one day.

When Sarami was in the grip of hysteria, even the entire womenfolk of the neighbourhood could not curb her. It took five or six stout, strong-bodied hunks to pin her to the ground, their eager hands groping, probing, squeezing, caressing, assuaging her body. After the spell passed, she would sit up, chastened, her face back behind her veil, biting her tongue in regret. Much as her blood boiled at the sight of the lusty young fellows crowding around her like vultures around a carcass, she had only herself to blame for making a spectacle of herself. What evil spirit had gotten into her and prodded her into such a shameless show!

In the beginning Raghu Tiadi and the relatives thought that perhaps an evil spirit had temporarily possessed Sarami or a sorcerer had cast a spell on her. Some said it could be acute stomach ache or some kind of extreme physical pain. But Sarami didn't respond to any cure — neither medicine nor exorcism. The doctors proved as helpless as the exorcists. In the end, people came to only one conclusion: 'The girl is shamming! Can't you see how quickly her pain vanishes once four or six young men hold her down? What does that mean? She's dying for you-know-what, the bitch, the immoral bitch! Poor Raghu Tiadi, he brought shame on himself by marrying a third time. But a wife who isn't satisfied with her lawfully wedded husband, be he old, ugly or pockmarked, is a whore to the core.'

Sarami couldn't prevent tongues from wagging. The only way out was to stop having hysterical fits, but that was something over which she had no control. The bouts came over her with embarrassing regularity, sometimes three or four times a month, in spite of having hardened her mind to stone. The stronger her resolve, the more determined her efforts to avert her eyes from men who made eyes at her, the more intense her afflictions. The very young men she kept at bay were the ones to feel, fondle, caress and squeeze her back to her senses. Could she ever tell them the truth? Why couldn't she keep her mind in check? Why was the mind so devious?

Time passed — weeks, months, years, decades; and Sarami's afflictions lessened and then suddenly disappeared altogether. She became normal. Her life became normal. In due course she became a mother, then a mother-in-law, and finally a grandmother. But the scandal of her youthful disgrace was not entirely forgotten or forgiven. Sometimes when there were quarrels, the relatives and neighbours did not shy away from rubbing it in. Sarami couldn't answer back, for she indeed had had that horrible disease when she was newly married.

The other day when the young second wife of old Manu Rath was wallowing in the grip of hysteria, the whole village turned up to witness the drama. Four or five hefty young fellows were told to hold her down. That's what she needs, the immoral bitch, people openly commented. Poor Manu Rath's fair name was in the mud.

Sarami, old, bent, shrivelled, stood a little straighter, as if to get a kink out of her back, and looked around. She knew them — the ones who had their saris over their heads and easy judgements on their eager lips. She knew them all inside out, the depth and extent of their chastity and fidelity, or rather the lack of it. Gathered here to castigate Manu Rath's wife, eh? That was a crime in Sarami's eyes. If it was a crime on the part of a young woman not to be satisfied with her old, decrepit husband, it was a bigger crime to expose her sad failing in public.

'Listen you all!' She faced the crowd, her brittle voice catching from rage. 'The young woman here is suffering from an abominable affliction. Pity her by all means, but give her the respect she deserves. Praise her for her conviction, for she didn't give up the principles of chastity and fidelity and rush to seek solace in clandestine affairs. That's why the fire within her drives her crazy sometimes. There are many women present here who took the easy way out to douse their fires, but not this poor girl. She did not want to open her doors to other men and keep pretending she was as virtuous as a Sita or a Savitri. You dare denounce her just because she didn't? Come on, ladies, come, come my pretties, my beauties, come and swear on the heads of your husbands and sons that not a single dirty thought ever flitted across your minds!'

She paused and added, 'Society is cruel to women. Like cattle, girls are given away to old men against their wishes. They have no say in the selection of their mates. Why? Don't women have minds? Are they all body and no mind? Have they been made only to eat, work and bear children? Yes, the body can be satisfied, but not the mind. And a dissatisfied mind can never extinguish the fire raging within. So in the end it's society which compels a woman to acts of immorality. A few who decide not to fall from their convictions convulse occasionally like this girl here. All you Sitas, all you Savitris, all you virtuous whores — have you no pity that you dare assemble here to castigate this poor little thing? Why are you so eager, so enthusiastic to witness her shameful plight? Get going. Go away. Leave before I give out all your dirty little secrets. Do you think old Sarami doesn't know what each of you has been up to?'

The women were hushed. The contempt in Sarami's old withered face was as dark and dense as their hidden sins.

The poor young wife of Manu Rath lay like a wick burnt from end to end — alone, away from the crowd, aloof as it were from society itself. Sarami hobbled over to her and sat down by her side. With her dry, decrepit, wrinkled hands she gently wiped the stains of the stigma from the forehead of the young woman. But could she be rid of a stigma for a sin she had never committed in the first place?

Ramachandra Behera

The Cage

That was the year the bear menace had reached new heights in our area. A student in the lower primary school at the time, I, along with my father visited the town zoo, said to be the biggest in the country. The bears had wrought havoc on the sugarcane fields in our village; worse still, they had attacked and maimed several poor woodcutters in the forest. And since ours was the only well-to-do family in the area, my father was practically forced by the neighbours into buying a gun. Of course for a long time Father couldn't think of it, but then the bears became truly unbearable, and the last bastion of Father's resistance fell when half a dozen of them banqueted on our sugarcane field one night. The next morning Father went to town to buy himself a gun and since I had created a fuss he took me along. That was how I got to see the biggest zoo in the country.

I folded the newspaper I was reading and dropped it beside me on the sofa. It was almost ten. Mahendra was still closeted in the toilet. Three days had passed since we had come to town, and we had already seen all the places worth seeing except the zoo. We had saved it for the end. Then we would get back to the college both Mahendra and I had recently joined as lecturers. The visit to the zoo was to be the culmination of our little holiday. And now

Mahendra was taking too long in the shower and I was getting bored.

I picked up the paper again and quickly glanced at it. Suddenly I remembered something that got me laughing so much I began to perspire, tears in my eyes and a knot in my stomach. I couldn't remember ever having had such a fit of prolonged laughter. How many years had passed since the incident? I wondered. Father bought his gun, we visited the zoo and returned home. Overnight I had become a kind of hero in the eyes of my village friends. Inspired by their wide-eyed wonder and curiosity, I spun innumerable yarns: for a thirty-paisa ticket you could sit on a lion or a tiger and take a ride around the zoo. Didn't they bite you? Of course not! I answered airily, moving my hand over my body as though I was rubbing oil into it. Come closer and take a look, do I have any toothmarks on me? Well, I rode a lion for ten minutes. Not only that, I held an ice cream stick in one hand during the ride. What's an ice cream — a lion cub? I laughed and laughed. Oh God, what fools! I could even have bought a lion cub, only Father said I couldn't have one until I finished school. You're one hell of a lucky fellow, my friends commented, but look at our fathers, they are such bloody cowards, they are so scared of bears, what would happen if they had to chase lions and tigers!

As I recollected all this now, a sense of anguish clouded my mind. Where had my childhood gone? Where had those days vanished to, when every word you heard or spoke was true? How wonderful the world was then — there was nothing that strained your belief. Everything was real, and nothing was impossible; no barriers to what you could believe. Now you couldn't tell such innocent lies; even if you did, the thrill would be missing and you might even feel a little guilty. What changes the years had wrought!

'Wake up,' said Mahendra, breaking my reverie. 'We're late.'

We locked the room. Mahendra tugged at the lock several times to make sure it was secure. Never depend on anyone was his cardinal principle.

'We'll take a bus to the zoo,' I said, as we went down the stairs.

'This hopping in and out of taxis should stop. You've got to board crowded buses to know the soul of a city.'

'What did you say — go by bus?' Mahendra turned up his nose. 'Do gentlemen go about in buses in this horrible city? The buses are full of criminals and diseases of every kind.' And after a pause he added, 'I've put on clean clothes, damn it. I don't want them spoiled.'

Clean clothes had nothing to do with a visit to the zoo. At least I could see no connection between the two, but I did not complain. Mahendra waved down a taxi and gave him the directions. We were at the zoo in fifteen minutes.

The place looked the same, unchanged. What I saw now was what I had seen years ago when I was a child. Nothing out of place. The same clear demarcations, the same boundary walls, perhaps the same trees and gardens, and even the same roads. The lake, the rivulet, the birds, the animals were the very same. But an overwhelming feeling of sadness crept over me.

There were cages and cages everywhere. So many prisons. Everyone in its own cell — from beautiful birds to tigers, from lions to reptiles. Buy a ticket and see the animals you might never have seen before.

But why was I so sad all of a sudden? Why did the cages dampen my spirits? The animals I had seen when I was a child must have died in these cages, and the animals I was seeing today were perhaps the offspring of those others long dead. Born in captivity, they would die in captivity — their life, as everyone else's anywhere, was cramped between the milestones of birth and death.

It was only two in the afternoon, but I was dead tired already. Mahendra kept up chatter about God knows what, but I could respond only with a desultory yes or no.

'Let's have tea,' I said. 'I'm very tired.'

Mahendra agreed and we walked to the zoo restaurant, which was already full. It was while we were having tea that the incident occurred.

The sirens suddenly started wailing. Before we could understand what was happening, we found the bearers throwing down the plates and glasses and running for their lives. Droves of sightseers ran every which way. The restaurant phone rang. 'Come on inside,' someone shouted. 'A lioness has escaped from her cage.'

We shot out of our chairs. The tables overturned, the cups and plates clattered down to the floor. Over the public address system came waves of frantic announcements: 'Climb the trees. Or swim into the middle of the lake, or get into a house. There's a lioness at large.'

There were hundreds of us inside the restaurant already. It was suffocating. People thumped on the door from outside. 'Go away,' someone beside me said. 'There's no room in here. Go climb the trees.' More pounding on the door. Desperate cries. And the same old answer: 'No room inside!'

What an incredible change within minutes! Outside, all had gone quiet with anxiety. As though a terrible force of destruction was suddenly looming from somewhere and confronting this tiny globe of ours.

I looked up at Mahendra and nearly burst out laughing. He was pale, drained of blood, his clothes crumpled and dripping with sweat.

'What the hell are you smirking at?' he said, irritated. 'Don't these zoo buggers have any sense? A bloody hungry beast is on the prowl and instead of pumping a bullet into it the buggers are asking people to climb trees or jump into the lake! The bastards are playing with our lives!'

There was a strange cacophony of shouts and screams, of wailing and weeping, with snatches of Hindi film songs issuing from the restaurant radio all the while. The crowd was tense. Who's playing with whose lives? I wondered to myself. The lioness with human lives, or humans with hers? Whose life is more precious? But I remained silent. The pitiable condition of the people around me was highly amusing.

Over the public address system came the announcement: 'Beware, the lioness is heading towards the restaurant. The zoo authorities are taking steps to shoot it.'

A hush fell over the crowd; the fear of death stole over their faces. One could hear their heavy breathing.

'Look, look,' said someone. 'It's coming this way.'

Standing near the window, we looked out and saw a tired and emaciated lioness walking slowly towards the restaurant. Was this the mighty beast of the jungle? We all tried to inch away from the window.

About fifteen metres from the restaurant the lioness stopped and squatted on her haunches, facing us. What was she thinking then — that she was the mistress of all she surveyed? Was she? Was she free? Had her ancestors belonged here? Or did she have nothing to do with it?

But looking at her, I wondered at the sudden reversal of roles. Until a few minutes ago she was in and we were out. Now we were in and she was out, and she watched us, hundreds of people in a cage. She in, we out; she out, we in. What a strange predicament! I tried but couldn't find words to express my feelings to Mahendra.

Then it occurred to me that the zoo authorities were trying to shoot the lioness, and strangely enough I felt quite agitated. Poor thing, she'd now pay with her life for having transgressed her limits, for having forgotten her captivity, for having desired what was forbidden. The cage was her heaven — her haven, why had she bartered away her life for the momentary excitement of temporary freedom? Wasn't she aware of the heavy price she'd have to pay?

The lioness slowly stood up and opened her mouth to growl. We could see right down into her insides, but if she wanted to growl we heard no sound. She just let out a silent groan.

She turned and walked off. The same unhurried steps, the same air of indifference. Maybe she wanted us to know she was through with everything, she no longer looked forward to anything in life, she had snapped her ties with the world.

After she had disappeared from sight, the cacophony started. 'That's Rosie!' We heard the boys working in the restaurant say over the din. 'She was born here. Her mother was born here too. Rosie delivered a litter of cubs a few months ago, but they all died.'

I looked out of the window.

Rosie was nowhere in sight.

We were close to being asphyxiated. Fear prevented us from bursting out of the room. Just then we heard gunshots — one, two, three, four. Shortly afterwards came the announcement: 'No danger now. The beast has been killed.'

We spilled out of the restaurant, soaking with sweat. Mahendra's face was distorted with anger and irritation. It amused me no end and I was about to make a wisecrack when a sense of sadness came over me. All around us was the hurrying mass of men, women and children, their nerves shot. A few minutes of captivity and fear had given them such a jolt!

'Come on.' Mahendra pulled me by the hand.

'Where?' I asked in surprise.

'Let's leave. I badly need a wash and a change of clothes. I feel so dirty. God, how long did we spend inside that stinking restaurant?'

'Leave me alone,' I said, freeing my hand. 'I don't want to go back right now.'

'What do you want to do?'

'I want to see the dead animal.' I started walking. 'I want to see Rosie.'

He followed, but made it clear he was fed up with me.

I walked to a knot of people and pushed my way into it. The sight took my breath away. Rosie lay dead, right in front of a closed cage. Perhaps she had tried to get back into it. There were four bullet holes in her body, but not a drop of blood. Why had they wasted so many bullets on her?

We returned to the college. In the train I lay on an upper berth and mulled over Rosie. I felt angry and helpless. Rosie had turned the last page of her life, a mysterious, saddening last page. She hadn't hurt anyone, let alone tried to kill them. All she had wanted was a couple of minutes of freedom, a couple of minutes outside the confines of her cage. But then why had she tried to sneak back into it? There was no plausible answer. And what was that expression on her face — was it regret? Or joy at liberation from the shackles of life? Who could tell? Maybe the zoo authorities had taken the right decision: a wild animal who was so eager to get back into its cage did not deserve pity. But was Rosie any different from a human being?

After I got back home, on a sudden impulse I entered the room where Father's gun was kept. I was a small boy when he had bought it and I could not lift it then. Now I could. I picked it up and held it as if I was going to shoot. The only consolation, I thought, was that my hands wouldn't tremble now to press the trigger.

Nrusingha Tripathy

Hunger

When Neha awoke, the sun had climbed high in the sky and was beating down fiercely on her. A ferocious wind had sprung up. She was afraid she was about to be set on fire. Where was she? The sand had got into her hair, pricking her scalp like thorns. She raised her head and looked around. Serrated stretches of sand lay ahead of her, beyond them undulating dunes, and faraway a range of sand hills. What was she doing here all alone? Where were her husband and the rest of the tribe? There was no sign of a living thing in the vast sandy expanse. Only blinding heat and deafening silence. What was she to do? She felt death rushing towards her from the sand hills, with open arms to embrace her. One more minute, and it would be upon her. She hid her head between her knees and broke into a sob.

Her tribe had lived in the desert from time immemorial. They lived in tents and made a living selling leather bags, reed mats and mirror-work skirts in the villages fringing the Thar. They often moved across the desert: sometimes for three days, at others for seven or eight, as they travelled from one village to another. They trudged on foot, all thirty of them — old men, old women, young men, their wives and children. Their only camel carted the tents, cooking pots, clothing and rations.

Twenty-year-old Neha had married a young man from the tribe three years ago. When her parents died shortly after her wedding, her husband had become the centre of her life. The first few months of marriage were ·bliss. Although she was not very beautiful she was young and possessed what men said was an inexplicable charm. But things began to change once her husband found out that she was barren. They tried several remedies. They even went to a hakim who carefully examined them both, but the medicine he prescribed was so costly that they had to walk away disappointed. Since then Neha could feel her husband's love for her dwindling fast. It was as if she alone was to blame. He never missed an opportunity to taunt her: once a desert, always a desert! Life had become quite unbearable for her, though she did not spare any effort to keep her husband happy.

A gust of wind blew over her, like sandpaper on her face, neck and arms. Suddenly in a flash it all came back to her. The tribe had set out from an oasis in the evening with enough provisions for the five-day journey that lay ahead. The moon was nearly full and walking across the desert was a sheer delight. They had walked until midnight and then slept in the open until dawn. The falling dew had soaked them to the skin. That was about the only bath they could hope to have in the desert. They had resumed their journey, taking a break only in the evening. And that was when the sandstorm erupted, the worst she had ever seen. Like cotton in the wind the group scattered; the wind blew them away from each other. She felt somebody twirl a rope around her and jerk her up into the sky. That was just before she lost consciousness. How many days had passed since then?

Thirst parched Neha's throat. If only she could have a drop of water, she prayed. Was this her fate — to be slowly consumed by thirst, hunger and a merciless sun in this vast endless desert? Where was her husband? Had he tried to stick with her? Or had he seen it as a chance to abandon her in the middle of nowhere?

Fatigue weighed her down. She wanted to bury her face in the sand and lie down again, letting the sun do the rest in a couple of hours. But a sudden resolve made her jump to her feet and break into a run.

She had walked for nearly two hours when she saw a path. Hadn't they walked along it yesterday? Yes of course, but in which direction? A wave of helplessness engulfed her and tears welled up her eyes. She would walk as long as her feet could carry her, she decided, towards where she thought the end of the desert was. If she was destined to die, she would anyway.

It was then that she saw the miracle: a camel, some way off in the distance. Was somebody coming to her rescue? She rubbed her eyes in disbelief. No, it was a miracle, not a mirage. She rubbed her eyes again. Oh God! Perhaps she wasn't destined to die, after all.

Dilwar could hardly believe his eyes. Was it a vision? Impossible! In the last ten years he had crisscrossed the desert many times over but had never seen a woman on her own. After finishing his studies, with no job in sight, he had started to trade in provisions — mostly out of a sense of pique against a society he thought had dealt him a rotten hand. He carried his merchandise from one oasis to another; the profit wasn't much, but that didn't matter. He had decided to live as he wished, on the edge of things and without the cares of a family. As he urged his camel forward, he eyed the woman over: she was not only young but beautiful too.

She stopped by his camel and whispered hoarsely, 'Water!'

'Who are you? How did you get here?'

'Tell you later. Give me water first, for heaven's sake. I'm dying.'

To Neha it was not just water but the nectar of a new life which soothed her flaming body.

'I'm headed for an oasis two days away,' Dilwar said after he heard her story. 'If you wish, I'll take you there. Climb up.'

The camel lurched forward.

It was a novel experience for Dilwar. Never before had a woman practically perched on his lap, pressing against him. All the women he had known before were whores. But someone as beautiful as this woman for company? No, never before. Her face and neck were red from the sun, and her breasts rose and fell gently with the rhythmic roll of the camel. But it was her feet that sent shivers through him — dainty, shapely and bronzed. A wave of desire swept over him, and he placed his hand on her shoulder.

Neha jumped off the camel.

'But why?' asked Dilwar pleadingly, a bit shame-faced.

'I refuse to go with you, if you do that again,' she said, her voice catching. 'I don't care if I die. Besides, I'm a married woman.'

Dilwar lit a beedi. 'All right, I'll keep my hands off you. Come now, climb up. We've a long distance to go.'

Two hours later they stopped. Dilwar pitched his tent and carried his food and drink inside. Then, without a glance at her, he began to devour his meal of bread, meat and dates.

'I'm so hungry.' Neha burst out in a sob. 'Can't I have a piece of bread, please?'

'No,' Dilwar said harshly.

Neha stared at him unbelievingly. Was this fellow a human being or a demon? Didn't he have any compassion or pity? There was plenty of food. 'You know I haven't had anything to eat for the last two days. And all the food you have in front of you could easily last the two of us three days. How can you be so heartless?'

Dilwar drank some water and cleared his throat. 'There's this hunger you've had for two days. Just two days! But there's another kind of hunger that has been gnawing at me for the last two weeks. How about that? Look, you've got the food that can sate this hunger of mine, but I don't want it by force. That's not my way. Can't we come to an understanding? You give me what I want, and I give you what you want. If you're agreeable, come have this piece of meat. If not, well, all you'll get is an occasional drink of water. Just enough to keep you going.'

'I don't want your food.'

They resumed their journey in the evening and began telling each other about the highs and lows of their lives. Neha hoped that after listening to her sufferings Dilwar would melt with pity, but dinner passed exactly as lunch had — and the conversation ran along much the same lines. She went to sleep with a drink of water.

She suddenly awoke in the middle of the night to find Dilwar sitting only a hand away from her, his stares piercing her body. She shrank away. Was this the prelude, the lull before the storm? 'Why aren't you asleep?' she asked. 'You aren't hungry, are you? Why do you sit and stare at me?'

'Stares don't violate you, do they? Surely they can't make you lose your chastity. But tell me, why do you think you'd be less virtuous if you let someone other than your husband touch you?'

'That's just it — I *would* lose my morals. That's what I've been taught to believe,' she said. 'But there's one thing. You and I know that my husband's missing. For all I know he might be dead, so I'm willing to marry you. You may marry me and sate your hunger.'

'Marriage be damned!'

'Is it because I'm barren?'

'That's got nothing to do with it. I just don't believe in marriage. Nor in having children and raising a family. Marriage is a millstone. It's a fetter. Man was made in the image of god to live in freedom, and it was only for social stability that marriage evolved as an institution. There's no other purpose behind it. But look at what's happening around you. Aren't people already far too cruel and heartless? Aren't they surrounded by tragedy, destruction and confusion? In my next life I'd hate to be born again as a human being.'

'Even though I can't bear you a child, I'd always be devoted to you and look after you. And always remain faithful to you. That's not enough?'

'That's it, that's it — faithfulness! Fidelity! What bondage! Your whole life is spent protecting each other from what you think are threats from others. You want to own the person you marry, heart and soul. It can never lead to freedom.'

'What rubbish!' she said. 'Just what are you gabbing about?'

'After the first flush of pleasure you even begin to hate each other. Well, in most cases, at least. I don't want that to happen to me. I don't want to hate you. Or any other woman for that matter. For me, a woman is like a shrine, a temple. We visit temples, we do not live there. And don't we worship the earth as a goddess because it produces food which satisfies the hunger of our stomach?'

Neha found him too abstruse. She rolled over on to her stomach and buried her face in her hands. 'All right, go on, stare at me to your heart's content.'

They were up before the sun and, hiding behind the squatting camel, washed themselves. Dilwar cast several sidelong glances at Neha as she rubbed the dew into her glowing skin.

The last leg of the journey began. They were quiet. They stopped around lunchtime, and Dilwar served her a helping of bread and meat. Neha was surprised. What had made him soften? His face was solemn and she could not summon enough courage to ask him. They ate in silence, and rested and started as soon as the evening fell. Late in the night they stopped, had dinner and lay down on the sand under the moon. Not a word had passed between them since morning.

Dilwar awoke with a start. Neha was sitting beside him, running her fingers through the hair on his chest.

'What do you want?' he asked.

'You,' she said. 'Hurry.'

The moon sank in the sandscape and in the pale penumbral twilight the man and the woman, wrapped around each other, formed a wondrous picture in the vast expanse.

'Tell me what made you change your mind?' Dilwar asked.

'I wanted to make you happy. Nothing, I thought, could be nobler than making a good man happy. If *that's* what he wants. But tell me, were you really so hungry for me?'

'I was. I still am. This is a strange hunger — this awesome hunger of a man for a woman. The hunger in your belly is nothing in comparison.'

'After an hour or two we'll reach the oasis,' she said, 'and you'll quickly forget me.'

'Never,' he said. 'For me, you're a shrine. One doesn't forget a shrine. I'll always cherish the memory.'

Clasping each other's dew-drenched body, they made love again.

Yashodhara Mishra

Moonlight

What had happened last night was not the first time; Manjushree, trusting, vulnerable to cajoling and coaxing, sometimes too gushing for her own good, had tripped once again. And there had developed a familiar ring of predictability about it: Vijay, her husband, would gently press her for information about before she was married; sometimes she managed to deflect the questions, sometimes she resisted, but sometimes she simply upped and threw caution to the wind. It was the ardour, the enthusiasm she always brought to bear on the retelling of perfectly harmless snippets that made every little reminiscence seem like a major revelation and left Vijay miffed. Disaster always had the soft footfalls of a cat; she didn't hear them until it was too late.

Time hung heavy in the afternoon and as, she embroidered flowers on her daughter's frock, Manjushree tried to recollect what had happened. It was like a spool of tangled thread. Their conversation had taken several twists and turns, swerved around many a treacherous bend before inevitably, if suddenly, it struck the forbidden reef.

When she awoke in the middle of the night to change her daughter's nappy, she saw a shaft of silvery moonlight on the bed. It was fresh and soothing, almost alive. The window curtains had been gathered in a knot at the top of the grill to let in fresh air. She looked out, mesmerized. A fat moon, a slice of pale blue sky, some fluffy white clouds, and away at the end of the road the silhouette of eucalyptus trees. Just like the backdrop to a tender love scene in a college drama. The feeling made her so fluttery, so oozy with romantic visions that she forgot her housewifely shame of having spoilt the mutton curry, always a Sunday dinner delight, and the impending blues of a Monday morning — getting her son, now muttering in his sleep, ready for school, complete with tie, shoes, schoolbag, tiffin box and water bottle, before the school bus stopped in front of the gate and honked; she even forgot that Vijay, her husband for five years, who lately had been putting on weight, was sound asleep beside her. She leaned over him and ran her fingers softly down his neck. He stirred.

'How can you sleep?' she whispered. 'Wake up, wake up and see. The moon. Just see, have you ever seen anything brighter?'

Very soon he had rubbed the sleep out of his eyes, and they were merrily talking together. Manju experienced a sharp thrill as she described how she and her friends in the ladies hostel would go to the terrace and sing under a full moon until late at night. Vijay remembered that he and his moonstruck friends had aimlessly roamed the campus, talking shop and discussing girls. 'If only I had had thou beside me,' he added, his voice still husky from sleep, 'instead of them guys!'

'Now you have me beside you, but you find me very unattractive, don't you?' She pouted coquettishly.

'Don't get me wrong, darling.' His voice had a shade of indifference. 'But we didn't ever get to romance each other in the moonlight, did we? I'd have gladly given an arm for the pleasure of walking the campus with you.'

Strange but true, Manju thought. It may not be a matter of deep sorrow or lasting regrets, but it was something which couldn't be lightly wished away either.

Sometimes when Vijay and his friends met in the evenings to play cards, with Manju acting the gracious hostess and plying them with plates of hot pakoras, Vijay laughed with evident pride and wondered aloud: 'I just can't understand how people go in for arranged matches. How do they learn to live with perfect strangers?

Well, my Manju and I — we were each other's choice, yessir.'

Ironically, in the four years of college the one and the only time Vijay had spoken to Manju was when he had picked up his courage on the very last day to speak to this beautiful girl who sang so soulfully on the stage and emitted bolts of lightning around her when she walked down the corridors. He did not expect to ever see her again. 'You might not know me,' he had said by way of introduction. 'I'm Vijay Patnaik, captain of the college cricket team. More important than that, I'm an ardent admirer of yours...I adore your voice. How well you sing! I just wanted to say goodbye...We may not meet again...I've just landed a job in Rourkela.'

And who in the college didn't know Vijay Patnaik the cricket captain? His father was a well-known lawyer and their house in the heart of the town was a huge two-storey mansion. And now, before he had finished college, Vijay had found a plum job, too.

Two days later he wrote, proposing to her. More than Manju it was her mother who was swept off her feet. Manju let herself float in the current. The effusiveness of her sisters was delicious, the envy-laced congratulations of her friends and neighbours oddly appetizing. She had made a wonderful catch, everyone said, she couldn't have wished for any better.

After the wedding she came to Rourkela with her husband and set up home in his flat. Always smartly turned out — never once during the college years had anyone caught her slovenly dressed, or with unkempt hair and oily face — she had highly individualistic ideas about doing up the house, but quickly grasped the importance of striking a middle path. She would have loved to have her hair bobbed, but thought better than to shock her husband; it was of course another thing that she did achieve the desired effect by a new hairdo.

It was only after being married to Vijay for sometime that she learnt he had been one of her most ardent, albeit secret, admirers.

'Whenever I found out you'd be in the college drama, I'd be in the auditorium hours in advance just to grab a good seat. And I had eyes for no one but you. The moment your part was over, I'd start fidgeting, dying to leave the place.'

Sometimes he could be a big tease.

'What I could never understand was why instead of singing solo you agreed to join the stupid choruses, la-laing, ho-hoing with those silly, dimwit girls. Those clots, they were all ridiculous, if you ask me.'

Sometimes Manju, smug in her sense of security, would let herself get carried away with Vijay's enthusiasm.

'There was once this little hiccup, for instance. Poor Nirmala hadn't learned her lines and had to depend entirely on the prompter. She was so jittery and nervous that she went and said many of my lines as well. As you can imagine, I was in a funk. I had to improvise like mad. You remember the play, don't you, the one we staged under Mr Patra's direction?'

'How can I ever forget it? That bloody Maqbool played the role of your father and took full advantage of it. He could hardly keep his paws off you. He must have put his hands on your shoulder no fewer than ten or twelve times.' Vijay remembered everything.

'Oh! No. Not that many times, I swear. Just once or maybe twice. Believe me, not once did he dare do it during the rehearsals. And I had no way of fending him off on stage.'

'If only I had landed his role! I'd have shown the audience how to act, how to emote. The stage would have drowned in a flood of filial love.'

Manju would giggle, nestling against Vijay and wondering whether to tell him another juicy story but would stop short. She was aware of the thin glass wall between them, just a whisper away; the slightest mindlessness, a little carelessness, and it would break, hurting them both. But at times she would get so carried away that she would not heed the tiny tinkling intimations of the glassy divide and plunge ahead. And once she had begun, changing the course of the conversation was not easy, with a keen sportsman like Vijay in the fray.

And that was how it had happened last night.

'Are you asleep, Manju?'

'No.'

'You woke me up and now you're dropping off. That's not fair.'

'I'm wide awake, I tell you.'

'Why are you quiet, then? Say something. Something interesting.'

'About what?'

'Anything. Your college life, your friends.'

She relaxed, let her guard down. It was so pleasant to chew the cud, to kick the ball.

'No, no, you tell me. Tell me all about the girls you wanted to romance in the moonlight.'

'What did my wishes matter? You know me well by now. I was ten times shyer in those days. My conservative parents would have cut me into pieces if I had been up to mischief.'

'Don't play the innocent, my dear! Remember the story you once told me of the midsummer night when all those girls, your cousins I mean, gathered on your terrace?'

'Oh, that? Of course I remember it. But that's an old story and I've milked it for all it's worth. Come on, Manju, you'd better tell me something about yourself.'

'What haven't I told you yet?'

'A lot. For instance, whether you ever took a walk in the moonlight with some fellow or other.'

'Well, I never did.'

'Come on, you had an army of admirers.'

She was not sure whether it was a compliment or a complaint. It was like this every time he mentioned admirers. His body beside her was so warm, his hand on her hair so reassuring, his whisper in her ear so tantalizing.

'Come on, Manju. Come out with it. There are many things about you I know nothing about. And I want to know everything, every little thing concerning you, when I was nowhere in the picture. You can share a secret or two with me, can't you?'

She could hear the glass wall demur. What was it that lay ahead — an abyss camouflaged with blades of green? She had better be careful.

'Didn't you ever take a moonlight walk with Ramesh?' Vijay persisted.

'Ugh!' Her voice was heavy.

'Ugh won't wash, my dear. Tell us the truth. I promise I won't take it amiss. Strange how it never occurred to me before to ask you about it. Surely you did enjoy one moonlight walk with our man Ramesh!'

'Never!'

'Hey, don't let your hackles rise. Cool down, take it easy. Think. Look back. You may have forgotten about it.'

'I told you I never went out with him.'

'What kind of love was it then?'

'Whoever said anything about love?'

'All right, all right, for the record it wasn't love, though I know it was.'

'If you're so sure, then there's nothing to talk about.'

'Manju, be a dear. Don't get so het up, please. You're spoiling the fun, the mood for earthshaking confessions.'

Manju remained silent.

'But Ramesh was head over heels in love with you, wasn't he?'

'Why do you ask if you're so sure?'

'The whole college knew. You were in love with him too, if only a little, but out of fear of the wild-tempered harridan that was your hostel superintendent...'

'Why did you want to marry me if you knew all this?'

'Somehow I could never take it to be true. But tell me, wasn't there a little something between you two?'

'Oh, nothing but friendship.'

'And what is friendship but mild love!'

'In your lexicon, perhaps.'

'I know nothing of mild love. In my book love is passionate, wild.'

Manju tied several knots and snapped the thread between her teeth, letting out a sigh. Oh, college life. In the whole college only four or six couples were in love and they flaunted it too. The rest merely derived vicarious pleasure from unbridled gossip. Whatever it was between Manju and Ramesh, the whole college believed it was love. Vijay did, too. But she knew there was no future in it; she could never get close to Ramesh, his conservative brahmin parents would never accept her. After her marriage to Vijay she had never had any regrets over her failed love, nor had she ever felt a twinge of guilt. But every time her husband quizzed her about her relation with Ramesh, she economized a little on the truth, and wasn't exactly sure why. And yes, she did think of Ramesh sometimes. But then there were so many other things she sometimes thought about. And if she spoke about them it was not so much out of the desire to unburden herself as out of a wish to relive those romantic moments.

'You remember the play in which I was the heroine?'
'And Maqbool your father?'
'Not that one, silly. I'm talking about Shravani, which we staged in the third year...'
'Wasn't Deepak the hero?'
'No, it was Ramesh. Have you really forgotten?'
'Go on.'
'Don't you remember Bula Patnaik's threat to disrupt the play? Well, we had put on our make-up quite early and the play was to start as soon as the first chorus was over. We were all keyed up.'
'How come you were not in the chorus? You who loved la-laing, ho-hoing in every chorus?'
'I'll keep quiet if you don't stop pulling my leg.'
'Sorry, go on.'
'Bula Patnaik and his gang were true to their words: they started the ruckus even before the chorus had ended. They went and blew the fuse. As the whole place plunged into darkness, we were in a panic. Keep your cool, we were told, everything's under control and the electricity will be restored in five minutes.

'There was that long verandah at the back of the stage, and beyond it, the open field. We began to pace about, Ramesh and I, saying our dialogue aloud. The big blooming moon was so bright that you could count the leaves on the deodars. Suddenly Ramesh said, "The deodar leaves remind me of your hair."'

Manju stopped.

'Go on,' said Vijay, after a moment of tense silence.

'Before we had realized it we had walked all the way to the back of the library building. I had left my cardigan behind, and my teeth began to chatter in the cold. "I didn't know it was so cold outside," I remarked, wrapping myself with my hands. Ramesh promptly took off his coat and put it around my shoulders. "Feeling better?" he asked, his hand briefly encircling my waist.'

'Go on.'

'I glanced at my watch. Only a few minutes had passed. I said people might be looking for us, and we returned.'

'Aren't you leaving something out?'

'Leaving out what?'

Vijay's voice dropped to a sibilant whisper. 'Didn't Ramesh kiss you? Tell me the truth. I won't mind it. After all it was ages ago.'

'Believe me there was nothing.'

'Hold me and swear.'

Manju stiffened. Her hand which lay across Vijay's chest slipped off.

'I'll never tell you a thing if you go on this way. Remember you said you wouldn't get angry.' Her voice had changed.

'Who says I'm angry?' Vijay laughed. 'Come, snuggle up.'

It was a dry, brittle laugh.

Next morning Manju awoke late. The sunlight was hitting the bed. Her heart skipped a beat.

'My, I've never slept so late,' she said apologetically, stretching her body. 'Why didn't you wake me up?'

'Hm,' said Vijay. He was through with his toilet, and stood in front of the mirror, putting on his clothes. He looked solemn, his face shut to her.

She recognized it as easily as a well-remembered algebraic formula. Vijay's reflection in the mirror was as cold and stiff as a photograph.

She began to hurry through the chores. Somehow she got her son ready for school and then whipped up a breakfast. As she prepared to lay the table, she was surprised to find Vijay putting on his shoes.

'I'm afraid I can't eat,' he said, his voice distant. 'I'm not feeling too well.'

'What's wrong with you? Have a piece of toast...'

'Please. I'm going to be late for the office.'

He walked off in a huff, leaving her with the plates in her hand. Now it hardly mattered if she ate or not. She took a bath, rubbed a pinch of powder onto her face, put a vermilion dot on her forehead and supervised the maid's work. There was a lot to tidy up. Sometimes her nosey neighbour, Mrs Mohanty, dropped in early without notice. How thrilled she would be to see an untidy house and Manju in a dishevelled state!

In the afternoon she packed Vijay's lunch and sent it to his office and busied herself with sewing. But the thread came off the eye of the needle repeatedly. Fed up, she jabbed the needle into the cloth and pushed it away. She began to wonder. How did she dredge up something new from her eventless life to spice her tales? Why did a perfectly innocuous reminiscence create an ugly situation every time? Was it a kind of unconscious desire on her part to test the solidity of her marriage or to prick the bubble of a placid life?

In the evening Vijay, back from the office, hastily packed his bags. 'I'm leaving for Cuttack tonight. We're playing an important match. Don't expect me before Saturday?'

She was hurt, although she did not betray any sign of that. 'Why didn't you tell me before? How long have you known?'

Vijay did not reply. His attention was riveted on folding his clothes.

Manju fetched his toilet kit. She hesitated a little about saying anything but went ahead. 'It isn't fair. You've no right to sulk. First you lead me down the garden path, and then when I admit some little thing you take it amiss.'

Vijay made a wry face. What was she gabbing about? 'What surprises me is that you have something different to reveal every time!' he said icily, shutting the suitcase with a bang.

As the tea brewed, she watched the blue flame of the fire through a film of tears shimmering in her eyes. Never trust anyone, she vowed, like so many times before. Words uttered at such moments of togetherness, on a rare moonlit night, are not to be trusted. Never get carried away. And why blame Vijay? The poor fellow has to carry the burden of acting the husband in broad daylight!

Vijay gulped down his tea. 'So long,' he said, without looking at her, and walked out of the house. She watched him cross the verandah and go down the steps and the small path leading to the gate.

In the following three days Manju had the ripe fruit plucked from the guava tree and prepared jelly. She had enough time to sit with Mrs Bose and listen to her collection of new records, and help her son with his lessons. More than once she had a strong urge to write some letters but didn't know to whom. Her sisters, all married, were caught up in their own affairs. And why bother poor Mother? As a nurse she was on her feet the whole day and came home tired to her bones. She needed to be able to enjoy whatever little rest she got, now that the problem of getting her girls married was off her mind. There were college friends, some right there in Rourkela, whom she ran into now and then in the market and movie halls. She was in touch with a few, but whoever she wrote to these days she did so only to confirm their belief that she led a perfect, happy life. She tried to remember her father, long dead. His was a kindly face. In sharp contrast, mother's was a weary, sweaty, anxiety-scarred face, which her spotless white uniform and brisk manners did nothing to enliven. When she was young Manju had always shrunk away from her. Home was oppressive. The only place where she felt good was school and then college. The moment she was out of the house she felt light-headed and fluffy, as if she had grown wings.

She thought of Vijay. She could not have hoped for a better husband. She had no fears when he was around. Perhaps it was this that had made her forget her limits, the fact that she must be cautious when dealing with her husband.

On Saturday afternoon she wore her lustrous hair in an attractive coiffure she had only recently picked up and put a string of jasmine around it. Her eyes never left the road in front of the house. When Vijay stepped out of an auto, she rushed out to welcome him.

'We won,' said Vijay, displaying his pearly white teeth below his jet-black moustache.

Manju heaved a sigh of relief. 'I knew you would.'

Later that night, after the children had fallen asleep, Manju, her chores finished, found Vijay at the table, his suitcase open before him, looking out the window. Outside, there was no moon. As soon as she went a little closer, he rose to embrace her. Manju sensed he was trying to drape something around her shoulders. It was a new sari.

'My, what's this?'

'For you. When I was taking out the presents for the children, you didn't even ask me if I had got anything for you.'

'You don't have to get me something every time.' Her voice caught. 'I'm not a child.'

Vijay tightened his arms around her. 'Manju, I love you. I love you more than I love my life. Don't you believe me?'

Manju's eyes fell on the open suitcase and the clutter on the table. She pulled down the window curtain. Her gaze travelled to the wall. A spider was busy repairing a broken web.

'You didn't answer me, Manju.' Vijay's whisper in her ear was ticklish. 'Don't you love me? Don't you trust me?'

'Of course, I do.' She nodded her head. 'Who else would I love and trust?'

She watched the spider. How quickly it had repaired the damage! Now it sat back, secure, motionless. What does a spider do to avoid being entangled in its own web? she wondered.

Jagadish Mohanty

A Sita in the Ashok Forest

A dying colliery, people say. No, more like the Ashok Forest, says Pratima. Remember the Ashok Forest? That was where poor Sita was imprisoned.

Pratima is a nurse. A Six hundred and thirty rupees basic salary a month, to which are added the dearness allowance, the variable dearness allowance and the incentive bonus of ten percent. Plenty, in a manner of speaking. So what ails the poor girl, what's the cause of her sorrow? Why does she wallow in self-pity, why does she think of herself as a Sita in the Ashok Forest?

Pratima's Soliloquy

My life is empty of all joy and happiness, its pristine whiteness sullied by globs of dirt. Of course, nothing better could have been expected in this godforsaken colliery. Here people spend as much or maybe more than what they earn — and they earn handsome amounts, mind you, compared to others — and just a week or so after pay day they head for the Afghan moneylenders. No one makes a serious attempt to improve the quality of his life.

Did I ever imagine I'd get stranded in a hole like this? It's an awful place, a barren patch, nothing will ever blossom here; and I'm trapped in a silent house, with nothing but memories to go over, over and over again.

The house, my house. Three living rooms. An inner courtyard, a kitchen, a storeroom, a toilet. What do I need so much space for? I've nothing to fill its void with. Sometimes I wish that the house was chockfull of bric-a-brac and that I had a man, someone after my heart of course, and maybe a little child. I lie on bed and dream, and my eyes well up with tears.

I live alone, so all I really need is just one room. For a long time after I moved in here I never opened the windows of the rooms I didn't use, until I found white ants having a merry go at the woodwork. The curtains too had been eaten. Since then I've made it a point to open the windows every morning and dust them, check the curtains and air them. But that's about all, the rest of the day the windows stay shut.

The place my house is located is called Number Eight by the locals. Named after the pit which was once operational here. It had to be closed down after water began to ooze out of its depths. Until then the place hummed with activity and bustled with people; some people thought the colliery was a blessed heaven, but after the mine was closed just about anyone and everyone who could pull wires with the administration moved on to better places. Those like me who couldn't, stayed behind.

I have very little contact with my neighbours. There's one Murthy — a Telegu fellow and a bachelor. I don't know his full name, I haven't spoken a word with him ever. Then there's a certain Singh. He has a big, thick moustache, and he looks every inch a goon; whenever we run into each other he asks, 'How are you, Sister — all right?' His accent betrays his Bihari origin. I don't know his full name either. He too lives alone. Then there are a few others I know only by sight. Some say hello, some flash a smile, some enquire if I am doing fine.

When I first landed here, a horde of women from the colony descended on me, in a gesture of good neighbourliness. They asked about my home, parents, marital status, the cost of my saris, and praised their husbands. Only later did I realize the real purpose of their visit: acquaintance with a nurse might come in handy some day. A few of course came out of sheer curiosity. Anyway the neighbourly visits soon dwindled and then stopped altogether. Of the whole lot I can count on my fingers the ones I remember — Mrs Jadav, Mrs Sinha, Mrs Srivastava, Miss Mohanty. The rest I've forgotten.

Hospital duty is eight hours. The doctor usually reports late, so there's plenty of free time; the actual grind never exceeds five or five and a half hours. The rest of the time you sit, chat and laugh. And then you go home to your little prison, cook, tidy up, wash clothes, browse through much-thumbed novels, fiddle with the transistor radio — anything, just any damn thing, to kill time. But is it easy to kill time? The clock stops, time dilates. Like a midnight train plagued by constant chain-pulling; despite blowing whistle after whistle, it hardly chugs ahead. Wistfully I look forward to the morning station — when will the train reach there? I turn, I toss, I sit up on my bed; I fiddle with the radio, I move the pointer from one dead centre to another. The room I'm imprisoned in expands, looms ever larger; the blast of emptiness rings out.

That's my life, in a nutshell, in the Ashok Forest. I can't get along with my neighbours. I don't even try. In the evenings, when smoke curls up from the coal ovens all around my house, I get out of breath. And that's when I feel what a big blob of dirt this colliery life is and how utterly devoid of freshness life is in the Ashok Forest.

The Ashok Forest. It's got a romantic ring to it, hasn't it? It feels so good to imagine yourself as a wilting Sita. But where's Ram, where's the rescuer in my life? I entered the Ashok Forest much before I could pick out a Ram. I could have, though. There were many men hovering around me, but nothing worked out, nothing came very close to anything serious, no one stopped by long enough to contemplate marriage.

In the last year of school there was this friend of mine, Vishnupriya, whose elder brother caught hold of me one evening and insisted in the presence of others on feeding me a handful of rice puffs. I felt shy, but I did open my mouth and his moist fingers brushed across my lips. The sensation stayed fresh for days, and anytime I wanted to I could feel his moist fingers on my lips. God knows it fed many of my dreams. It also inspired the first, and also the last, story I ever wrote.

It started fading when I finished school and went to Cuttack to train as a nurse. And there, Mannadidi, one of the senior girls, warned me: Beware of the roving eyes in the medical campus. Show the slightest unmindfulness and they will gobble you up alive. Don't ever let your guard down.

But did I heed her words of caution? Maybe no one got wind of it, maybe the only three people involved in the whole thing were God, Amit and myself, but I did steal into the Female Ward one night, eluding the watchful eyes of the sisters and attendant. I thought I'd just speak a few words with Amit, who was on duty there, but I let him lead me to the deserted post office behind the pharmacology lab and make love to me. The pleasure was as great as the accompanying pain, and I came back to the hostel crushed under guilt and had to invent a lie that I had been to see a distant aunt in the Female Ward. That night I could hardly sleep, gripped by fear and fathomless joy. Luckily it was my safe period.

Shortly afterwards Amit drifted away. Men continued to seek me out, but I played hard to get. Amit's betrayal drove home the lesson. Men were pariahs, taboo, to be kept at a distance; bring them a little closer and you start to melt like wax yourself. The heat they give off, the men. Hungry eyes followed me everywhere, but then the training came to an end and I landed this job through the employment exchange. And here, ever since I came, life has been awful — lonely, cocooned in a dense fog of despair. So much for my life in the Ashok Forest.

In Front of Pratima's House

Here comes Pratima, wrapped in a white sari. Tired, weary, her hair dishevelled and flying in the breeze. Plastic chappals. Long, chipped fingernails, remnants of cheap nailpolish on them; the coat of talcum powder coming off her face in patches, rivulets of sweat; the kohl fading from the rims of her eyes; cheap jewellery dangling from her ears; a bare neck; two glass bangles on her right wrist and a watch on the left; the watch stopped ages ago. Pratima is in limbo.

No past, no present, no future; everything's the same to her. Her eyes seem drowned in a bottomless pool of fatigue. Her white cap dangles limply from her left hand. In her right hand she holds a purse and a small ladies handkerchief, with which she wipes the grime off her face from time to time.

Pratima stops in front of her house. She opens her purse, takes out a bunch of keys and chooses one, leans forward on her toes, grasping her cap and purse between her teeth, inserts the key into the lock and turns it. She pulls down the latch and pushes open the door.

Pratima's Sitting Room

When the door creaks open, Pratima puts one foot inside. Outside, it's getting dark. The light switch, behind the door, is on the left. She turns, stretches her right hand, gropes around awhile and flicks the switch on. The room is flooded with light. She closes the door and stands for a moment looking down around her feet. The postman always pushes the letters under the door.

There's no letter but a piece of paper. Pratima is a little surprised. She still has her cap in her left hand and her purse in her right. Transferring her purse to her left, she juggles both and stoops down to pick up the paper.

It's neatly folded in four, and seems to have been pulled out from a lined notebook. The handwriting's no great shakes and a couple of spelling errors jump out at her at a casual glance. Oh my, it's a letter, a letter that didn't come in the mail; somebody's slipped it under the door.

She begins to read. On the top is a regular epigraph:

> Some love one, some love two
> I love one, that is you.

And below that:

> Queen of my heart!

She crumples it into a ball and holds it tightly. She knows what it is. Letters like this she had received in piles during training. Her heart begins to beat faster and faster. Her mouth goes dry.

Pratima's Bedroom

Curtains in the windows, shutting out the outside. A single mattress on a string cot; an ugly old tin trunk in a corner squatting on bricks; a cheap leather suitcase on top of the trunk; an attache case on top of the suitcase, wrapped in a cover made out of old clothes; on a shelf a small tin of talcum powder, a bottle of face cream, a bottle of shampoo, a bottle of nail polish, a few bangles in a cardboard box, a picture album; the empty box of a wall clock on another shelf. There are a few much-thumbed, dog-eared novels, some by Bibhuti Patnaik, all covered in yellowing newsprint, with Pratima's name written in bold letters on top.

A large mirror on the eight-by-eight wall. A wooden clothes-stand in a corner, with a few clean saris, neatly folded, hanging from it, the straps of the brassieres tucked underneath the saris peeping out. Folded blouses and petticoats. A hand-knitted cardigan. A picture of neatness. Everything in order. An overpowering feminine smell and presence on top of it all.

Pratima walks into her bedroom. She does not bother to change her clothes. She switches on the light and the fan. Depositing her cap, purse and keys on the top shelf, she walks to the bed and sits down, leaning against the wall. She slowly loosens her fist, and the ball of paper drops on to the bed; she unfolds it and smoothens it across her thigh, reading it again.

A Love Letter for Pratima

   Some love one, some love two
   I love one, that is you.
   Queen of my heart!

The day I first saw you I don't know why but I fell in love with you. Your image constantly haunts me. I see you everywhere, in my dreams too.

Dear Sister, why do you laugh and chat so much with those two good-for-nothing pharmacists at the hospital? One of them, the one called Das, is one helluva sonofabitch. He receives letters from any number of girls. I found this out from the post office. Eight to ten letters a day, no fewer. Who do you think write to him, if not girls?

And that other fellow, that Khuntia — well, he had an affair with Sister Hira. The whole colliery knew about it. Imagine how I felt the other day when I saw you sitting on the same bench as those two characters, chatting away nineteen to the dozen. Dear one, they are out to trap you. Beware!

That doctor chap is no good either. Do you know he doesn't get along with his wife? Well, he too has his eyes on you. Beware!

My Queen, don't be cross with me for coming out with all this. My only desire is your safety and well-being. I am pining for you like a chakor bird does for his mate. I lost my heart to you at the first glance, remember. I dream of you, oh so many dreams — but alas, when the dream's over and I awaken, I find myself painfully alone in my bed.

Flower of my love, I want to tie the knot with you. Are you willing? Can you give up everything for my sake? Will you be mine? If you are willing, then place a brick in front of your house when you go to the hospital tomorrow morning. That will be the sign, and in my next letter I will divulge my name and address. Suffice it to say we have met each other — not once, but several times. You have given me injections no fewer than five times. Looking forward to your consent.

> Tea for milk, milk for tea
> I for you, you for me
> Thirsting for your love,
> Your unknown friend.

Pratima's Reaction

Who sent this outrageous letter, who? How many such stupid love letters have I received so far? This one of course has come after a long, long time. The last one was in Cuttack, which I've left behind, together with my old life. It seems another life now. Who in this dead colliery...?

Who can it be? The letter reads like a young greenhorn's. A boy of sixteen, or seventeen. Oh mother mine, is he younger than me? Look at the handwriting and the spelling errors. And a marriage proposal to boot in the very first love letter! I don't even know the fellow from Adam! Look at his lurid style: Queen of my heart, flower of my love — what nonsense! Who does he think he's writing to — a high school girl? How dare he propose marriage? If he has courage, why doesn't he come forward and introduce himself first? The marriage proposal can wait. Why has he taken to writing letters? Who'll believe I got a letter from a young boy I don't even know? Everyone will think I must have led him down the garden path.

What if he comes over now? Suppose he comes and knocks and when I open the door... suppose he simply barges in and... he...! Oh mother mine, I'm alone, the colony's so deserted that no help would turn up even if I were to scream. What if he turns out to be a regular hoodlum? What will I do then, what?

Who can it be? Not Murthy, oh no; it can't be him. Not Singh either by a long stretch. Neither of them know Oriya. And the fellow says I have given him injections. Now who are the young boys who have regularly been to the hospital? Oh damn it, I can't remember a single face. How can a nurse remember the faces of all the people she's given injections to?

Can it be Das? Or Khuntia? One or the other, or both together, might have done it for the heck of it, who knows? You can't trust men. What will I do if they decide to barge into my house at night — oh God! I received so many of these damned letters in medical college but I was never so scared. What's the matter with me? Why am I so nervous? Is it because I live alone, because there's no one around to come to my rescue? Oh, how will I protect myself? Sister Kanaka, that irrepressible tomboy of a trainee nurse, who once hit a house surgeon for a misdemeanour and sang a bawdy song in front of a professor, what could she do when two drunken louts from Mangalabag pinned her down to the floor in the ENT ward? If the ward attendants hadn't responded to her frantic screams she'd have been raped. But how can I ward off an attack if and when it comes?

Pratima in Bedroom

Pratima in bed, lying on her stomach, her legs bent and raised and shaking spasmodically. Her face buried deep in the pillow.

She raises herself on her elbows, opens her eyes, fishes out the letter from under the pillow and reads: *I am pining for you like a chakor bird does for his mate. I lost my heart to you at the first glance, remember. I dream of you, oh so many dreams — but alas, when the dream's over and I awaken, I find myself painfully alone in my bed.*

She folds it. Her uniform crushed, her feet dirty, her hair tousled, she sits like a log, makes no effort to prepare tea, does nothing to start dinner. It's seven o'clock already. She does not look at the radio, does not fiddle with it to tune in Radio Ceylon.

Her fingers close around the letter and her fist tightens into a knot again. Her head droops and her face burrows into the pillow. She raises her legs and rocks them. Suddenly she gets up and turns the whirring fan to a faster speed. She stands in the middle of the room, but only for a moment, then she goes back to the cot and slumps down onto the bed again. Her fist opens. She smoothens the letter and reads on: *Flower of my love, I want to tie the knot with you. Are you willing? Can you give up everything for my sake? Will you be mine?*

She crumples the letter. A smile spreads over her face, bringing a little colour to it. She gets up and walks to the shelf, empties the cardboard box containing the bangles, places the letter at the bottom and puts back the bangles and then the box. She looks at herself in the tiny hand-mirror, runs her fingers through her untidy hair. Like a Sita in the Ashok Forest, she whispers to herself. Yeah.

Why does she repeat it to herself? Why does she repeat it and then burst out laughing bitterly?

Epilogue

The next morning as she started for the hospital, Pratima stopped by her door, her legs heavy and ready to send down roots. She remembered the letter, looked around and saw a broken piece of brick lying nearby. She started. She then picked it up and threw it as far away as she could. She surveyed the surroundings carefully again. No more bricks.

In the hospital she could not take her mind off the letter, no matter how hard she tried. She viewed everyone she met with suspicion — it could be anyone, just anyone, who knows. But no one seemed likely, even remotely.

It occurred to her that the broken piece of brick she saw in front of her house might have been left behind by a child who came to play. She needn't have panicked.

When she went back to her house at twelve o'clock, there was no brick, broken or whole, in sight. She pushed open the door of the house and looked down at the floor. Nothing there.

At three o'clock she returned to the hospital, and until six thought of nothing but the letter, and then it was time to go home.

When she opened her door in the evening she searched the floor again. Somewhere in the recesses of her heart she had a lurking hope that there would be another letter. No matter how much she would have loved to pretend the contrary, she longed for a letter, which would have felt like the gentle brushing of moist fingers across her lips. The floor was bare.

Days passed, one after another after another. Pratima went to work, returned home, stared at the floor, hoped for a message scribbled in royal blue ink on lined paper from a notebook. She never got one.

Months passed. Pratima continued to take care of her hair, cooked her meals, washed her clothes, kept her rooms spanking clean, changed her bedsheets frequently, did her duties at the hospital quite diligently. Her time passed — mornings, afternoons, evenings. Night after night she lay on the bed with the transistor radio on her bosom and listlessly moved the knob from one end to the other, not tuning in to any station in particular. She strained her ears to pick out the sounds of the dark: the chirping of crickets, distant drumbeats, the whirring of the fan, the commotion at the neighbours. A life lived alone is a life wasted, she often whispered to herself. A life of sorrow. Like the life of a Sita in the Ashok Forest. A life of lingering pain. She would lie wide awake late into the night, her breath hot and ragged. Sometimes she would get up and walk to the shelf, take down the cardboard box and retrieve the letter from underneath the bangles. A piece of paper torn from a lined notebook, a message scribbled in royal blue ink. *Flower of my love, I want to tie the knot with you. Are you willing? Can you give up everything for my sake? Will you be mine?* She would read it slowly, with a strange sensation of someone moving his moist fingers across her lips. Shaken to her innermost core, she would close her eyes and whisper: Oh, you little coward, why didn't you ever write again?

Sivapada Swain

The Couple

It was around twelve o'clock that he remembered the outing they had planned. Another hour or two of solid work and he could take the afternoon off with a clear conscience. Lately the office had begun to weigh on him; sometimes he was so harried that he wished he didn't have to work so hard, but he knew he was already a prisoner of the reputation he had made for himself as an honest and hardworking officer. No matter how much he cribbed, work he would.

The curtain parted and the peon came in with a slip of paper. He glanced at it and with a slight nod signalled for the visitors to be shown in. A moment later two greasy, middle-aged, fat men entered the room, with an exaggerated show of deference. He asked them to sit down, opened the file and studied it, turning the pages slowly. When he began to examine the businessman, the fellow kept his mouth shut and let his lawyer do the talking. This began to irritate him. He stopped the questioning. Then the lawyer submitted a long written statement. He read it carefully, noted the points and slapped the file shut.

'All right,' he said. 'You may go now. I can't take a decision right away. I'll have to think it over.'

'When do we get back to you, sir?'

'You don't have to. The decision will be communicated to you by post.'

'Sir,' the lawyer hemmed and hawed. 'Sir, if there's anything you need, please do remember us.'

'What?'

The businessman opened his mouth for the first time. 'If I can be of any service, sir...'

He politely dismissed them; there was no point in losing one's cool. If eight years in the job had taught him anything it was not to be provoked by such veiled offers. He rang the bell for the peon and asked him to take the file away.

As soon as the visitors left, he turned his attention to the pile of mail and jotted down notes on some of the letters. Then, out of sheer habit, he looked up at his notebook. Of the seven targets he had set for himself, he had taken care of four already. No mean achievement, he thought.

Just then the phone rang.

'Hello?' he said distantly.

'Guess who!'

'Isn't it rather early? The movie begins at three, doesn't it?'

'Listen, will you get mad if I suggest something? Do we have to see the movie at all?'

'I knew you wouldn't be able to get the tickets. I told you to leave it to me. I could've sent my peon.'

'It's not the tickets. Just that I'm not in a mood to watch a movie. If you agree I'll give the tickets to someone else.'

'All right.'

'But movie or no movie, we are going out. I want to eat out today.'

'Lunch or dinner?'

'Lunch, of course.'

'Where?'

'Peter Cat.'

'Oh no, not the same old place again! All right, I'll wind up in fifteen minutes flat. Will you meet me here? Or would you like to wait at the restaurant?'

'You don't exactly look overjoyed when I show up at your office.'

'Don't I? Hey, you're most welcome. I'd really love it if you came over. But promise not to laugh too loudly. And not to send my poor devil of a peon running up and down the stairs ten times for tea.'

'Thank you very much. I'd much rather sit in the restaurant.'

'All right.'

In the middle of the meal, she stopped, rolled her eyes mischievously and said with the effervescence of a sudden remembrance, 'You forgot to order your potion of poison!'

'Not really. I've got to get back to the office.'

'No way. It's past three o'clock already.'

'I wish I had left a word. Well, never mind.'

'No, you'd better go back to your office if it bothers you so much. Who knows, there might be a huge pile of work waiting for you.'

'Work can wait,' he said with a smile. 'Don't bother. It's all right.'

She smiled. 'It's always all right with you, isn't it? It sounds so funny. All right. All right. Isn't that a habit with you?'

He smiled, waved to the waiter and ordered a gin-and-lime. All right, my dear, he thought to himself, that's the end of the damned discussion. All right. Over.

Lunch over, they walked out of the restaurant, and he hailed a cab. When he gave the driver the address, both knew what was coming. A sense of awkwardness overtook them. During the ride she looked past him. But he stared at her unabashedly. She had a beautiful face and an even more beautiful body. When their eyes met he smiled and she lowered her face blushing. He held her hand; after a half-hearted protest she gave in.

They reached their destination, he paid off the driver and took the lift to his friend's flat on the seventh floor. The attendant answered the door, and with a smart salute bustled about, tidying up the bed, fluffing up the pillows, and switching on the air conditioner. He had the quiet air of efficiency of someone who knew his job well.

'Will you need anything else, sir?' he enquired.

'No, thank you. That's all right.'

'May I go out for a short while?' They knew that the man would be away for more than a couple of hours. A good man, a man of some sense; god bless him.

He bolted the front door and hurried to the bedroom. She was sprawled on the bed with a magazine. He padded over to the bathroom. When he came out she was standing near the window looking out, wrapped in thought. She looked distant and all the more ravishing for it. He tiptoed over to her and put his arms around her. He could feel a shiver running down her body. He ceremoniously guided her to the bed, already looking forward to the blessed fatigue, the wonderful languor that would follow the exertions.

After it was all over he could barely keep his eyes open and, turning his back on her, fell asleep in a minute.

'Wake up, wake up.' She shook him. 'You've slept long enough.'

He rubbed his eyes and smiled at her. The curtains were drawn and the darkness inside was moist. For a moment his eyes travelled to the oil painting on the wall and then to the TV and the mirror. He swung his legs down and sprang up with a litheness that surprised him, scrambled into his clothes, switched off the air conditioner, drew aside the curtains and opened the window. Then he came back to the middle of the room and surveyed the surroundings. Magazines and newspapers lay scattered all around. He picked up a glossy and, pulling a chair closer to the bed to put up his legs, flipped through the pages. He lighted a cigarette. He knew there was an ashtray somewhere, but was too lazy to look for it and flicked the ash on the grey carpet.

He was on the phone when she came out of the bathroom humming a tune. She sat down opposite him, watching him with a bemused smile. He put the receiver down.

'Who did you call?' she asked with studied casualness.

'My wife.'

'My, aren't you a loving husband! How I envy your wife.'

'It should be the other way round.'

She smiled.

'All right.'

She smiled some more.

'Now, now, my dear, instead of perching on the bed like a dainty little queen how about making us some tea?'

They were having tea when the attendant returned. They chatted for a while. Then he began to fidget a little. It was time to leave. It was already half past five. But she seemed to be in no hurry. No hurry at all. Of course she didn't have a single good reason for hurrying.

'How come you never give me a decent gift, huh?' she said suddenly. 'You always bring me books, which I never read anyway.'

'Why must it always be the men who give presents? Look, why don't you give me a present for a change, huh — a pair of shoes or a pullover, for instance? Oh boy, how I'd love to have a good pullover this winter! Have a little thought for this beggar, ma'am.'

'Would you believe it, I've been dying to knit a pullover for you. But what's the use? You won't be able to take it home. What would you tell your wife?'

'If a hand-knitted one would give us away,' he said, suddenly grinning, 'I wouldn't mind a readymade one.'

She gave a little smile. There was a touch of sadness to it. He was stung. He felt sick and his gall was up. Why can't he tell it from the rooftops that his girlfriend Savita Srivastava has given him a pullover? Why, why? Won't he ever find the courage? Will he have to keep the affair hidden forever? How demeaning, how humiliating!

Afterwards, in the cab, he knew he would be home late, maybe very late, when he heard her wondering aloud: 'Is it all right with you if we spend a few minutes at the Strand?'

'All right. I guess it's all right with me,' he said.

The river looked glorious in the twilight. All the benches were taken and there were people everywhere. He saw an obese middle-aged Marwari man and his bloated wife with their peanut-munching children behind them like waddling ducks; a slim, bearded young man with a sling cloth bag and an intense look raptly admiring a frisky young girl who chattered incessantly; a Sardar and Sardarni doing a fast clip, obviously on a trimming mission.

They walked far away from the crowd and stopped under a tree. He looked up at her. The bewitching temptress of an hour ago now looked like an un-worldly nun.

'You know something,' she said, looking up at the sky. 'Something interesting happened the other day. A group of people dropped in at our office and one of them, an elderly gent, I can't recall his name, suddenly began to sing your praises. My heart started beating so fast that I was afraid it would explode. I wished I could tell him how well I knew you. I feel so proud when you're praised. But of course I couldn't breathe a word. Not a word. No sir, I simply couldn't.'

The sky changed colours. The river murmured. The breeze became gentler. Suddenly he sensed a hint of danger. Things were getting a little too emotional and complicated. The sooner he left the better.

It was almost eight when they finally left the river bank and caught a cab. She snuggled up to him. Every time the cab stopped at a traffic crossing he felt a twinge of embarrassment. People from neighbouring cars avidly watched them.

After dropping her at her place, he headed home, but got out of the cab almost two streets away and began to walk, stopping at a street corner shop to buy paan and a pack of cigarettes. He chose the shorter route through a dirty, unkempt park long abandoned by the genteel folks of the neighbourhood. It was eerie. The whole place was overrun by grass and weeds; the fountain in the middle was dry. As he drew closer he could make out three or four women hovering around it. Whores? Hijras more likely. At a distance he could see another bunch of people. Customers? he wondered. They looked so hesitant, so undecided. He couldn't see their faces, only the glowing tips of their cigarettes. A peanut-seller suddenly emerged in front of him from somewhere, he gently brushed the fellow aside and quickened his pace. Home was only a short street away. He began to wonder what lies he would have to tell.

'Had one of those stupid meetings my whimsical boss calls so often at the end of the day,' he said. 'I called home twice but the line was busy.'

'The phone is dead,' said his wife. 'Have you forgotten? I met Saxena and Sarangi. Both came home ages ago. How come they didn't tell me about the meeting?'

'What have you been up to?' He was indignant. 'I don't like you to go quizzing people every time I'm a little late. And if you must know, Saxena and Sarangi work in a different building. Ours is one gargantuan department.'

'Don't ever be so late again,' she said. 'It scares me to death. I'm alone the whole day with not a soul to talk to and I look forward to your coming home.'

He held his wife, thin, pale, almost bloodless, and ran his fingers through her hair. 'Never again. My word.'

She smiled wanly.

'The lift's out of order,' he said. 'How did you get to Saxena's flat — climbed the stairs? The doctor has advised you not to, remember?'

She buried her face in his shoulder.

'Be a good girl until the lift's repaired.'

'I'm so lonely,' she said.

'All right, no office tomorrow. I will take the day off. That will make three days in a row, with Saturday and Sunday coming up. At the end of it you'll be so sick of me that you'll think of ways to get me out of your hair!'

She looked up at him and a brief smile flitted across her pensive face. It hurt him, for a moment she looked so much like a frail little waif.

Later, long after his wife had drifted into sleep, he lay awake on the bed. Sleep eluded him. Finally, he rose and walked to the window overlooking the balcony and opened it. Waves of moonlight and a gentle breeze wafted into the room like blessings. The bed rippled. He remembered his wife's smile.

He came back to bed and sat by her side. 'Are you asleep?' he called softly. 'Wake up. Come to the window and see. There's a lovely moon tonight. And it hangs so low. I can pluck it for you.'

She did not answer. Everything suddenly felt dead and gone.

Kamalakanta Mohapatra

The Thief

The headmaster wrote furiously till he had covered a whole sheet. His pen dipped into the ink pot from time to time and scratched on the paper. To Sasank the sound was familiar — like Mother's muttering under her breath when she was annoyed with Father.

When the headmaster had finished the letter, he pulled the drawer so vigorously that it came out and thudded onto his lap. Sasank smiled to himself: it must have hurt the old fellow a good deal. He stood there with the same drooping face as before, his back to the wall. School was over and the children had all left.

The headmaster rummaged in the drawer, found an empty envelope, folded the letter, slipped it in and sealed the envelope. Presently he looked up at Sasank. His face was ugly with anger. From the way he thumped the envelope, Sasank knew how the headmaster longed to spank him. Poor headmaster! As the son of the top government officer in the town Sasank often escaped beatings at school, this despite his parents' exhortations to the headmaster whenever they met: 'Cane him by all means; don't hesitate to if he's up to any mischief.'

In a high-pitched voice, the headmaster called Neelamani, the peon entrusted to shepherd Sasank to and from the school, as if the fellow was in another country. Neelamani was behind the door, his baggy khaki pants visible.

'Give this letter to your memsahib,' the headmaster said. 'Not to anyone else, mind you. And let me know tomorrow whatever the memsahib has to tell me. Right?'

Neelamani nodded vigorously as though he had understood the full import of the headmaster's words. 'Yes sir. This letter will go only into the memsahib's hands. Do you think I don't care about my job?'

Pointing at Sasank, the headmaster said, 'And deposit your illustrious little master with the memsahib. Now that he knows about the letter he might vanish, and good god, all the blame will be put on me. Hold him by the hand — right?'

'Yes sir,' Neelamani said enthusiastically.

'Now are you sure you know what you've got to do?' The headmaster sighed. 'God alone knows who can trust you!'

'No sir!' Neelamani protested feebly.

'No what? Now tell me what you're to say?'

On the way home Sasank tried to cajole Neelamani. 'Neeli, I don't feel like going home so early. Mother must be asleep. Carry on home if you wish; I'll get there in an hour or so. There's a fair on near the Gadachandi temple which started yesterday. Have you been to it?'

'Little master,' Neelamani said. 'So many letters are being sent home, but you don't seem to mend your ways.'

'What do you mean? What's the matter with you, old man? Tell me — are you a friend or an enemy?'

'Enemy? My dear little master, how could you think of me as your enemy? I'm sure you've been up to some terrible mischief at school. Please, please let me hear about it.'

'Let's drop in at the fair, I say.'

Neelamani hesitated. 'Little master, I've got to go to the market after handing over the letter to the memsahib. There's nothing at home for the pot to boil.'

Sasank rummaged in his pocket. 'Pinch something from our

house on the sly — I'm sure that's not a big problem for you. Let's see if the grocery peddlers are around. I've a fifty-paisa coin and two twenty-five-paisas on me. With that you can manage a bit of shopping, can't you?'

Sasank and Neelamani headed towards the Gadachandi temple. No one was selling groceries, only fancy goods and snacks, and one lone man was surreptitiously selling toddy from an earthen pot.

'Neeli, how about a drop or two?' Sasank asked.

'No, my little master.' Neelamani protested weakly.

His mild remonstration gave Sasank some hope. He knew he could make Neelamani do what he wanted, as usual.

'Come, come,' Sasank said. 'Just a small glass!' He pulled Neelamani towards the liquor seller. 'No one will know.'

'I'll be fired, little master,' Neelamani protested again.

'Come, come, why are you such a joker?' Sasank pretended a laugh.

'I'm doomed if the headmaster learns about this; doomed too if the memsahib finds out!'

'That's only if anyone is the wiser! Let's see what that baldie chappal-thief of a headmaster has written in the letter. Give it to me, I won't eat it.' Sasank dipped his index finger into Neelamani's tumbler and tasted the drink. 'Tastes good. You want another small glass?'

Neelamani smiled as he watched Sasank piss on the roadside and smear the wet mud on his forehead. 'You know, little master, you don't have a knack for stealing. You'll do well to keep off it.'

'Shut up!' Sasank bellowed.

'It's an art. Not everyone has it in him.' Neelamani laughed and took a crooked cigarette from his shirt pocket.

'You've gone and pinched Father's cigarettes again!'

'But who taught me that art?' Neelamani croaked. 'The day the sahib gets wind of it I'll be fired. I'm doomed.'

Sasank kept quiet.

Lighting the cigarette, Neelamani continued, 'As I said — it's an art. Do you know how I filch washing powder from your house?'

He broke into a broad grin. 'I pour a good quantity of powder into a paper funnel and rush into the bathroom; half I put into the bucket for your clothes, and the other half I roll into a bundle and tuck it into my dhoti. Then, after pottering about for a while, I rush into my quarters on the pretext of finding out what my poor wife is up to. My day's made when I pour the powder into the sari-ends of Chima's mother. You know, little master, my Chima wets his bed and floods the thin mattress every night. And his clothes stink if washed only in water. Little master, I've bared my soul to you, don't go and tell the memsahib! You tell her and I'm doomed! My family would be your responsibility then. Tell me, do I steal washing powder just for fun?'

'Chima's quite a roly-poly lad, I say,' Sasank said. 'Just like a tomato, eh?'

'Heh, heh. A tomato!'

'Neeli, why, aren't you already a little unsteady?'

'Not at all, little master. My legs are quite steady!'

'That Chima boy is still sucking at his mother's breasts?'

'He's not even seven months old, sir! Let him have all the mother's milk he can get for two more years.'

As they walked along, Neelamani gave a sudden start.

'Little master, we're almost home. Go ahead, I'll follow you. If memsahib sniffs the booze, I'll be doomed.' He crouched down by the roadside to pee.

Sasank stopped.

'Go ahead, I say,' Neelamani entreated. 'Little master, my dear little master, walk on ahead. I promise I won't give the memsahib the letter. Is that all right with you?'

Sasank toyed with the idea that after reaching home he'd sneak into Neelamani's quarters and tell his wife that something had fallen into his eye and could she please bare her breast and squirt some milk into it. Nothing like human milk for cleansing the eye!

Sasank's mother was very worried and was pacing up and down the verandah.

'Why are you so late?' she asked, when she saw Sasank. 'All the other children came back ages ago. I was wondering whether my illustrious one had forgotten his way home and forayed into some tribal village sucking his mean little thumb.'

'Fine! Keep reminding me about it, when I've almost given it up!'

'Come in and see who's turned up.'

'Who?'

'Come inside and see.'

'Ma,' Sasank said. 'One thing, Ma.'

'What?'

'No, nothing.'

'Come on, tell me.' She looked at him closely.

'Well, no, nothing.'

'I hope you haven't sullied your name in school!' His mother's voice was suddenly filled with anxiety.

'Why should I sully my name?'

'If you've any good sense, you'll tell me rightaway what mischief you've been up to. Come on now, confess. Oh, I wish I were dead. I'm tired of your doings!'

'Honestly, Ma, I haven't done a thing.' Sasank hugged her. 'Believe me — see, I swear by my eyes.'

'A curse on my fate. How I wish I were dead!' she muttered, as she walked away to the kitchen.

Grandfather, Sasank's mother's father, was taking a walk in the garden between the flowerbeds. He was visibly happy to see Sasank. 'Hello Smartie, how're you?' he asked cheerily.

'Grandpa, why didn't you bring Grandma along?'

The old man smiled, revealing his toothless gums. 'Why should I? What if somebody stole her! There're thieves around, I'm told.'

Sasank could sense that his mother and grandfather had been discussing his deeds. Unfazed, he said, 'Come, I'll show you the local market.'

'Forget the market, show me the temple. I'm told you've an important shrine here.'

'I've just come from the temple. Let's go to the market. There's a shop where you can get very good dosas.'

'Where will we get money to buy dosas, my dear?'
'I have some.'
'How much? Where did you get it?'
Just then Mother came out from the kitchen. 'Sasank, tonight Grandpa will sleep in your room.'
'That's all right,' Sasank said, and then turned to the old man. 'Tell me, Grandpa. What do you know better — ghost stories or detective stories? You'll have to tell me one at bedtime.'
They crossed the garden and reached the gate.
'Grandpa, take a good look at the rose bush on your left.'
Casting a glance at the plant, Grandpa said, 'Why?'
'There's a secret about it!'
'What's the secret?'
'Tell you later. Don't forget to remind me about it in five or ten minutes.'
'All right.'
'Take note of this tree too,' Sasank said, pointing at the sprawling banyan tree spreading its canopy over the compound wall. 'Its trunk is hollow. No one knows about it. Can you guess what's inside?'
'A bird?'
'Wrong. Guess again'
'A snake?'
'No. Something else. Wait, I'll ask you a riddle first. Try to give me the right answer. Here it is: name the one thing people all over the world die for.'
'Food.'
'Wrong. I'll give you another chance. Think hard before you answer. I can give you a clue. The thing could be either metal or paper.'
'Let me think about it; meanwhile you answer my question. If one egg takes five minutes to boil, how many hours will seven hundred and eighty-nine eggs take?'
'What kind of a riddle is that!' Sasank grunted. 'Wait, I'll do some quick mental arithmetic. Just you wait.'
Grandfather laughed and took a snuff box from his vest pocket. A crumpled two-rupee note fell out with it.

'Grandpa, tonight you'll sleep in my room, won't you?'

When Grandfather said he would rather go home alone after the evening prayers at the temple, Sasank returned to find his mother sitting on his bed weeping. His elder sister — back from her dance-school — held her hand, trying to console her.

Before Sasank could retrace his steps and escape, his sister spotted him and shouted, 'Here he comes! Here comes the moon of the family!'

Mother continued to weep. Amid sobs, she lamented, 'Why am I not dead? What an illustrious son I carried in my womb! What sin did I commit in my last life to deserve this boy?'

His sister grasped Sasank's hands pulling him closer. 'Ma, go ahead and break the hands that steal! That'll cure him.'

Wiping her nose and eyes with the end of her sari, Mother looked at Sasank in anger. 'Not even a week has passed, and you've done it again. You had sworn by touching me. How I wish I were dead!'

'The headmaster's a swine!' Sasank muttered, freeing himself from his sister's grip. 'Am I to blame for whatever happens at school? I'm accused of everything!'

Running her hand on his head, his sister piped up sarcastically: 'Yes, indeed! There's lot of glue here. No wonder the accusations stick!'

'Is it written in the book you've stolen that stealing is wonderful?' his mother asked. 'You know, Gautam Buddha never ever stole anything in any of his avatars? Do you know that?'

'I do,' mumbled Sasank.

'You do?' Mother's voice choked. 'Then why do *you* steal? I can't understand you. Just pick up a kitchen knife and cut me into pieces, and then go and steal to your heart's content!'

That night, when Sasank and his sister were having dinner, Father came back from the office. Noticing his wife's sombre face, he said, 'What's happened?'

'Have your dinner first,' she said. 'Afterwards you can hear about the great deeds of your illustrious son!'

'What deeds?'

'Go have a wash. Don't wait for my father, he hasn't got back from the temple yet.'

'I went to the market to look for some hilsa fish for your father, but didn't find any.'

'It's good you didn't. It's sankranti today.'

Sasank hurried through his dinner and tried to get up quickly.

'Why do you wolf down your food instead of chewing it?' Father said. 'Don't you know man can't chew his cud like cattle can. See how nicely your sister's eating!'

'Sasank, rinse out your mouth and come and sit here,' Mother said. 'Let's discuss the matter in your father's presence.'

'What's happened?' Father said, as he took off his shirt. 'Out with it.'

'The headmaster has sent another letter,' Sasank's sister chipped in.

'Shut up!' Mother snapped at her. 'If you've finished eating, get up and go to your room.'

'Has the little fellow been up to some mischief again?' And before he could get an answer from his wife, he pulled Sasank by his ears and hollered, 'Spill it out, boy, before I tear off your ears.'

'I haven't done a thing,' protested Sasank.

Father gave him a stinging slap. 'You haven't?'

Sasank was taken aback. Father hadn't struck him for a long time. He started to sob.

'This boy's heading for jail!' Father despaired. 'A watermelon today, a pumpkin tomorrow, and then maybe something big the day after! Tell me, what have you stolen from the school this time?'

'A book,' whispered Sasank.

'What book?'

'*The Jataka Tales.*'

'Only one book?'

'A whole pile.'

'A whole pile!' Father broke into a chuckle.

Sasank couldn't help but smile. Father always liked people who laughed along with him. He often guffawed, and, when he was alone, Sasank mimicked Father's boisterous laughter.

Another slap and Sasank's head spun around.

'How many books all told?'

'Haven't counted,' replied Sasank. A string of snot ran down his nose. He struggled to sniff it back up.

'See, see, the little sahib doesn't even bother to count!' Father suddenly began to speak with a theatrical flourish, as if addressing an invisible audience. 'Did you steal the key or break open the almirah?'

'Neither!'

'Then how did you remove the books?'

'I slipped my hand between the doors.'

'But why did you steal?'

'To read.'

'You could have asked the headmaster.'

'The headmaster has said the library books won't be lent out.'

'And so you stole!'

'I would have put them back.'

'You enjoy stealing, don't you?'

'No.'

'You hate it?'

'Yes.'

'Then why do you steal?' Father gave him a hard kick on his behind. Sasank keeled forward, his face barely missing the plates. He burst out crying.

'Leave him alone,' Mother intervened. 'Don't trouble yourself any more. Go have a wash.'

'Find out the price of the books from the headmaster and send him the money first thing tomorrow morning,' Father said. 'God, this thief will clean out my house!'

Grandfather returned home just then. 'Who's going to clean out your house?'

Sasank's mother carried him to his room. 'Come, my dear,' she said with a hug. 'Let me tell you something.'

Sasank wriggled out of her grasp. 'Keep your fake love to yourself. Aren't you the one who got me a beating?'

'Why did you get the beating — don't you ever think about, ever wonder about these things?'

'That's because you got Father excited!'

'I? How did I do that?'

'You mentioned the headmaster's letter.'

'But why did the headmaster send the letter in the first place?'

'It's all because I needed to read some good story books.'

'Don't sidetrack the issue! The headmaster complained about my darling because he stole the books.' She patted his cheek.

'That baldie chappal-thief has made up stories to malign me.'

'But that's because you gave him a chance to do that.'

'He makes a mountain out of a molehill!'

'Is stealing a nice thing?'

'No.'

'What comes to you when you steal?'

'Punishment.'

'What else?'

'Shame.'

'And for the parents?'

'Humiliation.'

'People will gossip that so and so officer's son is a thief; beware of him, don't ever let him into your house.'

'They'll say that.'

'And what else?'

'They'll wonder how his parents can stand him!'

'And how will we feel?'

'Mortified!'

'And what else?'

'You'll hang your heads in shame.'

Sasank had all the answers. Whenever the catechism began he felt his home was school and his mother, a teacher. He cheered up a little because Mother looked happy with his answers.

His sister hung back to listen. 'Ma, ask him where thieves go when they grow up.'

Without waiting for Mother to repeat the question, Sasank took off with a perverse flourish: 'They go to jail, hand-cuffed; their limbs are broken by the police; they're made to do hard labour; they weave carpets; their teeth break from eating rice mixed with stones; and when they're released, everybody avoids them.'

'You can rattle off all that in one breath, can't you?' Sasank made a face at his sister. 'Drop dead. Tonight.'

'You're a thief, you'd better drop dead,' retorted his sister. 'Mother and Father will then heave a sigh of relief.'

'You don't have to worry your head about your parents!' Mother snarled at her daughter, as she made Sasank's bed.

Father and Grandfather sat down to dinner and Mother served them. Sasank rolled in the bed from end to end and tried to count how many times Father had thrashed him. He seldom spanked, but when he did, he did a good job; and that's why his beatings hurt more. Mother's routine slaps had become a joke.

Sasank tried to eavesdrop.

'Let him go with Father to the village and study there,' Mother said. 'Not only will he have to pay more attention to his studies, maybe he will stop stealing.'

'Thrash him from time to time and he'll be all right,' said Father.

'God knows my hands are sore from beating him.' Mother sighed. 'It doesn't have any effect on him.'

'The trouble is one minute you blow hot and the next you blow cold. I'm not surprised he's hardened. If you want to thrash him, do it so that he takes to his bed for two or three days. Don't give him a look of pity. Only then will you know what a good beating can do! But with you it's a gentle slap now and five minutes later all syrupy fussing!'

'I can't be so heartless and cruel.'

'If you can't handle him, don't talk about it.'

Mother appealed to Grandfather. 'Did you hear! That's his way — I'm to blame for everything!'

Grandfather had finished his meal. 'Let Sasank come with me. He'll soon mend his ways in the village.'

'But he's still a child!' Father said. 'He can't manage in the village.'

'He's already almost ten years old!' Grandfather said shortly. Sasank beat his head against the pillow.

'Our village school is good enough,' Grandfather continued. 'Every year more than half a dozen of our students write the scholarship exams.'

'Forget the scholarship,' Mother said. 'Let him only give up stealing. That'll be more than enough. Did I tell you what the little devil did last gamhapurnima?'

Father, who had got up to wash his hands, stopped in his tracks. 'What did he do? You never told me! If nothing is brought to my notice, what cure can I prescribe? The treatment has to be timely!'

Sasank felt breathless. His mouth dried up. Oh God, he groaned. Let Mother not come out with *that*! Anything but that! May words fail her. May a wasp sting her!

'On the morning of gamhapurnima the postmistress came and invited me for lunch,' Mother began.

'Oh, you've a postmistress here, do you?' Grandfather remarked.

'No, no. The postmaster is such a quiet mouse that his virago of a wife calls the shots; so everyone around here refers to her as the postmistress. Gamhapurnima is a big festival for them. I'd failed to turn up at her house last year and for months she had put on a long face. So this time I thought I'd make up with her. Around eleven in the morning, after sending Neelamani with two seers of sweets and a basket of fruit, as I was getting ready to leave for their place, our illustrious son materialized from nowhere. For quite some time I'd been scared to take him along with me to anyone's house. Who knew he wouldn't lift something there? So I told him — darling boy, you'd better stay home, I'll be back in half an hour. But he was determined to accompany me. Helpless, I made him swear he wouldn't touch a thing at the postmistress's house.'

Sasank recalled the incident. For one thing, he hadn't really touched Mother when he'd given his word, but only her sari-end; for another, after saying aloud, 'Ma, I won't touch anything at the postmistress's house', he had added in silence without pausing for breath, 'Heck, I'm not swearing anything'. So that day Sasank was as free from scruples as Mother was from worries.

Mother went on with her account; Father and Grandfather made comments now and then. In the next room, his sister turned on the radio and listened to songs, perhaps jotting them down. She and Pranab, an older boy at school, periodically exchanged their song books. Smothered by Pranab's steady supply of chocolates, Sasank had not tattled to Mother about it.

Sasank plugged his ears with his fingers. A little later, he took them out, and then shoved them right back in again. Mother's voice sounded like the muffled roar of a distant ocean. He felt numb.

Unplugging his ears, he strained to hear. 'Just two rooms,' Mother was saying. 'A bedroom, and a sitting room.'

Sasank grew impatient. Mother had a knack for going into every little detail. Same with Father. A story was not just one story, it was many; if it concerned an individual, there'd be the inevitable details about his father, his uncle, his aunt-in-law's sister-in-law's father-in-law, and so on and so forth. Sasank closed his ears again and recalled the fateful afternoon he had spent at the postmistress's house.

Mother was being treated lavishly by the postmistress. All the other ladies sat huddled around her. Mother was laughing and talking very animatedly for a long time. Sasank felt very happy. Mother rarely laughed; she always worried, always laboured away at something; always feared that her children, particularly Sasank, would tarnish the family's good name. Everyday, when Sasank returned home from school, she would invariably ask him, 'Boy, have you done anything today to shame us?' She lived on the edge of morbid fear. Watching her now, Sasank decided he wouldn't look at a thing in the postmistress's house, let alone steal anything.

Standing on the verandah, he dredged up gobs of phlegm and spat them as far as he could. Despite repeated attempts he failed to clear the beautiful siju bush in front of the house. When his mouth was dry from spitting, he began to count the shoes collected on the doorstep. Eleven pairs. He tried to guess the owners. He didn't think Mother's pair was the costliest. Her left chappal was more worn out at the heel than the right one. Someone had come with a brand new pair, even the price hadn't been removed.

Bored with counting shoes, he went into the house and found the postmistress doubled up in laughter. Mother too was laughing hard. The postmistress's maidservant was serving them hot steamcakes. 'Serve the boy first,' the postmistress told her.

Sasank drank in the aroma of roasted turmeric leaves; he longed to devour a few stuffed cakes. But he was too restless to eat.

'Ma, let's go home,' he said.

'Didn't I tell you?' Mother said, not looking at Sasank. 'If Ma has a good time, it's too much for my children. Oh, what lovely children I have!'

'I want to go to the bathroom, Ma.'

'Well, if you want to go to the bathroom,' the postmistress said, 'you can use ours. Your mother has come to our place after such a long time, we won't let her leave so soon.' She took him through the bedroom to the courtyard and pointed out the toilet.

Because of what he had said, Sasank was forced to go into their stinking toilet. He stood there, first counting to a hundred and, in case that was too little, again to two hundred. While he was doing that he broke up a wasp hive on the wall. He dipped his left hand into the water of the old tin bucket and left the toilet.

Okra and chilli plants fringed the postmistress' courtyard. The okra was young and tender. Finding no one around, Sasank plucked one and ate it. No sooner had he entered the bedroom than he heard laughter and high-pitched discussion. He felt too shy to go into the gathering because Mother would immediately ask, without batting an eyelid: 'Did you have loose motions?' In their house, there was a joke about loose motions ever since Sasank had messed the bed.

He stopped in the middle of the bedroom. There was a cot pushed against the wall on the right. From a clothes line above the head board hung a variety of clothes. But the left side of the room seemed like a different world: there was a small table and on it an electric lamp, a stack of books and a bunch of pens in a glass tumbler. Sasank's eyes fixed onto the pens. His heart rose and sank.

He went closer to the table. Whose pens are these? he wondered.

The postmaster's, or his son's? He picked up a Plato and slowly unscrewed the cap. The nib was worn out and the ink had dried. He put it back in place and picked up another — a red Teko. It was filled with red ink and Sasank drew two lines on his palm and put the pen back. There was a blue Writer, but Sasank didn't even touch it. He had never considered a Writer a worthwhile pen — it was cheap, squat, and didn't contain much ink; it leaked if you ran about with it in your shirt pocket; the nib never became as smooth as you liked. A Writer had once been bought for Sasank, but within a couple of days he had broken the nib, dented the cap with his teeth and thrown it away. Another pen, slender as his little finger, stood like a dwarf beside the Writer. And at the very end, towering over the lot, was an unparalleled beauty, in all its elegance, which Sasank had purposely kept outside his field of vision. His eyes gleamed at the sight of it — a flaming red pen with a golden cap and a dainty clip, but a little fatter and tougher than any he had seen. Sasank picked it up and held it in front of him and read: Parker.

So this was a Parker! Sasank drooled. Mother often said Father had been given a Parker as a wedding present; someone in his office had borrowed and never returned it. A Parker was the costliest pen in the world, its nib made of gold; when the nib broke people took it to the goldsmith and melted it down, and with the gold made themselves rings. The pen didn't need ink to be poured into it; a few squeezes of the rubber tube inside the steel container and it filled up.

Sasank brought the pen close to his nose and sniffed. It gave off an aroma of paan zarda mixed with sweat. He flared his nostrils and took a deep breath. His hands were wet. He felt the pen slipping out of his hands.

From the sitting room came the clink of cups and saucers.

Sasank took his fingers out of his ears. He was curious to know how far Mother had got.

'I was surprised that the headmaster should come to call on *me*,' she was saying. 'What could have made him do that?'

She was preparing paan, and there was the sound of betelnuts being shredded by a nutcracker. Sasank felt irritated that Mother should go into all those useless details. She could never tell a story straight.

'The poor headmaster, he was so apologetic. "Memsahib, the matter shouldn't reach the sahib's ears!" What was it that would bring the world crashing down, if it reached the sahib's ears I wondered. The headmaster stood on the verandah, scratching behind his ears as if he had committed a grave sin. He wouldn't listen to my repeated requests to take a chair and remained standing. He bit his tongue when I asked him if he would like a cup of tea. I was amused by his behaviour. Why was he so tense, what could be the reason?'

Sasank pulled out the pillow from under his head and pressed it over his face. Mother's voice was now hardly audible. It had never crossed Sasank's mind that the baldie chappal-thief of a headmaster could so easily do him in.

Sasank was in no mood for school on the day following gamhapurnima. The whole of the previous night he had dreamt of pens. In his dreams the pens had grown wings and flown around like birds. Sasank had tried to catch them, but they always remained just out of his grasp. He had slept fitfully and every time he got up he had felt for the Parker under his pillow. He decided that instead of going to school he would hide in the garage and scribble five or ten pages with the pen.

But Mother had packed him off to school: 'Oh, you're beginning to shy away from your studies too? Oh, how did you come into my womb? Who are you? An imp? Must you always misbehave?'

Had it been some other day Sasank would have pretended to go to the school and instead headed for a tribal village up in the hills, where as the sahib's son he commanded a lot of respect and where in the past he had asked the buxom tribal girls to dance and sing for him. But today all he wanted was to be left alone in the garage with the new pen.

But Father's jeep had broken down and the mechanic was

expected anytime. Sasank decided to go to school. He took the pen from under the pillow and put it in his schoolbag.

He didn't say the prayers at the school Assembly. While others sang *Ahey Dayamaya Vishwa Vihari*, Sasank ogled Labanya, the daughter of one of his father's subordinates. Labanya was saying her prayers with her eyes closed, her breasts rising and falling and the curls near her ears swaying gently in the breeze.

'An important announcement!' the headmaster said, after the prayers were over. 'There'll be a pen competition today. The student whose pen is judged the best will receive a prize.'

The school was agog with excitement. Never before had a competition like this been held: it was always a handwriting competition, or games, or body-building, or exams. Sasank had never won a prize in any of these.

'The competition will be held after recess,' the headmaster continued. 'Those of you who want to take part should write their name and number on a piece of paper, and clamp it to the clip of their pen and submit them in my office. You can enter more than one pen. There won't be any classes in the last two periods and the results of the competition will be announced then.'

The little interest Sasank had for his studies evaporated when he heard the announcement. The image of the Parker danced before his eyes. The pen flew around like a golden oriole; it strutted about like a crane on spindly legs. The backdrop changed from blue skies to grassy fields. It was like his dream the night before.

Suddenly the arithmetic teacher asked Sasank a question and his reply made the students in the class burst into laughter. Sasank couldn't fathom why.

'Your head's full of cow dung!' the teacher commented.

The bell rang for the tiffin break. All those who had only their tawdry little Writers or ink-spewing old Platos — very few had a smart-looking Wilson, or a sleek Pilot, which had hit the market only recently — wrote out their name, number and class on a small slip of paper and, after placing their pens on the headmaster's table, slipped out to the nearby pond to take potshots at frogs. They asked Sasank to join them, but he refused. He opened his tiffin box.

Mother had sent suji instead of paratha and potato chips which he loved. He didn't eat.

Labanya came over, full of love. Sasank didn't attempt to nibble her cheeks as he did every time he had a chance. The two rupees he had filched from Father's pocket a week ago had now dwindled to four annas.

'Would you like to have a dosa?' he asked her.

Labanya nodded. 'How many pens are you entering in the competition? You've two lovely pens, haven't you? I'm sure your pink Pilot will get the first prize.'

'Is a Pilot still considered a good pen!' Sasank said. 'The best pen in the world is a Parker. Then there are Shaeffers, then Hero, then...'

Labanya began to sulk for no reason. 'I won't love you any longer, nor will I marry you when I grow up. Off with you!'

'Father gave me a Parker yesterday.'

'Show me!'

'Why should I show it to you for free?'

'Come on, show it to me. Please, just once. Or else we won't be friends any more!'

'First show me your...!' Sasank looked around and planted a wet kiss on her right cheek.

Sasank took the pillow off his face to find out where Mother was.

'As if it were a competition,' she was saying, 'the headmaster had a good look at all the pens and found the one the postmaster had described. And on the slip of paper stuck to the clip was the name of our illustrious son.'

'A capital idea!' Grandfather laughed aloud, as though it was a humorous tale. 'How the hell did he hit upon such a bright idea!'

Mother broke into a laugh. 'It takes a thief to catch a thief! You know what's been the rumour at the school for the past month? It seems the headmaster was caught stealing shoes! He'd gone out and left his tattered chappals behind; he walked away with someone else's new pair! Since then this boy of ours has been chanting: the baldie's a chappal-thief! Whether it's true or false, only Mother Ganga knows.'

'Like teacher like taught!' Grandfather observed, and they laughed aloud.

After catching his breath, Grandfather reminded Mother, 'What happened after that? You said the postmaster's pen was retrieved. Then?'

Sasank felt that they were laughing not so much at his theft as at his ineptitude. He kicked the pillow in anger and covered his head with the bed sheet.

Mother's voice was still audible.

In the last period but one Sasank was summoned to the headmaster's room. The headmaster stood, resting his enormous scrotum on the edge of the table, the pens in disarray before him. It suddenly dawned on Sasank that the competition was all a hoax. He cursed himself. How had he failed to see through such a simple ruse?

But he wasn't one to give up easily.

'Do you know the postmaster has beaten his son black and blue?' the headmaster ranted. 'No, why should you! The poor boy has taken to bed. Had the postmistress not intervened, the postmaster would have beaten the boy to death. And all because of you.'

'Sir,' Sasank said. 'This pen is not the postmaster's, it's my father's. I brought it from home on the sly to enter it in the competition.'

'How did you know there'd be a competition?'

'I didn't. After your announcement I went home during recess to get it.'

'But the school peon saw you and Labanya in the classroom during recess! Shall I call him over and ask him?'

'But this pen is my father's. He'll beat me to a pulp if he doesn't find it tomorrow.'

'Let him! The trouble with you is that you haven't been spanked enough. Being the darling son of an important officer, you have had a cushy time in school too.'

'If my father looks for the pen, I'll tell him you've taken it away. At least I'll not be the one to blame.'

The headmaster looked a shade uncomfortable.

Feeling too warm under the bed sheet, Sasank tossed it aside. Now he didn't have to strain his ears to listen to the conversation. Father was speaking in his big booming voice: 'Well, well, well. Only now do I understand why the headmaster rushed over to my office, panting and puffing.'

'Did he?' Mother enquired. 'Why did he do that? You didn't tell me about that.'

'How would I know the fellow had come to conduct an investigation into my worthy son's pen-stealing? He kept fumbling and scratching behind his ears; and when I asked what had brought him to my office at that late hour, he said: "Sir, you haven't visited the school in a long time, please visit whenever it's convenient; the fences are broken down and stray cows have eaten the few trees and plants; please give us a grant to mend the fence." And he asked for a character reference for his son who's going to apply for a job in the railways. I called the stenographer over and told him to type out a testimonial that such and such a person, son of so and so, whom I've known for so many years and so many months, is a hardworking, devoted young man, and has a good moral character. The headmaster was very restless. He sat on the edge of the chair, and beads of sweat dotted his bald pate. Then suddenly he started babbling: "Sir, you've so many pens, but you must have a Parker. It's the king among pens." I was a little surprised. The man's behaviour was certainly very odd — why did he suddenly mention pens? I thought of giving him a stern look, but then I thought why hurt the poor fellow. So I said, "A Parker's prohibitive. Besides, you can get it only in the black market." The typed character certificate was brought in, and as I was about to sign it with my pen, he fished out a lovely pen from his shirt pocket, unscrewed the cap, fixed it on the bottom, and ceremoniously held it out to me. "Sir, please sign it with this pen." I took the pen and signed. What else could I have done — told him that he'd better keep his bloody pen? It was a lovely pen, indeed. Pushing the certificate and the pen towards him, I remarked, "Don't forget to tell me when your son gets the job." And with profuse thanks he left.'

'But the headmaster didn't breath a word of it to me!' Mother was surprised. 'All he told me was — madam, it's a secret, only you and I know about it. What about the postmaster and postmistress? I asked. He said they didn't have to know. It was enough that they got back the pen, they should be happy with that.

'By then I was overcome with shame. While leaving, he even added — "madam, please forgive me for saying this, but please do keep an eye on Sasank, he's turning out to be an incorrigible thief." Mother choked. 'How did such a demon come into my womb? What ghost or spirit was fluttering around when I conceived him! Father, when you get back to the village, please consult a good astrologer and see if there's any hope for him.'

It had never crossed Sasank's mind that his fate would be decided so quickly. He heard Father tell Grandfather: 'Let him go with you to the village tomorrow. With the blessings of God he might give up stealing. If he doesn't change, he'll go to jail when he grows up. He'll be the one to suffer, what does it matter to me? I'll promptly disown him.'

Sasank took the pillow from near his feet and buried his face in it. A cold wave of banishment crept over him and he shuddered.

'Pack a few of his clothes in my suitcase,' Grandfather said. 'Nothing much. Whatever else he needs can be bought in the village.'

Sasank cried out in anguish.

Father set out on tour the next morning. His bedroll and suitcase were already in the jeep. The peon accompanying him had come dressed in a white uniform.

Father called Sasank over before getting into the jeep. He held him close. 'Now you realize! Because you wouldn't quit stealing you're being packed off to your grandpa's place. Parents don't love children who steal. Promise me you'll try and be a good boy.'

'I promise,' said Sasank.

'You won't ever steal again?'

'Never.'

'If I hear you've given up stealing, then next year I'll bring you back. You like the school here, don't you?'

'Yes.'

Sasank wished Father would leave early, so that he could travel at least twenty or twenty-five miles before the sun became hot enough to make his eyes water.

Father bent down and touched Grandfather's feet and got into the jeep. Turning to Mother, he said, 'Don't worry if I'm not back in three days.' Then running his hands over Sasank's head, he added, 'Obey Grandpa and Grandma. Be a good boy, right?'

Without any provocation, Mother suddenly piped up, 'If only your son had heeded such advice, he wouldn't have been sent away.'

Two hours after Father left, the bus came and stopped in front of their bungalow. They all came out of the house.

'Grandpa,' Sasank's elder sister said. 'Warn Grandma that she should be careful. This boy can steal the kohl from her eyes.'

Sasank made a face at her. 'Drop dead, sister.'

'I hope you haven't stolen anything of mine? I just can't trust you. Mother, have you checked his bag?'

Mother was in tears. Wiping her eyes with the end of her sari, she hissed: 'Don't tease the child. You know he's being packed off because of a bad habit.'

Grandfather gave a snort of a laughter. 'Daughter, the way you talk it sounds as if he's going to jail, not his grandfather's place.'

'Grandpa!' his sister chimed in again. 'Don't they beat thieves black and blue in the village? Aren't their faces tarred? Aren't they made to sit on a donkey and paraded around?'

'Shut up or else...' Mother screamed. 'As if *your* achievements are any less noteworthy!'

Mother bowed down by the wicket gate of the garden to touch Grandfather's feet. She held Sasank in her arms and kissed him copiously. Sasank tried to wriggle away. Grandfather's suitcase was lifted to the roof of the bus. The driver honked once but briefly, as though his hand had accidentally touched the horn.

As they boarded the bus, Sasank's sister tucked a bar of chocolate into his hands.

Two seats in the front row had been reserved for them. Sasank sat near the window. The bus moved. He waved. His mother and sister waved back. The bus gathered speed. Their bungalow slipped out of sight.

After some time they left the town behind. Hours went by and the day grew hot. A woman craned her neck out of the window and vomited. People seated behind her grumbled and shouted. A small child started bawling. The bus sped on.

Sasank saw tears rolling down Grandfather's eyes.

'What is it, Grandpa?' Sasank said. 'Are you missing Ma? You love her, don't you?'

Grandfather smiled. 'It's the hot air that makes my eyes water.'

'Why didn't you tell me earlier? I've got just the thing for you.'

'What is it?' Grandfather took out his snuff box from his vest pocket. It was a beautifully carved silver box. Sasank suddenly longed for it. Grandfather took a snort of snuff.

Sasank sneezed. He produced a pair of dark glasses from inside his shirt.

'Yours?' Grandfather was surprised.

'Put them on, you'll feel better instantly.'

'But whose are they?'

'They'll soothe your eyes.'

'Tell me the truth: whose are they — Father's?'

Sasank didn't answer. He dipped his hand again into his shirt and took out his sister's song book. The pink cover was wet with perspiration. Sasank said, 'Sister has copied down some lovely songs from the radio. We'll keep singing them throughout the journey. Sister once said this notebook was dearer to her than her soul!'

Sarojini Sahoo

The Rape

Not that Suparna and Jayant never had any fights; they had their fair share like any normal couple, but nothing out of the ordinary, nothing very bitter, certainly nothing irreparable. Sometimes they were about the kids, sometimes about a domestic problem — but they did not last more than ten or fifteen acrimonious minutes, invariably followed by an hour-long sulk, which then melted like snow, and before they knew it the day had resumed its easy pace, its pleasant ordinariness. Even cruel words like selfish, domineering, independence, profligacy, uneconomical, bandied about during the quarrel, did not exactly explode like bombs; by evening everything was forgotten.

But today's was unlike anything before. Suparna was surprised how quickly it had taken on sinister proportions, and the damn thing had happened before she realized it. She had got out of bed early, still groggy with sleep, and meandered in and out of the bathroom and then into the kitchen to light the fire for morning tea. As the water began to boil, she methodically cracked her knuckles, stretched her body and let out the yawns trapped inside her. When the brew was ready, she went and slipped her hand inside the mosquito net and gently shook Jayant awake. Tea in the open courtyard was still a beautiful ritual, something they loved to begin their day with.

'I had a bizarre dream,' Suparna said between sips.

'What about?' Jayant asked. 'I didn't have a pleasant dream either.'

'Not the kind you might think. This was the strangest I've ever had.'

'Let's hear.'

'Well, well, I did it with Dr Tripathy. I don't know how, but we were somehow thrown together, and we flitted from place to place looking for a lonely nook where we could be alone. But everywhere there was somebody or the other. Eventually of course it happened.'

'What happened?'

'He made love to me.'

'I wish I could too,' Jayant guffawed. 'Not to you, to somebody else.'

A ghost of a smile lingered on Jayant's face, but Suparna noticed it had clouded over. That lasted maybe a minute and then Jayant was his jovial old self again, but she sensed it was a put-on. He was simply trying to laugh it away, to show there was nothing to his flippant remark.

The dream was bad and had caused Suparna a twinge of guilt, but Jayant's remark was worse. She had had no intention of startling or hurting him when she came out with it; the whole thing had cropped up just like that, entirely unpremeditated. She had no idea that it would upset him. Although he swore several times it meant nothing to him, she was not reassured. She observed his smile — it was forced, like something he had plucked from somewhere and planted on his bitter lips.

She gulped down her tea and got up. The matter was best quickly buried. On another day she would have argued vehemently: 'What! You don't think I'm free to dream? Can I control what I dream?' Life, of late, had become a little too claustrophobic, a little too suffocating. As if taking advantage of her indifference, sloth and lethargy, life had confined itself to this house sitting on a small slice of land. The outside world had even begun to scare her. And to think she had once fancied herself being reborn as a bird, a free bird in her next life. Had she ever imagined a life confined to four walls, one day like the next, her twenty-eighth year the same as her thirtieth or thirty-third?

Immersed in the house-keeping chores of making hot rotis for her husband, correcting her son's lessons for school, taking care of her daughter's skin, teeth and hair, she had completely forgotten the rebel she had once been. During a college picnic to Dhabaleswar, she had sat on the river bank, defiantly smoking a cigarette, scornful of the sly innuendoes of her classmates. Who was that fellow — some Das Adhikari or something — she had confronted? 'What do you boys take us girls for — cows or sheep? Can't we smoke a cigarette if we want to?'

For three years following her marriage she had not dreamt of giving in to the repetitive banality of everyday life, of limiting herself to her husband's world, and had hopped from Cuttack to Bhubaneswar to Puri. 'I'll suffocate in this world,' she had told her husband. 'Jayant, I need the earth, the sea, the sky.' She found jobs a fetter, but decided to get one anyway and landed herself a fairly cushy offer. But about the same time she became pregnant and when the doctor advised complete rest for five months, she had had to give it up. How those five months had altered her life! New experiences overtook her. She became a mother and forgot all about wanting to be a free bird. She should have taken to her wings again, maybe with her first-born strapped to her back, but somehow she didn't. Then came the second child, a girl. The son's smiles, the daughter's impishness, the deep and untroubled sleep following her husband's vasectomy, all made her forget. She forgot Saul Bellow and Garcia Marquez; she forgot Sam Pitroda and Shabana Azmi and Anantha Murthy. Without the slightest twinge of inhibition she began to gossip with the neighbours: the Mohantys could make a kilo and a half of curry out of just half a kilo of mutton; she, Suparna, had received plenty of gold jewellery at her wedding and had added considerably to it since; every time she looked into the Pradhans' quarters she saw the husband either picking lice from the wife's hair or scouring the pressure-cooker. It all came so easy to her.

The milk van stopped in front of the house and the driver

honked the horn. Her three-year-old son came running inside. 'Ma,' he screamed. 'The milk van!' Suparna was surprised at herself, how could she dwaddle so long over washing the dishes; she spent more than thirty minutes over what should take no more than ten. The overnight milk bowl was still inside the fridge and there was no time to scrub it clean. She picked up another bowl, asked her son to hold two rupees for her, ran a hurried comb through her hair, smoothed down her sari, stole a brief glance at herself in the mirror and went out. The driver gave her a broad grin: 'Were you still asleep or what?' She gave him a sick smile.

She rushed through the cooking and had breakfast ready before eight. Jayant seemed to be in a hurry. When he was ready for the office, she put down her toothbrush with the dollop of toothpaste she had already squeezed onto it and walked to the gate to see him off.

'I gave you Littil's stool examination report yesterday, remember?' Jayant said. 'We will have to see the doctor today at ten. I'll try and sneak back from the office for an hour. Be ready.'

Before Suparna could say anything, he had revved up the scooter and sped away.

Another routine would overtake her now, she knew, one which would first involve spanking the children for no reason and then bribing them with chocolates, hot crispies and toys. There were lots of household chores to see to besides. The drawing room to be tidied — there were crumbs of bread and globs of curry not only on the floor but on the table, on the sofa set, everywhere; Jayant encouraged the children to eat breakfast with him but never bothered to stop them from making a mess as he himself would be engrossed in watching the morning TV — the bed to be made, the milk to be boiled, the living room floor to be swept and swabbed with a wet rag, a semblance of order to be restored to the whole place. Then there was the water filter candle to be scrubbed and cleaned, rice and dal and vegetables to be cooked — all before Jayant came back at ten o'clock. And she would have to shop at the green grocer's before starting cooking. She felt numb.

As she made the bed she felt tiredness overtake her. She threw herself on the bed, wondering whether she shouldn't hire a servant again. But servants caused more headaches than they relieved, and with a servant around the whole day would be spent under a pall of irritation and mutterings under the breath. She had been so happy when she had seen the back of her last servant some four months ago! The rigours of housework had melted down the rolls of fat around her waist and now she was back in shape. The only problem she faced was not having someone to keep an eye on the children. The other day, when she had been a little distracted, her daughter had picked a used ampule of distilled water out of the drain and chewed it up. It had taken a distraught Suparna quite an effort to extract the pieces of glass from the child's mouth. Her tongue was lacerated in several places and her stool had to be rushed to the doctor's for examination.

With a heave Suparna got up from the bed and went into the drawing room. The son and daughter were in the midst of a roaring fight. She broke it up and banished them to separate rooms to play with their own toys. Then she picked up the broom and started sweeping the floor. Cooking could wait, she decided.

She wasn't halfway through her chores when Jayant returned. 'I shan't be a minute,' she said, hurrying to change her clothes. She had misplaced the almirah keys and it took some time to locate them. Jayant, moody, jumpy, irritable, stayed by the front door. 'Done, done,' she babbled repeatedly. 'Through. I shan't be a minute.' When she looked for her shoes she found a thick coat of dust on them; she hadn't used them for a long time. She looked around for something, a brush or a piece of cloth, to wipe them but found nothing, so she hit them against the floor before slipping them on. Then she hurried out, closing the door and locking it.

It was nearly eleven by the time they reached the clinic. It was the busiest hour and there was already a long queue.

'Now you understand why I wanted you to hurry?' Jayant hissed.

'I couldn't do that simply because of Your Highness' command,' she snapped. 'Who do you think does the chores?'

Jayant grasped his son's hand and said, 'We'll wait outside. You take Littil inside and show her to the doctor.'

'Both Dr Tripathy and his wife seem very busy.'

For a long time the doctor wasn't even aware of Suparna's presence in the room. She inched closer to his table, one chair at a time. The doctor would now and then lift his eyes from the patient he was examining, his gaze one of pure contemplation, and look abstractedly around. Suparna tried to catch his eye with a nod of her head but nothing seemed to register. In real life Dr Tripathy seemed so different. In her dream he had appeared a lot younger, almost youthful, with scarcely a wrinkle on his forehead, and certainly much taller than his actual five-foot one or two, definitely not so solemn, nor so weary and irritable. She noticed that nearly half his moustache had already turned grey. His face in her dream was oddly handsome, as if carved by a sculptor, albeit not a consummate one.

Her turn came.

'What's the matter?' the doctor enquired.

Suparna gave him the run down on how her precious daughter had tried to eat a glass ampule.

'You should keep an eye on young children,' remarked the doctor, his voice a touch unpleasant. Then he pushed back his chair and stood up, asking her to bring her daughter into the examination room. There he made the little girl lie down on the table and began to feel and press her stomach. The girl started kicking and flailing her arms about. Suparna held down her hands and legs to keep her still. When the doctor inserted a tongue-depressor into Littil's mouth, she turned her head this way and that, and Suparna had a hard time pinning her down. The doctor did not quite mask his irritation when he showed Suparna how to hold the child. His examination was thorough and meticulous and he took his time over it. Then he said there was nothing the matter with the girl. Suparna was greatly relieved. She offered the doctor his fee but he waved it away. He didn't even prescribe any medicine. Suparna picked up the stool report from his table, folded her hands in a namaskar and walked out.

She found Jayant pacing the road in front of the clinic. The son was bawling for chocolates. Jayant ought to have met the doctor, she thought. She would have liked him to be with her when the doctor examined their daughter. She bought chocolates for the children and returned home.

Later that night, all the housework done, Suparna closed the back door, locked the front gate, gave herself a wash, poured two glasses of water from the filter and took them to the bedroom. The milk had cooled down and she put the bowl inside the fridge; the clothes had dried and she took them off the line, folded them and put them on the rack; the TV, the fan and the lights in the drawing room were still on and she switched them off. She checked the front door once again before getting into bed.

'If you want to read, switch on the bedside lamp,' Jayant said.

Although she would have loved to read for a while, she was totally worn out. 'I'm dog tired,' she said. 'I can barely keep my eyes open.'

She got inside the mosquito net and found the children spread-eagled in the middle of the bed. She straightened them out and moved them to their places. It took some effort. Jayant could have lent a hand but he didn't. As she lay down she felt his hand around her waist. Oh God, no, she thought, stiffening. Not tonight. Didn't he see how tired she was? She gently pushed his long hand away. But the hand crawled back again. This time she repulsed it firmly.

'So you met your Dr Tripathy today, eh?' Jayant said, with a snort of laughter. 'And your dream came true, did it, huh?'

Suparna started. It was like a stinging slap. Did Jayant mean what he said? Or was it just a sick joke? Whatever it was, it did not lessen the sense of humiliation that began to overwhelm her. Being raped couldn't have been any worse.

Notes on the Authors

Acharya, Santanu Kumar was born in 1933 at Calcutta. He taught chemistry in various colleges in Orissa before retiring as Registrar of Utkal University. He is the author of ten collections of stories and nine novels. *Mana Marmar (1962), Durbara (1965), Adina Baula (1978), Sharpayana (1989),* and *Chalanti Thakura (1994)* are some of his well-known collections of short stories. His major novels are *Nara Kinnara, Satabdira Nachiketa, Tinoti Ratira Sakala,* which form a trilogy, and *Sakuntala.* He has been the recipient of the Children's Literature Award of the Government of India (1961 and 1963), the Sarala Award (1987), the Orissa Sahitya Akademi Award (1970) and the National Sahitya Akademi Award (1993). An English translation of *Nara Kinnara (Saints and Satyrs)* is in process.

Behera, Ramchandra was born in 1945 and educated in Utkal University. He teaches English in Kendrapara College. He has written two novels and six volumes of short stories, among which are *Dwitiya Smasana, Abashista Ayusa, Omkara Dhwani, Banchi Rahiba, Bhagnansara Sapna.* His plays have been broadcast by the All India Radio, and he has won the Vishuv Award (1981) and the Sarala Award (1992).

Das, Jagannath Prasad was born in 1936 at Banpur, Puri, and educated in the universities of Utkal and Allahabad. A Homi Bhaba Fellow, he holds a doctorate in the art history of Orissa and has published seven collections of stories, besides nine volumes of poetry, one novel, *Desa Kala Patra,* and five plays. Among his prose works which are available in English translation are *The Magic Dear* (Vikas, 1984), *The Forbidden Street* (Vikas, 1987), *Spider's Web* (Vikas, 1990) and *The Prostitute and Other Stories* (Har-Anand, 1995). He spurned the National Sahitya Akademi Award given him in 1991.

❈

Das, Kishori Charan was born in 1924 and educated at Cuttack and Patna. Besides 14 collections of short stories, he has written two novels and two volumes of poetry, including one in English, and several books of essays. *Bhanga Khelana (1961), Manihara (1970), Thakura Ghara (1975), Bhinna Paunsa (1984), Dhabala Akash (1994)* are some of his well known short story collections. He has received the Orissa Sahitya Akademi Award (1976), the National Sahitya Akademi Award (1976), the Sarala Award (1985) and the Vishuv Award (1992). Among his works available in English translation are *Death of an Indian* (Prachi, 1984), *Wild Peacock and Other Stories* (Grassroots, 1985), *The Prayer Room and Other Stories* (Sahitya Akademi, 1993) and *The Midnight Sun and Other Stories* (B R Bublishing Corpn., 1993). He has edited the collection, *Modern Indian Short Stories*, Vol. IV (1983) for the ICCR and recently an anthology of modern Oriya stories for the National Book Trust.

❈

Das, Manoj novelist, columnist, short-story writer was born in 1934 in a Balasore village by the sea. His first book, a collection of poems, was published when he was in his early teens. As a student, he participated in the Afro-Asian Students Conference at Bandung in 1956. His novels and short stories are widely available in English translation. The notable ones among them are *Farewell to a Ghost* (Penguin, 1995), *The Submerged Valley* (Batstone,UK, 1986), *Man Who Lifted the Mountain* (Spectre, UK, 1979), and the novels *A Tiger at Twilight* (Penguin India, 1992) and *Cyclones* (Facet, New York, 1987). He has received the National Sahitya Akademi Award (1972), the Orissa Sahitya Akademi Awards (1965, 1989), the Vishuv Award (1971), the Sarala Award (1980) and the Sahitya Bharati Award (1996). He is currently Professor of English in Sri Aurobindo International Centre of Education, Pondicherry.

❈

Faturanand (1915-95), better known by this nom de plume rather than his real name Ramachandra Mishra, was one of Orissa's most popular writers. In spite of the serious physical disabilities he suffered from all his life, ever since he passed out of the Medical School in 1931, he wrote prodigiously and published over twenty collections of humorous short stories and belles lettres. Notable among them are *Sahityachasa* (1959), *Mangalabaria Sahitya Sansad* (1963), *Sahitya Beusana* (1984). His autobiography *Mo Phuta Dangara Kahani* (The Story of My Leaking Boat, published by Eastern Media Ltd., 1989) continues to be a bestseller. For over twenty years he helped edit *Dagar*, the literary monthly founded by Laxmikanta Mahapatra.

※

Mahapatra, Bijay Prasad was born in 1938 and educated in the universities of Utkal and London. A linguist, he has published two volumes of essays and seven collections of short stories, notable among which are *Kandheinka Galpa, Purira Galpa, Prema Galpa, Adinia Galpa,* and *Kalapana Golamara Galpa*. He won the Sudhanya Award in 1993 and the Vishuv Award in 1994.

※

Mahapatra, Laxmikanta better known as *Kanta Kabi* for his lyrical poetry, was born in 1888 and educated in Ravenshaw College from where he graduated in 1913. From early youth he suffered from leprosy which put paid to his higher studies. He could not participate in the freedom movement for which he had the greatest sympathy. The English translation of his novel *Kanamamu* (One Eye Uncle) was published by Orient Longman earlier this year. His collected works have been recently reissued. His contribution to children's literature is considerable. He founded *Dagar*, a major literary journal of the 50s.

※

Mahapatra, Nityananda son of Laxmikanta Mahapatra, was born in 1912. He had no formal education, having dropped out of school early in life. He is the author of six novels and more than five collections of stories. He received the National Sahitya Akademi Award (1987) for his novel *Gharadiha*. After the death of his father, he edited *Dagar* for more than two decades. Politically active until 1970, he served as a cabinet minister in Orissa in the late 60s.

※

Mishra, Krushna Prasad was born in 1933 and educated in the universities of Utkal, Banaras and Toronto. He taught philosophy in Utkal University until his death in 1994. He was the author of three novels and five collections of short stories. *Mounabatira Ratri, Kritadasir Kavya, Niagra* and *Devajani, Aranya O Upabana* are notable among them. He founded and edited *Manas,* a literary journal, for over a decade.

❁

Mishra, Yashodhara was born in 1951 and educated in Utkal University. She is the author of three collections of short stories, *Dwipa O Anyanya Galpa, Janharati,* and *Delchanahari.* She received the Vishuv Award (1975), the Orissa Sahitya Akademi Award (1990) and the Katha Award (1996). She teaches English in a Bhopal college.

❁

Mitra, Bamacharan (1925-1976) pursued a career in law after a long stint in government service. He was the author of several collections of short stories among which *Mitra Galpa, Mitra Kalpa, Pasanara Prana, Nara Chhanchana, Aseem, Swapna Siddha* and *Bata Mahapurusa* are well known

❁

Mohanty, Binapani was born in 1936 and educated in Utkal University. She taught economics in several colleges of Orissa before retiring in 1994. Author of two novels and twenty-two collections of short stories, she has received the Orissa Sahitya Akademi Award (1970) and the National Sahitya Akademi Award (1990). Her major story collections are *Kasturi Mruga o Sabuj Aranya, Anya Aranya, Pata Dei, Shakunir Chhaka,* and *Ekaki Puraskar.* An executive member of Orissa Sahitya Akademi, and founder-president of Women Writers of Orissa, she lives in Bhubaneswar.

❁

Mohanty, Gopinath (1914-1991) was born in Nagabali, Cuttack, and educated in the universities of Calcutta and Patna. He was the first ever recipient of the National Sahitya Akademi Award when it was instituted in 1955 for his novel *Amrutara Santana.* He won the 1974 Jnanpith Award for his novel *Matimatala.* Among his twenty-four novels are *Paraja, Danapani, Harijan, Rahura Chhaya, and Laya Bilaya.* He published twelve collections of short stories, two biographies, three plays, five volumes on tribal language and culture. He translated seven works into Oriya including the Soviet Land Nehru Award winning translation of Maxim Gorky's *My Universities* and Leo Tolstoy's *War and Peace*. Among his works available in English translation are *Paraja* (Paraja) (OUP, 1987), *The Survivor* (Macmillan, 1996), *Ants and other Stories* (United Writers, 1979), *The Bed of Arrows and Other Stories* (Sahitya Akademi, 1995) and collections of stories. In 1991 he was conferred the Padmabhushan. For a spell in 1986 he was the Adjunct Professor of Anthropology in San Jose State University, USA.

Mohanty, Jagadish was born in 1951, and has written two novels and seven books of short stories. *Ekaki Ashwarohi, Dakshina Dwari Ghara, Deepahare Dehkinathiba Lokatiye, Nian o Ananya Galpa* are among his well-known collections of short stories. He won the Vishuv Award (1985) and the Orissa Sahitya Akademi Award (1990). He lives and works in a colliery in south Orissa.

Mohanty, Surendra novelist, critic and journalist, was born in Purushottam, Cuttack, in 1920. An active politician for over three decades he was a member of the parliament for two terms. He edited *Kalinga* and *Sambad*, both daily newspapers, from 1966-1970 and 1988-1990 respectively. His four novels include *Andha Diganta* and *Nila Shaila*, for which he won the National Sahitya Akademi Award in 1970. He published eleven collections of short stories; among them are *Mahanagarira Ratri, Krushnachudar Hasa, Mahanirvana, Maralar Mrutya, Sabuj Patra O Dhusar Goplap*, etc. He wrote a two-volume history of Oriya Literature and critical works on Fakir Mohan Senapati, besides a biography of Madhusudan Das, the founder of modern Orissa.

Mohapatra, Godavarish poet, short-story writer, journalist, was born in 1899. For decades he edited *Niankhunta*, a bitingly satirical magazine, which he founded in the early 50s. He won the National Sahitya Akademi Award for *Phula O Kanta*, a collection of verse. He passed away in 1965.

Mohapatra, Kamalakanta was born in 1953 and educated in Utkal University and Banaras Hindu University. He has published a collection of stories, *Palabhut*, (1984) and a novella, *Photo*, (1990). He has translated the selected works of Fakir Mohan Senapati, Kishori Charan Das and Jagannath Prasad Das in English and Jean-Paul Sartre, Isaac Bashevis Singer and Gabriel Garcia Marquez in Oriya.

Panigrahi, Bhagabati Charan (1907-1943), younger brother of Kalindi Charan Panigrahi, is remembered for his lone collection of stories, *Shikar*, which was published posthumously. A communist by political persuasion, he spearheaded the popular revolts against the British imperial rule.

Panigrahi, Kalindi Charan novelist, short story writer, poet, critic and journalist, was born in 1901 and educated in Ravenshaw College, Cuttack. Among his five novels are *Matira Manisha*, (Sons of the Soil) available in translation in English and fourteen other Indian languages, and *Luhara Manisha*. He published four collections of stories which included *Sagarika*, *Rasiphala*, and *Sesha Rashmi*. A long-time executive member of PEN, Sahitya Akademi and many other literary institutions, Panigrahi was honoured with the Padmabhushan.

Patnaik, Akhil Mohan was born in Khurda in 1927. His father, Bankanidhi Patnaik, was a well-known writer of his times. Patnaik a keen debator and left-wing student leader, was educated in Utkal University. He practised law until his death in 1982. Of his six collections of stories, as many as four were published posthumously. He won the National Sahitya Akademi Award in 1981 for *O Andhagali*. He also wrote two plays, a travelogue, and a book of poems. He edited *Samabesh*, a literary journal, until his death.

Patnaik, Rabi (1935-1991) was a geologist, who wrote around four hundred short stories which are available in seventeen volumes. Notable among them are *Raga Todi*, *Andha Galira Andhakara*, *Hiranya Garbha*, *Bandhya Gandhari* and *Bichitra Barna*. He won the Orissa Sahitya Akademi

Award in 1984, the Sarala Award in 1991, and the National Sahitya Akademi Award posthumously in 1992.

❊

Rath, Chandrasekhar was born in 1929 in Bolangir and educated in Lucknow University. He taught English in several colleges and was for a couple of years the editor of the *Sun Times*. An immensely popular speaker in the lecture circuit, he is the author of three novels, one book of poems, thirteen volumes of essays and twelve collections of short stories. Recipient of the Orissa Sahitya Akademi Award twice (1980 and 1981) and the Sarala Award in 1982, the National Sahitya Akademi Award in 1997, his major short story collections are *Aswarohir Galpa*, *Anya Eka Sakala*, *Bagha Sabara*, *Ete Pakhare Samudra*, *Samrat o Anyamane*, and *Sabutharu Dirgha Rati*. The English translation of his novel *Yantrarudha* (Astride the Wheel) will be published by Macmillan later this year.

❊

Ray, Pratibha novelist and short story writer, was born in 1944. She has published eighteen novels and seventeen collections of short stories. She received Sarala Award (1989) and the Moorti Devi Award (1993) for her novel *Yajnaseni*, which is available in English translation (Rupa, 1995). A selection of her stories in English translation is scheduled for winter publication this year. In 1985 she received the Orissa Sahitya Akademi Award for *Shilapadma* and the Vishuv Award for life-time literary achievement in 1995. She teaches educational psychology in Ravenshaw College, Cuttack.

❊

Ray, Rajkishore was born in 1914 and educated in the universities of Patna and Calcutta. He taught Oriya for over thirty years in various colleges before joining the directorate of higher education. He is the author of fourteen collections of short stories and a book of one-act plays. *Madhyannar Marupathe*, *Panka-chandan*, *Manar Mrunala*, *Bikacha Satadal*, *Bana Jyotsna* are some of his well-known collections of stories.

❊

Roy, Satchidananda Raut poet, novelist, critic and essayist, was born in 1916 in a village in Khurda district. He began his literary career early at the age of eleven. Author of nearly 40 books, his output embraces volumes of poetry such as *Pandulipi (1932-47)* and *Kavita (1962)*, considered by critics as the precursor of modernity in Oriya Poetry, *Swagata* and *Kavita (1969)*. His best known short story collections are *Mashanira Fula (1947), Matira Taj (1947), Chhai (1948),* and *Nutan Galpa (1990)*. He has lectured in several universities in the USA and visited many countries of the world. He has been awarded the National Sahitya Akademi Award (1964), the Jnanpith Award (1986), the Sahitya Bharati Award(1997), and conferred the Padmashri in 1962. Among his works available in English translation are *The Boatman Boy and Forty Poems* (Modern Review Press, 1955) and *The Short Stories of Sachi Rout Roy*. The National Sahitya Akademi has recently published a selection of his poems edited by Jayanta Mohapatra. He lives in Cuttack.

Sahoo, Mohapatra Nilamoni novelist, essayist, critic, and short story writer, was born in 1926. Educated in Utkal University, he taught Oriya Literature for over thirty years. Of his 29 collections of short stories, *Abhisapta Gandharb* won the Sarala Award (1993) and *Brundavanar Sesha Dhup* the National Sahitya Akademi Award (1984). He lives in Bhubaneswar.

Sahoo, Sarojini was born in 1956. She teaches Oriya in Belpahar College. She has published five collections of short stories: *Sukhara Muhamuheei, Nija Gahirare Nije, Amrita Pratishkare, Tarali Jauthiba Doorga,* and *Chaukatha*. She received the Vishuv Award twice (1980 and 1993).

Senapati, Fakir Mohan father of modern Oriya prose, was born in 1843 in Mallikashpur, Balasore. He had a varied career. Largely self-taught, he became a clerk in the government salt office, an accountant's assistant in the ship-chandlering and sail-making business of his uncle, a schoolteacher, a part-time printer and journalist, a nationalist and popular agitator, and an administrator in the feudatory states of Orissa. After his retirement from service in 1896 at the age of fifty-three, he began to write. He wrote four novels, among them the satirical masterpiece *Chha Maan Atha Guntha*, an autobiography and a collection of stories. Of his novels,*Chha Maan Atha Guntha* (Six and One-third Acres of Land) has been translated into English four times and yet another, and possibly the most authoritative, translation by Jatindra Nayak is scheduled for publication in 1998. Senapati's *Selected Stories* (edited and translated by Leelawati Mohapatra and K K Mohapatra) was published by HarperCollins in 1995.

Swain, Sivapada was born in 1952. He attended Utkal University and Delhi University. His maiden collection of stories is being readied for publication.

Tripathy, Nrusingha was born in 1945 and educated in Utkal University and Allahabad University. He is the author of six volumes of poetry and a collection of stories, *Manonibesh* (1994). For over a decade he edited *Nabalipi*, a literary magazine.